LP F SLEEMAN
Sleeman, Susan, author.
Seconds to live

S0-ACS-679

SECONDS
TO
LIVE

Center Point
Large Print

Also by Susan Sleeman and available from
Center Point Large Print:

Fatal Mistake
Kill Shot

**This Large Print Book carries the
Seal of Approval of N.A.V.H.**

HOMELAND HEROES | BOOK I

SECONDS TO LIVE

SUSAN SLEEMAN

Fountaindale Public Library
Bolingbrook, IL
(630) 759-2102

CENTER POINT LARGE PRINT
THORNDIKE, MAINE

This Center Point Large Print edition
is published in the year 2020 by arrangement with
Bethany House, a division of Baker Publishing Group.

Copyright © 2019 by Susan Sleeman.

All rights reserved.

This is a work of fiction.
Names, characters, incidents, and dialogues are products
of the author's imagination and are not to be construed as
real. Any resemblance to actual events or persons,
living or dead, is entirely coincidental.

The text of this Large Print edition is unabridged.
In other aspects, this book may vary
from the original edition.
Printed in the United States of America
on permanent paper.
Set in 16-point Times New Roman type.

ISBN: 978-1-64358-462-1

The Library of Congress has cataloged this record
under Library of Congress Control Number: 2019950834

To my mother and father,
Geraldine and Rodney Becker

If only . . . I could share this moment and my joy with you. You could hold this book in your hands, and I could tell you that your outstanding example of hard work and dedication have made not only this book possible but many others. I could hug you one more time and tell you how much I love you and miss you . . . if only.

CHAPTER 1

One mistake. That was all it took to put Dustee's life on the line—death right on her heels.

She glanced over her shoulder into the murky night, with shadows shrouding the tall city buildings. She searched the soupy fog. Looking—seeking the man tailing her. A thick wall of fog blocked her view, but he was there. She could feel him. Feel the evil. The anger. The desire for revenge. Following her, his footsteps silent and deadly.

Phantom, he called himself, had been hot on her heels since she'd gotten off the bus, reaching out to grab her. She'd bolted into a group of fellow riders strolling down the hill. He'd hung back, his hoodie up, hiding his face. He lurked like a whisper of her imagination. But she hadn't imagined him. He was real.

Terrifyingly real.

Her stomach knotted tighter, twisting into a stiff ball of agony. It *should* be knotted. She deserved it. She'd done this to herself.

What made her think she could break the witness-protection rules? Be the exception and get away with it? She was forbidden from using any electronic device to access the internet. But it had been too long. She couldn't help herself. The library computers called to her. Now Phantom had found her, and she'd put both her life and her twin sister's life at risk.

Stupid craving for an online connection. She shouldn't have given in. Definitely not. She had to get away from him. But how?

She focused ahead on the winding road leading into the city of Portland. She picked up her pace. Hurrying. The clip of her spiky heels on the concrete sounded like machine-gun fire.

Run. Faster. You're so good at it.

Running from everything. From her past and nearly being incarcerated by the FBI. They offered a deal instead. All she had to do was help them take down Phantom. She'd jumped at the chance to help bring in the notorious hacker, but he outed her, and she had to go into the Witness Protection Program to stay alive.

Now he wanted to kill her, brutally, like the last person who'd tried to infiltrate his organization.

She didn't want to die.

Oh, please. No.

She picked up speed.

Click. Click. Click. The staccato bursts of her pointy heels rang through the air, a beacon for the man hot on her trail. She paused to kick them off. The pumps she'd been so excited to buy only a week ago tumbled down the road in front of her. Shoe over shoe, the rainbow-dyed leather disappeared into the curtain of fog kissing the asphalt.

She slowed to take another quick look over her shoulder. Other riders had turned off, and he'd silently moved closer, his hand in his pocket like he had a knife. One to slice her open, as he'd done with the last person who betrayed him.

Her heart raced, threatening to explode and paralyze her.

She swallowed hard and took off running. The sidewalk was cool against her feet, the roughness biting into her tender skin, but she didn't stop. Not even when sharp rocks cut into her flesh. Or when she heard his footfalls echoing into the night and pounding closer.

Closer.

Disappearing was her only hope.

She ran. Harder. Her breathing labored. An alley lay a few feet ahead, beckoning her. She careened around the corner, catching her fingers on the rough brick of an old seafood shop to keep from plummeting down the incline.

She picked up her pace, searching for a hiding spot—somewhere he wouldn't think to find her. Her chest burned, and she labored to gain even a sip of oxygen. She couldn't keep this pace up for long, but if she didn't, he would catch her.

He'd tower over her. His ghastly eyes glazed with the anger of betrayal. Filled with the darkness of revenge. A weapon. Pointed at her. Warning that she was about to die. That he was going to feel the relief of revenge.

Help. Oh, help.

Who would help her? She'd made a huge mistake. She was on her own.

She searched both sides of the narrow alley. A dumpster. Trash cans. Cardboard boxes. Her gaze settled on a big grate in the back wall of the fish market, the sour smell of rancid seafood almost suffocating her.

She ran to the spot. Assessed the grate.

The vent was large enough for her body. She released the catches on all four corners and tugged hard. The grill suddenly popped out. She fumbled with the cool metal. Catching the grate before it hit the ground, she set it down silently to slide her fingers into the slatted openings.

Balancing the grate, she tucked up her legs and wiggled into the yawning duct. She clasped the steel tightly and jerked it back into place. Holding it with one hand, she dug out her phone and scrolled to the number for Taylor Mills, the Deputy U.S. Marshal assigned to her protection.

The call connected. Rang. Once. Twice.

C'mon. C'mon. Answer, Taylor. Please! You always do.

Footsteps pounded down the alley, coming closer.

No. Not yet.

One more ring.

Phantom was almost to her hiding spot. She had to end the call before the screen's light gave her away.

She punched end and silenced her phone. Taylor would call back. Dustee was sure of it—as sure as she was that she had to escape Phantom. Taylor was like that. The best person Dustee had ever known. Selfless and caring.

Dustee's fingers on the grate cramped, but she clung tightly.

Phantom's footsteps halted nearby. Eerie quiet settled over them.

She caught a glimpse of him through a sliced opening. His face was shadowed as he stood tall. Strong. Searching the area. Looking for her. For a hint to her location. For anything, even the barest of clues.

Anger and hatred emanated from his body. Finding her was personal to him—so personal— this could be the end for her.

She didn't want to die.

Please, no.

Her heart raced. Faster. Faster. Pounding against her chest like the heavy beat of a conga drum.

A sob crept up her dry throat. Pressing hard. Begging for release.

She bit her lip to keep from crying out. From letting him discover her location. Tears welled up. She swallowed hard.

Waited. Waited.

The silent night pressed in on her.

He turned. Faced the wall. The grate.

Please. Oh, please don't let him see my fingers. Please.

Deputy U.S. Marshal Taylor Mills's phone rang twice from her purse, then stopped. She sighed at the welcome silence. If one more witness needed her today, she would lose it. Any need. Even a quick phone call to talk about their loneliness in the Witness Security Program, a conversation she had on a daily basis.

She closed her condo door and twisted the dead bolt. She was alone. Blessedly alone. At least physically. For the moment. In the condo she bought only a year ago, filled with all her favorite things. Comfort things. Too bad she was never here to enjoy them.

Her phone sounded again.

"Please, not again. I can't even tonight." She dug deep to find the person she wanted to be and answer it—the person who put the needs of the people in WITSEC before her own. She helped them adjust to a new life in hiding, forget their pasts, and succeed while under protection of the U.S. Marshals Service's Witness Security Program.

Hah, you're one to talk. Try forgetting your own past for a change.

Preparing to cringe, she looked at the caller ID. *Oh. Good.* Not a witness. Her friend Lisa.

"Lisa." Taylor tried to sound enthusiastic,

honestly she did, but she didn't pull it off. "Did you just call and hang up?"

"No. Why?"

"I missed a call and was worried it might be important."

"Wouldn't your caller ID show you who it was?"

"It's a number I don't have in my address book. Could be a telemarketer, I suppose." Still, Taylor worried someone's life might depend on her having answered.

"You sound stressed out," Lisa said.

Stressed? Taylor had reached a point where no word existed to explain her anxiety level, and she would need to create a new term to define it.

"Tough day at work," Taylor replied and left it at that. She wanted to say more but couldn't. Lisa didn't know that Taylor was a WITSEC deputy. Few people did. Many lives depended on WITSEC deputies. All were sworn to secrecy so they couldn't inadvertently lead someone to a witness. That made it hard to have a real relationship of any kind. Including romantic. Not that she was even thinking of romance in her life. A topic she couldn't even begin to ponder now.

"So, what's up?" That cheery voice she was trying to conjure up finally appeared.

"I wanted to ask if you'd like to catch a late movie."

"Tonight?" Taylor glanced at the clock, the hands nearing nine. "Late is right. I have to work tomorrow."

Lisa snorted. "Since when did you turn into my grandmother and go to bed so early?"

"That's me. Grandma Taylor. Been working sixteen-hour days. At my grandmotherly age, I need my beauty rest."

"That rough, huh?"

"I literally haven't had a minute alone in weeks." Taylor tried to remember a period of time lately that she'd had solely for herself. Nothing came to mind. Nothing. Not a single moment in recent days. Sure, she slept alone. Showered and dressed alone. That was about it.

Every moment of every single day she was on call with the goal of protecting her witnesses from dangerous people who wanted them dead. That meant she had to be sharp all the time. A late movie wouldn't help with that. "If you don't mind, I'm gonna pass. Maybe we can grab dinner on Friday."

"Sure. No worries." Disappointment lingered in Lisa's tone. "You know, I wasn't going to say anything . . . but seems to me like you need a vacation."

Boy did she. "I think you could be right. Maybe Friday we can talk about doing something together."

"Talk about it is all you'll do," Lisa muttered.

Taylor wanted to argue, but she was slow to pull the trigger on big things. Okay, maybe on a lot of things. She was risk averse most of the time, thanks to losing her brother, Jeremy, when they were teens.

"Let me know if you decide to bail on me." Lisa ended the call.

Guilt heaped itself on Taylor's head. She was such a bad friend. Not on purpose. She really cared about Lisa and wanted to be a better friend. But her witnesses were always in potential danger, and they had to come first. She had no idea why Lisa put up with her, but thank God she did.

Taylor headed for her bathroom. Usually seeing the space's cool, gray muted tones with bright white and silver accents was enough to lower her stress a notch, but not tonight. Not after the day she'd had putting out fire after fire.

She started the faucet running and dumped in a liberal dose of bath crystals. The lavender beads swirled in the rushing water, and the room instantly smelled like a magnificent garden. Perfect. A long soak in the tub would do wonders for her attitude and ensure a good night's sleep.

Just one hour. Sixty minutes. Three thousand and six hundred seconds of warmth and bubbles. For her and her alone.

After all, the odds of a witness having a major

catastrophe in the next hour were low, and if the person who'd called really needed her, they would call back.

Taylor had to risk leaving them on their own this one time to maintain her own sanity.

CHAPTER 2

"Ten thousand dollars. That's what a witness's life is worth on the dark web." Disgusted, FBI Agent Sean Nichols shoved back from a desk in the U.S. Marshals Seattle field office.

He stood, raising to his full six-foot-three height, allowing him to meet head-on the questioning gaze of Barry Eisenhower, the Immigrations and Customs Enforcement Special Agent in Charge of the Cyber Crimes Center, also known as C3.

Eisenhower rested against the wall and ran a hand over dark hair, buzzed close to his scalp. In his fifties, he was still fit and lean and wore his pricey black suit well. He narrowed his eyes. "Just so I'm clear. You're saying what I think you're saying. The WITSEC database was breached and witnesses' personal data was stolen."

Sean gave a calm nod when really he wanted to shout, *Heck yeah, that's what I'm saying. It's crazy horrible, and people will die if we don't act fast.* But he didn't want to draw the attention of the few deputies still working, and that statement was equivalent to crying out, *The sky is falling! The sky is falling!* And he was no alarmist. Although if there ever was a time to be one, a breach of thousands of people's secret identities would be the time.

"That's exactly what I'm saying." Dropping into the chair, Sean pointed at the computer screen showing a site on the dark web, a deep layer of the internet available only by using a special browser. "The data is already for sale for ten grand a pop. How the hacker decided on that amount I have no idea. Doesn't really matter. Criminals seeking revenge against witnesses who testified against them are sure to pay it. Especially some of the big crime families or drug cartels."

Eisenhower ground his teeth. "How did this happen?"

"I won't know until I have complete access to the WITSEC database files. Right now I have only basic login credentials, and I need to see the actual database and logs."

"If you can't access all the files, then how did you confirm the hack?"

"I came across this website and created a bogus witness in the database." Sean pointed at his monitor. "Then I came back to the hacker's website and requested the contact information for my made-up person. Ten thousand dollars in bitcoins later, the hacker gave me the data I'd just entered into the database."

"Dark web." Eisenhower sneered and shook his head. "No matter how long I do this job, I'm still amazed by the dark web."

Not Sean. Not after the years he'd worked in computer forensics. Nothing amazed or shocked him anymore, not even the dark web. Most people didn't have a clue that only five percent of the internet was available for public viewing, with many private, hidden layers making up the remaining percentage. The dark web was one of those layers where criminals set up shop and prospered by selling illegal products and services.

Eisenhower moved closer. "I mean websites to buy nearly anything, and not simple websites but sophisticated ones like that one. It gives even Amazon a run for their money." He shook his head and jabbed a finger at the screen. "Look at that. They have customer service and product reviews. Seriously, what person in the market for illegal guns or drugs or even stolen identities stops to write or read reviews?"

"I hear you, sir," Sean said. "But honestly that doesn't matter right now. The hacker has real-time access to witnesses' personal information. We need to get the database offline as soon as possible. Then I need to figure out whose identities are compromised so that deputies can intervene before witnesses are hunted down and murdered."

"And then we need to find this jerk." Eisenhower pushed off the wall and took a firm stance.

Here it comes. Eisenhower would issue an edict

sending Sean back to his current assignment of researching the explosion of internet-facilitated weapons sales on the dark web. He didn't mind that task. It was his area of expertise after all, but he had a high-stakes issue literally staring him in the face. It would be the investigation of the year, and Sean wanted in on it. Shoot, he wanted to take lead, finally achieving one of his elusive goals. But he wouldn't let his supervisor see how important this was only to have him yank it away.

Eisenhower widened his stance. "I would suggest we hand this breach off to the Marshals and get you back to your assignment. Thing is, you're the most qualified person in DHS to lead an investigation of this magnitude. Plus the hack poses an imminent threat to lives, making it a top priority. As of now, you've got lead if you want it."

Sean suppressed a victorious smile. Even with Eisenhower's blessing, that didn't mean Sean was in. He was part of the C3 elite Cyber Crime Unit that included ICE, FBI, DHS agents, and Deputy U.S. Marshals located in D.C., with additional agents embedded in law enforcement offices all across the country. Sean was sure the Marshals would fight for lead on a hack of one of their databases.

He sat forward. "You think the head honchos at the Marshals Service will go for that? I wouldn't if I were them. I'd do anything to be the one to apprehend the criminal who threatened my witnesses."

"It's my job to convince them that you're better than any of their staff, and it's in their best interests to let our team handle the breach." Eisenhower's persuasive skills exceeded any Sean had witnessed before. Odds were good that Eisenhower would make that happen. Still, there was bound to be tension with the Marshals.

"I'll cancel your training for tomorrow so you can focus on this," Eisenhower added. They'd traveled from D.C. to Seattle to do a West Coast training on detecting cyber intrusions, ironic considering this situation. "And I'll get the access you need when I notify the Marshals Service of the breach."

Sean gave a clipped nod. "Any idea how long that will take?"

Eisenhower glanced at his watch. "I'll start at the top, but at this time of night, I'll have to hunt someone down. They'll have to do the same thing. And so on. You know the drill. The big machine never moves as fast as we would like."

Frustration had Sean shooting to his feet. These witnesses were counting on him now. Him! He couldn't let them down. "Lives are depending on us moving faster. At a minimum we need to contact the database administrator and have it taken offline before additional data is stolen."

"Then I need to get to it."

"After I have access to the files and have a handle on the size of the problem, I'll let you know the resources I'll need beyond the RED team." Sean was already thinking about assigning tasks to his teammates on the Rapid Emergency Deployment team, fellow FBI agent Kiley Dawson, Deputy U.S. Marshal Mack Jordan, and FBI Analyst Cameron Linn. They were already at the hotel, but he would get them back to the office ASAP.

"Be sure you're only working this investigation, not the Montgomery Three case." Eisenhower eyed Sean.

"Understood." Sean lifted his shoulders into a firm line until his boss walked away, then his thoughts shifted to the Montgomery Three investigation where the team had failed big-time. After months of work, they were still unsuccessful in locating three abducted teens in Montgomery, Alabama. Becky, Felisha, and Izzie—girls just learning who they were and beginning to discover who they might be—were still missing.

Was it over for them? Were they alive and waiting for Sean to find them?

He should have worked harder. Smarter. Faster. Before Eisenhower pulled the plug and closed the investigation. Everyone on the team was still bitter about how things went down and couldn't leave it alone. How could they when the faces of these innocent girls haunted their dreams?

Sure, Eisenhower had forbidden them to work on the case. So what? The missing teens still needed them, and they wouldn't give up until the girls were found. The team got together off-site each week to work old leads. Eisenhower knew what was going on, yet he'd turned a blind eye.

But now? With this hack? That changed things. Heads would roll if he caught them even talking about the Montgomery Three during this investigation.

No matter. If a lead turned up, Sean wouldn't promise not to talk about it.

But now he needed to get moving on the hack. Discover the list of vulnerable witnesses and make sure they were protected. He glanced at his watch. Nine-thirty. No biggie. The team remained on call twenty-four seven and would respond.

He grabbed his phone and tapped the keys.

Urgent. New assignment. Report to office immediately. Confirm text received.

The affirmative responses came quickly, and his teammates arrived within thirty minutes. Looking wide-eyed and alert, Kiley was the first one through the door to the small room. Not unusual for the team night owl.

"You look jazzed about this assignment." She dropped her computer case on the desk and twisted her dark, nearly black shoulder-length hair into a bun and stabbed in a pencil to hold it in place. Her working mode, she always said.

She eyed him. "Well, what are you waiting for? Tell me about it."

Excitement over a new challenge hummed through his veins. He wanted to share, but they were a team. That meant not showing her favor and letting her in on it early simply because she was a longtime friend. "We'll wait until the others get here."

"Aw, come on." She dropped into a chair and pulled an energy bar from the pocket of her cargo pants. "We've been friends for years. You can tell me."

"Nice try, but no." He smiled at her but wouldn't give in. "This is so big I want everyone to hear it at the same time."

She chomped a bite of her bar and crossed her arms, chewing and staring at him. She liked to control every little thing and being in the dark about their assignment put her on edge, but he couldn't help that. He had to be the kind of leader he always knew he would be once given the chance. One who played fair.

Sporting a frown and rubbing his eyes, Mack entered the room. He held a can of Red Bull, his go-to drink, which was crazy if you asked Sean. Mack was always on the move and looking for a thrill—he didn't need the help of stimulants.

"This better be important." The words dragged out in his deep Texas drawl. He dropped onto a chair as if he had all the time in the world, and

24

his long legs stretched out making the small computer room feel even smaller.

"It's important." Sean left it at that even though he wanted to say more. He and Mack had been in competition since the day they'd met, and Mack repeatedly pushed Sean's buttons, leaving constant tension between them.

Scratching his full beard and yawning, Cam strolled in. "Figures. I decide I'm finally going to get to bed at a decent time tonight and then you call."

"Define *decent*." Mack lifted the Red Bull to his mouth and chugged.

"Midnight," Cam said.

"Nothing decent about that." Mack propped his scuffed cowboy boots on a chair. They looked like he'd just climbed off a horse at one of the rodeos he occasionally entered.

"Right, I forgot. Old men like you need far more sleep." Cam laughed and perched on the desk. "And energy drinks to keep up with the rest of us."

Kiley frowned at them. "Give it a rest, guys. Sean has something important to tell us."

Sean would like to think she was trying to help him out, but in fact she'd spent more of her life with computers than people and didn't like small talk and was moving them on.

He looked around to be sure no deputies were within hearing range. "It goes without saying that this is for your ears only. At 20:00 I discovered that someone hacked the WITSEC database and confirmed that they're selling witnesses' data on the dark web for ten grand each."

Kiley shot up in her chair. "Seriously? For real? Hacked?"

"Seriously."

"Man." Cam shoved a hand in his dirty-blond hair, already a tangled mess. "On a difficulty scale of one to ten, hacking that system is like, what, a twenty? Not many people could do that. Besides me, of course." He puffed up his chest and grinned. Cam was easy to work with, but he made sure people recognized his skills. Sean believed it came from Cam being the middle child in a family of five.

"No kidding. It's a stellar hack," Kiley said, awestruck. "Could be his motive for doing it. Just to say he could. Well, that *and* the money he's making from selling the data. That's a hefty price for one record."

"Agreed," Sean said. "But I figure the hacker's testing the waters with this amount and will adjust as time goes on."

Mack dropped his boots to the floor to sit forward. "Please tell me we got the assignment and we're gonna go after the jerk who did this."

"We did, and we are."

Kiley clasped the arms of her chair. "And you're taking lead?"

"I am." Sean glanced at Mack and found the frown he expected.

"So where do we start, boss?" Kiley asked.

Sean explained the details of how he'd discovered the hack. "Eisenhower is obtaining access to the logs, and until then we can only speculate on an action plan. But we all know gaining access to a tightly controlled database like this one is only possible with inside help."

"Something we need to watch for in reviewing the files." Kiley took another bite of her energy bar and chewed thoughtfully.

"Either way, it's the work of an extremely sophisticated hacker," Cam said.

Sean agreed. But who? "There's only one hacker I can think of who could pull this off."

"Phantom," Kiley said.

"I'd love to have a crack at nailing him." Cam's eyes narrowed. "He's been on the top of C3's most-wanted list for years. Seriously, the only thing they have on him after all that time is a witness sighting of a man fleeing a raided warehouse in Philadelphia where they found Phantom's hard drives and the partner Phantom's suspected of murdering."

"Been a while since we worked an investigation where a hacker turned killer," Kiley said. "They're few and far between."

Sean nodded. "It's also been a while since we went after a seriously paranoid hacker

27

like Phantom. This guy gives paranoia a new meaning."

Kiley frowned. "He thought the partner was trying to take over when in fact the partner hadn't done anything wrong."

"I heard something happened in his childhood to make him this way." Mack rubbed a hand over his wide jaw covered in whiskers, a ruddy red that matched his hair. "And he thinks everyone's out to get him. He's tuned in to even the remotest possibility of that and is ruthless when it comes to someone betraying him. Which is why we don't know more about him."

"What information did the recovered drives contain?" Kiley asked.

"Nothing of value in the hacking world." Frustration deepened Cam's voice. "He had a disk-wiping program running. By the time techs arrived on-scene there was virtually zero hacking info left to find. They did gather communications where Phantom calls out this partner and threatens his life. Agents tried to track the communications, but it didn't lead anywhere."

"Go ahead and get his physical description for me," Sean said. "It's at least something to start with."

Sean turned to Mack. "Once Cam obtains Phantom's file, check to see if they ran a ViCAP search on the murder. If not, run a current search and get the particulars entered. Maybe we'll come up with a similar murder."

Sean didn't need to explain ViCAP to Mack or anyone on the team. They were all familiar with the FBI's database designed to track and correlate violent crime information, especially murder. Current cases could be compared to others to see if their killer had struck before.

Finally looking alert, Mack set down his Red Bull can. "We should also consider witnesses in WITSEC. The majority of them were engaged in criminal behavior before they entered the program. It's not farfetched to think they might exploit their situation."

"Yeah. I can see that," Sean said. "Someone with strong hacking skills forms a grudge against the deputy assigned to them or simply hates their new life."

Kiley's eyebrows rose. "And that's a recipe for someone motivated to breach the system."

"Hang on. I'll check for any witnesses whose past crimes involved hacking." Sean logged into the WITSEC database and searched for anyone fitting the criteria. Several names populated the screen, but he quickly reviewed the details of their crimes and there was only one person with the skills to perform such a difficult hack. "One name fits the bill. A Dustee Carr, currently located in Portland, Oregon."

"Portland." Mack arched an eyebrow. "That's

a three-hour drive at max. We can interview her while we wait for database access."

"I'll go." The thrill of the hunt had Sean sitting forward, and he scanned Dustee's case notes. "Check this out. She once partnered with the FBI in an undercover sting to bring in Phantom."

Kiley leaned forward as well. "What happened?"

"She came close to infiltrating his organization, but he caught on to her and threatened her life."

"After he brutally murdered his partner, there's no doubt he'd follow through and kill her," Kiley said.

"Is that why she's in witness protection?" Cam asked.

"Yes." Sean turned to the team. "A connection to Phantom *and* WITSEC with the same person? That's highly suspicious."

Mack scowled. "Phantom could have her on his payroll. Offer her more money than she'd ever see in a legitimate enterprise. The whole WITSEC thing could be a smoke screen for her to help him gain access to the database."

"I need to head to Portland right away," Sean said.

"Good luck with that." Kiley shook her head. "If you want to talk to her, you'll need permission from the deputy in charge of her security, and that'll likely take a VIP to approve."

"We'll see." He turned back to the screen to

access the deputy's contact information. He took one look at the data and sat back, stunned.

"No. No way, Sean Nichols." Kiley scooted her chair forward. "Don't you gape at the screen like that and not say anything." She pushed past him to view the record. "It's Taylor? The deputy is Taylor Mills?"

"Yeah," Sean said, trying to make sense of it. "What're the odds of us knowing the deputy in charge of this suspect's protection?"

Cam shifted, planting his tactical boots firmly on the floor. "She was a big help on the Montgomery Three investigation—getting Harold Wilson settled safely in Portland and keeping him alive." Their prime witness in the investigation feared the person who abducted the girls would come after him, and he refused to talk until he was placed into witness protection.

"She's the best of the best." A fond smile erased Mack's scowl. "That's why I asked Eisenhower to have Wilson put under her protection in Portland."

Taylor and Mack had been friends since deputy training academy, so of course he would recommend her when they'd needed to place Wilson somewhere safe. But friends or not, Sean had agreed that her stellar qualifications and record made her the right deputy to take on Wilson's protection. And she had the necessary clearance to be read-in on the investigation and become a temporary member of the RED team so she could help coordinate between the team and Wilson for the duration of the investigation.

Sean had formed a virtual friendship with her during the investigation, and they'd kept it going. Yet he'd never met her in person. Never talked to her. Mack handled all of that. Sean had never even laid eyes on a picture of her, despite the many times he was tempted to find one, but they'd agreed not to do so. To remain semi-anonymous. An odd relationship to be sure, but it was working.

"Want me to give her a call and tell her you're on the way?" Mack asked.

"No!"

Kiley's eyebrow rose nearly to her hairline, and she gave him one of her famous interrogating stares.

Sean had kept his relationship with Taylor from them because of his unease with Mack, and Sean didn't need them to discover it now. If it got back to Eisenhower, Sean would be off the investigation without question. No way he would let that happen.

He took a breath to calm his nerves. "You can't tell her about the hack on an unsecured line, and I don't want her sitting for hours and wondering what I need from her."

Mack nodded, but a frown said he didn't much agree with Sean's plan.

Sean tried to turn his thoughts back to the investigation, but all he could think about was heading to Portland to see Taylor.

Taylor.

He lived in D.C. She lived in Portland. He never expected to meet her face-to-face.

Never.

Well, that was about to change.

"I'll get that file you need, but it'll take all of an hour, if that long," Cam said, already sounding bored. "What else do you want us to do while you're gone?"

"Would be good if you familiarized yourself with the WITSEC program. That way, when we get access to the logs and code, we'll be a step ahead."

"And the training tomorrow?" Kiley asked.

"Eisenhower's canceling it." Sean stood. "Hang tight while I request your access to the database."

The Assistant Chief Deputy U.S. Marshal was burning the midnight oil, and Sean went to his office to arrange the necessary permissions, all the while his thoughts remaining on Taylor.

He really would see her. *Unbelievable.*

He imagined stepping into her office. Saying hello. Her surprise. Would it be a good surprise for her or a bad one? He really didn't know. It was odd to even think about seeing her. She'd probably have the same reaction.

She seemed to get him in a way no one else did,

and he'd shared personal things that he hadn't told a living soul. A cold ball of dread formed in his stomach, and he grabbed a roll of antacids he made sure to carry in his pocket since the failed Montgomery Three investigation. He popped a minty tablet into his mouth and chewed.

Could he even look at her and not think about all he'd shared? He hadn't yet given her details, but he alluded to things he'd hidden from so many others. His mother's habitual lying. Her betrayal of everything a mother stood for. His fiancée's recent affair with his best friend, confirming for him that almost everyone lied, or if they didn't, he lacked the ability to figure out which people didn't and had the misfortune of surrounding himself with people who did.

For all he knew, Taylor was one of those people—a liar—and he hadn't figured it out yet. Would she prove him wrong, or was he about to find out she was exactly like the others?

CHAPTER 3

In a warm robe, her fingers pink and wrinkled from the hour spent in the tub, Taylor grabbed her phone and studied the missed call. She'd recently seen the number, but who did it belong to? She ran it over in her mind a few times.

"Duh!" She smacked her forehead. "Right. Dustee."

Her witness had changed her phone number yesterday because she'd given her last one to a guy named Wally who wouldn't quit texting and calling her.

"Sigh. Of course it would be you, Dustee." Taylor entered the number into her contact list. She wanted to be sure the next call would register with Dustee's name, as there would be a next call. Another. And another. She phoned all the time. Like *all* the time. Complaining about most everything, frequently getting into battles with her twin sister, Dianne, and Taylor ended up refereeing the fights. Dustee had spent most of her teen years behind a computer and hadn't developed strong social skills or any skills other than computer hacking. So she might be twenty-four, but she was very immature and acted like a spoiled teenager much of the time.

Taylor concentrated on positive thoughts and

tapped the number. No way she'd lose the peace she'd found in her long soak, and complainer or not, Dustee deserved Taylor's best effort. The call went directly to voicemail.

"Dustee, it's Taylor," she said, not sorry Dustee hadn't answered. "If you still need me, give me a call."

Taylor hung up and sat down at her laptop to transfer photos from her phone that she'd taken during her lunch break. She opened the first one of an elderly couple walking hand in hand, smiling at each other, love glowing on their faces. She tried to concentrate on cropping the image, but her mind kept going back to Dustee.

Taylor liked spending what little free time she had enjoying her photography hobby, but guilt had her closing her computer and reaching for her phone again. Why did she have to be such a people-pleaser? Her biggest flaw.

Taylor tried calling Dustee a second time and got her voicemail again. She could give up or she could call Dianne. She always knew what her twin was up to. Taylor dialed the number.

"Taylor, thank goodness." Dianne's relieved voice blasted through the phone. "I was just about to call you. Dustee should be back by now, but she's not. I don't know what to do."

"Back?" Taylor made sure she sounded calm, but worry took purchase in the pit of her stomach.

"From the library," Dianne said. "She's been

36

going there every night lately. Says she needs time to chill alone. I think it's a good idea. I know I appreciate the time alone too, but tonight . . . I don't know what happened. I keep trying to call her, and she's not answering."

Alarm bells went off in Taylor's head. "Do you think she's using the library computers?"

"I wondered the same thing. Even asked her about it. She said she wasn't, but she's really struggling with internet withdrawal. When she comes home from there, she's in such a good mood. So maybe. Yeah. Maybe she is."

Taylor glanced at the clock. Quarter after ten. "How late is she?"

"The library closed at eight."

Missing for two hours. A problem? "She could've stopped for something to eat or to grab some groceries."

"No. No way. After the shoe incident, she's broke."

Right, the shoe incident. How could Taylor have forgotten? Using the money earmarked for her share of the rent, Dustee had spent seven hundred dollars on designer pumps last week. A typical, foolish Dustee move. Dianne was right. Her sister didn't have even a dollar to her name right now.

Taylor's warning bells grew louder, ringing like an entire bell choir in her head, and she ran to her room to get dressed. "Which branch does Dustee go to and how does she get there?"

"She takes the bus." Dianne shared the library's location and Dustee's usual route.

Taylor wedged the phone between her ear and shoulder to pull on a pair of jeans. "I'll go look for her. You stay put with the doors locked and call me if she comes home."

"Do you think something bad happened? Like maybe she *did* access the internet and Phantom found her?"

Taylor did. She totally did. But she wouldn't admit it and scare Dianne even more. "Let's not worry about that yet. You know how flaky Dustee can be."

"You're right. Let me know what you find."

"You can count on it." While Taylor hated hanging up on Dianne when she was in such a worried state, keeping the connection with her would only slow Taylor down.

Father, please. Please let Dustee be safe. I should have . . .

"Stop. Don't waste time beating yourself up. Plenty of time for that after Dustee is found." She tossed her phone on the bed and put on the first shirt she found, a bright pink knit top. She covered it with a leather bomber jacket for warmth and to hide her holster, allowing her to carry and not raise suspicion from anyone she might run into. She snatched up her phone to pull up the bus stop closest to the twins' apartment, then raced for her car, grabbing her purse and credentials as she fled.

The streets were nearly deserted, and she made the trip from suburban Beaverton to Portland in record time, even with the dense fog. She'd have loved to run with lights and siren, but she had no clear-cut reason to do so and didn't want to risk distracting the few motorists who were out and cause an accident on foggy roads.

She parked outside the twins' apartment building and took off on foot, following the most direct route toward the bus stop. The overcast night, the fog, the mist so typical for April in Portland made a simple walk feel ominous and foreboding when in fact the neighborhood was safe with good walkability. That was one of the reasons the twins chose to live here. The rent was a bit higher than they should've committed to, and they often struggled to pay it, but thankfully they hadn't been late in the six months since moving into this apartment. Even with Dustee's shoe mistake.

Taylor climbed higher up the hill, where the dense wall of fog lifted a bit. No sign of Dustee. Up ahead on the shoulder, she spotted what looked like a pair of women's pumps.

Dustee's shoes?

Taylor kicked into gear, charging uphill, panting with the exertion it took to scale the steep incline. She squatted by the rainbow-colored shoes, size nine, kicked off and lying there discarded. Her heart dropped. No doubt these were the shoes that caused the disagreement between the twins last week.

Had Taylor's worst fear come true? Had she let her guard down for just an hour and something bad had happened to someone under her care?

No. Please. No. Let her be okay.

Panic gripped Taylor. She couldn't move. *Think.* That old familiar blanket of guilt over her brother's death settled over her. She struggled to take a deep breath, the thick air clogging her throat, and she wanted to collapse in a heap.

No. Stop. Get a grip. Focus. Dustee needs you.

Taylor swallowed hard. She had to keep it together. Find her witness. No matter what.

Picking up the shoes, she stood and looked around. No other sign of Dustee, but no sign of foul play either. Had someone come along in a vehicle and abducted her? Maybe she'd struggled, and that was how her pumps ended up beside the road. What other explanation could there be for Dustee leaving such expensive shoes behind?

Taylor couldn't think of a single one, but she could be wrong and Dustee hadn't been abducted. Only a thorough search of the area would tell for certain. Taylor had passed an alley on the way up the hill, a place where Dustee might have hidden if she feared for her life. She could still be there. Maybe hurt. Bleeding. Terrified. Calling Taylor on the phone, and Taylor hadn't answered. Then Phantom finding her. Finishing her off.

Please, no.

Adrenaline burned through Taylor's body as she sprinted toward the alley. She stumbled. Righted herself before making a crazy nosedive down the incline. Maybe this was what had happened to Dustee. Someone followed her. She'd bolted. Gotten off-kilter. Kicked off her shoes to run faster. Hopefully, Taylor would find her in the alley.

She hung a right at the fish market on the corner, home to her favorite wild-caught salmon, though now the fishy smell only made Taylor's stomach roil. She entered the alley, her free hand resting on her gun. She eased cautiously into the space.

"Is anyone here?" she shouted but resisted saying Dustee's name in case someone was lying in wait for her.

Taylor heard movement ahead. She searched the fog. Nothing moved in the haze. She dropped the shoes and drew her weapon, bracing it with both hands. She moved deeper into the narrow space. Thick fog clung to the ground, swirling around her ankles and dampening her clothing. If Dustee was lying injured or dead, there was no way Taylor could see her.

A noise clanged ahead, sounding like something crashing against metal.

Fear constricted Taylor's heart. "Hello?"

"Help—I'm here!" Dustee's frightened voice came from deeper in the alley.

She was alive! Dustee was alive!

Thank you. Thank you. Thank you.

Taylor's heart lifted, then immediately dropped again. Dustee might be alive but she could be seriously injured. The urge to rush toward her witness's voice grabbed Taylor by the throat, but caution was always the name of the game for a law enforcement officer in a risky situation. And always her manner of operating.

"I'm coming. Hold on." Taylor took slow steps, her heart pounding. Just ahead, she could make out a white grate lying on the ground. Ah, right, the clanking sound. She saw a large duct opening cut into the wall of the fish market.

"Dustee? Where are you?" Taylor called.

"Here." The dejected voice came from inside the duct.

Taylor bent down. Found her witness folded over and lodged inside.

"I'm so glad you came." Dustee exhaled a shaky breath. "I'm stuck and dropped my phone. I can't reach it."

"Why are you in there in the first place?"

"Phantom was chasing me."

Taylor's mouth fell open, and she fired a look around the area, searching for the hacker. "How do you know it was Phantom?"

"Who else would be stalking me?"

Gun still in hand, Taylor squinted into the fog. "Stalking as in tracking you for some time or just tonight?"

"Just tonight."

Phantom could still be nearby, and he was a ruthless killer. Taylor had to take precautions. Their safety came before freeing Dustee from the duct. "I'm going to clear the alley to make sure he's gone, and then I'll come back for you."

"I'm sorry." Dustee began to cry. "I messed up big-time."

"You used the computers at the library to access the internet, didn't you?"

"Yes."

Taylor opened her mouth to chastise Dustee, but her eyes were wide with terror. Taylor wouldn't add to her misery. "I'll be right back."

She made her way carefully down the alley. Step after step into the misty darkness, her gun raised. She flipped open the dumpster. Found it empty and sighed in relief. She ripped lids off trash cans. Kept moving. Finally, she came to the entrance of the alley and surveyed the next cross street.

No one. No Phantom. They were alone.

Breathing deeply, she rushed back to Dustee and holstered her gun before aiming her phone's light into the duct. Dustee flinched, but not before Taylor saw her red-rimmed eyes and big tears rolling over high cheekbones. A natural blonde with striking bone structure, Dustee was a real beauty. Model pretty. As was Dianne. They couldn't go anywhere without drawing attention. Some of it unwanted, but much of it acknowledged and exploited by Dustee. She leveraged nearly everything, but not right now. Even if she'd accessed the internet and perhaps alerted Phantom, she was the victim here, and she was wedged in tight.

"I hope I don't have to call the fire department to get you out of there," Taylor said.

"It would be embarrassing, but um, *hello! Hunky firemen.*"

Taylor rolled her eyes. Still, she had to admit that Dustee's humor helped lessen her worry. "And what logical explanation could I offer them for your predicament other than the truth? You know I can't share your WITSEC status with anyone, so you'd better hope I can get you out."

Dustee's lip trembled. "I'm sorry. I am. Honest."

Taylor stowed her phone. "I know you are, sweetie. I know. Press down now as tightly as you can and I'll pull on your feet. Can you do that?"

"Yes." Dustee flattened out.

Taylor grasped Dustee's ankles and tugged hard, inching her forward until her bare feet rested on the pavement.

"I can take it from here." Dustee maneuvered herself all the way out and collapsed on the ground. She lifted her arms overhead in a stretch, those big tears returning.

"I thought he was going to find me. I thought I was going to d—" Her voice broke, and she drew her knees up to her chest. She wrapped her long arms around them, her body convulsing with gut-wrenching sobs.

Taylor squatted and patted Dustee's back. "It's okay. You're safe."

"B-b-but he knows where I am n-n-now." Her wailing increased.

Right. Not good. "Did you give out your actual address online?"

"No."

"Okay then. Your apartment is still safe for now, but we need to get over there. Dianne is alone, and Phantom could show up."

Dustee sobered instantly and got to her feet. "Let's go."

"Let me grab your shoes to protect your feet." Taylor jogged back to where she'd dropped the pumps.

In Taylor's opinion, the shoes were nothing special. Just basic leather pumps in a rainbow of colors. Taylor could appreciate a nice pair of heels, but how in the world did these cost so incredibly much? And why was Dustee so desperate to own them that she'd risk being evicted from her apartment? Not that she really had to worry about that. Dianne was a saver, and Dustee counted on her sister to bail her out all the time. Why would this incident be any different?

Dustee stepped into the shoes. Taylor was five-foot-nine, but in the pumps Dustee towered over her as she glided like a runway model toward her apartment.

Hand on her weapon, Taylor set off while continuing to check their surroundings, searching for the hacker who'd brutally murdered his partner. "Are you sure it was Phantom who tailed you?"

"Who else would it be?"

"What about Wally?"

Dustee shook her head. "Wally's short. This guy was much taller. Plus his body language didn't say he was a man interested in romance. I've seen that before. This wasn't that. He looked rigid and angry."

Taylor wasn't certain you could get all of that from the way a guy approached, but Dustee knew men's advances and surely believed it. "Regardless of who it was, your internet visits compromised your identity, and I can't take a chance in leaving you here."

"You're going to move us? Change our names again?" Dustee gaped at Taylor.

"Yes. If my supervisor doesn't kick you out of the program for violating your MOU." Taylor didn't need to explain, as Dustee knew every witness was required to sign a Memorandum of Understanding before entering WITSEC. The agreement outlined the witness's obligations

46

upon admission to the program, and that included acknowledging that if they violated said amendment, it was cause for being removed from the program.

"Kick us out?" Dustee shot a panicked looked at Taylor. "But Dianne didn't do anything wrong."

Exactly. "Maybe not but her status is dependent on yours, remember? You screw up, you both pay the price for it." Just like every other time, Taylor thought but wouldn't add as she was already being tough on the stressed-out woman.

"I-I . . ." She started crying again and sniffled. "I really did it this time, didn't I?"

"Yes." Taylor let the word hang there for the next block, giving Dustee time to grasp the magnitude of her mistake. "I'll go to bat for you, though. You know that, right?"

"I hoped, but even I can see this time I don't deserve a second chance."

"I'm thinking of Dianne."

"Yeah. Help us. For Dianne." Dustee swiped her forearm over her eyes and jogged up to the apartment door to unlock it.

Once inside, Taylor engaged the dead bolt behind them.

"Where have you been?" Dianne charged her sister and swept her into a hug. The pair were identical, even down to their hairstyles.

"No time to explain," Taylor said, trying to

convey her sense of urgency. "I need you both to pack a bag. Fast. I'll arrange for backup and then we're out of here."

"A bag? Backup?" Dianne turned to Taylor. "I don't understand."

"Your new identities are blown. You'll have to relocate. Grab only what you need for a few days. I'll have the rest of your things packed and shipped."

Dianne opened, then abruptly closed her mouth. Opened it again and shook her head. "Wait. How were our identities blown?"

Taylor glanced at Dustee, who bit her lip, clearly not ready to admit her actions to her twin. Fine, Taylor would have to do that. But not now. "I'll explain later at the office, where you'll be safe until I find you a new home."

Dianne gaped at Taylor and wrung her hands.

Taylor took Dianne's arm to steer her toward her bedroom. "Come on. Let's get you packed."

"I'm sorry," Dustee called after them.

Dianne jerked free and spun to face her sister. "You did this, didn't you? You couldn't stay away from the internet. Broke the rules. Now Phantom is after us again. You're ruining my life, and I'll never forgive you."

"I know, and I don't deserve forgiveness," Dustee said quietly.

Taylor wanted to rail at Dustee for the poor-pitiful-me act she was putting on. At least Taylor thought it was an act. It was her go-to method to play on Dianne's sympathies, who usually fell for it.

Not Taylor. "Okay, both of you. Move! Now! We can iron out your differences once I know you're *safe*."

They stood unmoving, staring at her.

Taylor got it. Dianne's life had taken a serious change in course and she had to process it. But now wasn't the time to sort out her emotions. Now was the time for action.

Taylor took Dianne's arm and directed her into her bedroom. Taylor found a suitcase in the closet and opened it on the bed. She eyed Dianne, who continued to stare blankly.

Taylor needed to break through her shock to make her move. She got in Dianne's face. "Fill it, Dianne. Now! While I check on Dustee. Do you understand?"

She nodded woodenly and started throwing clothes from a dresser drawer into the suitcase.

Confident she would keep packing, Taylor hurried down the hall to find Dustee opening a matching suitcase, tears streaming down her face. Would Dustee actually realize for once that she'd been extremely foolish to risk her agreement with the agency—and her sister's life—all for an internet fix?

Maybe. Even if Dustee was tossed out of the program, Taylor hoped that since Dianne had done nothing wrong, she would at least be able to continue in WITSEC. But then Taylor didn't think Dianne would be willing to leave her twin for any reason, not even to protect her own life.

And that meant it was up to Taylor to make sure Dianne stayed alive, no matter the cost.

CHAPTER 4

Taylor peered out the apartment window. Phantom could be out there. Watching. She didn't see anyone lingering near the building, but the street was shrouded in a blanket of fog so thick that she could barely make out the parking lot. If Phantom truly was trailing Dustee, they would never see him. He'd earned his nickname. He was too smart to be seen. Too smart to be caught.

Two of her fellow deputies rolled up, lights running and spiraling into the murky night. She charged outside and down the walk, glad to see her friend Deputy Roger Glover climb out of his vehicle. One of their best deputies, she could trust him with her life. The other deputy was a fifteen-year department veteran, Jim Coates. Another trustworthy and skilled law enforcement officer. She brought them up to date on the situation and quickly positioned them at intervals along the apartment's walkway.

Taylor was likely being too cautious, but never before had any witness who followed the program's stringent rules been killed. Taylor wasn't about to be the first deputy in the history of WITSEC to have that happen.

She hurried back inside, and keeping the twins between her and the building for safety,

Taylor rushed them to her car. Adrenaline burned through Taylor's body, and her heart thumped hard as she quickly got them on the road with the other deputies flanking their vehicle.

"Is all of this really necessary?" Dustee asked from the back seat, sounding bored now.

"Necessary?" Dianne's voice rose a few octaves, and she swiveled to look at her sister. "It wouldn't be if you'd followed the rules. But no. You can't do it, can you?"

Taylor couldn't have said it any better. She glanced in the mirror to see Dustee's reaction. Her expression was tight with remorse, but then she'd acted like that in the past only to turn around and do something ridiculous.

"I'm sorry." Anyone who didn't know Dustee would believe her sincere tone. "I don't know what more you want me to say."

Dianne crossed her arms. "How about that you're done putting me in the line of fire? That you'll never endanger my life again for some selfish whim?"

"I won't."

"Pinkie promise." Dianne held her little finger out to her twin.

Taylor had seen their childhood ritual too many times to count. In the end, it never meant anything to Dustee, and she broke her promises left and right, but for some reason it still comforted Dianne.

She was mature, responsible, considerate, and a true pleasure to protect. Dustee suffered from ADD but hadn't been diagnosed until she was an adult. Their parents had told her often enough that they wished she'd behave more like Dianne, and when Dustee couldn't manage it, she'd taken the opposite approach to life. Dianne felt bad about the ongoing criticism heaped on Dustee, and Dianne had enabled her sister's outlandish behavior. Now it was ingrained. Dianne still enabled Dustee, but at times Dianne desperately wanted to tell her sister off and claim she never wanted to see her again.

Still, no matter how much Dianne protested, Taylor knew she wouldn't cut off a person who was like a part of her physical being. For Dianne's sake, Taylor would do all she could not only to keep them safe but together.

Taylor concentrated on her mirrors and their surroundings for the rest of the drive and didn't let up, even when she safely trailed Jim into the secured parking structure. She hustled the twins up to the conference room and sat them down next to each other.

Safe. They were safe. For now.

Thank you.

Still, they were mad at each other, and Taylor needed to get them talking and ironing out their differences. She opened her mouth to start the reconciliation process, but the room closed in on her.

"Go ahead and work this out," she barely got out as her throat started to close. "I'll be right back."

She bolted into the hallway. Everything hit her at once. The danger. Dustee's near brush with death. The high stakes Taylor faced every day. The worry. The fear. The loss of her brother. All of it, taking her breath away.

Her legs collapsed, and she slid to the floor. She'd almost lost a witness. Almost had one murdered. Why? Because she wanted a soak in the tub.

Selfishness. Pure selfishness. Exactly like her brother, history repeating itself.

Hadn't she learned anything with his loss? Carefully thought out every move—every step— every day?

Yeah, until tonight. And look what happened.

A brutal killer had tracked Dustee down, and the twins could have died. Both of them. It was by God's grace, not Taylor's good sense, that they lived to see another day. She had to work harder. Do better. Put her focus where it needed to be. Not on herself or her life. Not on what she wanted, but on her witnesses. Only on her witnesses.

"Taylor! Good. I'm glad I found you." Alison, a perky blonde and their section's administrative assistant, charged up to Taylor's cubicle not long after Alison arrived for her early morning shift. "There's an FBI agent in reception to see you."

"Seriously?" Taylor wasn't expecting any visitors, much less someone from the FBI, and she wasn't in the mood to deal with one of their agents. "I'm working on Dustee and Dianne's relocation paperwork. I really don't have time for a visitor."

"He says it's urgent, and he's not leaving until you talk to him."

"But I—"

"You have to go out there." Alison, a usually sweet and easygoing woman, narrowed her eyes. "He planted himself in a chair, and he means business. He's not leaving."

Taylor sighed. "Did he say what this is about?"

Alison shook her head. "But he's not leaving until he talks to you. I know that much."

"Fine." Taylor resisted sighing again. "I'll give him five minutes. What's his name?"

"Sean Nichols."

Taylor's jaw dropped, and it took everything she was made of to recover. "Sean's here?"

Alison's eyebrows rose. "You know him?"

Taylor nodded, but *know* wasn't the right word. Could she truly know someone she'd never met in person? She doubted it, but she did know quite a lot about him. His likes. His dislikes. His past. His fears. His hopes. They'd been online friends for months now, and it was such a relief to have a friend who understood what it was like to work a high-stress job, and eventually they'd poured out their struggles to each other. Since they lived on opposite sides of the country, the relationship seemed safe. It was easy to confide in him and nice to have a caring person share her burden. So yeah, maybe she *did* know him.

Regardless, she was about to meet him face-to-face.

Sean. He was here. Really here.

She started to speak but had to swallow hard as the words stuck in her throat. "Tell him I'll be right out."

"Perfect." Alison turned to march through the busy bullpen, her short skirt swishing. She always looked fresh and put-together, and today was no exception. Something Taylor might have managed herself, if she'd put on makeup and done something with her hair after her bath and hadn't spent her night refereeing the twins' argument.

She ran her fingers through the tangled mop to settle a few wayward strands into place and strode across the room. Feeling the bulky bomber jacket, she whisked it off and hung it over her arm. If only she had time to do something more with her appearance before meeting him for the first time. But why?

She wasn't interested in a romantic relationship

any more than he was. Which was why the online friendship was ideal for both of them. Caring at a distance—removed. It felt less real than a relationship where you sat across a table to share a meal. Or went for a walk. Or even simply hung out. Less permanent and less able to wind up hurting either of them.

Excited and terrified at the same time, she paused near the narrow window next to the door. The man she'd been friends with for six months sat tall in a plush chair, his feet firmly planted on the carpet. He wore dark jeans, a white button-down shirt, and a navy corduroy jacket, but oh, he wore it all so well. His long legs were coiled, and a sense of power and strength emanated from his body. His hair was brown, cut short on the sides, a bit longer on top with a slight curl. But it was his eyes . . . man, those eyes.

They held Taylor in place. Brown. Nearly black. Piercing and yet gentle at the same time. How could that combination even exist? It wasn't possible, was it?

Her love of photography made her fingers itch to take out her phone and snap a picture, but a good shot required the flash, and the glass would reflect the light. Not to mention that he would see her do it.

He shifted his focus and looked her squarely in the eye. Blood rushed to her head. She should look away, but she couldn't. She could easily imagine those eyes fixed on her and only her for the rest of her life.

Her breath caught in her chest. Seriously, did someone suck all the oxygen from the space?

"Is everything okay, Taylor?" Chief Inman asked from behind her, but she still couldn't look away from Sean.

Okay? No, it wasn't okay. Her heart was doing backflips in her chest, for goodness' sake. Right here in her office. Her workplace.

"Sure, fine," she finally got out, and heard Inman walk away.

She rested her hand on the doorknob, started to turn it, but stopped. The moment she stepped through that door and talked to Sean, things would change between them. Change drastically, and she doubted they would ever be the same again.

CHAPTER 5

Sean sat forward. The woman watching him had to be Taylor. After all, if he were in her shoes, he'd be there with his face plastered against the window too. She opened the door and put a hand on the jamb, pausing as if uncertain how to proceed. What her problem was, he had no idea—coming closer to him was the only course of action he could prescribe. Real close, giving him a better look at her eyes. At her face. At *her*.

She started his way, a graceful glide over the carpet. He pegged her at five-foot-nine, and her strawberry-blond hair was straight but flipped up at her shoulders. She wore a form-fitting pink top over dark jeans. The bomber jacket slung over her arm did nothing to hide her curvy figure. She stepped up to him, her gaze assessing him with a burning intensity. Her almond-shaped eyes were brown and bottomless, making his heart pound.

"Sean?" she asked, and he couldn't find anything coherent to say in response.

He never imagined the woman he'd been chatting and emailing with could be this attractive, this captivating. He'd only known that she was special and a good friend, someone who supported him when he was down. Who helped him work through issues in both his private and work lives. Who shared his joy when life went right. But man, seeing her was a kick to the gut. She had an innocence to her, mixed with a world-weary look that he found incredibly sexy, and he didn't want to look away.

"Something wrong?" Her mesmerizing eyes narrowed in confusion.

"Wrong?" he repeated.

"You're staring. I got called out last night and haven't had a chance to freshen up. I apologize if I look like Frankenstein." She chuckled, but the joke fell flat.

If this was how she looked after an all-nighter, if he saw her again when she was fresh and rested, he'd be a goner for sure.

She raised her eyebrows pointedly. "Did you want something, or did you drive all this way just to look at me?"

The receptionist snickered.

That brought him to his senses, and he snapped out of his trance to get to his feet. "Sorry. Been driving for hours and up all night. Guess I zoned out."

Right. Zoned out. So why did his vision seem extra crisp as he took in additional details like her full lips and cute nose?

Shake it off, man. This is ridiculous.

He smiled to ease her concern, maybe to break the hold she had over him, and held out his hand. "It's good to finally meet in person."

She clasped his hand. The warm connection to the woman who'd been a big part of his life for the last six months made him want to continue holding her hand, though she was already pulling it free.

"What brings you here?" She didn't sound happy about the visit.

He hadn't known what to expect, but he didn't think she'd be upset that he'd shown up. "I need to talk to you about one of your witnesses."

"Go ahead," she said.

What? They were such good friends online, and she wasn't even going to invite him in? "Not here. In private."

"I'm kind of up to my neck in alligators right now and don't have much time."

Something in her voice told him she'd been pushed hard to the breaking point and was barely holding it together. Something he could help her work through if she'd only contacted him. But for once she didn't. Why, he didn't know. But whatever she was fighting could be the reason she seemed distant, and her mood had nothing to do with him.

He could hope anyway. "Trust me. You'll want to hear this."

"Follow me." She went to the door and swiped her ID card through a wall-mounted reader. The door popped open with a solid click, and she led him toward a small conference room at a corner with glass walls on three sides. He had to force himself to look away from the sway of her hips, and he lectured himself all the way down the hall to keep their conversation all business.

She sat and pointed to a nearby chair, but he was too unsettled to sit close to her. He propped his shoulder against the wall and waited for her to say something to ease the tension quickly filling the room.

She dropped her jacket on the chair next to her and crossed her legs. "This is really surreal, isn't it? Meeting like this."

He nodded, trying his best not to stare at her long legs. "To be fair, I've had a few hours to think about it and just sprung it on you. I was in Seattle for a training and drove down."

"You could have texted or emailed."

Okay, maybe she was mad about *that*. "What I've come to discuss is too sensitive for a text or email. I didn't want to let you know I was on the way and leave you to worry for hours about the reason for my visit."

"That was kind of you." She smiled. Her eyes lit from inside, and her button nose crinkled to give him the barest of hints at the mischievous part of her personality he'd come to know. She rested her hands on her knee, looking more relaxed now.

"You mentioned you were having a bad day. Can I help?" It felt odd to ask this question in person, and yet it felt natural too, and he was glad to be here for her.

"It's a problem with a witness. I'm working through it." That was it. Her whole explanation.

Odd. She was always straightforward and willing to discuss her issues online. Maybe she was more uncomfortable with him than he thought. Or were they only online friends and it didn't carry over to the physical world? It was one thing to reveal only what you wanted to online, but something else to actually know someone in person.

"So who do you want to talk about?" she asked.

Right. Move on. Away from the personal. Keep on task. Exactly what he needed. "Dustee Carr."

"Dustee?" Taylor's foot dropped to the floor, and she sat forward. "What did she do now?"

Interesting. "Nothing, as far as I know."

She arched a brow. "Then why are you here?"

He moved away from the wall and planted his palms on the tabletop to convey the seriousness of his visit. "Before I tell you, you have to know this is on a need-to-know basis. No one besides you needs to know right now. Not even your chief. Got it?"

She nodded, but the tightening of her hand suggested he was scaring her when he never wanted to do that.

"The WITSEC database has been hacked," he began, deciding to come right out with it. "And the hacker is selling witness details on the dark web."

"Hacked? But how? Who?" She shot to her feet, her gaze searching the room as if she'd find the answers there.

He pushed off the table. "We don't know yet. That's why I'm here. This breach took some insane hacking skills, and the hacker had to have help from someone on the inside or by someone connected to WITSEC. That means I'm looking at everyone associated with the program with those abilities. Dustee is the only witness who could pull this off, so I'm starting with her."

He had to give Taylor credit. She didn't so much as blink at the suggestion. "You think she did this?"

He didn't . . . yet. "Isn't she banned from computer use?"

"Yes, but I found out last night that she's been using library computers and going online."

Interesting twist. "Then that gives her both means and opportunity."

She nodded. "But Phantom threatened her life. Why would she risk working with him?"

Good question. One Sean had spent most of the drive from Seattle thinking about. "Maybe he didn't threaten her. Maybe she's been working with him all along, and the two of them orchestrated things. You know, getting accepted into WITSEC to provide him an insider within the program."

"I . . . I . . ." Taylor shook her head and fell back into her chair. "I can't begin to think that's true. I mean, she hasn't shown even a hint of violating her agreement until now."

"She could easily do so without you finding out."

Taylor eyed him suspiciously. "Like how?"

"Use cash to buy a computer. Keep it at a locker at work and go any number of places to use free Wi-Fi. Or even use her work's Wi-Fi."

"I suppose, but Dustee lives with her twin sister, Dianne. I know she would've caught on and reported it."

"Wouldn't it be odd for her to tell you? The twin thing and all."

Taylor shook her head. "Not for Dianne. She would know it put their lives in jeopardy, and she's very protective of Dustee's safety."

Made sense. "Okay, I'll get a warrant to search Dustee's workplace and for the library network logs to track her movements online."

"You can get all that information?"

"Yes, unless Dustee used a VPN."

Taylor frowned. "I need you to explain that to me."

"It's basically a special IP address that prevents others from seeing the physical location a user logged in from." He gave the situation additional thought. "Or, as a former hacker, she might try to alter the library's security settings. Though their network is probably locked down tight, she has the skills to alter the settings."

Taylor's expression tightened. "If Dustee used one of these VPNs, then you can't track her movements online?"

"Exactly."

"I can't imagine she'd buy a VPN. She would have to know we could track that purchase and have proof she was violating her agreement."

Sean thought Taylor was acting awfully naïve for a deputy working with former criminals. "If she met up with someone locally to buy bitcoins with cash, she could use them online and hide any purchases from you."

Taylor nodded. "She would definitely know all about that."

"Right." Most hackers were intimately familiar with bitcoin, the virtual currency often used for illegal purchases, making it the payment of choice on the dark web.

Taylor ran a hand through hair that looked silky soft. "Dustee lives in a time warp. She acts like an out-of-control teenager most of the time and doesn't think about long-term consequences. Could mean she actually did get a VPN and bought a computer. I can check her credit-card bills and bank accounts for any large cash withdrawals."

Thankful for her cooperation, Sean smiled. "I don't want you to think that I have any evidence of wrongdoing on her part. But I also haven't seen the database logs or files yet. Which means I can't eliminate her potential involvement. I should have access later today. Right now, though, I'd like to question her about Phantom."

Taylor sighed. "So *that's* how he knew where she was—it actually wasn't her fault."

"What? You lost me there."

"Someone followed her last night when she left the library. She believes it was Phantom trying to kill her. She thought he'd somehow tracked her online, that she'd brought the attack on herself. But the database breach is most likely how he found her, right? He got her information from the hack."

Even more interesting. "Probably. Unless she lied to you and is working with him. Once we have access to the files, we'll know if her details were stolen."

Taylor clenched her hands together. "What about my other witnesses? Are they in danger?"

"Possibly. As is Dustee, if she isn't working with Phantom."

"No worries about her safety at the moment. She's in our conference room and won't be going back to her apartment again." Taylor's eyes, the color of dark honey, narrowed.

Her agony made Sean's gut clench. He had to shove his hands in his pockets to stop himself from reaching out to her. Online, he'd helped her work through painful problems, but he'd never had to see the pain in her eyes. The darkness lingering there cut him to the quick, and he wanted to do whatever he could to ease her emotional turmoil.

"I should warn my other witnesses." Her focus flashed back to him. "No, wait. What if their records aren't affected? I would upset them for no reason. Maybe panic them. But if I don't tell them, and their data *was* sold . . ."

He wished he could help make the decision for her, but there was nothing he could do except warn her of the danger and then make himself available as she worked her way through it. "You'll have to be the one to decide if you want to tell them to be more vigilant. But what if it scares them into doing something dumb? Like running?"

She nodded absently, obviously thinking about her people and potential consequences. She was committed to each of her witnesses. No matter the stunts they pulled, she did her very best for them. It was one of the things among many that he admired about her. Her loyalty knew no bounds, and until now, when she didn't seem to want him here, he thought he'd gained her trust and loyalty too. But had he?

He opened his mouth to ask, but then snapped it shut. He couldn't afford to be distracted by personal matters, and neither could she. *Focus.*

That was the word of the hour. Day. Week. If word of the hack got out, thousands of people in the program would panic and act hastily, putting themselves in even more danger.

He crossed the room and sat beside her. He caught a whiff of her fresh, clean scent. Reminded him of when his mother used to hang sheets on the clothesline in the backyard when he was little, and he ran through them. A time when his father was still living at home. When his mother didn't lie and cheat, but baked cookies and bandaged skinned knees. A time when he'd felt loved . . .

He blinked a few times. What was going on with him today? He must be more tired than he'd first thought, to be thinking about his mother. He closed his eyes for a brief moment and counted to ten, erasing his wayward thoughts, before opening them again. "You can't mention the hack to your witnesses. Not under any circumstances."

She leaned closer to him, and he could see a hint of black in her eyes, and the tiniest of birthmarks near her right ear. Like a little strawberry rose. His hand lifted to touch the mark as if it had a mind of its own, and he slapped it down on the table, the sound cracking through the small room.

She jerked back.

"Sorry," he said, but didn't try to explain. How could he do that when he didn't understand it himself?

She firmed her shoulders, and he was glad to see her worry dissipate a fraction. "Don't worry. I'm used to putting up a professional wall with my witnesses, and I won't say a word about the hack itself. But I might give them a heads-up and tell them to be more vigilant."

"That's your choice," he said, but wished she hadn't chosen to do so. "I'd like to talk to Dustee now if that's okay."

She nodded. "And you won't tell her about the hack either, right?"

"Not until I decide that she can be trusted."

"You should know. She's not the best at keeping secrets or at following rules. Hence her arrest. Telling her before this is all resolved might be a big mistake."

"Right. I keep forgetting that you work for the only law enforcement agency that puts criminals back on the streets instead of incarcerating them."

She lurched back, her mouth falling open.

Oh, man. Not good. "Sorry, that probably didn't come out right, did it?"

"Probably not."

"It's true, though. You've told me that yourself, at the end of a bad day."

She stiffened. "Not in those words, and I didn't think you'd use it against me."

"I didn't . . ." he started to say, but knew an explanation was pointless when he'd done exactly that. "I'm sorry. I was in the wrong. Still friends?"

She watched him for a long moment, and despite her questioning gaze, he loved looking at her. Connecting with her in the real world instead of the anonymous cyber world.

"This is too weird, don't you think?" She shook her head. "I mean, we've shared a ton of information about ourselves. It's like I do and don't know the man sitting next to me. Does that make sense?"

"Perfect sense. I feel the same way." *And I'm glad to see you, even if you don't return the sentiment,* he couldn't add without exposing himself to a world of hurt.

She took a breath and let it out as if blowing away his comment. "Thank goodness you're only in town for the day or this could get complicated."

Her continued rejection stung. "About that."

"Yes?" She fidgeted with the zipper pull on her jacket. She was as nervous as he was.

He found that oddly comforting. "If I believe Dustee's not working with Phantom, I plan to enlist her help in finding him, or whoever the hacker might be. And since it's looking like Phantom has shown himself here, it's likely I'll be in Portland until he's caught."

"What?" Her voice shot up an octave, drawing the attention of a deputy walking past the glass wall. "You can't work here. I . . . we shared things. Private things. Things I haven't told

71

others. Looking at you today, I'm reminded of them. I can't deal with bringing those memories up every hour of every day."

So *that* was it. Her emotional distance wasn't about him or about their friendship. They were still on solid footing. He could help with the way she was feeling, and hopefully their friendship would survive because he valued it more than anything else in his personal life. "I can work out of the local FBI office. That way you won't have to see me all the time."

"There's a problem with that," she said when he'd expected her to jump on his comment and embrace it. "Dustee is my responsibility. For her own safety, I plan to move her to another city as soon as possible."

Right. Her whole thing with protecting people to make up for the loss of her brother. "Sorry. That'll have to wait. We need her help. We can arrange for a local safe house, and I'll make sure she doesn't come to any harm."

"How?" Taylor stood and stared at him. "No one can promise that."

She was questioning his abilities? Really?

He got up to look her in the eye. "You know my skills."

"Sure, your stint on HRT makes you perfectly qualified." Of course she'd bring up his time on the FBI's Hostage Rescue Team. She'd been very interested in the details of that experience. Her eyes sparked, and she looked ready to fight him. "That doesn't ensure Dustee won't be harmed."

"Neither does moving her to another city." He took a beat of time to keep from showing his building frustration. "Look. This isn't negotiable, Taylor. My team wants Dustee's assistance. I want it too. If you're worried about Dustee, then partner with me and help protect her."

"I can't do that. I told you why. We . . . this . . ." She waved a hand between them. "It's too awkward. We'll have to find another solution." Expressions he couldn't decipher flitted across her face, but underneath it all lingered a thread of anguish.

Sean hated that he was the cause of her discomfort. Hated it more than he thought possible. They'd been together for less than an hour. Forget his overwhelming reaction to seeing her today. Forget that he found her attractive. That all paled in comparison to one fact.

He had feelings for her. Something he didn't realize until today.

Man, he hoped she would agree to work together, even though it wasn't a good idea for either of them. He wanted her here. By his side, supporting his efforts as he took lead on a high-stakes investigation for the first time, and he could encourage her in return. But if that didn't happen, he would still continue.

He had to do his job first—with or without her.

CHAPTER 6

Taylor led the way to the conference room, where Dustee and Dianne were locked in a heated discussion. Taylor had been gone for, what, thirty minutes? And they were already sniping at each other again. She wanted to lecture the women who were acting more like three-year-olds than adults, but she didn't want Sean to see how exasperated she was with her witnesses.

Funny thing, though. This was exactly the kind of situation she would share with him at the end of the day. She wouldn't use the twins' names, but she'd tell him the basic story. He would encourage her to take it in stride and go on. Then he'd make some joke and have her laughing. She loved that about him. He was like her own private cheerleader.

Had all that changed by meeting him in person?

"Well, hello there." Dustee slowly and suggestively slid her gaze over Sean.

A surprising flash of jealousy hit Taylor. She had no reason to be jealous of anything to do with Sean. They were friends—nothing more. And even if they were more, he would never go for Dustee. Not only was she a bit young for him, but she also wasn't his type.

Taylor ignored the comment and introduced the

twins. "Sean is part of ICE's C3 Cyber Crimes unit, and their elite RED team."

"Ooh." Dustee rubbed her hands together. "Handsome *and* an IT guy. Could it get any better?"

Taylor rolled her eyes. "He's here to talk to you about Phantom."

Dustee's smile evaporated. "What about him?"

Sean took a seat across from her. "You saw him last night. Can you give me a description?"

"Six feet. Really built. Tall." She chewed on her lip. "That's all I can tell you. Never got a clear look at his face."

"You once worked with the bureau to try to bring him in. Did you see him back then?" Sean asked.

"Never saw him in person."

"Tell me about your experience with him."

She jutted out her chin. "You're an agent. Look up the reports."

Taylor shook her head. How quickly her witness's mood had changed from flirty to belligerent. She was a volatile woman, and Taylor couldn't help but think bringing her in on this investigation would end badly. But then Sean was right. Dustee had skills far beyond most hackers, and if anyone could get to Phantom, it would be another unethical hacker who understood his thinking.

Sean didn't flinch or react at all to Dustee's

acerbic tone, giving him brownie points in Taylor's book. "I read the report, but reports don't include every detail. I'd like to hear it from you."

Taylor waited for Dustee to ignore him. Instead, she blew out a long breath and solidly met his gaze. "Not much to tell really. I was arrested for hacking, and your people agreed to let it go if I helped bring Phantom down. So I did. He was hiring for his team, and I applied. He took me on, and after four months of doing his bidding, he trusted me enough to share details of his next hack. It woulda led to his identity. So I reported it to the Feds, and that was it." She brushed her hands together as if brushing off the whole mess.

"But he wasn't arrested," Sean said.

"Nah. The thing is, he really didn't trust me. The hack was bogus. A test—and I failed. Then he threatened me. I'd covered my tracks online, but he still found me." She grasped her sister's hand. "So we went into WITSEC. End of story. No more contact with him."

"Until last night."

She scowled. "Right. That."

"Are you sure it was Phantom tailing you?"

She shrugged. "Can't be sure 'cause I've never seen him. No one outside his inner circle has seen his face. Closest I came was seeing a video one of your Feds once showed me of a dude running from them. The guy tailing me last night was the same size. So gotta figure it's Phantom. I mean, who else could it be?"

Sean tapped something into his phone, then looked up at Dustee. "You're not involved in anything illegal, are you?"

She clenched her fists on the table, looking like she did when she was about to unleash her wrath on Dianne. Then she pulled in a long breath and exhaled slowly between pursed lips. "I learned my lesson. I'm not doing anything I shouldn't—"

"Except using the internet at the library," Taylor was quick to point out.

"Yeah, but that's not illegal." Dustee crossed her arms and slumped down in her chair. "If you don't believe me, get the data from the network router at the library, and you'll see I didn't do anything wrong."

"Then how did he find you?"

"I don't know. Maybe he had an algorithm running to track my old account logins, and he captured the information when I logged in to one of my favorite forums."

"Using an old login wasn't a very bright thing to do." Taylor glared at Dustee. "Not to mention it's against your MOU to connect with people from your past life."

Dustee raised her hands, palms out. "I got it, all right. I messed up. You don't have to keep telling me."

Sean watched her for a long moment, and Taylor wanted to know what he was thinking.

"What about a VPN?" he finally asked. "Did you use one?"

Dustee rolled her eyes. "As if."

"Hack the library settings?"

"Not that I even tried, but they're locked down tight." She smirked. "I thought a big Fed cyber guy like you would know that."

"Some libraries aren't as secure as others, and someone as resourceful as you could find a way around weak security."

"Maybe, but you also gotta know Portland's a big-tech city, and our library computer settings are secure. But to answer your question, I didn't need a VPN. I was surfing the web. That's it."

Sean changed his focus to Dianne. "Do you have any reason to believe Dustee is spending her free time on computers—not only at the library?"

"How would I do that?" Dustee snapped. "Taylor could ask for my financial records and see I bought a computer."

"Bitcoins," Sean said.

Dustee shot up in her seat. "I didn't do anything wrong. How many times do I need to say that?"

Taylor wished she could be more open-minded about Dustee and trust her, but the woman continually fought the rules and pushed boundaries. Made Taylor's job harder than it needed to be. She tried to understand and extend the kind of grace she would want given to her in a trying situation. After all, computers were an addiction for Dustee, and she wasn't even allowed to own a smartphone. She had to use an old-fashioned flip phone instead. Going cold turkey on electronic devices held the same mental challenges as withdrawal from any other addictive substance.

But in Taylor's opinion, the ruling prohibiting Dustee from accessing the internet was fair. How could the agency ever trust her not to hack for profit again? The only way to ensure her cooperation was to prevent her from accessing the tool that could facilitate her life of crime.

"And we don't have a computer at our place," Dianne added.

"She could store it somewhere else," Sean said. "Like at work."

Dianne shook her head hard, her obstinate expression making her look more than ever like Dustee. "She hasn't been out of my sight long enough to do something like that."

Sean's eyebrow quirked. "How do you know how long it would take?"

"I don't, but I do know Dustee. First, she wouldn't be having computer withdrawal, which she is seriously experiencing."

"She is," Taylor confirmed.

"And second, if she logged on to a computer, she couldn't stop after a few minutes. She'd get lost in her work. Be gone for hours and hours. Other than the library and work, she hasn't been away from the apartment long enough to do that."

Dustee glared at Sean. "Feel free to search my work locker. I have nothing to hide."

Sean gave a quick nod. Taylor didn't know him as far as reading his body language, but he seemed to be buying in to Dustee's story. So was Taylor, but she knew better than to fully believe Dustee. Not when she'd told very convincing lies in the past.

Many of Taylor's witnesses, like Dustee, were criminals, as Sean had pointed out, and they balked against following rules of any kind or telling the truth. So they often got in trouble, and Taylor became their surrogate mother. She was the one person who cared enough to come to their aid when they messed up and help them find their way out of a disaster, typically of their own making. Like tonight.

She was mom all right. She even made sure the witnesses had shelter, food, and jobs that they actually showed up to, providing them income to pay their bills and keep them from turning to crime again. That should be enough, but she also helped them work through their emotions, and maybe, just maybe, helped them find happiness and joy again. Never mind that she didn't have a lot of that in her own life. She was content with helping others, right?

Sean sat forward and placed his hands on the table, his focus locked on Dustee. "I'll request a warrant to search your home and workplace. And for the logs for the library computers. Am I going to find anything?"

She continued to glare at him. "Sure. Tons of stuff. But nothing that will get me in trouble with Taylor. She already knows about the library."

"Okay, then say you're telling me the truth. If so, I'd like your help in locating a hacker. Might even be Phantom."

Dustee snorted. "Yeah, right."

"I'm serious."

"Only way to get to him is with computer access. I'm not allowed to use them. So sorry. No can do." Her snippy voice grated on Taylor, and she opened her mouth to say something.

Sean went on before she could. "I can have those restrictions waived while you're working with me."

"Seriously?" Dustee shot Taylor a look.

Taylor nodded. "He's right. We can lift the restrictions for the time you're working with Agent Nichols, but only during that time. And someone will be sitting right next to you, monitoring your every move."

Dustee was quiet for a moment as she studied Sean, her expression turning suspicious. "I don't know you. Means I don't *trust* you. So no thanks."

Taylor stared at her. "You're giving up a chance to do what you love best?"

"Like I said, I don't trust him. He could be setting up a trap to send me to prison. Wouldn't put it past a Fed to do that after I failed to give them Phantom. I'm sure more than one agent thinks I didn't follow through on my commitment and should be rotting behind bars instead of protected by WITSEC."

Taylor stared at her witness, trying to understand her reasoning, but Dustee had shut down, looking away from her. There had to be something else going on here. Dustee loved a challenge, and normally she wouldn't say no to an opportunity like this.

"Are you afraid because of last night?" Taylor asked. "Is that it?"

"Oh, I'm afraid all right." Dustee crossed her arms tighter. "But I wouldn't let that scare me off, not with Mr. Muscles here to protect me."

Another comment to ignore. Taylor could protect Dustee equally as well as Sean could. Muscles had nothing to do with it. Intelligence, instinct, and training—these were what kept Dustee alive.

"You trust Taylor, right?" Sean asked.

Dustee gave a half smile. "Totally."

"What if Taylor works with us? Would you agree to help then?"

"Now wait a minute." Taylor whipped her attention to Sean.

"Sure," Dustee replied. "After scaring me the way Phantom just did, I'd love to help put him behind bars. Finally get our lives back."

"We won't get our lives back," Dianne muttered. "You'd have to testify at the trial, and then he could still send someone else after you. So unless the dude dies, we're stuck in WITSEC."

"Oh, yeah, right." Dustee frowned. "I'll still do it because I want him in prison. *If* Taylor is with us."

"I . . ." Taylor caught herself and stopped before sharing her reason for not wanting to be involved in the hunt for Phantom. It was a personal issue with Sean, not a work issue, and she wouldn't say more in front of Dustee.

"Oh, I get it." Dustee slid so low in her chair that Taylor was surprised she didn't slip to the floor. "You're mad at me for the internet thing and don't want to have anything to do with me. I understand."

"No. That's not it. I . . ."

Dustee angled her body away from Taylor. Taylor might be exasperated with this woman most of the time, but she didn't want one of her witnesses to think she was so petty that she couldn't get beyond their mistakes.

Taylor knew what it was like to have someone hold a mistake over her head. It was painful. Nearly unbearable at times. In Taylor's case, especially painful because people she loved did the holding. She couldn't do that to Dustee. And even more important, she couldn't let Phantom get away with hacking the database and putting all the other witnesses' lives at risk.

"I'm in." Taylor met Sean's gaze, warning him with a single look that this was all business and nothing more.

But when a satisfied smile crossed his face, and his focus lingered on her, she knew she hadn't succeeded.

Okay, so that's the way it was going to be between them. She would need to be on guard every second of every day she spent with this man or she might find herself falling for him, and that was *so* not a viable option in her life. Not today. Not ever.

CHAPTER 7

"Don't ever do that to me again." Taylor issued the warning through clenched teeth as Sean closed the glass door to the break room. She'd brought him into this room on purpose. While she wanted the privacy, she also wanted people walking by to be able to see them or she just might strangle him.

He arched an eyebrow above those amazing eyes that were doing nothing for her right now. "Do what?"

"Oh, come on. You put me on the spot in there with Dustee." Taylor took a deep breath, inhaling the nutty scent of freshly brewed coffee lingering in the room. "There was no way I could say no to her without looking like the bad guy."

He clamped a hand on the back of his neck. "I'm sorry. It wasn't intentional. I'm just doing my job."

"But you didn't have to rush in like that. You could've asked to step out of the room and discuss it first so we could make the right decision."

He scowled. "Now you're sounding like Eisenhower."

"And that's a bad thing?" She poured a cup of rich black coffee and filled one for Sean without

85

asking, then handed it to him. "I thought you respected him as a leader."

"I do, but I get frustrated when he tries to stand in my way, like you seem to be doing." He pulled in a deep breath, his broad chest rising and falling. "Why waste time talking when the resolution is right in front of us for the taking. Take charge. Get it done. You know that's my motto."

She did know that, but she'd never had his motto applied to her. They were friends, after all. Shouldn't that make him more sensitive to her needs? The online Sean would've been. Clearly, she didn't know him as well as she thought she did. For all she knew, he spent time crafting his online answers, but here in front of her? He'd let his real emotions get to him and fired off his first response. His true response. His true self.

Still, she didn't want to snap at him again, so she stirred the cream, watching the white mix with black until a warm caramel color filled her cup. The two of them didn't resemble the coffee at all. They had completely opposite personalities and hadn't blended since he'd arrived. She liked him. Liked him a lot. As a friend. They had many things in common, but one of their main areas of disagreement was his not taking the time to reason things out before acting.

She took a sip of the creamy, warm liquid and lifted her face. He was watching her, that dark gaze carrying an intensity that both thrilled and worried her. "I don't pretend to know Eisenhower. But I do know that you threw caution to the wind and could have benefited from taking some time to think things through before rushing in."

"You, on the other hand, analyze everything to death." His words were slow and measured, his attention remaining locked on hers.

The intensity getting to her, she shifted. "But we're not talking about me here."

"Aren't we? If you could decide on the fly, we wouldn't even be having this discussion and wasting time." He took a step closer. "This investigation will move fast. It has to. Witnesses' lives are at stake. I want to work with you, but you'll have to keep up."

Ooh, he was so infuriating. Lecturing her like a rookie when she was perfectly capable of matching him.

She set down her cup and widened her stance. "I want to be clear, Sean. I realize your investigation is important. Critical even. And I'll support you. I always have. But Dustee is my top priority. If there are decisions to be made about her or her safety, I'll be making those decisions. Not you. Me. Understand?"

It was her turn to move closer, and she did, standing toe-to-toe with him. Her brain betrayed her, and she wanted to softly touch his face to let him know this feud was temporary and she cared.

He suddenly grinned. An adorable I'm-the-best-thing-since-sliced-bread grin, and you should not resist me. A let-go-of-your-anger-at-me grin and smile back. He couldn't have read her mind, so what was he up to?

Her lips started to turn up, and she clamped down to stop them. "What's so funny?"

"I like it when you're feisty. I've liked seeing it in our online chats, but in person? I have to admit I like it even more." He gently tucked a loose strand of hair behind her ear.

She stood mesmerized. Locked in heady emotions flowing between them. Losing track of time. Of everything but the warmth lingering on his face.

A conversation from the hallway filtered into the room, and her brain kicked in again.

What was she doing? They couldn't be having feelings for each other. Neither of them was looking for a relationship, but even if they were, he could never fall for her. She liked to plan things. He didn't. He would soon tire of her and look for someone more exciting. Someone who could keep up with his need for adventure.

She stepped back. "You're making this personal."

"I know it's unprofessional, but . . ." He shrugged.

She couldn't let this continue. Not at all. She had a job to do. Witnesses to protect. Lives depending on her. She couldn't get lost in his gaze, in him, so easily. "If we're going to be working together, we should set some guidelines."

He took a long drink of his coffee but didn't look away. "Like what?"

"I don't know off the top of my head." *Because the top of my head is in the clouds right now.* "For now, we should keep our focus on the investigation, but not let the tension get to us and mess with our friendship."

"I would hate for this investigation to ruin our being friends." A tight smile lifted his lips. "Seems like we might find ourselves on opposite sides here, but we both want the same thing. To make sure not a single witness is harmed."

She nodded. "I think if we keep the lines of communication open, we can make that happen and still come out friends at the end."

"I can do that, and I know you can too. But we have to make a point of remembering that when we disagree." He smiled.

She nodded her agreement and nearly sighed with relief.

"Are those for everyone?" He pointed at a box of bagels by the coffeepot. "I'm starving. I didn't stop to eat on the trip down here."

"Help yourself. I should have thought to offer."

"You were a little preoccupied." He sliced a plain bagel and lathered it with strawberry cream cheese.

Her stomach rumbled.

"You need this more than I do." He handed her the prepared bagel and didn't look up to see if she wanted it but grabbed another one with his free hand.

His actions felt so familiar. Easy. Right. Like they'd done this in the past when they hadn't even met before. She took it, and when her mind wanted to analyze that, she forced it back to the investigation. "When you're finished, we can get started on making a plan."

"I'll call to get the safe house under way so Dustee and Dianne don't have to sit in that room all day."

She took a bite of the moist bagel, enjoying the sweetness and smooth texture of the cream cheese. She wanted to comment about his taking over without consulting her, but she was all for making the twins more comfortable, and she appreciated the fact that he'd thought of their comfort. "Good idea to call. Then we can set up a plan for moving them and their ongoing protection detail. Plus we'll need to discuss the budget. Someone has to pay for all of this. And I'll have to read my chief in."

He watched her, his expression unreadable. Then he set down his bagel, dug out his phone, and tapped the screen. He asked for the special agent in charge of the FBI's Portland field office. She munched on the bagel and washed it down with coffee while tuning out his call and trying to gather her thoughts, but they were jumbled. She needed a whiteboard to organize herself. She could easily solve that problem. Next stop would be the conference room they often used for projects and investigations.

Sean finished his call and poured a second cup of coffee. "Safe house should be ready in an hour or two. An agent will pick up some groceries and clear the place, then wait for us to arrive."

She nodded. "I don't want to waste time while we wait. We should be planning, and for me that means a whiteboard."

"Conference room?" He took a long sip of his coffee.

"Yes. Follow me." Once in the room, she went straight to the whiteboard to start jotting down key points she would like to discuss before they moved forward. She chose a blue marker and made big bold strokes. The felt tip squeaked beneath her hand, and the familiar chemical scent filled the air.

"That's quite a list. Remind me never to leave you with nothing to do ever again." He chuckled and set his cup on the table, along with the bagel that he placed on a napkin.

She'd always liked his sense of humor, but she was focused now and had no time to joke around. "We should start by reviewing all information we have on Phantom. I have an extensive file in my office, and I'm assuming the agents who worked with Dustee have additional information."

"I already requested the file on my drive down here, but let me make a note to follow up." He tapped his thumbs on his phone.

"I'll have copies of my file made for you, and then we can review the information together." She marked her name next to the item, then pointed at the next one. "CCTV files."

"I can request video footage for the library, bus stop, and inside the bus," he offered.

"I have a source at TriMet. I'll do it." She jotted her name next to the action item and moved on to the third point before he could argue. "Budget. If my chief is going to free me up for the duration of the investigation and arrange safe transport, not to mention providing a twenty-four seven protective detail for the twins, then you'll have to pay for it."

He swallowed, and she watched his Adam's apple bob in a tanned and muscular neck. "Done."

"Just like that? No need to get approval from a supervisor?"

"We're the RED team. We've proven our worth and can approve most expenditures."

"Flexibility in spending is one thing," she said, "but you just agreed to pay the salaries for local officers to handle the transport. Plus my salary and a two-person protection detail for who knows how long. That won't come cheap."

"If it's what I need to do to get Dustee's expertise, then that's what I need to do." He attacked the bagel again and finished it with three bites.

Taylor didn't know what to say. If someone had made this same request of her, she would be completing a cost-benefit analysis. He obviously didn't roll that way, and it was his career and department's money, so who was she to argue?

She noted his name by the budget line item and added *Read Inman In.* "I'll need your permission to do that."

He sat forward and rested his elbows on the table to steeple his fingers. "I don't want you talking to him about it."

"Why?" She hated hearing the suspicion in her tone, but she was beginning to wonder if he was planning to micromanage and control every aspect of this investigation. If so, they would clash daily. Maybe hourly, for that matter. Again, so different from their friendly online conversations.

"The minute you break the news, he'll want to run it up the flagpole to his supervisor. But the investigation is on a need-to-know basis, and he really doesn't need to know."

"He does if you want my help or a protection detail for the twins."

"Actually, all he needs is a phone call from his supervisor, directing him to comply with our team's requests."

She gaped at him. "You're going above his head?"

"Not me. Eisenhower already started at the top. Management has been informed of the hack."

She set down the marker and planted her hands on her hips. "If that's so, then deputies should've received a communication to warn witnesses, and we didn't."

"I don't imagine that will happen until there's actionable information. If released now, it would send everyone into panic mode. And when people panic, they often get hurt."

"Management can't ignore the hack. What if one of the compromised witnesses is killed and the higher-ups could've done something about it? That would almost make them complicit in the death."

"Another reason why we have to move fast before someone gets killed." He grabbed his phone. "I'll get that warrant going for Dustee's workplace and the library computers so I can clear her. Once you check her finances, we can move forward."

There he went again, jumping in and starting when they hadn't even ironed out the whole plan. "I—"

A commotion in the hall captured Taylor's attention.

"I don't care, I need to talk to her!" Dustee's raised voice came from outside the conference room door.

"That's Dustee," Sean said. "She sounds freaked out."

Taylor resisted groaning. "Relax. She creates drama with most everything. She's probably hungry or something simple like that."

Taylor stepped into the hallway. Jim Coates had been assigned to babysit the twins, and he blocked Dustee's access to the room.

Taylor smiled at her fellow deputy. "It's okay, Jim," she called. "I got this."

Looking exasperated, he hurried away at a speed she'd never seen him move before. Dustee truly had that effect on people. Taylor willed herself to stay in place and do so with a patient smile.

"Taylor. Thank goodness. I just got a text. See . . ." Dustee held out her phone, her hand shaking. She latched on to Taylor's arm with her free hand, and fear radiated through her touch.

Something really was wrong, and for once, Dustee wasn't crying wolf.

Taylor looked at the phone. Her heart dropped.

You think you can run from me? No one makes a fool of me, Bridgett. I'll be there when you least expect me and pay you back for trying to out me to the FBI.

"It's from Phantom . . . using your real name." Taylor locked eyes with Dustee. "And he has your cell number. Phantom has your number."

Dustee nodded, up and down in rapid bobs born of terror. She tightened her grip on Taylor's arm, her fingernails cutting in. "And he's going to kill me."

CHAPTER 8

Back in the conference room, Taylor planted her hands on curvy hips, looking like a fierce mother bear protecting her cub, and Sean found her burning intensity even more appealing. He never expected to find her so attractive. She wasn't at all spontaneous or a go-with-the-flow kind of person. It was as if, by being so cautious, she was refusing to embrace all life had to offer, and he didn't understand that. He knew the reason. Her brother. Sean had often wanted to help her work through her lingering grief, but she wouldn't share the details. So he prayed for her. Every day. And watched for change, although she continued to struggle with the terrible loss she'd suffered.

"With Dustee's confirmation of Phantom's size and build, and now this text," Taylor said, totally oblivious to his thoughts, "it's a good bet he's behind the hack, and we should review the information we have on him. You know, get into his head. Make a plan to preempt any future attacks."

"Agreed." Sean dropped onto a chair and committed himself to giving her time to plan so that he didn't add to her stress. He opened his report on Phantom. "Not much is known about his childhood or upbringing, but we do know a few things about his behavior as an adult."

Taylor flipped through the folder in front of her. "Such as?"

"He seems to enjoy the publicity surrounding his hacking. In a search of the abandoned warehouse where they found his hard drives, they also found a box of news clippings. He was following himself in the news and had printed out internet stories. Including one about his missing partner. That was when the FBI started looking at him for murder, as well as hacking. The pages were ragged and worn from handling."

She turned to the disturbing photos of Phantom's murdered partner. "He removed the guy's tongue."

Sean nodded. "Our profiler thinks it's a message to others. That he would silence any-one who betrayed him or tried to help authorities find him."

She shuddered. "He's brutal for a hacker, right?"

"Yes, but these days hacking is big business, and just like the rest of the criminal world, there's more violence today than in the past—including infighting, with hackers trying to take over." He took a long breath. "And I'm just talking about hackers in our country. Don't get me started on other countries."

She looked horrified. "So Phantom's all about

sending messages, plus he likes to read about himself. Do you think he's hungry for attention, and that's part of his reason for coming after Dustee?"

Sean looked her in the eye. "Maybe, but his text sounds more like he's bent on revenge. Dustee betrayed him. Big-time."

"And revenge is one of the most powerful motives for murder, so we need to proceed with caution."

Sean was glad to hear she was taking this threat to Dustee seriously. "Before we talk about anything else, I want to point out that he isn't about to let anyone stop him. If you get in the way—"

"He won't hesitate to take me out." Her lips pressed together. "You too. During transport, we should wear vests and insist that Dustee wear one too."

"Agreed. And you need to be extra vigilant." He paused to make strong eye contact. "I care about you, Taylor, and I'm worried for your safety."

"I'm concerned for you too," she said, an innocent blush stealing up her face. "The entire team actually."

"Thank you." His heart warmed, taking in her heartfelt words, but he wouldn't continue this conversation as he could easily get lost in her gaze. "Our profiler says Phantom's self-image depends on the belief that he's smarter than everyone. With Dustee outsmarting him, he has a burning desire to prove he's better than she is. I think that was the point of his text to her. He wants Dustee to know he's the one coming after her. Probably wants us to know too."

Her forehead creased. "But why? It also tells us who to focus our efforts on."

"When he gets to Dustee—and in his mind there's no doubt he will—then we'll know he beat us. That's what he wants. For us to know he's behind everything." Sean could see he was scaring her more, but she needed to know the full extent of Phantom's wrath and abilities. "We have to remember he's bested law enforcement up until this point and proved he can murder someone and get away with it. He's certain he can do it again."

"Then we can't let him do it again." Taylor got to her feet and started pacing. "We need to get Dustee moved to the safe house, but he may be counting on taking her out then. No way will I allow a simple transport. We'll need local law enforcement assistance. That means it's imperative that we read Inman in on the hack."

Sean wanted to agree with her to ease her distress, but he had to keep this hack under wraps for now. "We can't read anyone else in at this point."

She lifted her chin and stared at him but

didn't speak. She didn't need to. He could read her thoughts. He respected her for the way she championed her witnesses. Her commitment and dedication were to be commended. Except, that is, when she let her past fuel her motive, taking it to extremes. Sure, she needed to be vigilant and extra careful, but telling Inman? Sean wished he could convince her to back down on that, but she wasn't one to back down in her personal life when she believed in something. He doubted she'd do so at work either. That meant he needed to find a compromise.

"What do you have in mind for the transport?" he asked when she likely expected him to argue.

"Most people think that witness transport is cut-and-dried, that we put our protectees in a car and just drive off. But that couldn't be further from the truth. We don't take any chances. Especially when the person who wants our witness dead could be watching, like Phantom might be. We need to confuse him so he doesn't have a chance to harm her."

"And how do you propose doing that?"

"We'll dress a variety of officers and deputies in hoodies of the same color. I'll make sure several people fit Dustee's body type. Then we'll have as many vehicles as possible departing and returning to our parking structure at a rapid pace so he doesn't know which vehicle she's riding in." Her expression came alive with the challenge.

He loved seeing the fire in her eyes. "You've obviously done this before."

"Several times for high-risk witnesses. Unfortunately, we don't have enough staff here to be effective, so I'll need to reach out."

Her plan sounded fairly elaborate, and the novice might think it was over the top, but Sean's training told him she was following proven procedures carried out by top-notch law enforcement personnel every day across the country. "Sounds like fun."

"Yeah, you'll like it. It's action, action, action." A smile curled her lips, her face lighting with a radiant beauty.

He bit back a groan over the surge of warmth in his veins and forced his mind to remain on the subject at hand. "I should be able to provide enough agents and cars to make it happen. We won't need to involve local PD, and reading Inman in won't be necessary."

"Sure it will." Taylor firmed her shoulders. "Dustee is a witness. I'm moving her under extreme circumstances. I'll be using fellow deputies to implement my protection plan at the safe house. He has to know."

"I could provide the protection detail too."

"I knew it was only a matter of time before you offered that, but no thank you." She crossed her arms. "We're trained in witness safety. Agents aren't. Dustee is my responsibility, and

I'll handpick the people on her detail from my coworkers."

Sean knew when to give in. "Fine, but I want to be there when you talk to Inman, and we give him the barest of information."

A satisfied smile crossed her face.

He shook his head. "I never took you as someone who would smirk over your victory."

"I'm not," she said, her grin widening. "I'm thinking about you trying to be vague with Inman. I promise you, it isn't going to fly."

She was probably right. Still, Sean would start out with the smallest amount of information required. "You'll need to be in the know on the investigation. I'll text Eisenhower and get you official clearance and bring you on as a temporary member of the RED team."

"Okay." But she sounded like she had reservations.

"It'll be great to have you on the team again. This time not on the other side of the country but right in the thick of things with us." He waited for her to respond, but she didn't say a word.

"Are you—?" His phone signaled a text from the team. He lifted it and saw Mack's name. "The RED team just arrived in town. They'll meet us at the safe house."

Taylor took a step back, a skeptical frown replacing her good mood.

He had to admit that seeing her in person was

great but also perplexing, as he was having a hard time understanding her body language. "What's the frown for? You know the team."

"Exactly. I do." She squared her shoulders. "You're all a force to be reckoned with. Everyone will want to weigh in on my protection plan. Maybe take charge, like you've been trying to do ever since you walked through my door."

She was right. He'd thought about the investigation more than he considered how she was feeling, and he didn't want her to think he didn't care about her. "I'm sorry. I know I've been pushy, and I'll try to curtail that. I promise. But I think it's good to have additional input on protection, don't you?"

She watched him for a long moment, her gaze drilling deep for something, but he didn't know what. "You have to remember who I am and what I do. Protection is a Deputy Marshal's primary skill set. No one does it better than we do, and honestly, we don't like being told how to do it."

He nodded his understanding. He wanted to put their friendship first. He really did. To put her first too, but he couldn't. Not with so many lives counting on him. So he wouldn't warn the team off. Not only did he feel responsible for keeping Dustee alive, but for keeping alive the one link they had to Phantom. If they lost Dustee, they might lose every chance at stopping the cyber creep, who didn't have any qualms about selling information that guaranteed people would die.

In the parking structure, Taylor ended her prayer for safety for all parties involved in Dustee's transport and flipped up her hood. The soft fabric of the new hoodie caressed the sides of her face and belied the tension surrounding her. She stood with Dustee and the other decoys, each dressed in nearly identical attire, their focus on high alert.

She glanced at Dustee, who looked lost since Dianne had departed for the safe house. Or maybe she was worried. Taylor sure was. She couldn't get Sean's comments about Phantom out of her head. She'd known he was dangerous, but now? Now she knew the full extent of his paranoia, and she had to up her game to keep Dustee alive. Taylor would give her life for her witnesses without blinking an eye, and she knew Sean and the team would do the same.

In fact, everyone in the parking garage would do so. They were the unsung heroes, men and women who put their lives on the line every day, like soldiers going into battle. This battle was in the homeland, because like it or not, there was a war on crime being waged in America, and she was glad to do her part to end it.

The final decoy vehicle with a hooded driver shot past Taylor and out into the busy Portland street. Rainwater hissed and spit under the tires.

The vehicle gained traction but lost grip and slid in front of Sean's SUV as he made his return trip, turning toward the entrance. He slammed on his brakes, narrowly missing the other vehicle, skidding across the slick pavement, plunging toward a solid concrete barrier.

Taylor sucked in a breath and held it.

His vehicle came to a sudden stop a foot shy of the barrier.

She exhaled, a long drawn-out affair. They'd done it. Successfully sent all decoy vehicles out, and no one had gotten hurt. Sean had come close, but he was a highly skilled driver. She was unreasonably proud of his defensive driving skills, and this wasn't the motherly pride she felt when her witnesses chose to do the right thing. Far from it.

He slid out of the SUV. His hand drifted to his sidearm, and he planted his feet in a wide stance as he surveyed the space. He stood tall and rugged, his shoulders thrown back. Taylor might've been arguing with him since he'd arrived, but right now she couldn't be more thankful that he was here and would be driving them to the safe house.

"Ready to go?" she asked Dustee.

She looked down and didn't speak.

"Nothing is going to happen to you," Taylor promised. "I'll be right beside you, and I'm armed."

Dustee looked at Sean. "I'd feel better if Hunky

IT Guy was by my side and you were driving."

Taylor gritted her teeth. Why did people automatically assume a big strapping guy could provide better protection than she could? Sure. Fine. He could out-bench-press her. Still . . . "Don't worry. I can protect you."

"Uh-huh."

"Let's go," Taylor snapped, and instantly regretted it.

Dustee arched a brow. "I do something wrong?"

"No. We just need to get going." Taylor pointed at the SUV.

Dustee took full advantage of a space filled with male agents and strutted across the parking garage, her head cocked with enjoyment as the men watched her glide toward the SUV.

"Ready to go, Hunky IT Guy?" she asked Sean, followed by a flash of her pearly whites.

"I have a name." He jerked the vehicle's back door open. "Agent Nichols or Sean. Please pick one."

"Ooh, testy. What's the matter? You feeling insecure with these other macho guys around?"

"Just get in." He ground his teeth.

She complied, and as Taylor approached, he met her gaze and shook his head.

"Don't expect it to get any easier." Taylor crawled over the vehicle's folded-down back seats, making her way to the large cargo area. Settling in, she drew her weapon.

Sean got them on the road, and she remained on high alert as he raced through town. She ignored Dustee's rambling and complaining, keeping close watch until Sean pulled up to the safe house without incident.

"Wait here. I'll be right back." She left Sean and Dustee in the vehicle and rushed up to the house.

A young agent opened the door and stepped back. An ill-fitting suit hung on his slight frame, looking like she could blow him over with just a puff of air. After flashing her ID, Taylor stepped inside. "I'm Deputy Mills. Our witness is in the car with Agent Nichols. Secure that door. I'm going to clear the house."

He tipped his head, and his slicked-back brown hair didn't move. "I already cleared the place, and so has the RED team hunkered downstairs."

"I appreciate your evaluation of the house, but I'm still going to follow through, Agent . . ."

"Snow. Agent Snow."

She nodded and moved to step around him toward Deputy Jim Coates, who was sitting on a sofa across the room. Snow didn't make it easy but stood his ground. *Okay, fine.* He had an attitude about her checking his work. If their roles were reversed, she wouldn't like it either. "This isn't personal, Agent Snow. Just doing my job."

Jim gave her a self-assured nod, and her

unease at having such a green agent at the door disappeared. She would have an experienced deputy on duty at all times. Jim would be here until Roger arrived for the graveyard shift.

She walked into the family room, which had a large fireplace and vaulted ceiling. She was glad to see blackout shades in every window, and they were closed tight. She strode down the hallway and quickly cleared the empty bedrooms, ending with the one assigned to the twins.

She knocked on the door. "Dianne, it's Taylor. We're here."

Dianne opened the door and gave Taylor a quick once-over, as if expecting her to be injured.

"Dustee's still in the car. Once I finish my sweep of the house, she can come in." Taylor smiled to ease her protectee's concern and searched the room.

"I always appreciate how detailed you are." Dianne sighed a long breath of relief. "Makes me feel safer."

And lets me sleep at night.

Dianne's stomach growled.

"Right, dinner." Taylor nodded. "We can get something started after Dustee is settled."

"Let me do all the cooking," Dianne suggested. "It's the least I can do."

Taylor didn't want to take advantage of Dianne, but the offer would make life much easier while staying at the safe house. "You do realize we'll have around ten people to feed, don't you?"

"I cooked for all our friends before WITSEC," Dianne said, "and I loved it."

"Then you're on. Mack loves to cook, and he might want to help, but I promise no one else will beg for KP duty. Agent Snow should have stocked the kitchen with fresh food by now so feel free to check it out."

"I'll do that." Dianne bolted for the kitchen, her face alive with a bright and eager smile.

Taylor's heart warmed at her protectee's excitement. She'd been lost since coming into protection, and God was using this tough situation to make her feel useful. Something He excelled at. Not that Taylor had seen much evidence of this in her own life.

Maybe because you haven't been looking for it.

Something Taylor might need to ponder, but she had no time to think about it now with Dustee still in the car. She took the stairs down to the large rec room, and spotted a round game table, foosball and pool tables, and an old upright piano. None of the team members noticed her, giving her a chance to assess the situation first.

Kiley was moving a chair from the seating area over to the fireplace, her wavy brown hair swinging over her shoulder. *Stress.* She was stressed. Sean mentioned that her secondary passion was interior design, and her need to decorate came out when she was under pressure.

On the far side of the room, Mack leaned

against the wall by the pool table, cue in hand. He was just over six feet tall, with short reddish-brown hair. Like many of the guys Taylor worked with, Mack's black tactical pants and cream-colored polo shirt with the Marshals Service's logo embroidered on his broad chest made him look law-enforcement tough.

"Cam, buddy," he said, staring at Cam, who was bent over the table, his tongue peeking out of the corner of his mouth as he lined up his cue. "Maybe you should hold off on this shot while Kiley color-coordinates the table for you. Then you'll manage to get at least one ball in the pocket before I slaughter you."

"Seriously, Mack." Kiley spun and shook her head. "That was *so* not funny."

Mack broke out in a good-natured laugh. Cam rolled his eyes and took his shot, banking the three-ball into a corner pocket.

A pang of longing hit Taylor. What would it be like to be a regular member of this group? To become friends? Daily coworkers? Sure, she'd been a temporary member in the past and was again, for now anyway. But with the team housed across the country, they'd mostly communicated via email on the Montgomery Three investigation, and she'd remained on the fringes of the group.

Nothing new to her. She'd been on the outside ever since the day of Jeremy's suicide. She'd gone from popular in high school to *that girl,* whose brother had taken his own life. No one knew what to do with her loss—with her. And with guilt coloring her every move back then, neither did she.

Even in college, she'd worried others might somehow discover she'd failed her brother. It carried into her adult life too. She could never be real. Never relax around other people and let the real Taylor come out. She'd only been able to do that with Sean because of their anonymity, and even then she hadn't shared the details of her brother's suicide.

She couldn't. Not without risking her friendship with Sean. And now he was here in Portland. In her world. Able to see her expressions and know when she avoided answering him. Know when she was holding back. With his perceptive abilities, she had to watch what she said, as it was going to be harder than ever to keep her secret.

CHAPTER 9

"Finally," Kiley said to Sean when he entered the basement family room.

He opened his mouth to mention that if Taylor hadn't needed to use such an elaborate transport drill—a drill Sean had to admire, as she'd planned it so well that it felt like a choreographed dance—and clear the house, he would've been down here sooner. But he wouldn't hurt her feelings by bringing it up, so he clamped his mouth shut and stepped to the side so that Taylor and Dustee could enter.

Mack set aside his pool cue and crossed over to Taylor, a broad smile on his face. Her eyes lit up in the way Sean had hoped they would've when he'd first arrived at her office, and a spasm of jealousy tightened his stomach. His response was illogical on so many levels, but he couldn't control how he felt. He could control whether he let others see his feelings though.

"Sorry you've had such a rough night and day." Mack drew Taylor in for a hug.

She went willingly into his arms. She rested her head against his shoulder and looked so content that Sean's gut churned even more. He should've been the one to offer her a hug. To be the friend she needed him to be, instead of some pushy agent needing to have his own way. He had a lot to make up for.

Mack released her. "Good to see you, Slim."

She wrinkled her nose and shook her head.

"What? Slim fits? I keep telling you you're a tall drink of water." He exaggerated the words in a lazy Texas drawl, which Sean had seen plenty of women find charming.

Sean needed the conversation to move on before he said something and hurt Taylor in the process. He cleared his throat. "Go ahead and have a seat, everyone, so we can get our meeting out of the way before dinner."

Dustee stepped past Sean and zoned in on Mack. "Well, hello there, handsome."

Sean saw her check Mack's ring finger. He wasn't wearing his wedding ring. A year ago, he'd split up with Addison Leigh—an ICE agent and former member of the RED team—but they never divorced. Why, Sean had no idea. All he knew was that when Addison could no longer work with Mack, she'd left them and they'd lost an amazing teammate.

"Go ahead and have a seat, Dustee," Sean said, before he had to embarrass her by saying Mack, and all the guys on the team for that matter, were off-limits to her.

She sauntered across the room, dropped onto the sofa next to Cam, and gave Cam a coy smile. Thankfully, he didn't react to her at all. He was the only non-law enforcement officer on the team, a computer geek in the nicest sense of the word, and as the youngest team member, he was the closest in age to her. She would have more in common with him. Sean didn't know what her deal was with the come-ons, but he would keep an eye on her and wouldn't let them affect the investigation.

He introduced her to the team, sharing their specialties, then sat on the arm of the sofa. "So go ahead and bring everyone up to date on what you know about Phantom and your encounter last night."

All eyes turned to Dustee, and she beamed back at them, obviously pleased to receive the attention. Sean waited for her to say something outrageous again. Instead, she succinctly recounted the same story she'd related back at the office. Not a bit of discrepancy between the two. If a person wasn't telling the truth, it was hard to recall every fact, so her ability to do so helped to ease Sean's anxiety.

She paused to take a deep breath, and a dusky shadow of fear darkened her eyes. "I should add that the biggest question I had when I worked with him was where he was born. It's possible he's of Russian descent."

Sean had read that in the files but wanted to hear Dustee's take on it. "Why's that?"

She firmly met his gaze, but her hands

trembled. "His code. We found a few Cyrillic letters left behind. Of course, they could've been false flags—just him trying to throw us off. He's known for that too."

Cam shifted to look at her. "So you think it's a good possibility he's not Russian?"

"Maybe." She bit her lip. "I just don't know. He's smart. Real smart, and I'm thinking he wouldn't make a mistake like that."

"If he used Cyrillic letters," Cam said, "then he would need the Cyrillic font on his computer."

Dustee nodded. "And if Russian *is* his native tongue, he'd probably write the comments using that font and translate them before deploying the code. Maybe he missed a few letters."

"But you don't think he's that sloppy?" Sean asked.

She shook her head. "Not the guy I worked with. This was found in his early coding, and he might not have been as careful back then. But that's just a guess."

Taylor sat forward in her chair across from Dustee. "Didn't you get a feel for his ease with the English language when you communicated with him?"

"We only chatted online, and honestly, he seemed foreign. But I could fake that if I had to, and like I said, he's crazy smart—like a genius— so I know he could fake it too."

Sean thought about his online communication

with Taylor. Could he have gotten away with faking a different nationality? He spoke fluent French and Spanish and could've probably pulled those off, but Russian was another thing altogether. It wasn't as common of a language for people from other countries to learn. Still, Phantom wasn't your everyday hacker, and he could've mastered the Russian language in order to better communicate with other hackers.

Something for Sean and the team to keep in mind. "As of now, we're not dealing with altered code, but if we find it, we need to watch for Cyrillic letters and false flags." Sean looked at Dustee. "Anything else we should know?"

"No. But his programming patterns are pretty ingrained in my head, and I'll keep an eye out for those. You know the drill."

Yeah, Sean did know the drill, but as lead on this investigation, he probably wouldn't be reviewing a ton of logs or code. He'd be too busy managing the investigation, and that included protecting everyone from a killer with an unquenchable desire to murder anyone who got in his way.

"Why don't we play a few rounds of pool, Slim?" Mack tipped his head at the pool table. "Erase some of the worry lines on your face."

"Sounds perfect." She smiled at her friend and went to select a cue. "But you're going down."

Mack laughed, and the sound of his joy cut the tension that lingered from Dustee's departure. An outsider might think Mack was callous to laugh given the situation they were facing, but law enforcement officers, her included, often used humor to diffuse uncomfortable situations. Without it they would burn out, and with the high stakes facing them, they needed a few minutes of downtime too. She would play one game of pool and afterward get to work reviewing her protection plan.

Mack racked up the balls, cracking them against each other. Kiley and Cam came over to watch, and Taylor grabbed a cue.

"Dibs on the winner." A mischievous grin quirked Cam's mouth, making him look even younger than his twenty-nine years. "About time I prove my mad pool skills."

"As if." Kiley smiled, raising cheekbones Taylor would kill to have, and Taylor was once again struck by Kiley's stunning beauty. Like Dianne, Kiley was oblivious to her good looks.

Taylor wanted Sean to join them, but he was glued to his phone in a hushed conversation in the corner, his shoulders rigid. This singular focus was not like the man she'd come to know online. It hurt her heart to see the demands of the job creasing his face, but a huge responsibility rested on his shoulders. The intense pressure was inevitable.

He suddenly shoved his phone into his pocket and strode to the piano in the far corner. He raised the lid and sat.

Taylor gawked at him. "Sean plays the piano?"

"He's actually good at it," Kiley said loudly, as if she wanted him to hear. "Especially for a dude who has no sense of rhythm on the dance floor."

With the mood Sean seemed to be in, Taylor waited for him to get mad, but he turned and grinned at Kiley.

Oh, man. Taylor drew in a sharp breath. He was good-looking before, but with an earnest smile and a happy glow to his face? He was devastatingly handsome.

"Everything okay, Slim?" Mack asked.

She tried to shift her focus to her friend but couldn't move a muscle, and if she could, she would likely be pulling out her phone and finding a way to take Sean's picture.

Mack studied her. "Oh, I see."

Cam pointedly cleared his throat. "Our fearless leader has that effect on the ladies."

"You're one to talk." Kiley looked him in the eye. Only an inch or so taller than Taylor, Kiley's posture was so perfect that she seemed taller. "How many different women have you dated this month?"

A wide smile brought out cute dimples in Cam's face, but his smile did nothing for Taylor. Nothing at all.

"Go ahead and break, Slim," Mack said. "If you can close your mouth and focus on the game, that is."

She'd been gaping like Dustee. A rush of heat started at her chest and rose clear to the top of her head. She busied herself with chalking the stick and listening to the music flowing from the piano, dragging her attention right back to Sean. He was playing something classical. Something that sounded and looked extremely difficult. High notes. Low notes. Runs on the keyboard. Beautiful and haunting at the same time.

"He unwinds that way," Kiley said. "And as a bonus, so do we."

Really? He'd told her he unwound with target shooting and archery, but piano? Nah, he'd never mentioned that. Here she thought she knew him so well.

"Have to say," Cam said, his eyes twinkling as he looked at Kiley, "your pillow and furniture moving doesn't help in the same way."

"And being a toy voyager does?" Kiley grinned.

"Hey, don't knock it until you've tried it."

"What's a toy voyager?" Taylor asked, honestly interested.

Kiley's muted green eyes were fixed on Cam. "He sends his *Game of Thrones* Lego figures to people, who then take them on trips and send back pictures."

"When you say it that way, it sounds stupid."

Cam frowned, his focus drifting to Taylor. "I want to travel. Just can't afford the time right now. So I send the Kingslayer places I want to go and then I get pictures back featuring him. I like it." He shrugged, looking uneasy.

"Sounds like fun." Taylor squeezed his arm. "You'll have to share your pictures with me."

Kiley groaned. "No. No. Don't ask. You'll never get away from him."

He gave her a playful look. "Just for that, I'll make you sit through them too."

She punched his arm, and Taylor was surprised at how at ease she felt with the team. Sure it was superficial and would disappear the moment they had work to do, but she was enjoying the interaction all the same.

Sean suddenly lifted his fingers from the keyboard, drawing everyone's attention. He dug his phone from his pocket, looking at the screen as he got to his feet. "It's a text from Eisenhower. The WITSEC database was taken offline this morning."

"So no additional data has been stolen," Taylor confirmed.

He nodded. "And my higher-level database access has been approved."

"Means we can finally get to work." Cam's boyish expression from a moment ago was long gone, replaced by an intensity that fit his standing as part of the RED team. "No more hanging out and wasting time."

"Soon." Sean crossed the room. "Our IT contact at the Marshals' office is cloning the WITSEC server now. We'll have access by morning. For now, though, I can download the database logs. We can get started on those tonight."

"Why a clone?" Taylor asked.

Sean turned to face her. "We can't work with or modify actual files. They're making a copy of the official server that hosts the database for our team to access instead. The only access to the database right now is still on the secured terminal at your office."

"You can't do it here?" she asked.

He shook his head. "We don't have any network access here. Too many risks of being hacked and giving away our location. Plus database access is restricted to authorized terminals only."

She didn't understand and opened her mouth to question him further when he preempted her with a raised hand. "I'll explain it all at your office. Shouldn't take us too long. If we leave now, we can be back by dinnertime."

"Sure," she said, though agreeing to be alone with him for any amount of time was akin to throwing fuel on a fire. And she'd rather not go out again today. She was hoping to use the time to review her security plan and look for holes.

"Let me grab my things," Sean said, not letting even a moment slow him down.

Taylor gripped the pool cue and watched him

pick up his computer case and settle the strap over his shoulder. He moved with grace and fluidity for such a big guy, and she could easily imagine him in action, chasing Phantom and taking him down.

She didn't know what she'd expected Sean would be like, but it was wonderful to put a face with the many conversations. Her friend, here in person. Now her, what, coworker? Yeah sure, but what else? Was there more? Did she want there to be more?

She forced herself to look away and found Mack watching her. He arched a brow but said nothing.

Had she been acting like Dustee again? Lovestruck? If so, she needed to cool it if she wanted the team to accept her. Maybe let her into their inner circle. And to keep herself safe from additional heartbreak.

Her phone rang, and she leaned the cue against the wall to dig it out of her pocket. She glanced at the caller ID and quickly answered, "Chief."

"Good." A sigh of relief flowed through the phone. "Glad I got you, Mills. Thought you'd want to know. Three witnesses were attacked today."

Oh no. "Three?"

"Yes. In Chicago, Dallas, and Minneapolis."

"Are they all right?" Taylor held her breath, waiting for the response.

"The Chicago woman's in intensive care. Hanging in there, but it's touch and go. The others escaped with only minor injuries."

Witnesses truly were in extreme danger. Taylor could hardly stomach the thought. She offered a quick prayer for the woman in Chicago, and for all witnesses in the program. "The attacks might not be related to the breach."

Inman snorted. "Come on, Mills. You don't really believe that, do you?"

She didn't like her boss's reply, but he was right.

Sean cast her a questioning look. She covered the phone and relayed the information.

His jaw muscle twitched. "Can he get us their names? The information might help us narrow down the witness list."

"Can you provide their contact information?" she asked Inman.

"I'll send it via secured email." An uncomfortable silence dragged out. "I know I have nothing to do with this investigation, but ticktock, Mills. Someone's gonna get killed if we don't get that list soon."

The office was dark, just as it should be at this time of night. Taylor couldn't count the number of times she'd needed information on a witness and come here after hours, but this visit felt different somehow. Maybe it was because Sean

123

was with her and she was still trying to figure out how to act around him. More likely her unsettled feelings came from Inman's call. Their witnesses were vulnerable. Every single one of them, and now that she was officially part of the RED team, she had to find a way to protect them.

She flipped on lights, illuminating the large bullpen with six desks, a small supervisor's office, a conference room, and a glass-walled room holding the computer deputies used solely to access the WITSEC database.

Sean headed straight for the computer. She followed and swiped her government-issued Common Access Card on the wall-mounted reader to gain access to the space, and she wasn't surprised to see her hand shaking.

"Hey." Hand on doorknob, Sean stopped to look at her. "Relax. We're safe here."

But she couldn't relax. Not with all the turmoil in her life right now.

"What is it?" Concern edged his voice as he rested his free hand on her shoulder.

She'd like to think his touch would make her feel better, but it didn't, and tears threatened to flow. She might be friends with Sean, but she was a deputy for goodness' sake and wouldn't cry on the job. She looked up at the ceiling until the feeling passed.

"Come on." His tone was a mere whisper, and he removed his hand to bend down to capture her gaze. "What's wrong? Let me help."

She truly was thankful that he was standing strong by her side. "The call from Inman has me spooked. I'm not actually responsible for creating the vulnerable witness list, but I feel this pressure to do something. To move faster. But we have nothing to go on. Nothing."

His brows pinched together. "Trust me. I know the gravity of the situation."

What a bad friend she'd been, thinking only of herself. He was in charge of protecting thousands of witnesses, while only two of her witnesses were in immediate danger. It took a strong man to handle such a big job and to do so with the confidence he'd been displaying. But his pinched look told her she'd erased some of his confidence.

She touched his arm. "I know I can't help with the technical things, but let me know if there's anything else I can do."

Sean nodded, just a quick bob of his head, but he didn't say a word as tension radiated from him.

"I'm sorry I gave you such a hard time today," she tried again. "I'm sure that didn't help things." His worry seemed to evaporate all of a sudden, and a soft smile played on his face. She had no clue as to the change in his demeanor. "Why the smile?"

"I liked seeing your tenacity today." His grin widened.

"Even if I was a pain to deal with?"

"Yeah. Even then." He cleared his throat. "I wanted to mention something, and now might be a good time, seeing as we're alone. I think it's best that, while we're working this investigation, we don't let the others know about our friendship."

Her heart dropped, and she didn't know how to respond.

"Wait. Don't jump to conclusions." He watched her carefully. "It's not because I don't want them to know about it. I'm proud to be your friend. But I don't want it to get back to Eisenhower. If he found out I have a personal connection to you, he's likely to overreact and replace me as lead."

"Okay." She knew he was just thinking about his job, so why did it sting? Maybe it was precisely because he was thinking about his job and not her, and that was what made it hurt.

Sean reached for her hand. "I'm sorry if this bothers you. I wouldn't hurt you for the world. You know that, right?"

Taylor thought through their past interactions, and she knew he meant what he was saying. She was just being overly sensitive. "I get it. And I'll do my best not to slip up."

"Thank you." He squeezed her hand. "And I'm sorry too. I've been a real bear all day."

"Yeah you were." She smiled.

His face looked like a little boy caught stealing a cookie. "I'm trying to do better, but if I let the job consume me, feel free to call me on it."

"Oh, I will." She laughed, and the tension in the room abated.

"If friends can't call you out when you mess up, who can?" He chuckled.

She loved the sound of his laughter. This lighthearted guy was the Sean she knew and cared for.

He pulled open the computer room door, and she followed him inside. Stepping into this space always gave her a feeling of importance. Not from the room's grandiose size—it was the size of a closet—but having access meant she was entrusted with highly sensitive and secure information.

Sean took a seat behind the computer, and she watched him insert his FBI CAC card into the computer's reader. A login screen appeared on the monitor, and she looked away to respect his privacy.

When his fingers stopped clicking on the keyboard, she turned back to see a long list of files opening on-screen. This page was nothing like the one she used to check records. In fact, she'd never seen this particular screen before.

She moved closer. "Mind explaining what you're doing?"

He nodded, drawing her attention to a small cowlick on the back of his head that she had to fight from trying to smooth down. "I'll be downloading logs for and queries made to the

WITSEC database. The logs will show the records accessed, who accessed them and when, and the location where the login occurred."

She didn't like to hear that. "That sounds like a lot of data to go through and could take days to review."

"We'll keep things manageable by looking only at the last thirty days." He entered the dates in the empty fields on the screen, then clicked to search. "But you should know, the site could've been hacked long before that, and the database administrator missed it somehow. In that case, we'll have to go back even further."

Dates aside, she had to admit to being a bit confused. "So these logs you're downloading, they'll tell you if the logins are legit or if it was Phantom?"

"It's a bit more complicated." He swiveled to face her, his knee connecting with her leg, and she jumped back. That earned her a raise of his eyebrows, but he continued, "Like I mentioned, logging in to the WITSEC database is limited to secured terminals. They're located at the Marshals' D.C. headquarters and field offices. There's no wireless login from home, or anywhere else for that matter. Not even the safe house."

"This makes the database more secure, right?"

He nodded. "Remote field offices have access via a VPN—a Virtual Private Network and encryption."

"Okay, that's clear as mud." She chuckled.

He gave a wry smile. "Think of it this way. It's like accessing your bank account when you use an ATM. There are two points of authentication just like here. Something you have, like your bank card, and something you know—your PIN. And it's all done at a specific location, using specific equipment."

She got it now. "With WITSEC, I have my ID card and password, and I use this computer."

"Exactly. So when your card is used, the program records that you logged in to the database and the actions you perform. The location of the access is recorded via the number assigned to each computer."

Taylor nodded, though she was still a bit confused. "If the only way to log in to the database is to use my card and an official computer, there couldn't be any unauthorized access, right?"

"Presumably, yes," he said, but his dire tone said otherwise. "We could have a deputy or another person in one of the offices working with Phantom. Plus there's always a cowboy who thinks he knows better and is above the rules, so he shares his card. That means we can't be certain the log reflects the actual person accessing the data, but we can be certain of the location. That can't be faked."

She let his statement settle in and didn't like the

implications. "So if database access is restricted to deputies only, that would mean—"

"We have a dirty deputy or slack security at one of the offices." He locked gazes with her. "Which means we could be looking at a deputy who works in this very office."

CHAPTER 10

Taylor slept horribly, tossing and turning, and despite the joy of watching the sunrise through her bedroom window, she couldn't shake the thought Sean had planted in her head. Someone in her office, someone she worked with every day, could be partnering with Phantom. She'd run through the list of deputies' names over and over during the night and couldn't come up with even one person she might suspect. But sadly, with all the duplicity she'd seen in her job, she had to admit that anything was possible. Still, she was dedicated to her coworkers and had to do something to prove there wasn't a dirty deputy in her office.

She picked up her phone and dialed their IT tech. Hershel was a night owl, and she would be waking him at this hour. Not something he would appreciate, but she needed to check for her own peace of mind.

"Hello," he grumbled.

"Hershel. Good. It's Taylor."

"Do you know what time it is?"

"Sorry about waking you, but this is top priority, and I wanted you to get started on it right away." She let the curtains fall over the window. "I promise I'll make it up to you. You name it, and it's yours."

"What do you need?" His voice had taken on a more civil tone.

"A copy of the office's security footage for the past month." Her request was met with an uncomfortable silence. "Is there a problem getting that to me?"

"Does the chief know you're asking for this?"

"Not yet, but I'll loop him in this morning." She rushed on before he could ask additional questions and put her off. "How soon can I get the files?"

His sigh filtered through the phone.

"I know you're overworked, but this is critically important for witness safety or I wouldn't be asking."

"Okay. Okay. I get it. I've got a few things I need to do first. I'll try to have the files to you by lunchtime, but don't hold your breath."

Her heart lifted at his willingness to produce the files without written permission from the chief. "Thanks, Hershel. I'll watch my inbox for it."

"Yeah, and in it I'll be naming my price." He disconnected.

He was for the most part a reasonable guy, but she couldn't predict his repayment demands. She hoped she could provide whatever he wanted.

She shoved her phone into her pocket and sat down to start calling her witnesses. Though scaring them was never her first choice, she'd decided she needed to warn them. She couldn't leak classified information. She'd just tell them to keep an eye out, and she'd check in on them on a regular basis until Phantom was caught.

She finished her calls, gathered up Dustee's financial files spread out on her bed, put them in her briefcase, and headed for the basement to review her findings with Sean. After the sunny bedroom, the basement felt dark, even with numerous small windows along the exterior walls. She swung around the corner to the family room and came to a stop.

The scent of microwave popcorn lingered in the air, and the team members sat in the same locations she'd left them in at 1:00 a.m. Sean had insisted she get some sleep, saying they would be heading to bed right after her. But this morning they wore the same clothes and same tired expressions. Obviously, they'd been up all night.

Sean looked at her from the couch where he sat with his laptop propped on his legs and a cup of coffee raised to his mouth. He choked on his sip but quickly recovered.

"You stayed up all night," she said, wishing they'd allowed her to help.

He set his cup on the table. "I wanted to get to a place where I could put Dustee to work today."

Taylor sat beside him and laid her briefcase next to her. "And did you get to that place?"

He nodded but didn't elaborate.

"Too technical to explain to me?" Hopefully this was Sean's reason and not him cutting her out of the loop.

"Exactly," he replied.

"Any leads on the hacker's identity?"

He shook his head, disappointment clinging to his every feature. He looked like he could use a hug. Nothing romantic, but an encouraging embrace. She would be glad to wrap her arms around him, reassure him that he was doing a great job leading the investigation, and convince him that he would find Phantom. Offering encouragement would be fine. The hug, not so much.

She tucked her hands under her legs instead. "I have every confidence that with you in charge, we'll find Phantom."

He leaned closer, as if he didn't want the others to hear him. "I appreciate your support. I want to do a good job here, but I have a feeling it's not going to be easy and will test all my skills."

"You've got this. I know it." She squeezed his arm and quickly let go to move them forward before she did or said something in front of the team to reveal her friendship with him. "What about the witnesses whose names were stolen? Any progress on that list?"

He glanced at his teammates sitting at the table. "We're working on it. Not progressing fast enough for my liking, but we're working nonstop."

"Those poor witnesses. In jeopardy and they don't even know it." She clasped her hands together. "You should know, I just called my people and warned them to be careful. And I plan to check in with them often."

He nodded, but his expression was blank, and she couldn't tell what he thought of her decision. Maybe he needed good news.

"I also finished reviewing Dustee's financial files, which I printed at the office last night. I went through her statements to track her income and expenses, and she's still as broke as I thought. No income beyond her regular salary." She tapped her briefcase. "I have the files here if you want to review them for yourself."

He shook his head. "She could be hiding the money."

"Yeah, I thought of that. The thing about Dustee is, if she has a penny to her name, she spends it on something lavish. If she was receiving big payments from Phantom, I would have seen the results of this."

"So you're sure she's clear?"

"As sure as I can be," Taylor answered.

"Okay. That's good enough for me. I'll still monitor her closely, but I'll allow her to work the investigation. We're all heading up to get ready for the day." He ran his gaze over her, lingering along the way. "Looks like you're already quite ready."

Worried the others might see the attraction in his eyes, she turned to check and found them laser-focused on their work. Good. "I could've stayed and helped out last night."

"Not much you could've done, and it was important you got some sleep. You look . . . um . . . well, refreshed. Perky even." He chuckled.

He might be ready to move on, but she wasn't. "While I get that your team doesn't think they need anyone, I am available to help. I might not be able to assist on technical things, but I could've made coffee, snacks . . . and cleaned up."

He looked at the table covered with discarded wrappers, cups, and microwave popcorn bags. "We get kind of messy, don't we?"

"I'll clean it up while you all shower."

"You don't—"

"I insist." She nearly snapped out the words.

Why was she so bound and determined to be part of this group? They lived a country away. She wouldn't see any of them again after they located Phantom, so what was the big deal? Seriously, what?

Sean squinted at her for a moment, then nodded. "Okay. Sure. Clean away, and thanks."

Mack started toward the stairway, stopping to rest a hand on her shoulder. "Morning, Slim."

She smiled up at her friend. "I'm expecting videos from TriMet and the library anytime now.

I could use some help going through them. Are you available?"

He jerked a thumb at Sean. "You'll have to ask our fearless leader."

She turned to Sean. "It really would be helpful."

"Sure," he replied, but annoyance flicked through his expression. Why, she didn't know.

"See you later." Mack strode toward the stairway, his shoulders thrown back and his steps purposeful. The uneasiness between him and Sean remained hanging in the air.

It seemed Sean didn't get along with Mack, and vice versa. Perhaps the two men were too much alike, both overly competitive. She hadn't noticed whether or not this interfered with their work, but then again her experience with them was limited to just the one investigation, and that wasn't in person where she might've seen the nuances in behavior.

"I love how your team is multi-agency," she said to Sean, feeling like she needed to stand up for Mack. "It was great to see the agencies cooperate in the Montgomery Three investigation. I especially appreciate that you have such a talented deputy on the team."

"Mack's good at his job and well-respected, I'll give him that." Sean sounded reluctantly impressed. "His fugitive investigation skills have helped us bring in many of our suspects."

"He told me Eisenhower added him to

your group when he came to complain about something the team did."

"Yeah." Sean frowned. "Not my finest day, but yeah. Mack was mad at how I handled an interrogation. Eisenhower defended me, but he liked the way Mack stood his ground too. Eisenhower saw the value of having a deputy with Mack's experience on the team. The rest is history." He closed his laptop and put it in his case. "FYI, we're heading into the FBI office at nine to start working logs and searching for modified files. I'll need Dustee to join us."

Taylor didn't like that plan. "I'd rather not have her leave the house and expose her to a potential attack. Can't she just do her thing here?"

Sean shook his head. "No access to the cloned server."

Taylor couldn't very well argue with that. "Then I'd like to send a decoy vehicle ahead of us. Just to be sure."

"I figured you'd want to do that. I already contacted Snow. He's on his way with a female agent to stand in for Dustee."

She nodded her thanks. "That's great."

"I aim to please." A grin spread across his face.

Despite her resolve to ignore her feelings, his consideration touched her heart. "Are you any closer to knowing when the hack occurred?"

"Not really, no. We reviewed the—"

"I need to talk to you, Sean." Kiley's voice came from behind.

Taylor had been so wrapped up in her conversation with Sean, she didn't hear Kiley approach. Taylor swiveled in her chair to look up at Kiley.

Kiley grabbed a white pillow from the end of the sofa, and after eyeing a club chair with a blue pillow, she quickly exchanged them.

Sean sat forward to zip his laptop case. "You have something else?"

Kiley karate-chopped the pillow to leave a V in the middle. "Maybe, but we should talk about it in private."

"No one can hear us down here," Sean said.

Kiley cast a pointed look at Taylor.

"Me?" Taylor clutched her hand to her chest. "You don't want to talk in front of me?"

Kiley nodded.

"But why?" Questions pinged through Taylor's brain. "Oh, I get it. You want to talk about deputies I might know."

Kiley didn't acknowledge or respond at all, but just remained there, shoulders back, lips pursed.

"The Marshals Service doesn't have dirty deputies, and our security is as tight as it can be," Taylor said, though she doubted her own words as soon as they left her mouth. She wished she'd received the security videos from Hershel already and could at least clear her coworkers of any wrongdoing. "The computers are locked up in every office with keycard access only."

"See." Kiley put a hand on her hip. "That's why I want to talk to Sean alone. If I say anything bad about a deputy, you'll argue with me and waste time when we don't have time to waste."

Taylor wouldn't give up that easily. "If I promise not to respond at all, will you share what you've found?"

"Fine." Kiley tilted her head, her long hair cascading over her shoulders. She sat on the coffee table and leaned forward. "As I've been reviewing the logs, the pattern of late-night database logins bothered me."

Taylor opened her mouth to ask for clarification, but then remembered she wasn't supposed to speak, so she fired Sean a questioning look.

"We found three offices with a high number of middle-of-the-night logins," he said. "Would that be normal for one of your field offices?"

Taylor shook her head. "Some logins, yes. In an emergency. But a large number? No. In my experience, that wouldn't be the norm."

"Cam and I thought the same thing," Kiley said. "So we're thinking that the hacker changed the log clock on these offices, showing logins at odd hours of the day to lead us astray."

"He can do that?" Taylor asked, not caring that she wasn't supposed to speak.

Sean nodded and locked gazes with Kiley. "The

minute we access the cloned server, I need you to look for any software updates that would alter the clock. We figure out how this change impacts the records, and just maybe we figure out who hacked the database."

CHAPTER 11

The sun shone brightly over the local FBI office, highlighting the brick structure near the airport. A spiky wrought-iron fence surrounded the building, and a security booth stood out front for guest check-in. Yet Sean drove past the main entrance as Taylor and Dustee gawked at the relatively new building. They wouldn't be entering through the front door.

For Dustee's safety, Sean had arranged to use the secured parking lot. He swung the car around back to the multilevel structure protected by an impenetrable barrier that had to be lowered for access. Mack and the other team members trailed them in a separate SUV. Sean parked and dialed Yancy Andrews, the assistant special agent in charge of this field office.

Tall and gangly with thinning gray hair that looked like he'd pasted tufts of it across his scalp, he was intensely focused as he met them at the door and reviewed their credentials before escorting them to a large conference room. Waiting for them on a long, polished mahogany table sat laptops with cords running to the bureau's network hub. For security reasons, the team couldn't use their own machines on this network, but they did have access to the cloned server via the computers here.

Andrews handed Sean a note card. "Login credentials for each computer."

Sean took the card and was grateful the ASAC had assigned separate logins. He could now easily track any untoward network use by Dustee.

"I've arranged for snacks and lunch to be brought in, and help yourself to the coffee." Andrews pointed at a portable bar with a coffeepot. Fresh pastries lined the top shelf, with the lower shelves containing the coffee-making supplies.

"Perfect," Sean said. "You've thought of everything."

"You have my cell number. Call me if you need anything else." Andrews started to leave, then turned back. "Oh, and Agent Snow will be right outside ready to escort you around the building when needed."

Sean nodded and clamped down on his lips to keep from spouting off. Dustee needed an escort, that he understood, but the others? No. They didn't need babysitting. They were trustworthy. Still, Andrews was only following policy, and Sean enforced the same rule regarding the transport of guests in his own office.

"Um, login credentials," Cam demanded from behind a computer at the end of the table. The guy might have a laid-back personality, but when it came to work, he could get pushy.

After logging Cam in, Sean made his way around the table to where Taylor sat next to Dustee. She'd dropped into a chair by the nearest computer and stroked the keyboard, her expression dreamy. He took a seat on her other side, but before he could log her in, his phone rang. He glanced at the caller ID.

"Hang on," he said to her. "I gotta take this."

"Of course you do." She sighed and slumped back in her chair.

Sean ignored her attitude and quickly answered the call from Gary Boyd, C3's phone analyst. "What do you have, Boyd?"

"The text to Dustee came from a burner phone," he replied in his usual no-nonsense tone. "No way we'll get owner information for a burner."

Though Sean had expected Phantom to cover his tracks, taking extra precautions by using a prepaid untraceable phone, he still didn't like having it confirmed. "Get a warrant for the telecom and request a call log so I can at least review the other calls made from that phone. Maybe those numbers will lead to more contacts and produce a much-needed lead in the investigation."

"Will do." Boyd sounded way too laid-back for Sean's liking.

"Telecoms can take their sweet time at responding. Keep the heat turned up on them until they comply. And get the log to me the minute you receive it."

"Understood."

Frustrated, Sean disconnected. "The text to Dustee came from a burner phone. Boyd will request the call log."

No one said anything. Why bother when it was the news they all expected?

"Now is it finally my turn?" Dustee's whine grated on Sean.

Taylor leaned forward and looked him in the eye. "We need a quick review of the rules before you sign her in."

"No surfing the web without permission," Dustee snapped. "Duh! I got it."

"Maybe we need to add an attitude change." Sean eyed her. "Because I really don't want to work with you right now."

"Sorry, but it's like I get it already." She sighed, long and drawn-out like a balloon deflating. "Quit harping on it. You can trust me."

Taylor shared a look with Sean that said they couldn't, and he had to side with Taylor. "Time will tell."

Dustee crossed her arms over her pastel tie-dyed shirt. "Log me in, and I'll prove it."

They'd discussed her role on the drive to the office, and she now possessed sufficient knowledge to get started without additional directions, so Sean entered her network credentials. He would keep a close eye on her. No telling what she might get up to. At least they'd restricted her permissions, and she couldn't see confidential information or overwrite files like the team could.

The computer finished logging in, her screen filling with a list of cloned server files. Her eyes brightened, and she cracked her knuckles and started typing. She was a beautiful woman, but in her element she moved to runway-model beautiful. Still, her looks didn't do a thing for Sean.

But the woman at her side, the one with the confident tilt to her head and eyes that were warm and vulnerable, the one who possessed a heart of gold and compassion that knew no bounds . . . now that was a face he could get lost in.

Maybe Mack could too.

Sean's gut tightened. He didn't like the way Mack kept touching her. She'd said there was nothing between them, that they were just old friends and coworkers. Still, Sean didn't like it. Not one bit. But it was his problem, not theirs. Gina's betrayal with his best friend left him doubting everyone. Not a good feeling. He valued Taylor's friendship. Now he might lose it because of this crazy attraction between them. An attraction he thought he could control. But man, when Mack touched her, Sean saw red.

Mack looked up, and Sean prepared himself for a scowl, but instead his teammate looked at Taylor. "I finished the first video, Slim. Which one do you want me to watch next?"

"I'm still on the second one," she replied without

looking up. "Go ahead and start number three."

"Roger that," he said, and went back to work.

Sean didn't like the pair of them working together, but at least they were right here where he could keep an eye on them.

Man, had he really gotten that suspicious? Not the guy he wanted to be for sure. When this investigation was over, he needed to do some soul-searching. For now, he'd settle for keeping his feelings under control and not hurting Taylor.

His phone rang. Perfect timing. He didn't recognize the number, but he needed the distraction so he quickly answered. "Special Agent Sean Nichols."

"Agent Nichols, this is Agent Bristow in Philadelphia," the woman said, her voice deep.

"Yes, Agent Bristow," Sean said, wondering why she was calling him.

"I worked Phantom's investigation. My ASAC said you'd requested our case file for your current investigation, and I thought you should know that I think Phantom is operating under the name Paul Jackson."

He remembered the name from the case file, but only because it was listed as the warehouse owner's name. "Why wasn't your theory in the report?"

"Because I didn't—don't—have concrete evidence to prove the connection."

"What *do* you have?" He tried not to sound suspicious, but he didn't manage it.

A frustrated breath of air came rushing through the phone. "The real Paul Jackson can barely use a smartphone, let alone perform a complicated hack. He's clearly not our guy. But I've recently heard mention of the name in hackers' circles on the dark web in connection with Phantom. I figure he decided to use Jackson's name. Maybe his entire ID."

Sean wanted to believe this, except he needed hard evidence to do so. "The real Paul Jackson could've put on an act for you. Downplayed his skills."

"No. No way. We thoroughly vetted him. Left nothing unturned."

Maybe she had something here. At least it was worth checking into. Especially since they didn't have a strong lead of their own. "Have you documented your findings in writing?"

"Absolutely."

"And are you willing to share your report with me?"

"If you think it will help bring this despicable guy to justice, you better believe I will."

Sean gave her his email address and thanked her before disconnecting. He looked at Dustee. "You ever hear the name Paul Jackson in connection with Phantom?"

She didn't look up from the computer. "Should I have?"

"No." He stood.

"Okay, people, listen up." He shared the information he'd just received from Agent Bristow. "Mack, I want you to leave the video reviews to head up this line of inquiry. Get a strong contingent of analysts in D.C. to search for the name Paul Jackson in connection with hotels, car rentals, et cetera in the Portland area. Check every flight manifest from Philadelphia in the last month. Trains and buses too."

"You got it." Mack's eyes lit with the thrill of the hunt as he grabbed his phone, while Cam and Kiley kept their heads down just like Dustee.

They were listening. Sean was sure of that. Multitasking to find the much-needed list of names.

"That's it! I've got it!" Kiley shot to her feet. "The software was updated two weeks ago. We were right. The update changed the way logs record time stamps."

"Systems change all the time," Sean said, trying not to get excited about this news.

"True that, but the update was done at 3:27 a.m., and we're talking a government database here." Kiley started pacing the length of the table. "No one is likely to alter code in the middle of the night unless the system was offline or there was a security breach, which the IT staff said didn't happen. And it most definitely wouldn't be altered from a remote location."

"Just to clarify," Taylor said, spinning around

to look at Kiley, "you're saying someone logged in from a remote office in the middle of the night and changed the program?"

Kiley gave a firm nod, her ponytail swishing.

"Then get on the phone to our Marshals' IT contact in D.C.," Sean said. "Verify that this wasn't an approved update, and we'll take it from there."

Kiley frowned. "You know they're going to say it wasn't authorized."

"I suspect so, yes, but I want to confirm before we commit any resources to that area. Meanwhile, Dustee can get started analyzing the code."

Kiley cast a skeptical look at Dustee.

"She knows Phantom's signature." Sean held Kiley's gaze, warning her that this wasn't negotiable and waiting for her to respond with her agreement.

She nodded, but turned away to straighten a picture of the FBI director on the wall.

"You didn't say which office the code update was launched from," Sean said.

Kiley looked over her shoulder at Taylor. "You're not going to like this. Someone at your office uploaded the update."

"No." Taylor shook her head and crossed her arms. "Not my office. You're wrong, Kiley. Totally wrong. The deputies I work with wouldn't do that."

Kiley jabbed her finger at the laptop she was

using. "It's right here on my screen, if you want to take a look for yourself."

"I don't believe it. It can't be true." Taylor's expression intensified, turning confrontational.

"I don't make mistakes, and I resent the implication that I did." Kiley fired a combative look at Taylor and took a step toward her, looking like she planned to deck her.

"Stop, both of you," Sean said. "The last thing we need is to turn on each other."

"But . . ." Taylor shook her head slowly. "It's . . . unbelievable."

"Sure, fine, I get that." Kiley lifted her shoulders into a rigid line. "You want to be loyal to your buddies. I understand, but don't make out like I screwed up."

Taylor sighed. "I'm sorry. I wasn't calling your abilities into question. Really, I wasn't. I'm just shocked. Maybe it would've been easier to accept if you'd shown me the information right off instead of just telling me."

"There you go. Putting it all on me again." Kiley crossed her arms.

"No, wait. I wasn't doing that. I'm a visual person and I . . ." Taylor stopped and shrugged.

"Try putting yourself in Taylor's position," Sean said to Kiley. "If someone said that one of us had illegally hacked the database, you wouldn't have simply questioned it, you'd be clawing their eyes out."

Kiley's anger vanished as quickly as it came, and she grinned. "You're right. I would. Sorry, Taylor. I overreacted. Not enough sleep, I guess."

Sean knew it went far deeper than that, and Kiley was likely still unsettled inside. Growing up, her mother was critical of Kiley's independent nature and constantly criticized her for it, then tightly controlled her life. Now, having her skills questioned was one of her hot buttons.

"I'm sorry too," Taylor said.

Best to lighten things up and encourage them both to let it go. "Good. Now that you've kissed and made up . . ." Sean paused and smiled.

The two women rolled their eyes at him, but the tension in the room evaporated as he hoped. "Time to get back to it."

Kiley sat down. "Okay. I'll get you a list of the people who accessed the database around the time of the software update."

"And if Phantom didn't modify that log," Sean said, his excitement starting to build, "we should finally learn the name of the deputy who did."

CHAPTER 12

Sean closed the file from Agent Bristow. Too bad there hadn't been more to her report instead of conjectures and theories. She'd warned him that she couldn't prove the connection, but he'd mistakenly hoped he would see something in her file that she'd missed. And Kiley struck out with the code changes. Phantom had made sure she couldn't pin the login down to a particular person. It was going to require a deeper investigation. Of course it was. Nothing came easy in the hunt for an elusive hacker.

Sean glanced at his watch. Nearly eleven o'clock, the minutes counting down until a witness was hunted down and murdered.

"Look at this, Dustee." Taylor pointed at her computer screen. "I found the right video."

Dustee swiveled to look, and Sean got up to peer over Taylor's shoulder. A unique scent of berries and vanilla wafted up and brought back the memory of her coming down the stairs that morning. She wore skinny jeans and suede boots with high heels and a purple knit top that brought out a reddish tint in her hair. She looked so amazing that he'd almost choked on his coffee.

She lifted a delicate hand and started a video playing of Dustee exiting a TriMet bus. A hooded man, head down, rushed after her. He grabbed her arm from behind, and she whipped around to shake off his hand.

"It's him, right?" Taylor asked.

Dustee wrapped her arms around her stomach. "Yeah."

"It's the guy who followed you?" Sean clarified. "You're positive?"

Dustee nodded but couldn't seem to summon the strength to speak again. Sean actually felt bad for the often acerbic woman, as she was obviously terrified of this man.

"Let's compare it to the old video that we got from the prior investigation," Sean said. "Can you pull it up?"

"Of course." Taylor accessed the file and started it running. This scene was dark and blurry, but Sean could make out a tall figure darting away from a run-down apartment building. "Has the same build as this guy."

"Agreed," Taylor said. "But there's no way to make a clear connection."

"Still, it's one more thing pointing to Phantom."

"Let's track the footage from inside the bus to see when and where he gets on." Taylor opened a file with a camera obviously mounted at the front of the vehicle near the driver. She set it to a slow rewind, and they watched riders get on and off until their suspect appeared on-screen, moving in reverse.

"That's him. I'll play it in forward motion now." She cued up the video with the suspect stepping into the bus, his face low and turned to the side. He deposited two dollars and a coin into the money slot but fumbled a quarter, dropping it to the floor. He bent to pick up the coin and fed it into the machine.

Sean pointed at the screen. "See how he avoids the camera. Like he did his research and knows where it's located."

"Something Phantom would do for sure." Taylor rewound the video, enlarged the display, then restarted it. "Does it look like he spoke to the driver?"

"Can't tell." Sean squinted, trying to make out details. "Odds are he didn't. He wouldn't want to draw attention to himself."

"I wish the feed was clearer," Taylor said. "Regardless, I need to interview the driver and get the outside video for this stop to see if we can figure out how he arrived. Hopefully, my TriMet contact can give me that too." She got out her phone to make the call.

Sean went back to his seat, but he couldn't concentrate. Interviewing the driver should be their next step. There was no way Sean would let Taylor go alone. Phantom could still be in the area. In fact, he might've seen Taylor last night when she came to Dustee's rescue. Taylor would be disposable to Phantom—just someone standing between him and his target—and he wouldn't hesitate to take her out. So Sean wasn't about to risk her life by letting her go alone.

"Now? You're sure?" Taylor's voice rose. "Okay. Great. Perfect. Get that footage to me as soon as possible."

She stood and shoved her phone in her pocket. "Video might take some time, but the bus driver is on his route right now. Enzo Russo is his name. I'll need to borrow your vehicle to go interview him."

Sean stood. "I'm going with you."

She cut her gaze to Dustee and gave Sean a pointed look.

Sean shifted his focus to the other end of the table. "Kiley, can you move over here by Dustee and keep an eye on her?"

"What am I, some baby that needs a sitter?" Dustee muttered under her breath.

"It's for your protection, as well as ours," Taylor replied.

"Yeah right," Dustee grumbled.

"I'm glad to do it." Kiley picked up her laptop, carefully moving cords to keep them from getting tangled.

Sean looked at Kiley. "If Dustee gives you a legit request to access the internet, then allow it and monitor closely."

Dustee shook her head. "I'm right here, you know."

Kiley sat. "And I'm here too, so cut me some slack."

Sean regretted foisting the job of babysitting on Kiley, but he needed to accompany Taylor on this interview.

"You can always call me if you need me," Taylor assured Dustee, her expression one of fondness mixed with frustration, which very much resembled a mother looking at a wayward toddler.

"Thanks," Dustee said, but her tone was filled with her usual sarcasm.

Sean didn't know how Taylor kept her cool around this woman, when he wanted to lose it most of the time. Sure, she was a victim of Phantom's revenge and deserved protection, but she didn't have to make it so hard to be around her.

"The rest of you, call me if anything develops," Sean said to his fellow team members, looking at each of them to communicate a sense of urgency. Then he gestured for Taylor to go on ahead of him.

She'd started for the door when her phone rang, and she stopped to pull it from her pocket. "I have to take this. It's my chief."

Sean stood back to wait, and he watched her answer and listen with an intensity he found admirable. But truth be told, he was focusing more on how cute she looked with her lips pursed. She really got to him. She was the first woman since Gina had cheated on him who made him consider finding a way out of his self-imposed dating exile.

She suddenly sucked in a breath, and her face paled. "When?"

Sean's stomach clenched. He didn't know what Inman was telling her, but when she planted a hand on the wall to brace herself, he started toward her.

"Of course, Chief. I'll be right there." She stowed her phone, looking like she might crumple to the floor.

Sean didn't care if touching her was a bad idea. He grasped her elbow and steadied her. "What is it? What's wrong?"

She took a fortifying breath, let it out slowly, her lips trembling. She looked up at him, seeming lost and tortured at the same time. "Someone broke into our office last night. Trashed my things like they were looking for something. Inman wants me to check my desk and files."

"Phantom," Sean ground out between his teeth. "Had to be him."

She gave a wooden nod, her wounded gaze never leaving his. "What if we'd gone later last night to download those files? We would've been there. He could have . . ." She closed her eyes tightly and shook her head.

Sean clung to her elbow when what he wanted

to do was draw her into his arms to offer comfort. But he couldn't even be sure that she would feel comforted. Not after the way she reacted to seeing him yesterday.

"We need to get going." She wrapped her arms around her stomach, and his hand fell from her elbow.

Acid burned in Sean's stomach. Too much coffee mixed with stress. He reached into his pocket for an antacid and inconspicuously popped the tablet into his mouth while organizing his thoughts. "We'll go straight to the office and interview the driver later. But I want additional team members to join us."

She frowned. "That's not necessary. Really. And even if it is, Inman probably wouldn't allow it. He knows I'm with you all, and he only asked for me."

"Then we don't ask for his approval," Mack said, already on his feet. "We just show up."

"And what about Dustee?" Taylor asked Sean.

"I need Cam to keep working on the list of endangered witnesses," he answered. "He can stay here with Dustee."

"Ooh, Cam and me." Dustee gave him a dreamy look.

Cam didn't notice, or if he did, he ignored it.

Something Sean was grateful for, as he didn't need to be dealing with Dustee's misplaced affections right now. "We need that vulnerable witness list ASAP. Sooner."

"I'm closing in." Cam kept his focus on his screen. "Should have it for you real soon."

"You're sure you want to move all our resources except Cam to that office?" Gnawing on her lower lip, Kiley started to rise. "Maybe we shouldn't all rush off, but take a moment to think about this."

Sean understood her apprehension. She liked to plan, to think things through before acting. Not something they often had the luxury of doing in their line of work, so Sean was used to acting quickly. He wouldn't change now. "The more eyes we have on the scene, the more likely we are to spot something the Marshals could miss."

Taylor propped a hand on her hip and stared at him. "That sounds very much like a slight to our team."

Sean was glad to see some of her color and feistiness had returned. "No slight intended at all. Just wanting fresh eyes on the place."

She gave a nod of understanding, and he waited for her to move, but she remained frozen by the door. She was probably thinking about what she would see when she arrived and didn't want to leave.

He felt her pain and wished they had time for her to work through her emotions, but they had to get going. He opened the door and stepped into the hallway. Agent Snow was leaning against the wall, and he instantly came to military attention.

Sean met the agent's questioning look. "We're heading out for a while. I'm assuming I have clearance to escort the others to the exit."

Snow bobbed his head and took a step closer. "Anything I can help with?"

"Not at the moment, but Dianne needs additional supplies at the safe house. Did you get her list?"

He nodded again, this time less enthusiastically.

"When you're freed up here, getting those items delivered is the best thing you can do for us." Sean encouraged Taylor to precede him down the hallway toward the parking structure. Kiley and Mack fell in behind them.

In the garage, Sean faced the team. "Taylor rides with me. That way we can go straight to interviewing the bus driver once we're finished at the office, and you all can come back here."

He waited for one of his teammates to point out that it didn't matter who they rode with on the way to the office as long as they took two vehicles, but no one said a word. They nodded and started toward the other SUV.

Taylor glanced back at the door. "You think Dustee will be all right here?"

"Security wise, yes." Sean led her to his rental. "I have the feeling if Phantom could get into this office—which he couldn't possibly do—Snow would do his best to defend her and keep her from harm."

"As we all would, but I get your point. He has that fresh eagerness I remember from my early days." Taylor frowned. "Not sure how long it's been since I felt that way."

A gust of wind whipped into the parking structure, and despite the sun highlighting the building, a nip in the air pierced Sean's jacket as he unlocked the SUV doors. "We may not be quite that eager, but we both still love our work, and that says a lot after all these years."

"We've done well in our careers." She stared over his shoulder, a faraway look in her eyes. "Except for the Montgomery Three investigation. Closing that case without finding the girls still bothers me."

The faces of the missing teenagers popped into Sean's mind. Not unusual. He thought about them often enough. They'd suddenly disappeared from the Vaughn house while Becky's mother, Vivian, was out, and the team had no leads except for a white van seen by Harold Wilson, who was now under Taylor's protection. Sean had always thought Wilson knew something and was the key to solving the investigation, but he'd been only minimally helpful. Even after Taylor questioned him a few times. Still, Sean thought Wilson could yet be pivotal in solving the case, and that meant this trip to Portland was a blessing in disguise.

"You know I'll want to talk to Harold Wilson while I'm here," he said, and opened her door.

Taylor's focus returned, and she shook her head. "Sorry. I can't let that happen."

Not the answer he expected at all. "Why not?"

She looked at him for a long moment, as if he were a challenging puzzle she needed to figure out. "Your investigation is officially over. That means you have no standing to request a visit with Harold, and I can't ignore the rules just because we're friends."

Again, totally not the answer he expected or hoped for. "How can you turn your back on those girls?"

"I'd do most anything I can to help find them, but you know I can't put one of my witnesses in danger. Not for any reason." She gritted her teeth and took a step closer to him. She was so close, he could feel her annoyance with him. "And honestly, you interviewed Harold many times before he came here. I've questioned him several times since. We've gotten no new information, so I can't see how talking to him again will help."

Sean took a beat before he let his frustration get to him and start an argument. "He was on their street the night they disappeared. He saw something that can help us. I'm sure of that."

She raised her chin. "Then why hasn't he told you?"

"Because I don't think he knows it yet," Sean said firmly. "That he didn't think it was important at the time, and it's locked deeper in his memory.

So how can I not talk to him again? And even if I do, I don't see how that would put him in any danger."

She looked like she wanted to sigh but held it in and swatted at a strand of hair that was blowing in the wind. "Sometimes even the most innocent of things can cause a problem for witness security. And that's why I'm not prepared to violate department regulations."

"Fine." Sean didn't want to give in, but she had a valid point. "I don't like your stance, but I can respect it, and I would never ask you to go against your department's regulations. But you *could* ask Inman for permission."

"Now that I'm glad to do." A tight smile crossed her mouth, but then evaporated as quickly as it had appeared. "But I have to warn you. He'll likely say no, and if he does consider it, with the case closed, he may need to run the request up the flagpole."

Meaning the request could get to Eisenhower, and Sean would be outed for working on the Montgomery Three investigation.

So what? For the teens, Sean would take that risk. "Just do what you have to do, because I *will* be interviewing Wilson before I leave town. You can be sure of that."

CHAPTER 13

Pushy. That's the word that kept scrolling through Taylor's mind on the drive to the office. Sean was pushy and used to having his own way. Was that because he was in charge of a high-priority case, or because the team's strong reputation often afforded them carte blanche? They were the rock stars of the law enforcement world. Agent Snow was a perfect example of someone who fawned over them.

She glanced at him. He clearly didn't want to discuss Harold any further. At least that was what the unyielding set of his jaw and hands firmly planted on the wheel told her. Fine. She didn't either. She sent an email to Inman as she promised, and until he responded, she would let it go. With the break-in, she figured his response would be slow in coming. Sean wouldn't like that, but she wouldn't push her boss right now.

She shifted to look out the window for the last few minutes of the drive. She'd grown up in the Pacific Northwest and loved the weather at this time of year. They frequently experienced light drizzle with a few sun breaks that shone gloriously through the many soaring trees. A rainbow often arched in the sky and reminded her that God was always there, even in the midst of a storm. Too bad she didn't manage to remember that all the time. Like now with her protectees facing such danger.

Sean pulled into the reserved lot and was out of the vehicle in a flash, striding around the front in his black tactical pants and boots. She studied him for a moment. Which Sean did she like best? The one who looked so fine in business casual attire yesterday, or this one who looked darkly dangerous? Didn't matter, as like him she did, even if he continued to challenge her decisions.

He opened her door, and Mack swung the other vehicle into the adjoining space. She wasn't eager to see her office trashed and so took her time exiting, but gave a nod of thanks to Sean for his consideration. Of course, that made him smile. She wasn't quite ready to let go of her frustration just yet and had to look away.

Mack came up beside her, his hands shoved in his black jacket pockets with a C3 logo on the chest. He wore tactical clothing matching Sean's, except she didn't find it all that interesting on Mack.

He patted her shoulder, and he smelled like the mints he offered to others. People rarely took one. Not surprising. They were strong enough to make your eyes water. Knowing his stubborn nature, that was why he'd chosen this particular brand. "If it's as bad as we're all imagining it to be, just say the word and we can come out to grab some fresh air."

She smiled her thanks and caught a scowl on Sean's face.

How could he not see what a good friend Mack was, and in turn a great guy? If she managed nothing else while with Sean, she hoped she could convince him of that.

In the elevator, Mack held out his tin of mints, and the others shook their heads. "Suit yourself." He popped one into his mouth.

"Seriously, man, how do you even stand those?" Sean faked a shudder, but then his expression turned serious. "Remember, no one but Inman is read-in on the hack. And he doesn't know about the connection we just discovered to this office. If I decide he needs to know, I'll be the one to tell him."

Taylor didn't like the thought of her boss having to hear that one of his team members had betrayed them. "Might be easier for him to hear it from me."

"Maybe. We'll play it by ear."

Sean said maybe, but it was obvious he wanted to be the one to inform Inman. Perhaps it was better that way. She really didn't want to have a deputy's betrayal associated with her, but if it turned out she could better break the news, then she'd do her job.

"Promise me you won't try to bully or upset him," she said to Sean.

"Me?" He honestly looked surprised.

"Um, Sean." Kiley shrugged out of a leather jacket, revealing a soft ivory blouse that emphasized her dark complexion. "I'm with Taylor on this one. When your focus is set on the end result, you can be a force to be reckoned with."

Sean looked like he thought they were ganging up on him. "Sometimes you have to be."

"Not with Inman, though, right?" Taylor asked.

"Sure, okay," he said, but sounded reluctant. "I promise to go easy on Inman."

His hesitancy gave her pause, so when the elevator doors opened, she hung back for a moment. But when the entire team stared at her, she got moving and spotted her friend Roger Glover standing outside the door. Just under six feet tall, he had flaming red hair, freckles, and muscles on muscles from working out to keep in shape for his role in fugitive apprehension. He wore khaki tactical pants and a fugitive task force T-shirt.

Taylor didn't participate in investigations often—like hardly ever—but at the Marshals' Training Academy she'd learned basic police work during the required ten weeks in criminal investigators' school. From that, she knew Roger was serving as the officer of record. His job was to document the people who were present at the crime scene before the investigation began and add everyone who came and went from the scene after that. A boring task, especially when he usually spent his days hunting down criminals.

She approached him. "How'd you get this job?"

"Just lucky I guess." He rolled his eyes. "Seriously, Inman arrived first and discovered the break-in. He kept everyone out of the office, so we hung out here until he came out. He ordered me to grab a box of booties and gloves from my car, then shoved the clipboard at me. He sent the others home and called you in."

Taylor nodded her understanding. "You're still on the schedule for Dustee's protection detail tonight, right? I don't trust her with just anyone."

"If this goes long enough, Chief will replace me." He looked past her at the others. "He didn't mention that you'd be bringing your whole posse."

"He doesn't know."

"Not sure everyone's welcome at our dance." Roger's forehead wrinkled, but she didn't try to argue with him as he could very well be right. He handed her a box of gloves. "Go ahead, glove up and put booties on while I confirm with Chief that they're allowed on-scene."

Sean pulled a pair of gloves from the box. "You two seem friendly. You never mentioned that you were close."

"Our desks are next to each other," she said. "He's a great guy and has an amazing family. And as an extra bonus, when I have a craving for

169

a home-cooked meal, his wife, Naomi, invites me over."

"Can't complain about that." He snapped on a glove.

She kept looking for an ulterior motive in his expression, but it seemed like he was trying to make up for his earlier behavior. Why then was she still upset with him? She'd have done the same thing if she were in his shoes. Law enforcement officers frequently had to be tenacious and aggressive. It was often what made them good at their jobs, and Sean was no exception.

Roger returned, Chief Inman trailing behind. Short but fit, he looked crisp in his black suit and white shirt. His expression was taxed and irritated, so Taylor quickly introduced everyone to move them along.

Inman ran a practiced gaze over the group before letting it land on Taylor. "I'm not sure what you hope to achieve by bringing the whole team here."

"A fresh perspective," she replied, quoting Sean. She couldn't very well admit he'd bullied his way into bringing everyone along.

"And Dustee?"

"She's safe and sound at the FBI office with Cam babysitting her."

Sean stepped closer. "Odds are good that your break-in is related to our investigation, and as such we'd like to take a look."

"With your influence, I'm sure you could have my supervisor on the phone in quick order, telling me to comply." Inman ended with a sharp look at Taylor. "No point in saying no and wasting everyone's time. Sign in and make sure you stay out of the way." Inman spun and went back inside.

Roger held out the clipboard. "He's not happy, and you are *so* going to hear about this later. In private."

Taylor knew Roger was right. "Hopefully it won't include a reprimand."

"You really think that's going to happen?" Sean asked. "Because if you do, I can—"

She held up her hand. "Save it. The kind of help you can provide will involve higher-ups, and that would only get me in more trouble."

Sean signed in, and as the others followed suit, he studied the card reader dangling on the wall and the shattered glass entry door. "Hey, Glover," he said. "You have a monitored security system, correct?"

"We do, yes."

"And did the alarm go off?"

Glover shook his head. "Whoever did this knew how to disable the system before the alarm sounded."

Sean met Glover's gaze. "Or they had card access."

"You think one of us did this?" Glover shook his head, his expression turning to granite. "You're way off base here, man. That's not possible."

Taylor opened her mouth, likely to mention their recent discovery of the hack originating from here. That was privileged information, and Sean couldn't have her tell anyone. Not even a trusted deputy and friend. He gave her a quick shake of his head. She caught on and closed her mouth.

"Has anyone contacted the security company, or were the intruders caught on video?" Sean asked Glover.

"I'm not sure on either point," Glover replied. "I do know that Inman has our tech person inside. The server room was broken into, and video files were erased. We may never know what happened."

Kiley stepped up to sign in. "Erased doesn't mean gone."

"Beg your pardon?" Glover asked.

She scribbled her name. "First, there should be off-site backup. Either in the cloud or a tape drive stored off-site."

"I wonder if Hershel does that." Glover looked at Taylor.

She shrugged. "If it's standard protocol, I'm sure he does."

Kiley held out the clipboard. "Even if some-thing happened to the backup, odds are good we can recover the files if they haven't been overwritten."

"You can do that?" Glover took the clipboard and passed it to Mack.

"Usually," Sean said. "But something tells me that the person who deleted these files knew enough to overwrite them."

"Still, if they weren't thorough, we may be able to find something." Mack clicked the tip of the pen absently as he looked at the form. "Unless they used a degausser to eliminate the drive's magnetic field."

"A degausser?" Glover asked.

"A large magnet passed over the hard drive."

"We need to talk to Inman about this," Taylor said. "Maybe he'll be glad I brought you with me after all."

"Let's find out." Sean gestured to the door.

She entered the office, and he followed close behind.

Glass crunched underfoot as she passed through the reception area, which remained untouched. Just inside the door, she came to a sudden stop, and Sean nearly plowed into her. She did a one-eighty, taking in the destruction. Her eyes landed on him, and the haunted look shot a flash of anger through his body. He knew that look. He'd seen it hundreds of times in victims' expressions. She felt violated, and a place that once had felt safe to her now felt out of control and dangerous.

It was one thing to see this anxiety in a stranger's face, but in the eyes of someone he cared for? A woman who'd been there for him through thick and thin for months. On his side and in his corner, and now, finding her way into his heart. That was another thing altogether.

"It's . . . I can't even . . ." The words came out in a fragile whisper. Way too fragile for this very strong woman.

Anger took full hold, and Sean's hands fairly vibrated with it. He was torn between punching something and hugging her close.

He'd experienced anger this intense only once. A year ago with his father when Sean shared his mother's lie. All his life she'd told him that his father wanted nothing to do with him, when in fact his dad had fought to be a part of Sean's life. He couldn't bear to see his dad's pain that day, and couldn't bear Taylor's now.

He moved closer to her. Instead of holding her hand and embarrassing her in front of her boss and the forensic staff, he touched the side of his hand against hers to let her know he was there for her. He didn't care if his teammates noticed, and notice they would. What he did care about was how Taylor was feeling and the deep scars this would leave.

She looked up at him, an excess of emotions warring to take hold in her expression, and she eased closer to him.

"We can turn right around and leave if you want," he said quietly. "No one will think less of you. Especially not me."

"I will, though." She took a deep breath, and in her eyes he could see her struggle with what she should do. "Marshals haven't backed down since the service was formed in 1789, and I won't either. Even when horrible things like this come too close to home."

He admired her spirit, one that her fellow deputies held, often pointing out that the Marshals Service was the very first law enforcement agency in the country. Still, he didn't move his hand, didn't walk away. Because as much as she was trying to sound strong, her body language said that she was still troubled.

"That's my desk." She pointed to the one on the far left. Every item had been tossed onto the floor, the desk tipped over, while the other desks in the space were still upright, and many of their items remained in place.

"I'm sorry, Taylor. I know this must feel like a terrible violation."

She nodded, her face still pale and pinched. "I should get to it."

The best thing for her now was to take action to right this situation, but as much as he cared for her, he couldn't let her do it. "You said Inman wants you to look through your things, but I'd like to talk to him before you touch anything."

She offered him a tight-lipped smile. "This is really throwing me for a loop, and I appreciate your taking charge."

"It's the least I can do after getting you in trouble with your boss." He grinned in an effort to lighten the mood.

Her smile still trembled but widened. Feeling she was on the upswing, he turned to his team to get them moving. "Mack, I want you on the security system. Evaluate its complexity and the skills needed to disarm it. Kiley, find their tech guy and the server room to do an assessment on those deleted files. And I want an image taken of Taylor's hard drive so we can look at it back at the office."

"Our tech guy is talking to Inman. Come on. I'll introduce you." Taylor led them through files strewn on the floor and commingled with office supplies to her boss, who was talking with a skinny guy sporting a man bun, goatee, and black glasses.

"Sorry to interrupt, Chief," she said, sounding apprehensive, "but the RED team would like to offer their help in recovering the deleted video files."

Inman's eyebrow rose, probably questioning how they knew about the deleted files. "We were just discussing that, and Hershel tells me there's no hope. They've been overwritten."

"All of them?" Kiley asked.

Hershel scratched his goatee. "Preliminary look says yes, but I need to dig deeper."

"Mind if I sit with you while you do?" Kiley asked.

Hershel eyed her suspiciously. "If Chief approves it, I have no choice."

"It's fine," Inman said.

Hershel frowned, raising Sean's radar. It wasn't unusual for other agencies to resent the RED team's interference and have an attitude, but Hershel's response could also mean he had something to hide. As IT support, he would have access to the database, and he possessed the best computer skills in the office.

Sean looked at Kiley and silently communicated to be watchful of Hershel.

She gave the barest of nods, then changed her focus to Hershel. "We also wondered if you've had a chance to image Taylor's computer. If not, I can help with that."

"I wasn't even planning on it." Hershel crossed his arms. "Is there something you know that I don't?"

"Hershel, why don't you go on back," Inman suggested. "And these guys will catch up with you in a minute."

Hershel eyed Kiley one more time before tiptoeing through the mess, heading for the back of the office.

"Not having been read in on the hack, Hershel

believes this to be a routine break-in." Inman turned to Sean. "And it doesn't look like the WITSEC computer was accessed, so it might very well be just that."

"Did Hershel tell you it wasn't accessed?" Kiley asked.

Inman nodded.

Kiley looked at Sean. "Want me to confirm that?"

"Please," Sean said.

"Wait." Inman's head jerked back. "You suspect one of my people of doing this?"

Sean couldn't have asked for a better opening to tell the chief about the breach. "You should know that this morning we tracked an unauthorized software update made to the database back to your office."

Sean waited for Inman to respond, something along the lines of Taylor's denial when she'd first heard the news. But Inman didn't move. Just stood staring ahead. "I'm guessing there's irrefutable proof of this or you wouldn't be mentioning it to me."

"There is."

Inman planted his feet wide, looking like a pit bull. "And now you think my staff is involved. Or maybe even me."

Sean nodded. "Your lack of reaction to my bombshell worries me. As does your defensive posture."

"You expected what?" He lifted his chin. "That I'd break down? Maybe shout. Declare my innocence. That wouldn't be good for my staff or the forensic techs on-scene."

Sean had to respect the guy. Here he was dealt a shocking blow, and he still thought of those he supervised. Sean could take a lesson from the man, but that wouldn't stop him from doing his job. "I've run into a number of supervisors in the past who tried to cover up employee wrongdoing, and I don't want to put you in a position where your actions might be called into question."

"With a smooth answer like that, you should go into politics." Inman shoved his hands into the pockets of his dress slacks. "I can see the value in accepting your help in this investigation. Let's just be sure you keep this breach to yourselves."

"No worries, sir. With our clearance level, we're experienced at keeping things quiet." Sean tried hard not to sound like he was rubbing their higher clearance in Inman's face. "If video files have in fact been deleted, I have to think that the person who hacked the database wanted to hide his access to the computer. So, as of this moment, we'll be taking over this investigation."

Taylor gasped, but Sean couldn't look at her. Not when he felt like he was betraying her trust, and he hated doing so. She brought him to the office of her own accord, and then here he was taking over. Sean would rather not do so, but after learning about the deleted videos, he had no choice. If he left the Marshals in charge, and there truly was a bad apple on their team, critical evidence could be destroyed.

And then Sean might never find the person who trashed this place and put that terrified look on Taylor's face. His gut screamed with the need to hunt him down and make him pay for what he did. So Sean would soldier on, no matter the collateral damage. "I can run this up the flagpole for official permission if you insist, but it would be easier if we came to an agreement right now."

Inman worked the muscles in his jaw but remained calm, at least outwardly. Sean had to give the man credit. "I know arguing is futile. What do you want from me?"

There was no easy way to say this, so Sean just went for it. "I'll need you and your staff to leave the office. I'll bring in ERT to process the scene, and then we'll secure the place. After we've finished gathering evidence and completed our evaluation, I'll turn the office back over to you."

Inman gave a tight nod. "I'll contact my staff and make sure they know they're not welcome here at the moment. Let me give you my cell number so you can call me the minute you finish."

He rattled off the digits, and Sean typed them into his phone. Inman gave Taylor a sharp look and exited. Sean glanced at her, and she was watching her boss walk away. She looked shocked. Maybe hurt. Maybe questioning what was to become of her office and her boss.

Sean faced her. "I'm sorry—"

"You promised . . . I trusted you, and then you do this? Unbelievable." She spun and stalked off.

Sean understood how she felt. He'd been betrayed enough times to get it. She wanted nothing to do with him right now, and he suspected she might *never* want to see him again, but the witnesses were counting on him to do his job. Even if doing it meant hurting this very special woman when that was the last thing he ever wanted to happen.

CHAPTER 14

Anger bubbled up, darkening everything within Taylor's view. The feeling strangled her, but she didn't know how to let it go. One thing was certain. She couldn't stand to be close to Sean at the moment, so she crossed the room to her desk. While she wanted to tear through her files to see if anything was missing, she couldn't touch a single item without Sean's permission. And she wasn't about to ask him for anything. Besides, he was deep in discussion with his team as if nothing had happened.

Why had she trusted him? Believed he was different than the deceitful witnesses she dealt with every day? A man of his word?

The group suddenly split up and strode her way with a gait that reminded her of movie heroes walking in slow motion. Their hair blowing back. Their strides powerful. Determination etched in already strong faces.

Were they coming to help her or throw her out like Inman?

She curled her fingers, letting the nails bite into her palms, and waited. Kiley and Mack passed her by, heading for the server room. Mack paused to offer a comforting smile and give her hand a quick squeeze.

Sean stopped next to her, his feet shoulder-width apart, his hands on his hips, looking strong and in charge, just as she expected. His expression was another story, though. Apologetic and sincere. And the eyes—she'd only just discovered she enjoyed looking into them—met hers. "I really am sorry about Inman. I know I made a promise, but once we found out about the videos being overwritten, I had to take over. You can see that, right? To protect everyone here except the dirty deputy."

She appreciated his effort to make up, but she was still mad and needed to process it before relenting. "I get it, but you could've taken him aside. Discussed it. Not taken over and tossed him out in front of the others."

Sean cringed. "You're right. I could have been more diplomatic. But when I saw the look in your eyes when you first discovered the mess in here . . ." He paused and shook his head. "I lost sight of everything but finding the jerk who tore this place apart and put that look on your face."

He cared about her, that was obvious. But his efforts were misplaced. "You really think you did this for me?"

"I do."

"Then you don't know me as well as I expected, or you would've known that I care about Inman and all my coworkers. That I would never want them to be hurt this way."

"What can I do to make it right?" He looked around the room as if searching for an answer. "I can apologize to him."

"That's a start." *But I need more.* What was the question that even she didn't know the answer to?

"I'll call him right after I get ERT and an agent out here to relieve Glover." He pulled out his phone.

Right. He was moving on. Getting down to business. She would follow his lead. "And what do you want me to do?"

He looked up from his screen. "Since I can't have you touch anything until after ERT finishes processing the place, there's nothing to be done here. Kiley's in charge of the technical files, and I've put Mack in charge of the physical investigation. That frees me up so we can go interview the bus driver."

"Sounds good," she said, and meant it. She really wanted to leave the vandalized office behind.

"Hang tight. I'll be ready in a flash." He let out a huge breath.

Did he think because she was talking to him that she'd forgiven him? Should she forgive him? He did seem truly sorry. Like before, she could understand that he had to take charge, even if his method of handling the situation still stung. But she couldn't so quickly let go of the fact that he didn't live up to his promise.

He soon finished his calls and smiled as he motioned for her to leave. She couldn't summon up a return smile, but instead made her way through the office.

"What happened in there?" Roger held out the clipboard so they could sign out. "Why did Inman bolt like that?"

She scribbled her name and passed the clipboard to Sean. She started to explain to Roger about Inman being sent home when Sean gave her a warning look as he signed the log. Though she wanted to tell Roger everything, she couldn't share even one detail. She waved her hand like it was no big deal. "We can talk about it tonight back at the safe house, okay?"

Roger nodded, pressed his lips together, and took a long look at her.

"See you tonight," she said quickly, then hurried for the elevator before he asked more questions.

Taylor didn't like being in this position with a friend, but her loyalties needed to be with the RED team right now. She didn't want to do anything to jeopardize their hunt for Phantom and securing the witnesses' safety.

Sean caught up to her, and the elevator ride was filled with tension, as was the drive through town. At the bus stop, she nearly bolted from the vehicle into the biting wind. Misty rain started to fall, and she huddled into her jacket. To distract herself, she got out her phone to take a few pictures of the trees glistening with rain.

Sean retrieved cash from his wallet for the tickets. She gladly let him pay, searching around the area for the perfect picture. Five additional people waited for the bus in the drizzle, their attention fixed in a daily commuter's glaze. A few had lifted their hoods against the rain, but no one held an umbrella. It might rain nearly every day from October through June in the Portland area, but it was often light, and Portlanders were known for shunning the use of umbrellas.

Sean bent his head away from the falling rain. "I don't know the last time I was on a bus."

Okay, fine. He wanted to engage in small talk. Probably better than the pain-filled silence that had lingered after she'd said goodbye to Roger. "I often take MAX—the light rail—when I go downtown for events. Never buses. But come to think of it, I don't know the last time I took MAX to anything."

"Job get in the way?"

She nodded.

"Me too. Even if we weren't both avoiding dating, we might be destined to live life alone." He chuckled.

She didn't like the sound of that. Not at all. Sure, she didn't want to date, but she'd never really considered the long-term consequences of her decision. Not really anyway. *Was* she destined to spend her life alone?

"Looks like I stepped in it again," he said. "You clearly don't think that was funny."

"It's one thing to decide to be alone, but to know it's my likely future? That it's beyond my control?" She ran a hand over her damp hair. "That's another thing altogether."

His smile fell. "You could be right."

Is this what you want for me, God? To be alone?

She'd honestly never asked Him. Not once. Just decided that after Jeremy died, a season without a significant other was her path. But now? Now what was she supposed to think? Was she letting her attraction to Sean color her thoughts?

The bus arrived finally, sloshing over the wet street, the brakes hissing as it slowed. The door groaned open as if it were too much effort to move. She waited for the others to board, then climbed the steps into the vehicle that smelled of the city and damp passengers. Bald and overweight, the uniformed bus driver's belly hung over his belt holding up blue uniform pants, and his matching vest strained the zipper. His nametag said *Enzo Russo*, the driver they were looking for.

"Afternoon." A pleasant smile crossed his chubby face.

As Sean fed dollar bills into the slot, she

displayed her credentials and introduced them. "We need to talk to you about a man who rode your bus two nights ago."

Enzo frowned. "Then you'll have to sit down and ride to the end of the route, because I can't get behind schedule."

"We could talk as you drive." Sean's coins clinked down the slot.

"Not happening. Security violation to have you in front of the line." He jabbed a thumb at a yellow painted line on the floor. "So either take a seat or hop off. Your choice."

"How many stops to the end?"

"Six."

"We'll sit." She smiled at him and went to find an open pair of seats near the front.

She scooted as far as she could toward the window to keep Sean from touching her, but he was a big guy, the seat small, and his leg pressed against hers. She was aware of every touch point. Every fraction of an inch where her jeans brushed his cargo pants. As much as she wanted to move away, being close to him also felt right.

How in the world could she feel this way when he'd just hurt her?

Ignore it. Ignore him.

She shifted her focus out the window, watching Portland's slick streets pass by and listening to the spinning tires rumble over brick-paved intersections. Leafless trees lined the street, laden with big fat drops that served as artwork in themselves. She thought to take out her camera, but for once she really didn't feel like snapping any pictures.

Seriously. This was crazy. She'd taken to admiring tree branches to stop thinking about Sean. She stifled a frustrated groan and grabbed her phone to open the bus video so it was ready to show to Enzo.

At the final stop, he parked, and after the other riders got off, he swiveled to face them. Sean let no time pass but was in front of Enzo in a flash.

She joined them and held out her phone. "I have video from your route that I'd like to show you. We're interested in the passenger in this clip. He got on at Twelfth Avenue in northeast Portland and off at the library. In the video, it looks like he talks to you." She started it playing. "Do you remember him?"

Enzo watched intently through thick wire-rimmed glasses. He started to shake his head, but then stopped and leaned forward. "Yeah. Yeah, I remember him."

"Did you get a look at his face?" Sean asked.

"Nah. He didn't look at me at all. Was a pretty rude fella."

"Didn't you find that odd?" she asked.

He rubbed his jaw. "Riders do weirder things than that. So no, that didn't seem odd to me. But his tattoo was unusual."

"Unusual how?" Sean asked before she could.

"First part of the design was on one hand, the second part on the other." He pointed at her phone. "You can see it when he picks up the quarter and puts both hands together on the machine."

Excited, Taylor enlarged the screen by Phantom's hands and rewound. The letter *L* with three horizontal lines to the left of it were tattooed on his right hand. His left hand lifted to drop the coin, revealing an *R* and a vertical line. He placed both hands together for the briefest of moments, and the lines came together to form an *E*.

"REL," she said, trying to work out why he would have that word, if it even was a word, inked on his hands.

She glanced at Sean. A spark lit in his eyes, but he didn't speak. Right. He had an idea of what it meant, but he wouldn't speculate on the meaning in front of the driver.

"I told him it was unique," Enzo said. "And I asked if it stood for something. He just mumbled, 'Mind your own business, old man.' "

"That was rude." And so very much like she would expect Phantom to behave. "Did he say anything else?"

"No. He just dropped the quarter in and marched to his seat. I remember him getting off at the library. He shoved someone out of his way.

Then he caught up to a young woman and took her arm. She jerked free and took off. I figured he was fighting with his girlfriend." He ran a shaky hand over his face. "Don't tell me he hurt that girl."

"No. She's fine."

"Thank goodness. I almost called it in, but then she left on her own, and I figured it was all good." He shook his head. "You see so much in this job, which is why I try to work the day shift if I can help it. The crazies really come out at night."

Another driver climbed the bus steps and eyed Enzo. "You planning to spend your break behind the wheel?"

Enzo shook his head. "If that's all, I gotta go."

"Can I get your phone number in case we have more questions?" Taylor opened a notes program on her phone.

"Sure, sure." He vacated his seat and shared his contact information.

She repeated it back to him to make sure she got it right and gave him a business card. "If you think of anything that might help us, give me a call, okay?"

He nodded.

"Thanks, Mr. Russo." She took a seat out of their new driver's earshot, and Sean dropped down next to her as the bus swung back into motion.

She wasted no time but faced him. "Seems like you have an idea what REL means?"

"It's a computer term," Sean said. "Basically means a relationship to something else. Since Phantom's into computers, at first it seemed like the most obvious explanation. But now, I honestly don't think it's that simple."

"Why not?" she asked.

"Someone as methodical and driven as Phantom wouldn't ink his hands and not have it mean something important, and it's a relatively innocuous word in the computer world."

She searched for a logical explanation. "Maybe he's reminding himself of a personal relation to something. Or it could be an acronym and the letters mean something."

"I'm betting on the acronym. He's aggressive. Bold. A risk taker. Not a people person. He turned on his partner after all, so I can't see him letting a relationship influence him."

She had to agree. "So we'll try to come up with an acronym."

"With only three letters and no real reference as a starting point, that'll be like looking for the proverbial needle in a haystack."

She didn't like the sound of that, but knew he was right. Still, she spent the remainder of the ride thinking about the acronym. When she stepped off the bus, she was no closer to having an answer. She wound her way through the riders waiting to get on and headed for the parking lot. Sean clicked the SUV doors open with his remote and climbed in, but as she opened her door, she noticed a man standing behind a nearby tree, furtively watching them.

His physique fit Phantom's build, and she knew she had to question the man, whoever he was. She started his way. He turned and fled.

She drew her weapon. "Police! Don't move!"

But the man kept going, picking up speed, in full flight now. She chased after him. He glanced back, revealing his face.

Shocked at seeing him clearly, she came to a stop and gaped after him.

He cursed and ran. Fast. Across the lot.

She came to her senses and began chasing him again, but with his head start and her shorter legs, he took a big lead and then vaulted over a wall too far ahead to catch.

She reached the wall and stopped to take deep breaths. Sean came barreling up to her.

"Phantom," she said, trying to catch her breath. "Call 911. Get the police on him."

He peered over the wall and dug out his phone. "Did you get a good look at him? Can you describe him?"

"I can," she got out between breaths. "I saw his face."

Taylor sat at her desk and stared at the photocopy of Phantom's sketch. The artist had captured his face exactly as she recalled seeing him. Hair the color of dark chocolate was combed forward and cut in an uneven line, dipping over his high forehead. He had a large, fleshy nose on a square face, and his eyes were dark too, though she hadn't been close enough to determine a color.

Sean had already distributed the sketch to Oregon and Washington law enforcement, the news media, the airport, and the bus and train depots. They'd run it through the FBI's facial-recognition program, but the software found no matches. She hoped someone would see Phantom's sketch on the news, recognize him, and call the special number set up by Sean.

She glanced up and spotted him talking with the team in the corner. She'd been so focused on the sketch, then evaluating and reorganizing her files, that she hadn't even noticed them gather. He waved her over, and she wasted no time heading over there.

He smiled when she reached them. "I was just going to come get you so we could review our findings. Did you discover anything missing?"

She nodded. "I'd started a file, putting together the paperwork for transferring Dustee and Dianne. It's gone. Not sure what Phantom thinks he can do with the file when it contained nothing of value to him."

"Maybe he thought it would delay the move," Mack said.

"Maybe." She had no idea of Phantom's motive

and didn't want to waste time speculating. "Anyone else find anything?"

Mack nodded. "The intruder isn't as skilled as we first thought. The office's security system is a simple system like you'd find in a home but with a card reader."

"Easy to disable then," Sean said.

"Easy if he has basic electronics skills, which we know Phantom has."

She didn't like hearing about their less-than-impressive system. "I'm surprised our security is so lax."

"Small offices like this one are low priority when it comes to budgets and pricey upgrades," Sean said.

"As is also true of the servers," Kiley said. "They're not SSD, and they're using tape backup with storage in an off-site location. Regular backups are done nightly, but Hershel only changes out the tapes every Friday."

Sean frowned. "So last night's video has been erased."

"Can't we retrieve the old files from the off-site location?" Taylor asked. "So we can at least review video for the day of the hack?"

Kiley shook her head. Her bun, held up by a pencil, came loose and the pencil dropped to the floor. She ignored it. "The intruder knew about the backups, and the tapes are missing. The storage facility has video. I've requested those files, but I suspect whoever took the tape knows how to avoid the cameras."

"We have no video then." Taylor tried not to sound frustrated, but after the sketch didn't return a match, she was disappointed and her emotions rode on her words.

"Not unless we can recover them." Kiley bent to grab her pencil. "Hershel was right. The suspect overwrote the files, which means we won't likely retrieve much, if anything. At this point, I know he targeted only the video files, but further review might reveal more files."

"And the WITSEC computer?" Taylor asked.

"Not accessed," Kiley said.

Taylor took a moment to process all the points mentioned. "I'm the last person who wants to admit this, but we have to be dealing with someone inside the office, right? Only an insider would know about the tape backup location and how to access the video files."

"Not necessarily." Sean's eyes narrowed. "If the intruder knew Hershel was your tech, he could have trailed him to the storage facility. And anyone with computer skills could locate the video files."

"So you don't think this is an inside job?" she asked.

"Oh, no, I do." He looked her directly in the eyes. "In fact, I'm more sure of it than ever. But I have no proof, and we have to consider all possibilities." He faced Mack. "Let's canvass the neighborhood and get any CCTV footage in the area."

Mack widened his stance. "I already have agents going door to door, and I've requested traffic-cam footage for last night and the night the database was hacked."

Taylor was glad to see Mack in charge of the break-in. His time working fugitive apprehension gave him the ability to think like a criminal and better help in the investigation. "What about forensics?" she asked.

"Several sets of prints were lifted, but then we'd expect that in a public office," Mack replied. "Thankfully, the office employees' prints are recorded in AFIS, so we can quickly eliminate their prints."

Taylor remembered very well having her prints taken and entered into the Automated Fingerprint Identification System when she first became a deputy. It was standard protocol for all law enforcement officers for this very reason. "But if one of my coworkers is behind the hack, then their prints will be eliminated."

Mack frowned. "True, but no one except Hershel should be using the keyboard and mouse in the server room. So any additional prints in that space would be suspicious."

"Not that we'll recover the intruder's prints anyway." Kiley shoved the pencil back into her hair. "If we're dealing with Phantom, he would've worn gloves."

"One thing that hasn't been suggested," Sean said, "is that Hershel could be our guy."

"Agreed," Mack said with a nod. "And that's why I had him give Kiley the lay of the land before banishing him from the office."

"Hershel continued to be belligerent with me as we worked," Kiley added.

"But that's probably because you're this super-agent, and he resented your interference," Taylor said, hoping she was right. "I mean, he's usually so timid and unassuming."

"As are many IT people, so that's not really a reason to eliminate him," Sean said. "In fact, the IT connection makes him a prime suspect."

Taylor didn't like them ganging up on one of her coworkers and wanted to prove his innocence. She looked at Kiley. "What are the odds that you can recover the deleted video?"

"You know I'm one of the best in the country," she replied. "But I'd still say my odds are slim to none, and Phantom will once again manage to evade us."

CHAPTER 15

Time rushed past in the FBI's small conference room. Sean struggled to breathe, as if all the air had gradually been used up and not replaced as the clock ticked down on potential murders of vulnerable witnesses. The database contained records for witnesses and their family members entering WITSEC since the program began in the seventies. Thousands of lives were at stake, and Sean desperately needed a strong lead.

He looked down the table at his team, all of them focused on their work. He couldn't ask for better associates. They'd finished processing the Marshals' office, boarded up the entrance, and turned it over to Inman. Returning the office to Taylor's supervisor had gone a long way in getting her to forgive Sean for his earlier mistake, which she did before going to check in with Inman. She needed to find out if he was upset with her for bringing the team to the office.

Kiley leaned back in her chair and stretched. Her blouse was rumpled, and she looked exhausted after their all-nighter.

Sean took a deep breath and let it out slowly. "Find anything in the deleted video files yet?"

"Don't you think I'd tell you if I did?" Kiley rubbed her forehead. Right. She was just as stressed as Sean. "You of all people know how this is nearly impossible. I'm looking at remapped sectors now. That's our best hope. Shoot, our only hope."

"Not much hope then." Sean hated how down he sounded. As lead on the investigation, the team would reflect his attitude. "And you, Cam? Are you anywhere nearer to giving me a list of compromised witnesses?"

Cam scratched his jaw, looking like he'd rather do anything but answer the question. "Closer, but not there."

"Before you ask me anything," Mack said, "I have only bad news. No Paul Jackson on flight manifests or any other transportation records we've searched. Sorry."

Sean had hoped for better news and wanted to let his frustration fly, but he refused to infect the team with his attitude. He had to get out of this room and blow off some steam. "I'm gonna get some air. Be right back."

Kiley nodded and looked thankful for his departure, confirming his need to improve his mood.

He stepped into the hallway and paced the carpeted floor. Thankfully, Snow wasn't back yet from escorting Taylor to the small conference room. It was going on seven o'clock in the evening and they'd learned nothing today to move the investigation forward. Sure, they were now fairly certain of Phantom's physical description so that someone could possibly spot him. The tattoo might lead to something significant, but right now it was too vague. Without any solid references, figuring out the three letters' meaning wasn't feasible.

Footsteps sounded in the distance, and Snow rounded the corner, Taylor behind him. Sean continued to pace.

She stepped into his path, forcing him to stop. "What's going on?"

Should he say something about his frustration or keep his big trap shut? She was his friend and a good sounding board. Or at least she had been until he'd broken his promise.

"You can tell me," she encouraged.

Was this an olive branch? Her way of saying they were back on solid footing?

He could talk to her. Make it casual, unimportant, not letting her know how much he feared failing at this assignment. How he was letting the investigation get to him and doing things he didn't want to be doing. Like push her. Be demanding. Break a promise.

Yeah, he wanted to talk to his friend. Alone. He fired a look at Snow.

"I get it." Snow nodded. "I'll make myself scarce." He made a precise pivot on squeaky soles and headed back down the hall.

When he was out of earshot, Sean faced Taylor

but didn't want to start with his issues and bring her down. "Everything okay with Inman?"

"Yeah. He doesn't seem mad at all, and there's no sign of anyone targeting my witnesses. Thank God for that." A luminous smile crossed her face. "So, what's going on with you?"

"It's no biggie. I'm just frustrated with the lack of progress. I'll be over it by morning." He hoped. "I didn't want to take it out on everyone so I came out here to walk it off."

"I wish I could help by giving you the TriMet video. My contact just called. She's working on getting the files, but she's held up by a technical issue. Still, she promised them in the morning."

Par for the course. "I hate having to wait. Because if we can find out where Phantom got on that bus, it could lead us to him."

"You know . . ." Her eyes narrowed. "Everyone's tired and hungry. Why don't we call it a night here? Head over to the safe house. We can grab some pizza on the way and take an hour or so to relax and unwind a little. Then get back at it. The downtime will do wonders for everyone."

He didn't want to waste even a second, but she was right. At this pace they were liable to burn out, and in the long run it could cost them even more. It would also be easier to talk to Taylor once he was in a better frame of mind. "Good idea. Except I won't stop for pizza with Dustee in the car. I'll have Snow pick up the food and let him eat with us as a reward for his help."

"He's gonna love that." She chuckled.

Sean smiled. "Why don't you get everyone packed up, and I'll send him for the pizza?"

She reached out to squeeze his arm. "We'll figure this out, Sean. I know we will."

He couldn't help but compare the woman standing before him to the sterner deputy he'd seen since he arrived. This woman had emailed and chatted with him so many times. This woman supported him and was honestly his best friend. Sure, the other team members were his brothers and sister, but they rarely talked about personal struggles. Certainly no conversations like the deep discussions he'd had with Taylor. Discussions of faith. Life's hurts. Disappointments.

"I've missed *this,* Taylor." He was surprised he could vocalize it.

Her forehead furrowed. "I'm not following you."

"The Taylor who's so supportive and doesn't argue with me about everything has been missing since I got here."

She tilted her head and eyed him. "I could say the same thing about you."

"Yeah, you could."

She stood watching him for the longest time, and he had no idea what she was thinking. Then she seemed to shake off whatever was consuming her mind. "Maybe we need to consciously agree to be more supportive and less contentious."

"Sounds like a good plan."

She frowned, and it hit him how face-to-face communication was so much better than chatting online. Here, he could see her facial expressions. Read what she wasn't saying, as much as seeing how she was responding.

"What is it?" he asked.

"I was just thinking about the conversation we keep having about seeing evil win way too often in our jobs. Phantom is the epitome of that evil. Looking at the pictures of his former partner again reminded me of that." She took a breath and slowly released it, all the while looking Sean in the eye. "He's like the killers my witnesses are hiding from. Now Phantom wants to give away their info to these butchers. It's not fair. Not fair at all."

"No, it's not."

"And there's no good explanation for any of it or reason why it happened."

Even though Sean agreed with her, he thought he should say something that would lift her spirits, because he suspected he was the one who'd brought them down. "God has a purpose, you know. A reason. And we need to trust that He's in charge and has a plan here."

He spouted off the words like a robot on autopilot when he wasn't sure he even believed them anymore. At least he hadn't seen much evidence of the good lately. Where was the good in the three teens still missing in Montgomery? Those families had no closure. Just pain and anguish. And his team? They were suffering too.

Taylor cocked an eyebrow. "And all this pacing and frustration out here in the hall means you're trusting Him?"

It was just like her to call him on his struggle. He dug deep for the right thing to say in response. Another platitude maybe. Anything to get them moving on. "Nah, I'm failing, but tomorrow's another day."

She nodded. "Trust even when you don't feel like it, and maybe you'll soon feel like it."

He thought back over their numerous conversations and the times he'd reminded her of that. Other times she'd reminded him. But they kept each other honest, and it worked. Most of the time anyway. But this was different. "It's so odd for us to be working the same investigation and both be in this position at the same time, isn't it? I'm glad we're here for each other."

"Me too." The smile he'd expected when he first saw her yesterday lit up her face. The smile that had filled his mind for the last few months whenever he imagined her face.

He'd been so tempted to Google her, but they'd agreed not to, and he didn't want to violate that agreement. Mostly he didn't want to see her because that would've made their relationship real and would've had the potential to hurt him. And, man, now he knew how much it would have done exactly that.

He sucked in a long breath, then another. He felt as if he were drowning in a lake of carbon dioxide.

"I'm glad we're friends," she said, and tightened her hand.

He nodded and resisted pulling her into his arms where he desperately wanted her to be. "I have a feeling this is going to get very ugly before it ends, and we'll need friends more than ever."

In the SUV's back seat now, Taylor rested her forehead against the cool window. Dustee sat next to her, trying to engage Cam in a conversation, but he replied from the front seat with single-word answers only, clearly not into it. Taylor wished they weren't just leaving the parking garage and didn't have a thirty-minute drive to the house and that pizza. She was starving and beyond tired. She didn't do well without regular meals, and she'd skipped dinner.

She looked at Dustee. "Maybe Cam wants to reflect on his day or think about the files he reviewed."

Dustee swung her focus to Taylor and rolled her eyes. "What's there to think about? He was looking at logs. Either they had the data he needed or not."

"He could be planning his work for tomorrow."

"You could ask me." Cam swiveled. "I'm right here."

Dustee pulled off her seat belt and slid closer to Cam.

Sean turned onto the street, and Dustee lost her balance, tipping to the side and falling over Taylor's lap. She started to push Dustee back into place.

A rifle report boomed. The window above Dustee's head exploded. Glass peppered the space. Pain razored through Taylor's arm, but she didn't care.

"Go! Go! Go!" Taylor ripped off her seat belt to throw herself over Dustee. "Are you okay, Dustee?"

"Y-y-yes."

Thank you.

"Be alert for another threat!" Sean shouted. "Call 911, Cam. Tell them we're coming in hot."

Taylor heard Cam make the call, but she wouldn't move. Not until Sean drove them to the nearest police precinct. They'd planned for this scenario. She'd marked out every precinct on the route and made Sean memorize them, never really thinking she would need the plan. They could go back to the FBI parking lot, but it would take too much time to lower the security barrier, leaving Dustee exposed.

Taylor held Dustee down, her body trembling as the miles melted beneath the speeding tires. Their vehicle swerved. Horns sounded, frantic, warning. They swerved again.

Sean was dodging in and out of traffic. "Brace yourself!"

Tires shrieked, and he took a hard corner. Taylor's head slammed into the door.

Cam's phone rang. "It's Mack in the other vehicle. They're in pursuit of the shooter."

The SUV slowed a fraction.

"Everyone all right back there?" Tension laced Sean's voice, but underneath it a solid strength told Taylor they would be okay.

"We're good," she replied, though pain shot up her arm.

Glass wouldn't have cut her flesh like a razor, and something had to have broken the window in the first place. Clearly the bullet had sliced through her arm. Hopefully she'd sustained only a minor wound, but blood continued to seep into her jacket, sticky and wet.

"ETA two minutes," Sean announced. "Hang in there."

"Can you get off me now?" Dustee whined.

"No," Taylor replied. "Not until we're safely inside a police precinct."

"Then at least shift a bit." Dustee grabbed Taylor's injured arm.

Pain coursed up her arm, and her vision faded.

Stars floated before her eyes. She clamped down on her lips and managed not to cry out.

"Your arm!" Dustee cried out. "It's bleeding. You've been shot!"

"Taylor?" Sean's panicked voice rose from the front seat.

Tears suddenly pricked Taylor's eyes, and she wanted his arms around her. Tight and secure. Reassuring her that she would be fine. That her arm would be fine. That might be what she wanted as a woman, but as a deputy she wanted to look back on this day and say she did her best to protect Dustee, no matter the consequences. And that meant staying strong and continuing to assess threats.

"Taylor." Sean's voice rose even higher. "Talk to me."

"I'm okay . . . just a scratch," she got out between measured breaths to keep him from knowing how the gunshot had shaken her.

"Call dispatch back, Cam," Sean demanded. "Make sure a medic is waiting for us."

"It's not nec—"

"I'll decide what's necessary," Sean interrupted, his tone brooking no argument.

The minute they arrived at the precinct, she would remind him that *she* was in charge of Dustee's safety. Not him. And Taylor wasn't going to sit down for a medic to examine her. Not as long as a gunman was hunting Dustee.

CHAPTER 16

Sean stomped the gas pedal. He could hardly breathe, knowing Taylor had taken a bullet. And most every officer who'd been shot said the wound was just a scratch when in fact it was often far more serious than that. While Dustee was still in peril, Taylor would do that for sure. She'd give her life for Dustee, and Sean was worried that might happen tonight.

He cranked the wheel hard left, regretting that the sharp turn added to her pain, but he had to quickly get them off the road and into a safe location. He took the final turn nearly on two wheels, then shot through the open gate. Officers with guns raised protected the entrance. Sean slammed on the brakes to make the hard turn into the police precinct's repair bay, bringing them to a rocking stop. The large garage door whirred down behind the SUV.

Sean didn't let a heartbeat pass, but was out of the vehicle and opening the back door.

"Taylor?" He ran his gaze over her body and cringed at the telltale dark blotch on her jacket.

She sat up. "Let's get Dustee inside. That bullet was meant for her, and I need to make sure she's safe from another one."

Sean pointed at the blood. "Your arm."

"Will have to wait." She scrambled from the seat and pushed him out of the way to help Dustee exit the vehicle.

"Where to?" Sean asked the nearest officer.

The burly guy crooked his finger. "Follow me."

Taylor took a silent, wide-eyed Dustee by the arm and got her moving while continuing to survey their surroundings. As did Sean, who charged ahead on the other side of Dustee.

They moved into a hallway, where the officer rushed across the tile floor and opened a door. "In here."

Taylor raced ahead of Sean and shoved Dustee into the small interview room and into a chair. Once Dustee sat, Taylor let out a shaky burst of air.

"You think that Phantom shot at me?" Dustee's high-pitched tone hinted at impending panic.

"Yes, but you're safe now so try to relax." Taylor squeezed Dustee's hand and gave her a smile, though her face was pinched with pain.

Sean watched them, getting angry at Dustee's ongoing neediness, expecting Taylor to help even after she'd been shot. But Dustee had come to expect such quality care from Taylor. She was ready to drop to the floor but insisted on calming her witness first. "We need to treat your arm, Taylor." He tried to sound gentle, caring, but his words came out like a barked command.

She took a long breath. Then another. Her

adrenaline was likely wearing off and the pain in her arm settling in. "Maybe you're right. The room is spinning, and I'm nauseous." She dropped into a chair and looked up at him. "I think I'd like to see that medic now."

Where was the guy?

"Be right back." Sean pushed past Cam, who was hovering in the doorway.

"Medic!" he called at the top of his lungs in the hallway. "In here, now!"

Even if he didn't know he was overreacting, the looks he got from the other officers told him he was behaving like a crazed man. His outburst was senseless, especially when he didn't even know if the ambulance had arrived. So what? Taylor had been shot. He could've lost her. She'd come to mean so much to him, and he couldn't stand to see her bleeding. Or the pain tightening her face. He couldn't care less about bringing Phantom to justice right now. Sean simply wanted to watch over Taylor and keep her safe.

How had he reached this point, so far removed from who he was?

Was God leading him in a new direction, or was Sean just giving in to his feelings when he should be focusing on his job? After all, even if he was inclined to get involved with a woman, he didn't have time for a relationship. He was too busy apprehending the criminals of the world and making them pay. Criminals like Phantom.

The officer who'd escorted them stepped calmly into the hallway. "Ambulance is a few minutes out."

Sean didn't want to wait a few minutes, but he had no choice. "My associate took a bullet. Get the medic down to us the second he arrives." Sean returned to the room to update Taylor. He found her trying to remove her jacket and wincing.

"Here, let me help," Dustee said, sounding so like Dianne that Sean had to blink a few times to be sure he was seeing the right twin.

She got up and eased Taylor's uninjured arm from the jacket. "Now, can you slide it down the wounded one?"

"I can try."

"It might hurt."

"That's okay. The medic has to see my arm." Taylor gritted her teeth.

"But they have scissors," Sean said, now at her side again. "They're a few minutes out yet. Why not wait?"

"And let them cut my leather jacket? Are you kidding?" Taylor looked up at him. "Besides, I want to make sure the bleeding has stopped."

"Then let me help you." He waved Dustee away, and she didn't protest. He took the collar of Taylor's jacket in his hands and stopped to look down at her. The pain still registered in her gaze but was tempered by emotions he couldn't put a name to. "I'll try not to hurt you."

A weak smile tipped her lips. "Don't worry. It's got to be done."

He gave a firm nod of resolve as he slowly brought the jacket down her arm.

She bit her lip and closed her eyes, taking deep breaths.

"Imagine a happy place and tell me about it." He lowered the sleeve inch by inch.

"I'm in a lovely field of lavender," she said, her voice dreamy. "The sweet smell is wrapping around me."

He was amazed at her ability to conjure up a beautiful place while he continued to inflict pain.

"The delicate purple blooms are standing tall over the plants with tiny fine leaves," she went on, her voice a mere whisper now. "I can run my fingers over the softness. It's like heaven on earth. God's place. Where peace reigns and people like Phantom don't exist."

"Done," he announced, thankful to have that over.

She looked at her arm. He followed suit. Blood saturated her sleeve in a large pool that also trailed down her arm.

Sean bent closer and studied the fabric. "Looks like the bleeding stopped, but with that quantity of blood loss, you have to know it's more than a scratch."

She nodded. "I hope it's superficial enough not to cause any muscle damage." She glanced at Dustee, who was now looking bored and tired.

"I need to call Inman and make arrangements for Dustee's protection."

She started to reach for her phone with her good hand. He rested a hand on her arm to stop her. "I'll do that. You just focus on getting this arm taken care of."

"I've got this." She jerked free and grimaced. "Dustee's my responsibility."

"I've never had anyone fight over me before." Dustee grinned. "Especially not cop people. I kind of like it."

Taylor looked like she wanted to respond with a sharp retort, but she got out her phone and dialed her chief. She arranged to have Glover come take over the detail, and Sean noticed she didn't tell Inman about her injury.

She shoved her phone into her pocket. "Roger's the only one I can trust in the office now, and I want you to escort them back to the safe house."

"No. I won't be going with Dustee. Cam can accompany her. I'm staying with you." Sean braced himself for an argument.

She didn't balk at all. A sure sign that she was feeling worse than she was letting on. He didn't like it. Not one bit. But what could he do? Nothing. And he felt helpless seeing her like this.

He squatted down by her knees, took her hand in his, and smiled up at her. "You look worried."

"Just concerned about permanent damage to my arm."

"We'll make sure we get the best doctor to look at it," Sean assured her.

Quick footsteps sounded in the hallway, and two medics rushed into the room. The first, tall and fierce-looking, approached Taylor with a clinical gaze. "I'm Ryan. Gunshot wound?"

She nodded. "Just a scratch."

"Then let me itch it for you," Ryan joked.

Taylor half smiled, then winced.

Ryan set down his kit and took out a pair of scissors to cut away her sleeve. He peeled back the fabric. Taylor gasped. Sean had to stifle his reaction at seeing the long, gaping wound stretching across her arm, looking grisly and far worse than he'd imagined.

Ryan sobered. "Let's get you on the backboard so I can pack your wound and transport you to the ER."

She nodded, but quickly stopped as if the room were spinning.

"Let me help," Sean said to the medic. He gently scooped her into his arms and knelt by the backboard to settle her in place. Brushing a wayward lock of hair from her face, he lingered a moment with his eyes locked on hers. "Everything's going to be okay, honey. I promise."

The wound looked too severe to make such a promise, but right now, with the pain etched on her beautiful face, her grimace, the tightness of her jaw . . . he would promise anything and everything, and find a way to deliver.

The young ER doctor named Pilcher probed the gash on Taylor's arm. "Good news is you didn't sustain any muscle damage and no vascular injury."

Though pain radiated up her arm, she gave a sigh of relief and heard Sean do the same from where he stood on the far side of her bed. She glanced at him to see a pinched smile. He'd been beating himself up over her injury, blaming himself for not foreseeing Phantom's attempt to take Dustee out. But Taylor hadn't seen it either. How could she? Phantom had never used a rifle in the past. At least not that they knew about.

"Does this mean it won't require a hospital stay?" Sean asked.

"Correct," Pilcher replied.

"You stitch up my arm, and I can get out of here?" she clarified, thinking it was too good to be true.

Pilcher shook his head. "Gunshot wounds run a high risk of infection. The bullet carries bits of fabric, et cetera with it. So I'm going to clean the wound and pack it."

"You're going to leave this big gash open?" Taylor asked.

He nodded. "You'll need to keep it clean and dry, and change the dressings regularly. Follow up with your doctor in a day or two for further evaluation."

Thoughts of seeing the gaping wound on a daily basis churned her stomach.

Pilcher sat back on his stool. "I get that it's a bit unsettling to have to re-dress such a wound, but—"

"I'll do it for her," Sean said.

She shot him a look. "You don't—"

"Perfect," the doctor chimed in.

Okay, fine. Let it go. Don't waste the doctor's time talking about it. She could discuss it with Sean at a later time. "We should get to cleaning it."

Pilcher looked at her chart. "Says here you're refusing pain medication."

"I'm still on duty and need to get back to my assignment as soon as possible. Tylenol should ease the pain."

Sean stepped closer. "Taylor, you—"

She knew what he planned to say and held up her hand to stop him. She wasn't leaving Dustee's care to anyone else for very long.

Pilcher looked up. "If you need me to write up a work excuse, I can."

"No thank you. Maybe you can apply a topical anesthetic before cleaning."

"Sure, Lidocaine will help, but pain meds can make it much easier for you."

"Lidocaine is fine."

"If that's what you want." Pilcher reached for

a syringe. "Just a few pinches and then we'll get started."

She took a deep breath, inhaling the hospital's antiseptic smell. She didn't want to imagine this doctor cleaning out a wound that was already throbbing worse than any injury she'd ever experienced.

"Okay, here we go," he said.

She gritted her teeth and closed her eyes. Liquid splashed into her wound, and she almost came off the bed. Could she really do this? Yes, for Dustee. It was her job. No sacrifice was too great for her witnesses.

"I'll need to remove debris deep in the wound and irrigate it again," he said, a frown in his voice.

She glanced over to see him take a long tweezer from the tray. She closed her eyes again and bit her lip to keep from crying out.

On the other side of the bed, a warm hand slipped into hers. She opened her eyes to find Sean watching her.

Concern mixed with compassion in his expression. "Why don't you tell me about your kitchen remodel?"

They'd chatted online about her upcoming project, and he'd shown zero interest in remodeling. He was offering to talk about it to keep her mind occupied. "I know you don't want to hear about that."

"Sure I do," he lied smoothly. Too smoothly.

"Start with the tile you chose. What shape is it again?"

She'd found herself drawn to him since the moment they met in person, but now his willingness to discuss a subject he couldn't care less about warmed her heart.

The doctor probed deeper. A sharp pain took her breath away, and her vision blurred. If she hoped to survive the cleaning without passing out, she would have to take Sean up on his offer to talk. "It's an ogee shape."

"Yeah, right, but what's an ogee look like?"

"It's a scallop or fish-scale design."

He screwed up his face into such a horrifically confused look that she laughed.

"You have to see it to appreciate it," she added.

"What color?"

"Pale gray."

"To go with the gray floors."

"You remembered my floor color?"

"I remember everything." He tapped his forehead, a grin spreading across his handsome face. "Steel trap."

"Oh, yeah? What color are the counters?" She arched an eyebrow.

"Um . . ." He cleared his throat and squirmed.

She almost took pity on him by giving the answer, but she was enjoying their playful banter, similar to how they'd interacted online.

"Gray?" he squeaked out.

She laughed again. "I haven't picked them out yet, so I never told you."

His eyes narrowed. "Trying to trick me, huh?"

"And it worked."

"You'll pay for that, you know."

"I'm shaking in my boots."

"You know I won't follow through. Not on this. Not with you." He lifted her hand to his mouth and pressed a soft kiss on the back of it.

The touch of his lips sent a warm trail to her heart. He leaned forward. Closer, his eyes maintaining a steady gaze, darkening, and mimicking her emotions. A tremor of excitement shivered over her, rattling her to the core.

"Thank you," she whispered, her voice shaky. "I know you wanted me to take the pain meds, but thank you for letting that go and being on my side."

He nodded. His gaze warmed, and his breathing grew uneven. Something powerful ran between them. Deep. Warm. Mesmerizing. She closed her eyes to savor the moment.

How could she ever go back to only chatting online with this amazing man?

"Okay, you're good to go," Pilcher announced. "The nurse will put your arm in a sling for protection."

She snapped out of her trance and looked at her arm now encased in a large bandage.

Pilcher eyed her. "I may be discharging you without work restrictions, but this wound is nothing to take lightly. Be sure you follow up with your doctor."

"She will," Sean said, still clutching her hand.

The doctor gave a firm nod. "I'll get your discharge paperwork in order, and I'll add a prescription for pain meds in case you change your mind."

"Thank you." She waited for him to exit and quickly extricated her hand from Sean's. She couldn't continue such an intimate connection with him when she had no plans to follow through on her feelings. That wouldn't be fair to Sean. But she couldn't just sit here either.

She got out her phone.

"Who are you calling?" he asked, sounding disappointed.

She'd take disappointed over hurting him by leading him on when there was no future for them as a couple. "I want to make sure Dustee made it back to the safe house and ask Roger to meet with me to do a thorough threat assessment."

"You think Phantom has the safe house location?" He took a few breaths and slowly let them out.

She needed to do the same deep breathing, but she ignored the rapid beating of her heart and focused instead on the mission at hand. "I don't know, but I won't risk it. If our assessment leaves any questions in my mind, I'll move Dustee without a backward glance."

CHAPTER 17

Taylor slept very little and felt drained of every ounce of energy. She was thankful that her injured arm remained tight in the sling and didn't move throughout the night or she wouldn't have gotten the little bit of sleep that she'd managed. Sean insisted she fill the pain prescription, but unless things suddenly worsened, she still wouldn't take the pills. Not while she was responsible for Dustee's safety.

She stood and adjusted the sling before stepping out of her bedroom. She'd tried to change her bandage but couldn't reach her upper arm without causing extreme pain. She didn't think it wise to be in close contact with Sean and thought to ask Dianne for her help. But Taylor didn't want her gunshot wound to scare Dianne further, which meant Sean would have to change the bandage.

Taylor descended the steps to the family room. Sean sat on the sofa, watching his group seated at the table, laptops in front of them. His arms were crossed, and a deep frown marred his face. She didn't like seeing the tension radiating from his body. She could easily imagine the online conversation they might be having right now. He'd tell her exactly how he felt, but in person he seemed to be a typical guy. Not overly communicative. She got that. It was much harder to express your feelings in person. So much easier to let them flow from her fingers onto the screen, where she could review and edit as needed, stopping her from saying the wrong thing, from coming across the wrong way.

And don't get her started on how seeing expressions and body language gave so many nuances to each word he uttered that she was often questioning every little thing. But still, she couldn't quit looking at him. He sat there larger than life. Handsome. Intense. A different man than the online guy, and she didn't know how to start the conversation.

"I can feel you watching me." He slowly turned to look at her. He grinned, a potent number that sent her heart racing. "Like what you see?"

She thought to lie, but telling the truth was always the best thing. "Actually, I do. I had no idea you were so good-looking."

"I thought I told you that. I mean, it's usually what I lead with." He chuckled.

She caught his joking mood, which she suspected was his way of dealing with the shooting. "I find it distracting."

"I get that."

"What? You know you distract women?"

"No. I find you distracting too."

"Oh."

"You're a beautiful woman, Taylor. You must know that."

"I know I'm not unfortunate-looking."

He burst out laughing. "Sweetheart, you are so far from that, it's funny."

"Um, can we change the subject?"

"Don't like it when the tables are turned on you, huh?"

"I can handle it. I just don't happen to think looks are all that important. It's what's inside that counts."

"But we already know what's inside from our online conversations. It's the looks that we're just discovering. Totally backwards from any other relationship I've ever had."

"Relationship?"

His smile wavered. "Friends. That's all I'm saying."

"Right. Friends who help each other out when we have a problem. Which is good because I need this bandage changed."

"Smooth transition. Gotta hand it to you." He held his hand out for a fist bump.

She tapped his fist and turned to leave, knowing he would follow her. She was acutely aware of him behind her. As she'd tossed and turned last night, she kept thinking about their interaction at the hospital. She'd come to two conclusions. She wanted more of the flirting and heart-melting emotions, and yet she definitely couldn't have

225

them. So what was the first thing she did when she saw him this morning? She flirted.

Seriously. That has got to stop.

Back in her room, she sat down on the edge of the bed where she'd already laid out the dressings and supplies. She eased her arm out of the sling.

He watched her every move. "How's the pain today?"

"Manageable." She held her arm out for easier access and made sure she didn't wince when every part of her wanted to. Because if he got even a hint that she wasn't doing well, he would likely try to sideline her.

He sat next to her and started unwinding the gauze. "I can't tell you how bad I feel about Phantom shooting you. If you'd died . . ." His voice trailed off, and he shook his head.

"I'm fine." She squeezed his hand. "Stop beating yourself up. You couldn't have known a reporter would get wind of the RED team working at the bureau's office and let the whole town know." She smiled to cheer him up. "And besides, agents are out looking for the bullet casing. If they find it, we might be able to lift prints or DNA from it. It could turn out to be the very lead we need."

"That's true, I guess, but I think Phantom would wear gloves."

She let her hand fall. "You're still frustrated with the slow progress we're making."

"We keep hitting brick walls." He lifted off the wound packing material.

She gasped at the pain but forced herself to focus. "Then let's talk out the leads. One by one. Maybe we can make some progress that way."

He reached for the gauze package. "Okay, the tattoo. I've been trying to figure out a meaning beyond the computer terminology. Can't come up with a thing."

"What about an algorithm to look at variables for the letters? I know you guys often write such things." She faked a shudder. "I just can't imagine how you enjoy doing it."

He looked at her and grinned. "And we can't imagine how you enjoy babysitting people like Dustee."

"Touché."

His smile disappeared. "Kiley's already run a program, and it returned an extremely long list. It's impossible to eliminate anything without additional information on Phantom."

Taylor's phone rang. She glanced at the screen. "It's Hershel."

She answered, and before she could question his reason for calling, he said, "I have the video files. The ones from the dates you requested."

Her heart lifted. "You do?"

"Yeah. In yesterday's craziness, I forgot I'd downloaded a copy to my laptop while I was getting ready for work. You can come over and look at the footage, or I can email the files to you."

She didn't want to risk Phantom intercepting the email and somehow finding out they had the files. "I want to see them in person. We'll be right there." She disconnected and looked at Sean. "Quick. Finish up my arm. Hershel has the video for the day of the hack."

From the safe house family room where Glover sat on the couch, Sean heard Dustee and Dianne arguing in their room. He wasn't about to get in the middle of a fight and was honestly thankful that it was too risky to bring Dustee with them to a location Phantom could be staking out. The rest of the team had already departed for the FBI office, though thankfully Glover had agreed to stay with Dustee until Sean and Taylor could return to transport her to the FBI.

"Thanks, Roger," Taylor said at the door. "I owe you one. Again."

"Those favors are starting to pile up. And this involves Dustee, who seems to be in her usual good mood this morning. My payback request will be huge." He gave Taylor a pointed yet humor-filled look.

She wrinkled her nose and opened the door. Sean stared at her for a moment, missing a similar easiness he'd enjoyed online with her that had all but disappeared since they'd met in person. Now it seemed they managed tension for the most part, and he wanted the former friendship back. Or maybe more.

He trailed her outside and held the SUV door for her. She rushed past him as if she couldn't wait to get to the office. He was eager to find their traitor too, but he wouldn't compromise her safety. They believed the bullet was meant for Dustee, but since Taylor had seen Phantom, he could be targeting her as well.

He glanced at her. "Just so you know, I'll be taking an indirect route this morning."

"But that will take longer." She tried to fasten her seat belt with one hand and failed.

He reached over to help. "I won't let Phantom take another shot at you."

"He was aiming for Dustee, not me, and she's not with us right now."

"Doesn't mean he wouldn't take the chance to eliminate Dustee's protection team. Or more specifically, you. You saw his face, remember?"

"Good point. Can you at least speed then?" She grinned.

He smiled at her good mood as he jogged around the front of the vehicle to get in behind the wheel. He didn't know how she could keep her good humor even when in physical pain, but she did, and he enjoyed just being with her for the drive.

At her office, they found workers repairing the glass door. They paused to allow Sean and Taylor access to the office. The space was buzzing with activity, as deputies and clerical staff had returned to work. Inman's office was dark, however, with Taylor's boss nowhere to be seen.

"What happened to your arm?" the receptionist asked Taylor.

"It's nothing," she answered evasively.

Sean eased up next to her. "You reported your injury to Inman, right?"

She didn't respond.

He tugged her to a stop. "You didn't tell him?"

"I left him a message last night. He hasn't called back." She slipped around Sean. "Hershel's waiting for us in the server room."

He caught up to her. "Remember, he doesn't know about the hack."

She nodded and entered the small room at the back of the office.

Hershel looked up. "I've got the video cued up for the night you requested. I don't know why you wanted this, but it's suspicious at best, and I'll need to turn it over to Inman."

Before he could start the video, Sean's phone dinged. He glanced at his text message. "It's from our phone tech in D.C. He's received the call logs we were expecting." He avoided mentioning Phantom's name in front of Hershel. "No calls made on the phone in question other than the one to Dustee."

"So much for hoping there'd be numbers to

help move the investigation forward." Taylor focused on the computer again. "Please start it playing, Hershel."

Sean stepped closer and held his breath as the video began to play. He didn't know any of the deputies in the office except Glover, so he didn't expect to recognize the traitor, but Taylor would. She thought she was prepared to see this traitor's face, but seeing the very person who'd betrayed their team was sure to devastate her even more and chip away at her earnest belief in people's goodness. At least it would do that to him.

The video came to life, and a man appeared at the office entrance. Okay, it was a man for sure, but his back was to them, the black-and-white footage fuzzy. The man swiped his ID card down the reader. Sean sucked in a breath and hoped the guy would turn. The door popped open. The intruder pulled on the handle. Pivoted. The camera caught his face.

Taylor gasped. "No. It can't be. Impossible."

"Glover?" Sean met Taylor's shocked gaze. "Roger Glover is our guy?"

"No." She kept shaking her head. "No, it's not possible."

"We left him with Dustee." Sean turned to leave. "We have to go."

"Hold on." Taylor shot a searching look around the room. "Roger wouldn't do this. He's likely at the office because of a witness."

"Are there additional files?" Sean asked Hershel.

He nodded. "A couple of cameras inside the building picked up his movements."

"Cue them up, and then leave us with it." Sean eyed Hershel, not giving him an option other than to do as told, and he got to work loading the video.

Taylor dug out her phone and dialed. "Dustee. Good. Just checking in. Is everything okay there?"

Sean watched, praying that Glover hadn't harmed her or taken her hostage.

Taylor sagged against the wall. "I heard you fighting on my way out. Go ahead and stay locked in your room. I'll be back soon and will talk to Dianne then."

Taylor lowered her phone. "Dustee's mad at Dianne, so she locked herself in her room."

Sean nodded. "Never thought I'd be thankful for one of her moods, but I am."

"Video's set." Hershel stood and walked out, closing the door behind him.

Taylor dropped into the vacated chair. "Good thing Hershel doesn't expect to be read in or he might not have left so easily."

Sean wasn't concerned about Hershel. His focus was totally on Glover right now. More specifically, the man's relationship to Taylor.

"Before we watch this next clip, tell me just

how good of a friend Glover is to you," he said, hating the fact that he needed to ask.

She looked up at him, a question in her eyes. "He's that work friend you can tell anything to, you know? I've also spent a lot of holidays with his family. Got to know his wife, Naomi. Even babysat their kids."

So they were close, and she had to be hurting big-time over the man's duplicity. "I'm sorry about this," Sean said. "For you. Not him. I know from firsthand experience how much it hurts to have someone you trust betray you."

"You do?" Taylor asked. "Why haven't you told me about this?"

"I don't like to talk about it." And he still couldn't say much. "It wasn't work-related and didn't involve a crime like this—unless you think a cheating fiancée is a crime."

"You were engaged?" Her eyes widened. "But I . . . we . . . we're friends. I thought you'd shared with me all the major things in your life."

Oh, man, he'd offended her by not telling her about Gina. He didn't want to cause her any more pain. Not at all. And he needed to fix it. Quickly. He thought about reaching for her hand, but she'd probably just pull it away. So he settled for offering his best apologetic look. "I'm sorry, Taylor. Very sorry. It's not something I've told anyone. If I ever did decide to talk about that time in my life, it would be with you."

She locked eyes with him, but he couldn't read her thoughts. "I know we need to watch the video now, but please say we can talk about it more when we have time."

"I'll try my best. Okay?" He waited for a response, but her expression remained fixed, and she didn't speak. Had he totally blown it with her?

Please, God, don't let that be the case. I need her in my life.

He took a long breath and searched for the right words. "I want to tell you about Gina, but I just can't. Not yet. I hope you can understand."

"I do, and I promise I won't push."

He squeezed her shoulder and was once again struck by what an amazing woman she was. A man would be blessed to spend a lifetime with her, building a strong family together, the kind of family he'd always wanted growing up.

She patted his hand and turned to start the video. He tried to force his mind back to work, but his emotions continued to churn until suddenly he wanted to explain. How odd. He'd never felt that way before. Not even a moment ago.

He opened his mouth to tell her something— what, he didn't know—when movement on the screen grabbed his attention. Glover swiped his card by the glass-encased room holding the WITSEC computer. He removed a flash drive from his pocket and inserted it into the computer, then took a bundle of papers from his jacket pocket, laid them on the table, and started typing.

Sean squinted but couldn't make out the text. "Zoom in so we can see the details on that page."

Taylor complied, and the image filled the screen with blurry but legible writing. Sean only had to read the first line of code to know the document contained programming details that would allow Glover to hack the system. Sean's body vibrated with anger. It was bad enough when someone outside the law enforcement community betrayed them, but a fellow LEO? Sean could barely contain his rage. How must Taylor feel? He took a deep breath to clear his head so he didn't do anything rash and make things worse for her. "He's our guy. No question."

She wrenched her hands together, and her tortured gaze met his. "I can't believe it. I just can't. You saw what a great guy he is. So helpful. Compassionate. Considerate. He has a terrific wife and kids. I just . . . there must be an explanation for this. There just has to be."

"The only explanation is the one right before our eyes," Sean said with conviction. "Roger Glover is following directions to hack the database. And worse yet, we left him in charge of Dustee's protection detail."

CHAPTER 18

Taylor's stomach churned, and the closer they came to the safe house, the more she thought she might actually throw up. She'd never known such a level of betrayal. Sure, her parents had turned their backs on her, and that was a form of betrayal, but she'd never really thought of it that way. This hurt, big-time, and she didn't know what she would say when she laid eyes on Roger. At least he hadn't harmed Dustee.

Sean parked near the house and reached for his sidearm.

She held up a hand. "No, Sean. No guns."

"We don't want to alert Glover," Inman said from the back seat. He'd arrived shortly after they watched the video and insisted on being present at Roger's arrest. Surprisingly, Sean not only agreed to let the chief be in on the takedown but thought Inman had formulated a sound plan.

"We approach the house like we've come back to get Dustee," Taylor said. "Tell Roger that Chief came along to discuss the safe house. Nice and casual. No need for weapons creating a hostage-taking scenario."

"Don't worry. I got it. Just checking the clip." Sean shoved his gun back into his holster and reached into the glove box for disposable handcuffs. "I'll cuff him so you don't have to take in one of your own."

She sighed, something she seemed to be doing a lot these past few days. But what a few days they'd been. Dustee was followed by Phantom. The database was hacked. She'd been shot. And now one of her coworkers, a sworn officer of the law and a friend, had broken the law and exposed the witnesses they worked so hard to protect to life-threatening danger.

"I'm so sorry about this, Taylor," Sean said. "It has to be hard for you."

"It is." She squared her shoulders. "But I can handle it."

Inman opened his door. "It's better we're here to take Glover in and question him. Hopefully he'll be more cooperative with us."

Taylor got out and marched toward the house. She wasn't looking forward to laying eyes on Roger, much less questioning him, but she did want to hear his explanation for breaking the law.

As they neared the door, Sean squeezed her hand, and she was thankful for his steadfast presence. He'd been there for her every step of this investigation. Would continue to be there for her, that much she knew. He was a man she could count on. But seeing him in person these past few days was probably the biggest stressor of all.

She started up the steps. They were here to arrest a coworker—a friend. She took gulps of air to calm herself as thoughts of Roger's wife and his two darling children crashed in on her. In the next few minutes, she'd irrevocably change an entire family's world forever. That outweighed anything she was personally stressed over. She offered a prayer for them, then unlocked the door.

Roger was sitting on the sofa, his phone in hand, but he shot to his feet and reached for his weapon. "Oh, it's you guys." He hissed out his breath and let his hand fall. "You might've texted me so I knew you were coming." He holstered the gun and shifted his focus to the kitchen, where Dianne was standing behind the counter. "It's okay. We're clear."

She nodded, but what Roger had done, and could've potentially done if they hadn't learned his secret, really hit Taylor then, and she felt her legs weaken. Would he have gone so far as to murder Dustee, or would he settle for giving Phantom access to her so he could kill her? Knowing Phantom, he would want to do the killing.

She gripped the wall, and Inman stepped in behind her.

"Chief," Roger said, his gaze questioning.

Taylor rested her hand on her sidearm. "We're here to arrest you, Roger. So please put your weapon on the table."

"Arrest me? Seriously? What's the joke?" He sounded and acted so innocent.

"You know," Inman ground out between clenched teeth. "Don't make this worse by playing dumb. Set your weapon on the table— now."

His face paling, Roger looked at his boss and blinked. "No. Really. What's this about?"

Sean stepped closer to Roger and planted his hand on his own sidearm. "Weapon. On the table."

"Do it, Roger," Taylor said. "Sean means business."

Blanching even more, Roger slowly lifted his gun from its holster and laid it on the coffee table.

"Your backup too," Taylor said. Like many other law enforcement officers, she knew Roger carried a second or backup gun they called a BUG.

He reached down to his cargo pocket, took out a smaller gun, and placed it on the table beside the other one. Inman wasted no time, but stepped forward and confiscated both weapons.

Sean moved in. "I'll be searching and cuffing you."

Roger responded with a glare. Sean not so gently pushed Roger up against the wall and performed a thorough search. Thankfully, Taylor didn't have to see Roger's face. Still, it was one of the hardest things she'd ever had to witness on the job. She'd seen some horrific things before, but never had she felt so violated. So betrayed.

Sean tightened the cuffs and turned Roger to face them.

"Why?" she asked him. "How could you do this to the witnesses? To us? To me? We're friends. You've destroyed that. Worse, you put thousands of lives in danger." She shook her head. "I can't even deal with this. It's just surreal."

He cringed and opened his mouth to speak.

"Save it until the interview." Inman sounded as disgusted as Taylor felt.

Sean grabbed Roger's arm and led him to the door. Taylor went to the kitchen to explain everything to Dianne. She was removing a pan of chocolate chip cookies from the oven, the sweet smell upsetting Taylor's stomach all over again. She sat on a stool at the island and waited for Dianne to turn around.

"What did he do?" She took out a spatula and started moving the chocolate-oozing cookies to a cooling rack.

"He's the person behind the hack."

Dianne's arm halted midair, a cookie resting precariously on the spatula. "He's Phantom."

"No," Taylor said. "But he was working with Phantom."

"You're sure?"

Taylor nodded with sad resignation. "We have him on video programming the hack."

Dianne settled the cookie on the rack and scooped up another one. "He seemed like such a

240

nice guy. Guess you never can tell about people, can you?"

"No you can't," Taylor said emphatically. "No you can't."

Sean divided his attention between Glover, Inman, and Taylor in a small interrogation room at the Multnomah County Corrections facility. Sean was surprised to see the jail stood in the middle of downtown Portland, but it was part of the county's Justice Center, so it made some sense.

Sean tried to relax, but his adrenaline was still pumping from moving Dustee and Dianne to a new location in much the same method as their first transfer. The local bureau had only one safe house, so Taylor rented a cabin under a fictitious name and used an ID that couldn't be traced back to Dustee or anyone on the team.

Inman had booked Glover and now sat quietly in the far chair, tracking Glover's every move. Given the tension in the room, Sean was concerned Inman would go off on Glover. Or maybe Taylor would too. Sean started the video recorder before that happened. He informed Glover that it was running, and Sean recorded his name and position, along with Inman's and Taylor's information for the record.

"Why?" Taylor asked before Sean could get the first question out.

Glover ran a hand over hair shorn in a military recruit style. "You're doing the questioning? Not you, Chief?"

She sat up straighter in her chair, her shoulders in a crisp line that a soldier would admire. "I'm handling this. Do you have a problem with that?"

"Come on, Taylor." He eyed her. "We're friends, and you're acting pretty hostile. I want to be sure I get a fair shake. Someone impartial."

"Seriously?" She shot to her feet and planted her free hand on the table, a grimace on her face, likely from the quick movement. "You're calling *me* out after what *you* did?"

Sean took ahold of her good arm, gently urging her to sit back down. She glared at him but relented, taking her seat. He wouldn't say a word on the video, but he gave her a warning look that he knew the camera wouldn't catch.

She took a long breath and eased it out between clenched teeth before offering a reassuring nod. She faced Glover again and clamped her free hand on her knee. "Why did you hack the WITSEC database?" Her tone was eerily calm now.

Glover slumped in his chair and picked at a hangnail on his thumb until it turned red and raw. "I can't tell you."

"Yes, you can." Her tone was rock hard. "We have a right to know."

"I know you do, but he'll . . ." Glover slid

deeper into his chair and shook his head. "I just can't."

"Phantom threatened you to make you do this?" Inman asked. "Maybe your family?"

Glover gave the barest nod of acknowledgment but didn't speak. Was he afraid that Phantom could access this recording?

"Then you have to tell us so we can protect them," Inman said. "He'll know you've been arrested and believe you're talking whether you do or not. We can bring you and your family into the program. Protect them."

Glover sat forward, his eyes on his boss. "You can't promise that. I'll need to go through the review process first and could be rejected."

"Trust me," Inman said. "If I say you're in the program, you're in."

Glover sat there. Not talking. Not moving. But emotions fought for purchase on his face, racing by so quickly that Sean couldn't begin to guess what the guy was feeling.

"Okay. Fine. We come into the program." Glover steeled his gaze. "But I don't say another word until I know my family's been moved to a safe location and we've signed the MOU. And I want to talk to my wife now."

"We need to know more first. This minute." Urgency laced Taylor's words. "Witnesses' lives are depending on it."

Glover crossed his arms and leaned back. "Like

I said. I'm not talking until I speak to my wife and I know my family's safe."

Inman turned to Taylor. "You've got your plate full with the twins. I'll take lead on bringing in his family."

"Sure. Yeah. That would be good." She shifted to glare at Glover. "But once he's ready to talk, I'll be doing the interview."

Sean had to give her props for being willing to face someone who'd hurt and betrayed her the way Glover had. If only Glover had reported the situation when Phantom first approached him, there could've been a much different outcome to this situation. But he didn't, and he'd lied to everyone. Just the kind of behavior that caused Sean's teeth to clench.

"We should get going." Sean gestured to the door.

Taylor leaned over the table and got in Glover's face. "You thought you were doing the right thing to protect your family, but you were wrong, Roger. You could've gone into the program then. Or we could've played this out with Phantom and arrested him. But now there are witnesses across the country whose lives are in danger. If one of them is murdered, you'll go to prison as an accessory. How could you put them at risk like that? And put such a black mark on our office's name? Betray all of us?"

"You don't understand." He tightened his arms, his biceps bulging against his sleeves.

"How could I understand? It's unthinkable." She paused a moment. "We were friends. Good friends. I would have found a way to help you." She stood and shifted her attention to Inman. "Don't forget, I want to be here when he talks. I can't wait to hear a better explanation for his reprehensible behavior."

"I'll text you," Inman replied.

She didn't look away. "Do I have your word that you won't cut me out?"

Inman nodded, and she pivoted so fast her shoes squeaked on the floor.

"Hey, wait up," Sean called after her. But she didn't slow down until she reached security and retrieved her phone and weapon.

"I know you're angry, but we need to talk about how to use this to our advantage. After we bring in Glover's family for their safety, we can use Glover's phone to communicate with Phantom."

"Set a trap." She stopped and looked up at Sean. "You think that will work?"

"Maybe. If Phantom wasn't watching the safe house and saw us haul Glover out in handcuffs."

"It's also possible that Phantom dumped the phone after he got what he wanted from Roger." Outside, she turned on her phone and it chimed a few times. She glanced at it. "The videos we requested for the bus stop are in."

"We can review them the minute we get back to the office."

She bit her bottom lip. "I'm in no mood to see Dustee and answer the million questions she's sure to ask. Do you think we can review the videos in another room?"

"I'll have Snow find a place and computer for us to use." Sean motioned for her to precede him down the hall.

On the drive over, he called Snow. And when they pulled up to the building, the eager agent was waiting for them at the door. He escorted them to the small conference room. "Hang tight. I'll go grab my laptop."

He rushed away before Sean could utter a word. "The guy is starting to grow on me."

"Yeah. Me too." Taylor settled in a chair, a faraway look on her face.

Sean sat next to her. "You're thinking about Glover."

"Actually, I'm thinking about his sweet kids. This will devastate them. It's all so sudden. Their life is good right now, and then *boom,* it all changes the minute we notify them of the arrest." Her expression glazed over, and tears filled her eyes.

"You're thinking about how your brother's death affected your family, and the Glovers will feel like their life disappeared just like your family did."

She nodded but didn't speak.

He wanted to encourage her to share but held

back. She'd made it clear in the past that she didn't want to talk about her brother, and he didn't want to upset her even more. He'd always thought she was hiding something from him, and now that he could verify this in her wounded expression, he was sure of it.

Would she drop a bombshell on him someday? Betray him too?

She took a shaky breath. "I hate what it will do to them, but I also want to see justice done. Roger needs to pay for his actions."

"But you can understand it, right? I mean, if he thought Phantom planned to kill his kids or his wife if he didn't cooperate . . ."

"I can't even imagine how awful that would be." She wrapped her good arm around her stomach. "But we were friends. He could have told me. We could have come up with something other than releasing witnesses' information. We know how to protect people better than any law enforcement agency around. His family would've been safe, and Roger knew that." Anger crept back into her voice, replacing the anguish and sorrow.

"From what you've told me, a lot of your witnesses struggle in their new lives. Maybe he didn't want that for his family."

"So because he didn't want to be uncomfortable, he exposes thousands of people to the criminals who want them dead?" She shook her head, the anger burned on her face. "Nothing justifies that. Nothing!"

"Here you go." Snow returned carrying his computer. "I hate to do this, but if you need to access our Wi-Fi, I have to be present."

Taylor offered him a tight smile, but the rage remained veiled in her eyes. "I just have to download a few videos. We shouldn't need anything else."

"Then go ahead. But like I said, I have to watch." He lurked over her shoulder.

She connected to her email provider and started the videos downloading.

"How's the investigation going?" Snow asked.

"Fine," Sean replied, as the rookie didn't need to know that they were struggling. "It's all still on a need-to-know basis."

"And I don't need to know." He frowned. "I get it, but if I knew what was going on, I could be more helpful."

"You're doing exactly what we need right now, and we thank you for that." Taylor's focus remained on the screen.

Snow's frown deepened, but he didn't continue the discussion, just stood back while the videos finished downloading. "If you'll give me access to the computer, I'll log out of the network."

Taylor slid away, and Snow quickly signed off and moved back. "I'll be in the hallway if you need access again." As he pulled the door closed, he muttered, "Restroom duty. That's why I got a master's degree."

"Now I feel bad for him," Taylor said, opening the first video.

"Hey, we were in his position once. He needs to learn the ropes, even if that involves escorting us to the restroom."

Taylor started playing the video, and they watched several of them before they came upon the one they needed. Phantom climbed out of the front passenger seat of a Honda Accord a few blocks from the bus stop where he boarded the bus to the library. The driver remained in the car.

"We may not be able to see his face, but we do have a license plate number." Taylor paused the video and tapped the screen, her angst replaced with enthusiasm as she looked at him. "Which means we can use DMV records and finally, finally, track Phantom down."

CHAPTER 19

The plan was set for the raid on the driver's house, and even before leaving the office, adrenaline raced through Taylor's body. She hadn't been on a high-octane op since her rotation in fugitive apprehension and had forgotten the intensity of planning. They'd completed a threat assessment of Fritz Dupont's house. Kiley and Mack had done a drive-by, revealing the suspect's car sitting in the driveway. The team had also reviewed the property's aerial footage and obtained a search warrant for the dwelling and car. Unfortunately, they didn't have probable cause for an arrest warrant for the driver. A search of the car and residence would hopefully provide the needed information.

"Okay, people." Sean stood tall at the end of the table. "We're a go. Remember. This suspect may be working with Phantom. Means he could be armed and dangerous. So keep your eyes and ears open."

The group mumbled their acknowledgment and got to their feet, except Cam who as an analyst couldn't go on a raid.

Taylor skirted around them to approach Sean, who was strapping on his body armor. "I'll need to borrow a vest."

He fastened the last Velcro strap and tugged on the fabric to settle the vest in place. "I wasn't planning on you coming along."

"What? Why on earth not?" Her shock traveled through her tone and drew attention from the team.

Sean gently took her arm and led her out into the hallway. He lowered his voice. "First, you're injured. Second, I can't have you there. You'll be a distraction."

"That's ridiculous." She would cross her arms, if not for the sling.

"No, it's not. You're not part of the team, and we have a rhythm. We have our signals, and we each know our job. You'll interrupt that."

"I get that . . . to a point, but I also know other LEOs go on raids with you. Means you know how to adapt."

He stepped closer. "Yes, but I didn't have feelings for those other LEOs."

"Feelings?"

A fond smile tipped his mouth. "You're my friend, Taylor. I care about you. You should know that."

She loved hearing he cared, but . . . "You're friends with your teammates, and you're not making them sit this out."

He groaned. "Okay, fine. I think it's more than friendship. My feelings, that is. So I can't have you there."

She couldn't even begin to deal with that

comment right now, not when they should be moving. "I'm coming along. We can stand here and argue, maybe miss our suspect, or you can get me a vest and we can be on our way."

"*Aargh.* You are so stubborn."

"As are you."

He stared at her, his concentration unyielding. "I'll get the vest, but you'll be right at my side through it all. Got it?"

"There's no place I'd rather be."

He arched a brow, perhaps searching for a deeper meaning in her comment.

"I meant that you're the best of the best," she clarified. "I'd feel safe near you."

"Right. Okay, the vest. I'll get it." He departed and soon returned with body armor that would fit her.

After she'd ditched her sling and put on the Kevlar, they piled into two SUVs and made the drive to Fritz Dupont's small bungalow. When Sean wasn't looking, she snapped a picture of him, capturing his fierce expression. Excitement had her hands trembling, but hopefully she got a clear shot to upload to her computer for a better look at the man who so captivated her.

They approached the house, and she stowed her phone while Sean parked down the street and got out binoculars to watch the house.

"No sign of the suspect." Mack's strong voice came over their earbuds. He'd circled the block and was now parked on the far side of the house. "Clear to approach."

Taylor didn't let a second pass, but jumped out, drew her sidearm, and headed up the concrete walkway. Sean remained at her side, his weapon in hand, the rest of the team fanning out to surround the house. Her heart pounded so hard she was surprised Sean didn't say he could hear the crazy thumping. He motioned for her to take the steps up to the bungalow.

At the door, Sean lifted his hand in a signal to hold. He pressed on his earpiece. "Alpha one in position," he said into the mic. "Alpha two, report when set."

She loved how sure he sounded. How strong he looked with his Kevlar vest and weapon in his hand. He was ready for anything, and if this op went sideways, he would make sure she stayed safe before protecting himself.

"Alpha two in location," came the response over her earpiece.

"Making contact." Sean knocked on the door.

They both stood to the side of the door to avoid a bullet that could pierce the door in this dangerous approach. And they continued to hold their guns, but at their sides so as not to alarm the person they heard coming to answer the door.

A skinny guy with shaggy hair and black glasses pulled open the door and looked at them, his head cocked to the side. He wore khaki pants and a corduroy blazer over a knit shirt, looking very professorial.

He eyed them like one might an unruly student. "Can I help you?"

Sean made the introductions and displayed his ID. Taylor tapped her free hand on her badge clipped to her belt. Pain raced up her sling-free arm, and she drew in a sharp breath.

Sean cast her a quick look before swinging his focus back to the man. "Are you Fritz Dupont?"

A seemingly pointless question, as they both knew this was Dupont from his driver's license picture. Still, Sean had to confirm the fact.

"I am," Dupont replied.

"Can we come in and talk?"

"About what?" His eyebrows rose over his thick glasses.

"An investigation we think you can help us with." Taylor smiled to try to disarm his concern.

"I suppose." He stepped back.

"After you." Taylor motioned for him to go back inside. No way would she ever turn her back to a potential suspect.

She holstered her weapon but kept her hand on it. Sean followed suit as Dupont led them to a compact living room filled with classic mid-century furniture boasting bright orange cushions. Bookshelves filled to overflowing ringed the room, and a desk with mounds of papers on it sat in one corner. No sign of any technology. Not even a tablet.

"Go ahead and have a seat," she said to Dupont.

He dropped into a plastic shell-type chair and stretched out legs that didn't seem to end. Sean remained standing, and she took a firm stance next to him.

"Are you alone in the house?" Sean locked his focus on Dupont.

Dupont lifted his chin. "Yes, but I don't know why you need to know that."

"Suspect detained," Sean said into his mic.

"Suspect? Detained?" Dupont sat forward. "What in the world? I haven't done anything wrong,"

"Kiley, stand watch out front," Sean said. "Mack, clear the house."

A chorus of "Roger that" came through Taylor's earpiece.

"Now, wait a minute," Dupont said. "Clear the house? I didn't invite anyone else in."

"No," Sean said. "But it will go easier for you if you allow them to confirm we're alone."

"I . . . I . . ."

"Do you own a 2007 Honda Accord with . . ." Sean got out his notebook and gave the plate number, redirecting the conversation.

"Yeah. It's outside. Why?" Dupont wrapped his arms around his waist, and it looked like he could circle his long, slender arms around his body twice over.

Mack entered the house. He gave a firm nod

as he passed Sean, Mack's focus pointed and intense.

Dupont blinked hard, apprehension lodged on his face. "Is this really necessary? I haven't committed any crime."

Sean ignored the interruption and kept on track with his questioning. "Were you driving your Accord on Monday night at eight o'clock near the Twelfth Avenue bus stop in northeast Portland?"

"Bus stop? No, I don't take the . . . Oh, wait. Yeah. I was." Dupont smoothed his hands down his pant legs, and they were trembling like frightened kittens. "I dropped off this guy I met at the coffee shop so he could catch the bus."

Sean took a step closer but kept a deadpan expression when she knew he had to be excited about the direction this conversation was going. "What's the guy's name?"

"Paul Jackson."

Taylor glanced at Sean, and he didn't let on that the name was important. "And you'd just met him at a coffee shop, then gave him a ride?"

"Not just. I talked to him a few times before then. I go there every night between five and seven to write. I work all day, but I'm a wannabe sci-fi writer. It's my time alone, away from the wife and kids."

"Which coffee shop?"

"Stumptown Coffee Roasters. It's on Harvey Milk Street."

"What kind of work do you do, Mr. Dupont?"

"I'm a high school guidance counselor. Why?"

"How are your computer skills?"

"Computer?" He glanced at Sean, then Taylor for clarity as he scratched his chin. "I can do the basics like text and social media. Type reports. Fill in forms at work. Word-processing. That's about it." He dropped his hand and cocked his head. "Why are you asking about my computer skills?"

"How exactly did you start talking with Paul?" Sean asked, continuing to ignore Dupont's questions.

"He approached me one night last week and made a comment about the action figure I had on the table. I keep one by my computer for motivation. I don't remember which one I had that night, but he recognized it. Then we talked a few times during that week."

"About what?"

"Well, my book. The current action figure. And then just stuff in the news. Weather. You know, small talk."

"Whose idea was it to give him the ride to the bus stop?"

"Hmm." Dupont tapped his chin and raised his face to the ceiling. "I'm not sure if I offered or if he asked."

"Think harder."

Dupont closed his eyes and muttered something unintelligible.

"What did you say?" Sean asked.

"I just was telling myself to think because this seems really important to you." He scrunched his eyes tighter. "It was seven-thirty, and I packed up my computer to go home. He asked if I'd made good progress. I said I had, and then he got up too." Dupont's eyes popped open. "Then he asked me which direction I was heading. I told him, and he asked if he could catch a ride to the bus stop. Yeah. Yeah, it was his idea." He paused and frowned. "Obviously this guy did something wrong. Am I in trouble? Or danger? My family . . . are they safe?"

"This man's a suspect in an investigation." Sean remained vague.

Taylor saw it as an opening to get involved. "We'd like to bring you and your family into protective custody until we can sort this out."

Sean shot her a surprised look. She should probably have talked to him about this before taking over and offering, but she believed Dupont's story, and she didn't want him to worry.

Dupont looked at her. "Like we'll be under arrest?"

"No, but you won't be able to leave the location we provide."

He clawed his fingers into his hair, locking on for a moment and then raking through to leave tufts sticking up. "For how long? My wife and I have to work. The kids go to school."

"I can't put a timeline on it," she replied. "We'll

protect you for as long as it takes to make sure you're safe. And we'll help with trying to clear you of any wrongdoing."

"But I told you, I . . ." He scrubbed a hand over his face. "I knew something was off about that guy. I shouldn't have given him a ride. My wife's gonna kill me."

Sean moved even closer, but he looked less fierce. "Off, how?"

"Just too friendly, I guess. I should've known he wanted something all along."

Sean looked like he agreed. "We'll also be impounding your car to process, and we have a warrant to search your house."

"My house!" Dupont shot up and shoved his glasses higher on his nose. "But he never came here."

Sean's forehead wrinkled. "All we have is your word that you aren't associated with our suspect. We'll be looking for connections to either prove or disprove your statements."

"Oh, man." Dupont shook his head. "My wife's really gonna be mad about that."

Taylor gave him a tight smile. "We're sorry, Mr. Dupont, but we have to follow every lead. If you don't have a relationship with our suspect, then you have nothing to worry about."

He groaned. "Tell that to my wife."

Mack entered the room again, this time pausing in front of Sean.

"We're clear inside," Mack said. "I'll clear the garage and join Kiley, unless you need me for something else."

"Go ahead." Sean directed his attention to Dupont again, and Mack departed for the garage. "Can you describe this Paul Jackson?"

"Sure, yeah. He's a few inches taller than me, so about six-foot-one. Looked like he works out. Like a lot. He has this really big nose. Kind of puffy looking. His hair's dark brown. It was combed forward and jagged in the front."

The description matched her drawing of Phantom, and Taylor could hardly contain her excitement. Sean exchanged a knowing look with her, a glint in his eyes.

"But with our recent cold snap he wore gloves," Dupont continued, "so you aren't going to find fingerprints in my car. Maybe that means you won't have to take it."

Sean shook his head. "He could have transferred secondary evidence from his clothing or shoes."

"Oh, right. I see stuff like that on the CSI shows."

"Sounds like you can describe him well enough for an artist to make a sketch," Taylor suggested. It was better for him to have the sketch made than to show him the one she had done, as he could feel pressured to confirm her drawing when it might not be the same guy.

"Yeah, sure." Dupont nodded and couldn't seem to stop. "I can do that. Glad to help."

"And I'll want you to write down every conversation you had with him," Sean said.

Dupont nipped on his lower lip. "I'll do my best, but honestly, I didn't pay this guy all that much attention. Like I said, small talk. Not exactly memorable."

"Do the best you can." Taylor gave him an encouraging smile. "Something he said to you could be the key to our finding and stopping him before he hurts someone."

Her phone buzzed, and she read a text from Inman. She looked at Sean. "I need to head back to the jail."

He nodded. "I'll take you. No way I'm missing that interview."

"Don't you need to stay here?"

He reached for her arm and took her aside. "I believe this guy's telling the truth. Except for prints or DNA from the car, we're done here. I don't need to stick around to have the car hauled in. Keep your eye on him and give me a sec to put someone else in charge. Then we can go."

She nodded, and he stepped toward the door. She considered any additional questions she might have as she moved back to Dupont.

"You seem nice." A weak smile narrowed his thin lips. "You believe me, don't you?"

Did she? "I'm not sure, Mr. Dupont. Your story

sounds good, but until we talk with the staff at the coffee shop to confirm it, and search your place, we'll have to keep an open mind."

"This is all so surreal. Like a dream. Make that a nightmare." He shook his head and couldn't seem to stop. "I don't break the law. I just don't."

She hoped he was telling the truth. "Once we have your family safely tucked away, you can tell us more. So use this time to remember as many details as you can. Everything will go better for you if you do."

"Okay. I can do that."

Sean returned with Kiley, grabbing Dupont's attention. He ran his gaze over her, and Taylor knew that look. He was assessing her as a woman in law enforcement, wondering if she might be easier to deal with than Sean.

"This is Agent Dawson," Sean said. "Tell her how to find your wife and kids, and deputies will pick them up. Then we'll arrange a formal interview at the office with you."

"Oh, man." Dupont sighed. "They're at her parents' house. My in-laws already don't like me. This'll give them justification for it."

Taylor felt sorry for the guy, but that wouldn't deter her from checking out his story and keeping him and his family in custody until they could be sure he was telling the truth and their lives weren't at risk.

Sean faced her. "Ready to go?"

Eager to question Roger, she nodded and marched out the door.

At the jail, a deputy led them down a long hall holding multiple interrogation rooms. Prisoners called out, shouting obscenities and more. She'd experienced unruly prisoners' often crass behavior in her detention rotation, and she had tremendous respect for the law enforcement officers who worked with them day in and day out.

"Have a seat. Glover's still being processed. Might take a few minutes before we bring him down." The deputy shook his head on the way to the door, muttering, "I can't believe he did this. He was such a stand-up guy."

Taylor couldn't defend Roger. She didn't even want to discuss her friend. Wait, was he still her friend? What was the protocol here? Did a person break off a friendship when someone was arrested, or did you see them through it? He'd lied to her. Betrayed her. Posed as one thing, but was another. Right now she couldn't imagine forgiving him, much less staying his friend.

I know, God. I know I need to forgive. To think about what you would do in this situation.

"You seem miles away." Sean leaned on the wall nearby.

"I was just thinking about Roger. We've been friends for years. A work friend, you know?"

Sean nodded. "Unless you mean work friends

like we turned out to be, because if so, you're really close."

"I don't think of you as a work friend. Is that how you think of me?"

"No. No way." He met her gaze and held it. "And I don't think *friend* is the right word anymore either."

How on earth should she respond to that? She couldn't. Not when she had no idea what she thought of their relationship. "So what do I do as Roger's friend?"

Sean arched an eyebrow. "Chicken."

"What?" Taylor blinked as thoughts pinged through her head.

He shifted from the wall, planting his feet firmly on the concrete floor. "Whenever I bring up the subject of us, you keep avoiding it. Avoidance never solved anything, and these feelings aren't going to go away, you know."

She wanted to be able to talk about the two of them—about how she felt—but she just couldn't deal with another emotional topic at the moment, even if her silence hurt him.

"Right now I need to focus on Roger. Figure out what to do. He betrayed my trust in the worst way."

Sean worked the muscles in his jaw and gave a clipped nod. "I'm sorry he put you in this position."

As predicted, she'd hurt Sean, and her chest

tightened at the thought. But she couldn't let go of her focus on Roger.

"How do I ever recover from what he did?" She shook her head. "One thing's for sure. It's not by being foolish enough to trust anyone else in the future."

CHAPTER 20

Sean wanted to gape at Taylor, but he held his emotions in check. His extensive experience with betrayal meant he should say something to help her, but he'd only told her a bit about Gina and that he was estranged from his mother, not all the details. He was embarrassed that these two women had fooled him. Him, for crying out loud, an FBI agent who should be able to recognize deceit. But no. He'd been fooled. Deceived. Call it what you want. He'd let them trick him.

But this wasn't about him. It was about Taylor. She was suffering, and he couldn't just stand by and protect his ego. He took a seat next to her in a chair bolted to the floor. "Can I give you some advice?"

"About?" Her hesitancy spoke volumes.

"Betrayal. Lying. How to handle it."

She sat back and assessed him. "Is this about your former fiancée?"

"Yeah, and more." He still wanted to leave it at that. He'd thought about telling her everything. Many times. But never did he imagine it would be in a jail. Still, they had time, so why not? "My mother was the first."

Taylor swiveled to face him. The intense interest in her expression rattled his nerves. He

266

wished he could slide his chair back, but it was bolted to the floor. He shifted to the side and casually hooked an arm over the chair.

"Tell me about her," she said softly.

He clenched his hands and focused on them to stem his anger. "My dad left when I was two. So it was just my mother and me. We were dirt poor. One paycheck away from living on the street. Then when I was seventeen, she was killed in a hit-and-run accident."

"I'm so sorry, Sean." Taylor rested her hands on his.

The warmth of her touch gave him the courage to continue, though he still couldn't look her in the eyes. "I was a senior in high school. Had a scholarship that included summer work-study and housing. All I had to do was figure out how to survive through the rest of my senior year."

"What about your dad? Did you try to get in touch with him to help?"

"No," he said firmly. "My mom had told me like a million times that after he left, he didn't want to see me. So I didn't look him up. I stayed in the apartment as long as I could, then lived in our car. I got a job at night that paid enough for food and basics and joined sports teams so I could shower at school."

She squeezed his hand. "That must have been hard."

He looked up at her. "Yeah, it was tough losing

my mom, but figuring out what to do for the next four months wasn't as hard as I thought it would be. The police never found the driver who killed my mom, so when I got to college I majored in law enforcement. I thought the FBI had the best resources to help me find the driver and signed on with them. FYI, I found him and brought him to justice."

"That must've felt good."

"Yeah, for all of a day, but then I didn't have a driving focus, and I was lost. No goal." As the memories played like a video in his brain, he shook his head to push the images away. "I suddenly realized I was totally alone and decided to go see my father. I didn't expect anything. I just wanted to show him how well I turned out, even without his support. To basically tell him off."

He got up, dropping her hand and keeping his back to her as he shared the painful part. "He showed me letters he'd written to me since the day he left through my high school years. They were marked 'Return to Sender' in my mother's handwriting. She'd lied to me all my life."

The pain knifed through him, just as it always did when he thought about her lie. He clamped a hand on the back of his neck and faced Taylor. "She cost me twenty-five years with my dad. The closest person to me. My mother. The one person I should've been able to trust. She betrayed me."

Taylor rushed over to him, took his hand, and

looked deeply into his eyes. "I don't even know what to say other than I'm so sorry. Truly sorry. Do you see your dad now?"

He nodded and pulled his hand free. "But that's not the point here. Betrayal is. And lying. And what to do with it."

She tilted her head. "What *can* you do with it?"

He steeled himself and locked the emotions back in the vault. "Forgive and move on, wiser and stronger. Then don't let yourself get close enough to anyone to be hurt again. That way you can avoid the pain."

"What about your dad?"

"He's in my life, but we're not close."

She studied him, long and hard. "And if you're not willing to risk getting hurt, where does that leave us?"

He could hardly believe that after all the avoidance, she brought this up now. "That's why I liked our strictly online relationship. It couldn't go anywhere."

"And now?"

"Now." He scrubbed a hand over his face and tried to come up with a response. "I don't know. Can I trust you, or are you going to pull the rug out from under me too?"

She stared at him, emotions racing over her face, giving him the answer he didn't want to see. She wasn't sure. Taylor. His friend. The woman he was falling for. Wasn't sure about how she felt about him. He couldn't chase after his feelings for her. He had to keep an emotional distance in the event they ended up wanting different things.

The door opened, and Glover shuffled in, his head down. Perfect timing.

Sean let out a sigh. Taylor continued to look at him, but then her lips pressed together as she shifted her attention to Glover.

He dropped into a chair and gave her a sullen look. "Let's get this over with."

She eased out a long pent-up breath and sat across from him. She took her time adjusting her sling, pressing her free hand flat on the table. She lifted her face, her concentration so deadly intense for an even-tempered woman that it shocked Sean. He was afraid she might verbally attack Glover. To preempt her, Sean quickly started the recorder placed in a cutout in the wall. He informed Glover that he was being recorded and got his permission to do so.

"Why'd you do it?" Taylor demanded.

Glover shifted uncomfortably in his seat. "If only I'd kept the burner phone he gave me, you could see for yourselves every communication I had with the jerk who made me do this."

"Why'd you get rid of it?" Sean asked.

"He instructed me to," Glover said matter-of-factly.

"He?" Taylor continued to glare at him. "You mean Phantom."

"His name in the text was Paul. That's it. I can't tell you if it's this Phantom guy you're looking for or not."

Paul. There was that name again, and Sean wished they knew more about him. "Is that the only way he communicated with you?"

Glover nodded.

"What about the break-in?" Taylor's voice remained laced with pain. "Were you part of that?"

"No. No way."

"Start at the beginning," Sean said. "Tell us how this Paul contacted you."

"I came out to my car one day and found a phone in an envelope." Glover clenched and unclenched his hands. "It contained pictures of my kids. On the playground. At school. With Naomi. At the grocery store. Gas station. You name it, he'd taken their pictures."

"He was telling you he could get to them," Sean said.

"Exactly. Then he sent a text to the phone. Like he was watching me and knew I had it in my hand. If I didn't do what he wanted, he would kill one or all of them. He sent me pictures of a man he'd butchered. Or at least he claimed to have butchered him." Glover described the photos in detail, which matched the murder of Phantom's associate.

Sean pictured a child butchered this way, and

acid burned up his throat. He reached for an antacid, but didn't want Taylor to see his distress so he let the pain fuel his determination to find Phantom.

"What exactly did he tell you to do?" Taylor asked, her anger in check now.

"He told me he would leave flash drives and directions for me to enter information into the WITSEC database. He said it was malware and he'd hold the database for ransom. If I'd known his real purpose . . ." Glover clamped his mouth closed and shook his head. "I don't know. I don't think I would have done the same thing, but I just don't know. They're my kids. *My kids.*" Tears formed in his eyes, and he scrunched them closed.

Taylor watched Glover for a long moment. "You were in a nearly impossible position. I get that. But you should have come to me. We could've brought your family into protection."

He stared at Taylor. "And then what? Start over somewhere new? No contact with our family and friends? I've seen that play out way too many times to inflict it on my own family."

"So you don't believe in the program your agency provides." Sean let his disgust flow through his words. He usually tried to contain his emotions in an interview, but as a law enforcement officer who'd sold out the agency, Glover was the lowest of the low in Sean's book.

"Oh, I do," Glover said. "It works great. We keep people alive who wouldn't make it a day without us. But the innocent people—the ones who simply witness a crime and have to go into the program—pay a huge toll. They did nothing wrong, and just like that, they're punished for it."

Sean sat forward and stared at Glover. "It would've been better than betraying your oath. Your coworkers. The witnesses."

Glover crossed his arms and leaned back in his chair.

"Fine. Clam up," Sean spat out. "That's what people like you do. Lie and betray and then shut down. I've seen it too many times, and you're a poster child for all of them."

Sean sat in the conference room staring at his computer. Since their follow-up interviews with Dupont and Glover, Sean had thoroughly vetted Dupont's story and reviewed the evidence from his house. He also picked up the video at the coffee shop where Dupont had met Phantom. While the footage failed to show Phantom's face, his body size, build, and other physical details supported Dupont's statement. The car might be another story after forensics processed it, but for now, they had nothing on Dupont.

"Yes!" Cam punched his fist into the air. "I've got it. The list. It's done."

"Excellent. Email it to me now." Sean's

computer dinged right away, and he downloaded the list containing 236 names. "Longer list than I expected."

Cam nodded. "Question is, did Phantom put all the names up for sale yet? I'll cross-reference them to his site on the dark web."

Sean nodded and quickly scanned the list, looking for Dustee and the three witnesses who were attacked the other night. He spotted all four names. Not a surprise.

"You found me, right?" Anxiety darkened Dustee's eyes.

Sean hated to tell her, but she needed to know. "Yes. Your record was accessed."

"So it really was Phantom who chased me, who tried to kill me." She wrapped her arms around her body.

Taylor swiveled in her chair. "I'm sorry, Dustee. I wish it wasn't so, but it's not really a surprise, is it?"

"Still . . ." Her voice cracked. "Hearing your name is officially on a hit list is totally different."

"Yes, I can imagine it is." Taylor reached for Dustee's hand.

She jerked it away to go back to her computer. "I need to work. I'm going to find his signature in these files and nail him. Make sure he goes away for infinity-plus."

"That's my girl. Put your anger to good use." Taylor smiled and changed her focus to Sean.

"I'll need the names of any Portland witnesses on the list."

Sean wasn't sure how to respond. She had to know the list should go directly to Eisenhower, and then he would distribute it. But that could take hours. Maybe a day. Sean couldn't bear it if during that time one of Taylor's witnesses was murdered. "Besides Dustee, there are two others on the list." He jotted the names on a sticky note and handed it to her.

She grabbed the note and jumped to her feet. "I have to call Inman. I'll be right back."

She bolted for the door, where Sean heard her ask Snow to escort her to the small conference room. Sean emailed Eisenhower the list, along with an update on the investigation. He replied right away, stating that the Marshals' IT staff were still reviewing other areas of the server, and if they located anything, he'd get back to Sean.

Sean mentioned the email to his team. "Other than the database modifications, anyone run across anything else on the cloned server to indicate additional tampering?"

Cam looked up. "I haven't had even a second to look beyond the database."

"Ditto that," Kiley said.

"And I don't have access." Dustee's belligerent tone had returned.

"The IT staff could be right," Sean said. "You

all keep on your tasks, and I'll take a look. See what I can locate."

"FYI," Kiley said, "I'm running an algorithm to scour the internet for any connection between Phantom, the coffee shop, and the bus-stop locations."

Cam cast her a skeptical look. "You really think you'll find something actionable?"

Kiley frowned. "It may be a long shot, but it's worth checking out."

"The idea is sound, Kiley," Sean forced out over a tightness in his throat.

And I should have come up with it. But I didn't.

Why? Stress. Distractions. Taylor. The case closing in on him. Pressure. Much like the Montgomery Three investigation. All of it weighing him down. Everyone was fully invested in this case, but sometimes that wasn't enough. Sometimes the bad guys still won and evaded capture.

It was all up to God, and as much as Sean wanted to trust Him, when Sean's mother died, he'd had to take things into his own hands. Become independent. Meant he often had a hard time trusting God to work things out. But if Sean had learned anything on the Montgomery Three investigation, he'd learned God was in control. Not him. God. That was true now, too, and worth remembering.

But please, God, not this hacker. Please don't

let him slip away. And don't let him kill anyone else.

Taking comfort from the prayer, Sean started reviewing files so that no witness in danger remained hidden. Hours passed, and his neck cramped, but he kept at the job, as did everyone else.

"It's Phantom!" Dustee swiveled her computer so the screen faced Sean and jabbed her finger at it. "See the false flag? He signed it with a stolen digital certificate. It's from Sphinx, one of Phantom's known enemies. He's tried to blame Sphinx in the past."

"Isn't proof positive," Cam muttered.

Dustee crossed her arms. "Add that with the other things I know about him, and I have no problem attributing this hack to him."

Sean wished it were that easy. "The process of attribution isn't that simple when you work for a law enforcement agency. We need more than this to officially attribute it to him."

"But you know I'm right, don't you?" She grinned at Cam.

"Oh, yeah." Cam returned the smile, showing what a good-looking guy he was and surely a temptation for Dustee.

"You need to get back to work and prove it," Sean said to Dustee. "Any hint of the Russian connection?"

She shook her head.

"Good job, though," he said to encourage her. "I knew you were the right person to find his signature."

She sighed and ran her fingers over the keyboard. "I'm gonna miss this when it's over."

Surprisingly, Sean felt sorry for her. "Maybe you can talk to Taylor about finding a way to help out in a supervised manner."

"Maybe."

"She really wants you to be happy, Dustee. That's what she's here for."

"Yeah." She shook her head. "I don't get it."

It wasn't Sean's place to share Taylor's strong desire to help others. "For one thing, she lives her faith."

"Right. That. She's never come out and said she's a Christian, but I can tell she is." Dustee sat unmoving, her hands poised over the keyboard. "I think because of her, Dianne's going to check it out."

"And you?"

"Yeah . . . maybe after this I will."

Sean knew the change in lifestyle would be harder for Dustee than for Dianne, but he was glad to hear her pondering it. He offered a prayer for both of them, then it hit him. Was he living his faith the way Taylor seemed to be doing? She displayed her love in most every action. Of course, he didn't know if she was acting that way because of faith, or if her guilt over Jeremy was what motivated her. Either way, God was using her to draw people to Him.

As if thinking about Taylor made her materialize, she walked into the room. She looked content in a way he hadn't seen since they'd met in person.

"I take it everything's okay?" he asked.

She nodded. "Inman and the team are working on relocating the compromised witnesses, and of course, Dustee is with me. Even so, I didn't tell the others to stand down on their vigilance yet."

He understood her hesitancy but wished she wasn't still concerned. "I hope the list has been distributed to all the offices by now and everyone's safe."

Taylor's smile disappeared, and she dropped into the chair by Dustee. "Do you think this is it, or will we find others?"

He hated seeing her good mood fade, but he had to tell the truth. "Anything is possible."

"I'll keep after it, Taylor," Cam said. "And if there are other names, I'll find them. You can count on that."

She smiled. "Have we heard anything new on Dupont?"

"The sketch artist is scheduled for morning," Sean replied.

Her phone rang, and she looked at the screen. "Odd. It's Inman. What could he want when we just talked?"

"Chief." She tipped her head to listen, and her lips pursed in that cute way Sean loved to see. Her face suddenly blanched, and she grasped the edge of the table, her knuckles turning white.

Sean's heart dropped to his stomach. Something was wrong. Totally wrong. Maybe it was something with one of the witnesses.

"We'll head out there right away." Her voice broke.

Sean wanted to fire questions her way, but he didn't want to upset her more. He pressed his hands on his knees and waited for her to speak.

She laid her phone on the table and looked up, the sadness in her eyes cutting him to the quick.

"The bus driver we talked to," she said. "Enzo Russo."

"Yes?" Sean held his breath.

"He's . . . dead." She shook her head. "He was brutally murdered tonight."

CHAPTER 21

The cold damp night bit into Taylor's body, and the street where Enzo Russo lay sprawled on his back steamed under the large Klieg lights shining harshly on his body. The mist added to the tension swirling in the air as Taylor and Sean signed in with the officer of record. Taylor scanned the mixed residential and commercial neighborhood in southeast Portland. She knew nothing about the area and had no idea why Enzo would have been here at this time of night.

She eyed the body, glad for the distance that kept the details out of view. She'd been so demanding with Sean, telling him she was coming with him to the scene when he'd wanted her to stay at the office, but now her last meal sat like a ball in her stomach, and she doubted her ability to move her feet forward and duck under the crime scene tape to approach Enzo's body. She'd seen murder victims exactly two times in her career, and both times she'd almost gotten sick.

"Ready?" Sean grabbed the yellow tape.

She nodded, but he had to see she was feeling queasy.

"You don't have to be here," he said softly.

She appreciated his quiet tone to keep the

officer of record from hearing about her reticence. "I'm good."

They moved closer, their steps echoing through the night. They passed an emergency response truck, the ME's van, an ambulance, and numerous police cruisers, their lights still flashing as if silently announcing the death scene. Local detectives, a crime scene photographer, uniformed officers, and criminalists swarmed like worker ants over the area, each of them with a specific job to do.

What exactly her job was here, she didn't know, but if this murder involved Phantom, she had to learn as much as she could to protect the twins. She gulped in moist air and slowly let it out.

"I'm right here beside you." Sean's hand brushed against and tangled with her fingers for only an instant. Anyone watching wouldn't have even noticed, yet his support gave her strength.

"Thank you." She offered him a small smile, but her lips trembled, betraying her emotions.

"Look away if you have to. No one will think less of you."

"Do you really think Phantom did this?"

He nodded. "You know Phantom's paranoia is through the roof. He saw us talking to Enzo and probably assumed he told us something. Phantom can't abide betrayal, and the need to silence Enzo had to be like an itch he couldn't help but scratch. Plus he's proven his instability in the past by having killed his own partner. And we both know that once someone commits murder, it's easier to commit another one."

"True."

"Like the text to Dustee, this murder just might be a message to us. To tell us he can get to anyone, anywhere."

"You really think Phantom was watching when we talked to Enzo?"

"After the shots he took at Dustee, it's clear he's keeping tabs on her and the people around her."

The thought of this killer watching her sent a deep shudder through Taylor. "Yeah, I guess so."

"We'll soon see if this killing shares the same MO as Phantom's partner." Sean marched up to the body and the detective standing over it.

Taylor took a quick look at the tall, thin detective dressed in a worn leather jacket over a white shirt and wrinkled khaki pants. His square face, silvery-gray hair, and large nose gave him an unapproachable vibe. He held out his hand to Sean. "Jesse Roderick."

Taylor shifted her attention to Enzo. One look and she spun away. She didn't care what anyone thought of her skittish behavior. Her actions were instinctual to preserve her sanity. She blinked a few times, trying to wash the image of Enzo's bloodstained body from her mind, but it remained, along with images of the murdered partner. The similarities stood out like blinking neon lights.

"It *is* Phantom." She quickly turned back but kept her focus on Sean. "He did this. The wounds are identical to those of Phantom's partner."

"That's pretty farfetched after only a peek at the knife wound." Roderick frowned at her. "Granted a wound of this severity isn't common, but I've seen it before."

"There's blood near Enzo's mouth. Check his tongue. Phantom cut . . ." Her stomach roiled, and she couldn't finish the sentence.

Roderick knelt down, but Taylor planted her focus on Sean. His face was tight. Angry. Most likely over the senseless murder. She'd been too upset at seeing Enzo this way to feel anger for the pointless killing, but now it boiled up.

"It's missing." Roderick got to his feet and turned to Sean. "Tell me more about this Phantom guy."

Sean didn't answer right away, likely deciding which of the investigative details to start with. "He's a notorious hacker who killed his partner a few years ago. He thought the partner was going to out him to law enforcement."

"I see," Roderick said. "So he silenced him."

"Ditto for Enzo here," Sean said. "Phantom rode Enzo's bus, and we interviewed Enzo as part of our investigation."

Roderick nodded, his expression that of a

seasoned detective searching for answers. "So you believe this Phantom dude saw you talking to Enzo and thinks he snitched?"

Sean nodded.

Roderick got out a small notebook and a pen. "I'll need your contact information and a copy of your reports."

"Sorry," Sean said. "You don't have clearance to be read in on our investigation."

Roderick raised his eyebrows, the many lines in his forehead squishing together, but he didn't speak.

"I have an evidence response team on the way," Sean continued. "They'll work alongside your team to process the scene."

"What? You're not taking over the investigation completely?" Roderick's sarcasm was probably called for, but Taylor didn't like that he directed it at Sean, who was just doing his job.

"I'll be conducting an independent investigation." Sean's forthright reply impressed Taylor. She knew he interacted with local law enforcement all the time and had experience dealing with them, and yet she could see how easy it would be to become sarcastic in return.

Roderick shoved his hands into his pockets. "Can you at least direct me to the case files for the prior murder?"

Taylor fired Sean a questioning look. He nodded.

"Give me your business card," she said to Roderick. "I'll email the detective's information to you."

He dug out the card and slapped it in her hand far more forcefully than needed.

Sean raised an eyebrow. She shook her head, telling him to ignore Roderick's behavior and move on.

"I'll also instruct the ME to compare this wound and the tongue removal to that earlier murder," Sean said.

"You think this is a copycat?" Roderick asked. "Not the real deal?"

Sean shook his head. "Just being thorough. I assume since you're touching the body and the hands are bagged, that the ME has examined the body."

Roderick nodded. "He and his assistant are grabbing the gurney."

"Did the ME provide a time of death?" she asked.

"Rigor hasn't set in so less than two hours. That's all he'll commit to at this point."

So they'd probably arrived before anyone had a chance to disturb the crime scene. Not that Taylor expected Phantom would leave much evidence behind. His ability to evade law enforcement for years proved he was too careful for that.

"With the tongue removed, we might get lucky and find the killer's DNA on the body," Sean stated. "That is, if the killer didn't wear gloves. Have you requested your forensic staff to swab for DNA?"

Roderick frowned. "I'll make sure the swab is completed."

A liberal dose of skepticism raced across Sean's face. "I assume the Portland Police Bureau isn't equipped to process the DNA, and it will go through the state lab."

Roderick nodded.

"State labs are usually backlogged. Will you rush that DNA, or should I take care of having it processed?"

"I've got it." Roderick clenched his teeth.

Taylor didn't think he had a right to be upset with Sean. Sure, Sean was dictating instructions and questioning the man, but again, that was Sean's job.

"I'll expect you to notify me the minute the results come in," Sean said.

"I'll do my best."

Sean ran a hand over his face. "Any witnesses?"

Roderick shook his head. "Uniforms canvassed the surrounding buildings, but if anyone saw anything, they aren't talking. Not unusual for this neighborhood. There's a sizable illegal immigrant population here, and they don't often trust the police."

Taylor tried to visualize Enzo visiting the neighborhood, especially on a dark and rainy night. "What was Enzo doing here? Does he live nearby?"

"No. We have no idea of his reason for being in this area."

"Who discovered him?"

Roderick pointed at a phone lying next to the body. "There was an anonymous call to 911 using his phone."

"I don't want anyone touching that phone before it's taken into evidence," Sean said.

Roderick's lips pressed into a white slash. "Look. I get that you all think you can run roughshod over me. Think I'm a peon. But I'm gonna give my sarge a shout-out and get him down here before we go any further."

"Sure, fine," Sean said. "I'd like to do this the right way—in a spirit of cooperation and sharing of what we're able to divulge. But know this. No matter how we handle things here, the outcome will be the same. I will get what I need for my investigation. You can count on that."

Sean kept his focus on the road during the drive back to the safe house, carefully navigating the foggy night and slick pavement. Taylor had locked her eyes on him the moment he'd exited the parking lot, and he could feel them resting there ever since. If she wanted to say something or talk, all she had to do was start the conversation. But he felt personally responsible for failing to apprehend Phantom before he got to Enzo, and he was in no mood to talk, so he didn't ask about it. Now, as he parked in the sloping drive, he wanted to know what was going on in that beautiful head of hers.

He removed the key and faced her. "What did I do wrong?"

"Wrong?"

"You've been staring at me since we left. It's like I have the plague or something."

She didn't answer, but sat there staring at him, her eyes glazed and vacant. She was thinking. He wanted to push her to speak, wanted to know what she was thinking. From his past experience, though, he knew she didn't often blurt out the first thought that came to mind. She weighed and crafted her responses. So he sat back and looked at the drive lined with evergreen shrubs, their leaves shiny with rain, to give her the time she needed.

"I don't know exactly," she finally said. "I guess . . . I haven't ever seen the side of you that you showed at the crime scene. You totally surprised me."

"What side?" he asked, confused.

"Over-the-top intense. A foe that no one would want to go up against. Intimidating."

"You mean with Roderick?"

"Yeah, with Roderick."

Sean ran through the conversation in his

mind. Maybe he had been over the top in his demeanor, but the investigation was everything. And Phantom needed to be stopped at all costs. "Roderick's a big boy, and I don't have time to worry about his feelings. I have a killer to catch. It's nothing personal."

"The LEO in me gets it. But as your friend . . ." She shrugged. "I've just never seen it."

"It seems to bother you."

"Not really. I mean, I should know you wouldn't be on the RED team if you were all wishy-washy, but the forceful and aggressive part of your personality doesn't jive with the guy I've gotten to know. That's all I'm saying."

He got her point, but . . . "I could say the same thing about you."

"Me? Aggressive?"

"Yes, when it comes to your witnesses."

She raised her chin. "Well, yeah, I have to be. They're my responsibility. I'd die for them if I had to."

"And keeping someone from getting murdered is my responsibility. Right now that's Dustee and all the witnesses. So I'm just doing my job like you are."

"You're right. I *am* different on the job, more forceful. I suppose that's something we didn't know about each other." She took a deep breath. "And the other Sean? The one who's my best friend? Where's he in all of this?"

"He's still here." He smiled and touched her shoulder. "I can tell one of my great jokes if you want me to prove it."

She held up her hands and mocked a horrified look. "Please no. Anything but that." She laughed, and the tension in her face washed away.

In a flash of a moment, the mood changed. The air heated up between them, charged with emotion. His brain refused to process, and he could hardly think straight.

All he knew was that he was looking at a beautiful woman who had slipped into his heart. First as a friend. Now, as what, he didn't know. Didn't care at the moment. More important, he knew he had to touch her again.

He raised his hand and cupped the side of her face. "I'm this guy, Taylor. The one who knows you and cares for you. I'll always be there for you. Always. I'm not going anywhere, no matter what Phantom or anyone else does."

Instead of a joyful response, she flinched. Had he gone too far by touching her so intimately? She didn't pull away. In fact, she nuzzled into his hand. But the horrified look remained in place, one mixed with sadness.

"What is it?" he asked.

She shook her head, tears glistening in her eyes.

He'd evoked something in her. Something big. What had he said to cause her to react like this? He racked his brain for an answer. Then a lightbulb went off. Her parents. Was she thinking about them? About how they'd blamed her for her brother's death and essentially abandoned her?

She removed his hand from her cheek, held it, and looked directly into his eyes. "I know you think you'll always be there for me, that you'll never leave. But you can't predict the future. No one can. We never know what we'll do when faced with a challenge or situation that's bigger than we are."

He didn't know how to respond. She'd put up a huge wall on this issue, and he didn't know if he could ever break it down or if he should even try. But he had to know if he was going to find a way to help her. Maybe asking questions would bring things out in the open.

"Please, tell me more about your brother's suicide," he encouraged.

She cringed and shook her head. "I've already told you."

"Yeah, in a cursory overview. But not about what actually happened. How you felt. Feel."

She released his hand. "What's the point in discussing it?"

"I want to help you get through it, but to do that, I need to understand why your parents would turn their backs on you. Did you have something to do with Jeremy's death?"

Her mouth fell open, and she gaped at him. "N-no. Of course not." She took a long, lingering look at him and then bolted from the SUV.

She hurried up the steps while he took his time searching through the shifting fog for answers. He'd obviously hit a nerve, and despite wanting to know what had happened, he'd leave it alone for her sake.

What a pair they were. Seemingly so right for each other, and yet neither of them could pull the trigger on going beyond friendship. He got the feeling she wanted to. He thought he wanted to as well, but no matter how much he thought about having a woman in his life, or even wanting such a relationship—as he was coming to learn he wanted with her—he knew it wasn't going to happen.

CHAPTER 22

The morning started out dark, rainy, and foggy, and the view outside the lobby window of the Portland Metropolitan Forensic Laboratory matched Sean's mood. He still felt responsible for Enzo's death, and he'd let it eat away at him all night long. Plus he hadn't let go of Taylor being shot. Changing her bandage each morning had reinforced that. Today, though, she visited the doctor, and he cleared her to remove the sling. Sure, Sean understood that he wasn't personally responsible for these things, but if he'd found and arrested Phantom first, neither of them would have happened.

The door behind Sean opened, and he glanced back to see a young woman peering at him through large round glasses. The brown frames matched her bangs and hair tied in two ponytails near her shoulders. She looked like a high schooler, not the experienced scientist he'd expected, but she wore a pristine white lab coat and was likely the person he'd come to see.

She crossed over to him, her sneakers slapping on the tile floor and echoing in the small space. "I'm Anna Coleman, criminalist. Detective Roderick called me in to head up evidence recovery at the Russo crime scene. I'll be walking you through our findings."

Sean shook her hand in greeting, introduced himself, then said, "And this is Deputy Taylor Mills."

Anna nodded at Taylor and spun. "Follow me."

Sean stepped back, allowing Taylor to go before him, and he had to admit to liking the gentle sway of her hips and the way her high heels made her legs seem about a mile long as she hurried after Anna, who moved rapidly through the building. At a second-floor lab, she swiped her card and opened the door to an organized and sterile work space with tall lab tables and stools in the middle of the room. Various computers, machines, and other equipment Sean couldn't identify filled the room.

Anna went straight to a large machine holding evidence hanging from clips. Sean had to hurry to keep up with the little dynamo.

She rested against the counter and boldly met his gaze. "I didn't necessarily ask you here to share our findings when I could have done that via the phone. But I wanted you to see our lab in person to give you confidence in our results."

"I don't know why I—"

She held up a hand. "The FBI's super lab in Quantico is the standard by which every other lab is judged. Your evidence techs made that perfectly clear at the crime scene last night and pointed out that you would want to wait for their results. But as you can see, we're nationally accredited, and I know by the time you leave, you'll be confident in our results and won't feel a need to wait on Quantico."

"You're right," he said, catching her off guard. "We are snobs when it comes to our lab, and visiting here helps allay any concerns."

"I didn't expect you to admit it, but I'm glad you did." She turned to the counter and tapped fingerprint cards lying there. "Our first task was to process the victim's phone for prints and DNA. We lifted several good prints, but unfortunately, they all belong to the victim. DNA hasn't finished running yet for the phone. We'll have that information later today."

"Great." Sean smiled. "Were you able to collect touch DNA from Enzo's body?"

"Not yet." She puckered her lips. "Detective Roderick charged the ME's office with collecting the DNA. He should've let me take a sample at the crime scene too, but he authorized the removal of the body before I could do so."

Sean didn't often feel the need to curse, but he had to stifle the urge to do so now. He thought he'd communicated a sense of urgency to the detective. Obviously not, and Sean would probably need to call Roderick and get him moving on other aspects of the murder investigation as well.

Anna squared her shoulders. "I called the ME the minute I discovered he'd taken the body. He said Roderick made him aware of the need for the DNA swabs, and he authorized me to take samples at the autopsy later today."

"Excellent," Sean said, and meant it. "I also asked the ME to compare this murder to a prior one. You might want to talk to him about that too."

"I'm glad to do so."

"Thank you for being so diligent," Sean said.

And thank you, God, for placing such a talented tech on our investigation.

Sean's phone sounded in Mack's ring tone. Anna frowned at the interruption. "Sorry. I don't mean to be rude, but I need to get this." He answered it and stepped away for privacy, leaving Anna and Taylor to talk between themselves.

"The artist just dropped off the sketch from Dupont's session," Mack said. "It's a close match to Taylor's suspect."

"So it looks like Taylor actually did see Phantom." Sean looked across the room at her. When he shared the news that she'd gotten close to Phantom, he could see it potentially freaking her out. He would try to break it gently to spare her more anguish. "Can you scan and email it to me?"

"Already did." Mack pulled in a long breath. "Also, the CCTV footage from the area around the Marshals' office shows one man accessing the building on the night of the break-in. No clear footage of his face, but his build fits Phantom."

"And the night of the hack? We have video of Glover inside the building, but was there any footage from outside?"

"Cameras caught him approaching the door. He didn't even bother to hide his face."

"He didn't think he'd get caught." Sean clenched his teeth at Glover's audacity. "Anything from the canvass?"

"Nothing actionable, but we have a few more doors to knock on."

Sean could only hope they would produce a lead. "I gotta get back to the forensic update. We'll talk more when I get back."

He hung up and returned to Anna, whose irritation seemed to be gone. She focused on him and continued, "Once I have the DNA samples, I'll process them and run a CODIS search." She didn't need to explain that CODIS was an acronym for the FBI's Combined DNA Index System, as everyone in law enforcement knew about the database of criminal DNA profiles. "The autopsy is scheduled for late afternoon, so running the samples most likely won't happen until the morning."

She grabbed a printout from the table and handed the papers to Sean. "Enzo's phone calls and text logs for you. It looks like he arrived at the murder scene because his daughter sent him a text saying she was in trouble and asking him to meet her there."

"His daughter?" Taylor looked at Sean. "Odd."

"I thought so too," Anna said. "So I asked the tech to do some digging to see if the text actually came from the daughter."

Sean folded the papers and put them in his jacket pocket. "You're thinking the killer spoofed the text."

"Yes," Anna said.

Sean let the thought settle in. Sending a text from an unknown source and pretending it came from Enzo's daughter was well within Phantom's wheelhouse. "I'll need the daughter's contact information so we can interview her."

"I'll email it to you," Anna said. "And now that you know we're legit, I can email the rest of our findings as we receive them." She grinned, and he could swear she really was only sixteen or so. "If you don't have any more questions, I'll walk you out."

Sean gestured for her to go ahead. In the lobby, his phone rang, and Kiley's name popped onto the screen. He stepped outside to answer on speaker so Taylor could hear what Kiley had to say. "You're on speaker, and I have Taylor with me. Tell me you have something."

"Maybe. I hope so anyway." Kiley's tone mimicked her hopeful words. "I added the location where Enzo was murdered to my algorithm, and it returned a picture of a guy who claims he's digging a tunnel under a famous hacker's house. Says the hacker is paying him big bucks to dig it."

"Tunnel?" Taylor's eyes narrowed.

Sean shrugged. "What's the connection to the address where Enzo was killed?"

"Chris Hall, the guy who posted the picture. His uncle owns one of the abandoned warehouses near the crime scene. Hall's been dumping the dirt from the hacker's house at this location."

Interesting twist. "And you think Phantom's the hacker?"

"Hall never comes right out and says that's who he's working for, but he hints at it."

Hope lit a fire in Sean. "Tell me you know where we can find this Hall guy."

"I traced him back to his parents' place. He lives with them. He's an unemployed IT professional, which in the Portland market where IT jobs are plentiful probably says a lot about him. And maybe why he's digging tunnels for money and living with his parents."

"Text me the address." Sean shared an excited look with Taylor. "And we'll stake out the house until the guy shows his face."

Taylor watched Sean talk on his phone, his free hand casually draped over the steering wheel. He'd driven straight to Hall's house, parked down the street, and promptly called Mack to tell him to interview Enzo's daughter. Now Sean was talking to the forensic tech who'd processed Dupont's car. She didn't have to wonder about the gist of the conversation. Not with his jaw clamped tight and this stakeout seeming all the more important.

She shifted her focus to Hall's place. All was quiet at the run-down bungalow. If only Hall would show himself. Not just for the lead, but she suspected that once Sean finished his calls, he would ask her about Jeremy again. She'd avoided his question about her brother one more time, though not successfully. Okay, fine. She'd lied to him. Told him she'd had nothing to do with Jeremy's death when, in fact, she had. And she wasn't a liar. But when he'd asked if she had a role in his death, everything in her cried out to protect herself. To deflect the question. Because when Sean heard what she'd done, he would turn his back and walk away exactly like her parents had.

She couldn't lose him. Not now. Not when she'd learned what a wonderful man he was, and that he cared about her too. But did that even matter when she couldn't enter into a relationship before she was ready to share the full truth about Jeremy?

Years had passed—fifteen to be exact—and still she was no more ready to do that than she was the day she'd told her parents about her actions. She could still see the horror on their faces and never wanted to talk about Jeremy again. Or even think about him. Well, not really. She loved thinking about their life before he ended his, and thinking about her mom and dad in those happier days as well.

Oh, how she missed them. In the worst way. In that deep, achy place she never wanted to visit, as it always brought tears. She had gone off to college and never returned home. At least not to stay. She'd parked across the street many times over the years to get a glimpse of her mother and father. She'd watched them climb into their car and head out to who knew where. Sometimes she came early in the morning to see her dad leave for work, his trusty thermos under his arm as always. She found an odd comfort there. But it always ended in tears over what might have been if she'd only made a better decision that day.

What if she *did* marry someday? Had children? Because of her actions, they would never know their grandparents.

Tears wet her eyes, and she looked away as Sean was ending his call. He'd shared about his difficult past and deserved to know about Jeremy, but she wasn't ready to open up and didn't want him to see her tears and start asking questions.

He placed his phone in the dash holder. "Lots of clean latents recovered from Dupont's car, but no AFIS matches. They did find cat hair, but it could've come from him or the other passengers Dupont hauled."

She nodded at Hall's house. "We could go knock on the door and see if Hall's home."

"I don't want to risk sending him to ground if he's not." Sean lifted his binoculars to view the house.

She looked at his strong profile, and the urge to touch him was almost stronger than she could control. She searched for something to say and ignored her feelings. "You should've brought Mack on this stakeout instead of me. With his fugitive apprehension experience, he'd be much better at it."

"Better at watching a house? Not likely."

"What's the deal with you and Mack?"

"What deal?" He lowered the binoculars and looked at her.

"You don't get along."

"I . . ." he started to say, then paused. "Addison."

"You blame him for their marriage breaking up?"

"No. I blame him for our team losing an incredible member," he said with force.

She had no idea the breakup had affected him so deeply, but he was way off base. "It's not Mack's fault Addison couldn't continue to work with him. He had no problem working with her."

Sean narrowed his eyes and shifted to face her. "Maybe because he's the one who wanted to split."

News to her. "Did they tell you that?"

"No. Just speculating."

"But they said it was mutual."

He arched a brow. "Then why did Addison have to leave?"

Taylor wanted to sigh, but that wouldn't do Sean any good. "I don't know, but you're blaming Mack because of something else between you two. Like maybe because he complained about you to Eisenhower."

Sean was silent for a long moment, and she waited for him to disagree.

He blew out a breath. "Maybe."

She was so glad to hear him admit it. "Wouldn't life be easier if the two of you got along?"

"Yeah."

"But?"

"No buts. I agree." He tightened his fingers around the binoculars. "I've tried to change, but I just don't seem to have the power to alter my opinion of him." He gave her a long look. "So where will you move Dustee and Dianne when this is over?"

She didn't want to let him get away with changing the subject, but if he didn't want to work on his animosity toward Mack, she couldn't force him to. And he hadn't pressed her to talk about Jeremy, so she would return the favor and move on. "I'm not sure where I'll put them. They're so different from each other that they'll want different places. But ultimately, it's my decision, and I'll try to find somewhere that's a good fit for both of them."

He watched her for a while, his lips parted, as if he felt compelled to speak but didn't want to or didn't know what to say next.

What happened to the easy conversation they'd always managed online? If it had been this tense, this uneasy, they would never have become friends. But then maybe they'd never needed to work through any deep personal issues. Sure, they discussed faith and that could get complicated, but they had the same beliefs so those conversations didn't cause disagreements.

"You know," he finally continued, "being a WITSEC deputy is the wrong job for you, don't you?"

Shocked, her mouth dropped open. "Why?"

"You're afraid if you fail one of your witnesses, they'll die just like Jeremy."

"Ah," she said, trying to remain calm when her heart had started racing. "I wondered how long it would take for you to bring that up again."

"And you're trying to distract me from it already." He cast her a sympathetic look. "All I want to do is to help you move past it."

She understood his motives were pure. That he wasn't being pushy here. That he had her best interests at heart, but she still couldn't tell him and risk losing him. "I know."

He tilted his head and studied her. "You ever think about how you don't want to let anyone else help, but you have to be there at your witnesses' beck and call twenty-four seven?"

Did she refuse help from others? She'd never noticed, but she did know she gave her everything to the job. "It's what the job requires."

"Maybe, but to the degree you take it?"

She really did appreciate how he looked out for her best interests, even though he was way off base here. "Put yourself in a witness's situation," she felt compelled to explain. "They've had to give up everything they know. Family. Friends. Jobs they like. They can't work in their chosen fields anymore. Even anything related to them. Some have kids who resent being moved, who rebel. How can I not give them my all?"

"I get it. They need you. But most of them are in that situation because of a choice they made. A choice to break the law, and they got lucky in that they aren't in prison because they testified against an even bigger criminal."

"You're right, but it doesn't make them any less deserving of grace and my help," she said, maybe trying to justify her actions when he was correct on her real motives. "To make their life in hiding easier."

He looked at her for a long moment. "We all live in hiding to some degree. You should know that. You're hiding from your parents."

"And you're hiding from what?" she snapped, letting her emotions get the best of her. "A father who you thought didn't want you as a kid, and now that you know that your mom lied, you don't know how to be with him?"

Sean jerked back.

His horrified expression tore at her heart. "Sean, I'm sorry. That was awful. Unforgivable. I don't like that you're right about me. I *am* hiding, but I don't want to admit it, and I took it out on you."

"It's okay." He clasped her hand between his strong fingers. "We both need to face the fact that people in hiding want someone to care enough to look for them, and we're no exception. Even if we don't like it."

Was he right? Did she want him to keep digging to reveal her issues? For her parents to come looking for her? To admit they were wrong?

Sure she did, but it wouldn't change anything.

She took her hand back and peered across the street. Time ticked by in silence. A heavy silence that felt overpowering. She was about to crack the window for some much-needed fresh air when the front door of the bungalow opened and a short, wide man lumbered down the steps.

"That's him," Taylor said, stowing her angst and reaching for the door handle.

CHAPTER 23

Sean and Taylor followed Hall to the end of the block, where he plopped down on a bus stop bench inside a small enclosure. *Perfect.* Sean was thankful the guy couldn't run from them like suspects often chose to do. Not that a man of his size could come close to outrunning either of them.

Sean stopped in front of Hall, blocking his escape. "You Chris Hall?"

He arched an eyebrow. "Who wants to know?"

Sean didn't want a prolonged dance, so he pulled out his credentials. "Special Agent Sean Nichols, and this is Deputy Taylor Mills."

Hall focused on Taylor, offering her a shy smile.

"Your name came up in our investigation," Sean said.

"Me?" His smile disappeared, and he reluctantly dragged his gaze from Taylor. "Where?"

Sean had the guy's attention now and wouldn't waste any more time. "You posted on the internet that you were digging a tunnel for a notorious hacker."

"Far as I know, digging's not against the law." He raised his pudgy face and poked out his chin. "And it's not a crime to post in forums online."

"But hacking is."

"I'm not a hacker." He shot to his feet so fast that he wobbled and had to grab a corner post of the shelter to steady himself.

"Maybe not." Taylor raised her shoulders and firmed her stance. "But you're associating with a wanted criminal. As such, we could take you in for questioning. You need to answer our questions if you don't want that to happen."

His eyes widened, then narrowed in a quick flash. "What do you want to know?"

"Start by giving us the address for the house where you're digging the tunnel," Taylor said.

"I don't know it." He sounded confident, but a tremor rattled his hand that had come to rest on his belly.

"Oh, come on," Sean said, wishing suspects would simply cooperate. "How do you get to the house to dig then?"

Hall glared at Sean. "He rents a car, picks me up on a street corner, and blindfolds me. He drives around for about an hour. Makes like a ton of turns to keep me from figuring out our location. Best I can say from using his wireless network for my cell is that the house is somewhere in Washington."

"You really believe that?" Sean eyed the guy.

Hall's forehead creased. "Sure, why not?"

If Hall couldn't figure this out, Sean was beginning to see why the man continued to be unemployed in the IT field. "If he works so hard to hide his house location, he's smart enough to spoof his router."

"Well duh." Hall slapped a palm against his forehead. "I should have thought of that. But honestly, I don't care where his house is. It's just cool hanging out with him."

Sean got out his phone and opened Taylor's sketch of Phantom. "Do you recognize this man?"

Hall glanced at the photo, then looked down and stabbed a toe at the concrete, acting as if watching his foot was more important than answering. Sean waited a few beats to give the guy a chance to respond, but when he lifted his head, his lips were compressed into a hard line of silence.

Sean jiggled the phone. "Refusing to tell us what you know about this man gives us cause to arrest you for accessory to murder."

"What?" Hall shot a look around as if searching for an escape route. "I didn't kill anyone. Or help kill anyone."

"If you don't assist us in locating this hacker," Taylor said, her tone quiet but powerful, "and the crime he's involved in results in murder—which is the direction it's heading—you'll be charged as an accessory."

"Fine." He crossed his arms and stared at her. "That's him."

Taylor fired a look right back in his direction. "Then we want you to help us find him."

Hall clenched his hands together, his mouth closed, and he didn't look like he intended to say another word. Just when Sean thought he'd have to haul out handcuffs, Hall sighed and said, "Tomorrow. I dig tomorrow."

Sean glanced at Taylor, and he caught a flash of excitement in her eyes. He felt the same way and wanted to pump his fist in the air to celebrate over finally having something to go on, but he wouldn't let Hall see his enthusiasm or the guy could use it against them.

Sean nodded at Hall. "You'll come with us now and hand over your phone for some modifications."

Hall's face blanched. "If you think you can put a GPS tracker on it, you're wrong. He does a sweep before we go anywhere. He'll kill me if he finds it."

"Trust me," Sean said. "I'm going to turn the tables on him, and he won't catch on to my methods."

"I don't know." Hall chewed on his thick lower lip. "He's pretty smart. Cautious. Like paranoid. And he's vindictive. I've seen the way he acts with people who don't follow his every command. And I've heard he killed someone." The last words came out in a whisper.

"And yet you're willing to work with him." Taylor shook her head.

"He's like this legend," Hall grumbled. "And I knew I wouldn't disappoint him, so no worries on my behalf. But this tracker. No. That he's going to find."

Sean was so over discussing their plans with the guy. "He won't find it, but it doesn't matter if he does, because you're going to pack a bag and move into our safe house until he's behind bars."

"No. No. No. No." Hall frantically looked around. "That will just prove to him that I helped you find him."

"Would you rather have that happen or wind up dead?" Sean held out his hand. "I need your phone."

"But I—"

Sean wiggled his hand. "Don't waste our time arguing. You're going to give it to us in the end so just do it now."

"Please." Taylor turned one of her irresistible smiles on Hall.

A dopey smile replaced his fear, and without looking away from Taylor, he set the phone in Sean's hand.

Sean woke it up. "And password?"

"Hotstuff," Hall said without so much as a blink of his eye.

Sean had to swallow down a sarcastic response and typed in the password. He made sure GPS was turned off, then located the texts and noted that Phantom had consistently used the same phone number when contacting Hall. Exactly what Sean wanted to see. He pointed down the street. "Let's get your things."

Hall stomped down the sidewalk, leaving a strong trail of body odor behind him.

Taylor coughed. "And we're going to get into a car with him?" she asked quietly.

"I'll open the windows," Sean said.

She grimaced. "I don't like the idea of putting him in the same house as Dustee, and not because of his smell. I don't want to give Phantom another reason to want to look for her location."

Sean agreed wholeheartedly. "With everything we have to think about, I'd rather pawn off Hall's protection detail to someone else anyway. Give me another safe house to put him in, and I'll be glad to send him there."

"I'll call Inman while Hall packs his things. With his connection to Phantom, I know we can find a place for Hall."

Sean ushered Hall and Taylor into the FBI's small conference room and left the door open in self-defense. He held up Hall's phone and looked at Taylor. "I'm going to get Mack started on this. I'll be right back."

He felt bad about leaving her in the room with Hall, who was staring at her like she was a nice big juicy steak, but prepping the phone was vital to finding Phantom. Acid burned up

Sean's throat, and he stopped outside the other conference room to chew an antacid. At the rate he was going through these, he would have to see a doctor for a prescription to control the problem.

Or maybe start trusting God to eliminate the worry.

All true, but he had no time to ponder that at the moment, so he swallowed the chalky tablet and entered the room where his teammates were seated behind laptops.

Sean headed straight for Mack but remained standing. "I've got a phone for you to infect."

That got Mack's attention, and he looked up. "I'm listening."

"Belongs to Chris Hall." Sean handed it to Mack. "Get a warrant for the telecom to install the FinFisher Trojan via a software update. It has to happen today. Phantom's calling Hall tomorrow." Sean explained Phantom's transport procedure.

Mack shook his head. "He's one suspicious dude."

"FinFisher Trojan." Dustee lowered the screen on her laptop. "That's spyware, right?"

Sean nodded. "It's packaged as an operating system update. We hope Phantom won't think anything of installing it, giving us control of his phone, and then we can track his location."

"Wouldn't it be easier to just follow him?" Kiley asked.

Sean shook his head. "He's too smart, and as Mack said, seriously too paranoid to tail."

"What about a drone?" Mack asked.

"He'd pick up on that too, and we'd just end up spooking him. This is our best bet." Sean pointed at the phone. "Also, Phantom's likely carrying more than one phone. So I want you to get authorization for Google to serve a reverse search warrant for the last date he transported Hall."

"Whoa, what's that?" Dustee asked. "I've never heard of it."

Sean wasn't surprised. It didn't often make the news because Google rarely agreed to participate. "Google will cast a geographic net based on the use of Android operating systems on cellphones and other mobile devices in the area and time where Hall is usually picked up."

"They give you a list of every cellphone in the area?" Dustee asked. "So like if I happened to be there, my number would show up?"

"Yeah, for Android phones," Cam joined in, his forehead furrowed. "And that'll be even harder to get than the phone update."

Mack peered up at Sean. "You think the judge will go for that?"

Sean widened his stance. "You're going to make sure he does. Involve Eisenhower if you need to. I also want you to recover all of Hall's texts to and from Phantom."

"At least that part will be easy," Mack stated. "I'll get started right away."

"Thanks," Sean said and started for the door.

"By the way," Mack called after him, "the prints at the Marshals' office came back and almost every print linked to staff. No match on the others in AFIS."

"And the server room?" Sean asked, hoping for some good news.

"Only Hershel's prints."

Sean expected that but couldn't say he wasn't disappointed. "And Enzo's daughter?"

"She didn't text him and has no idea why he was there or that he had any contact with Phantom outside of the bus trip." Mack frowned. "Poor woman was really torn up."

"A violent death is hard to recover from." Sean may have stated the facts in a level tone, but he was still struggling over his responsibility in Enzo's murder. "Let's get going on the warrants and make Enzo's killer pay. The rest of you keep working on the code."

Kiley's focus locked on him. "I never knew you could be such a taskmaster."

"I'm not going to let this investigation go cold like . . ." He didn't add the Montgomery Three. He didn't have to. Their tight faces said they got it, and Dustee's questioning arch of her eyebrow told him she planned to ask about it.

"I'll be in the small conference room with Hall

316

and Taylor or transporting Hall to a safe house," he said before she did. "Let me know the minute you get the warrants and the texts."

Sean returned to the conference room, and Taylor let out a long, thankful sigh.

"Sorry," he whispered as he sat next to her and across from Hall, who was still looking at her like he'd found his long-lost love.

"You better be," she whispered back.

"What're you two talking about?" Hall asked.

Sean wasn't going to explain anything to this man and fully intended to ignore any and all of his questions in favor of asking his own questions. "Tell me how Phantom first contacted you."

"In a forum." Hall fidgeted with a button on his shirt. "He posted about needing someone to help with a secret project. I thought I'd be doing some sick programming." He laughed, his belly rolling with each burst like waves onto a beach. "Boy was I wrong."

"Did you know who he was?" Sean asked, keeping them on track.

Hall shook his head. "He used a screen name. But I'd seen his other posts. Figured from the technical things he posted that he was a hacker. Then when we met, he was too paranoid for someone who was legit. I mean, I'm only digging a tunnel, and he does like this in-depth background check on me."

Sean wasn't surprised by the check, but the more he learned about Hall, the more Sean was shocked that Phantom associated with him. "Why did he choose you?"

"He actually liked that I couldn't keep a job." Hall grinned. "Said I was disenfranchised and would understand his work. But he never really told me about his work. He never really said much at all."

"Why was he building the tunnel?" Taylor asked.

"An emergency escape route. I figured as a hacker, he might need to get away from guys like you." Hall smirked.

Taylor frowned. "Is the tunnel finished?"

"No. But it's close. Maybe one more dig will do it, two if I stretch it out." Hall's snide grin returned.

Sean, feeling sorry for Taylor sitting under this man's obvious infatuation, had heard enough to make a final plan. He stood. "Hang tight. We'll get the protection detail set up and transport you to your new home away from home."

Hall's cocky attitude vanished. "You're sure Phantom can't find me there?"

"Sure?" Sean eyed the guy. "When it comes to Phantom, I can't be sure of anything except he's a master of evasion."

Taylor let the water sluice over her body. Just being with Hall for the few hours it took to get him settled and agents to arrive for his detail left her feeling in need of this shower. She wished she could clear the smell from her nose as easily. And maybe her brain from the way the guy kept coming on to her. Thankfully, Sean eventually shot him down by putting his arm around her and saying they were a couple. She liked the way she felt snuggled close to his side, his arm tightly holding her. Liked it way too much. His touch. The warmth.

Grrr. Stop thinking about him.

She scrubbed hard to distract herself and finished up quickly instead of lingering and letting her mind wander. She dried and applied her own bandage on the wound that was healing well. After dressing in yoga pants and a soft sweatshirt for comfort, she dried her hair and put on a bit of makeup. Not for Sean. For herself.

Sure, that's why.

In the family room, she spotted Sean sitting alone on a love seat, a laptop on his knees. He'd changed into athletic pants and a dark gray T-shirt. He seemed more relaxed, or maybe it was his casual clothing. Either way, she liked the look, and that he didn't appear as stressed out as before.

Should she just walk on by or join him? She didn't want to be near Hall, but his computer was a different story. She was curious about what the forum conversations contained.

Sean looked up and ran his gaze over her slowly. "Wow. You look fresh and comfortable all at the same time."

Her skin tingled with his compliment, though she wouldn't let it get to her. "I had to wash Hall's scent down the drain."

"Yeah, I showered too." He chuckled. "No wonder the guy can't hold a job."

She sat on the sofa.

"Need help bandaging your arm?" he asked.

She shook her head. "If I get it at the right angle, I can do it myself now without pain."

"So no more playing doctor?" He grinned.

She rolled her eyes but couldn't stop the laugh that escaped.

"I got a call a few minutes ago," he said, sobering. "They found the bullet casing."

"The shooter didn't police his brass." She was glad he didn't pick up his casing to keep law enforcement from processing it. "Odd, right?"

"It ejected into the hollow of a tree. Shooter probably couldn't find it and didn't want to risk hanging out there."

"Fingerprints?"

He shook his head. "And the slug was too mangled once it lodged in the SUV's door to analyze it, other than determine it was a .30-06. Likely chambered in a bolt-action hunting rifle."

"Wow . . . oh . . . wow." Her heart sank. "He meant business then."

Sean nodded. "Unfortunately, trying to narrow down a list of shooters with such a popular round is next to impossible. They did find a boot print at the shooter's stand and cast it. They'll get back to us if it leads anywhere."

No one should be able to shoot her and get away with it. No one. But it was looking like this guy might escape again. She looked down to gain her composure, and her focus landed on the computer on Sean's lap. "Is that Hall's computer?"

He nodded. "I've been looking at the phrasing of Phantom's posts to see if they match the tone of his emails from the old investigation."

"Can I see it?" She scooted next to him to get a better view of the screen. Or maybe in her mood, she wanted to be nearer to him. She couldn't be sure.

Sean swiveled the computer and raised his arm along the back of the sofa, allowing her to move even closer. Sliding nearer to him was surely a mistake. So what? She just needed to put her attention on the screen. "He used Ghost as his screen name. Maybe a play on Phantom."

"Yeah." Sean's breath was warm on her skin.

Ignore it. Ignore him. She started reading the posts. "The phrasing seems the same to me."

"Are you certain?"

She looked up at him and nodded, but gone was the bit of a hold she had on her emotions. Longing filled his expression, and she got lost in his eyes. She was vaguely aware of him setting the computer aside but intimately aware of his arm coming down on her shoulders, and his hand gripping her good arm to draw her closer. He shifted a bit. Lowered his head.

Her breath caught. He was going to kiss her, and she would let him. Not only let him, but encourage him. She raised up and lifted her hand to clasp the back of his neck, his skin warm against her palm. His soft intake of breath, his anticipation, thrilled her. His breathing became ragged.

He lowered his head, and his eyes closed. He gently touched his lips to hers, and an explosion rang through her brain. His kiss was slow and thorough, and she returned it measure for measure. Lost herself in it. Lost sight of everything around them. She'd never felt anything like this. Nothing at all came close.

His powerful arms slipped around her waist and pulled her tighter. She slid her arms around his neck, her injury aching, but she didn't care. She clung to him. Deepened the kiss. Wanted it to go on forever.

A door slammed in the hallway. Cutting through her fog.

Sean pulled back, his expression contrite and sad at the same time. "That was wrong. I'm sorry. I shouldn't have. We're colleagues. Friends. I don't want to ruin that, and there can be nothing more."

"Don't worry." She let out a shaky breath. "I wanted you to kiss me."

"You did?"

"Yes. I think I wanted it since I first saw you in the lobby. My 'friends only' feeling evaporated then, but I've been fighting it because, as you said, it can go nowhere."

"What if we ignored everything but this? You and me?" He stroked the side of her face. "How could we even have a relationship? We live on opposite coasts, and we both like our jobs too much to move."

"Which makes this even more impossible, and we need to be careful not to let it go any further or we'll both get hurt. And like you said, then our friendship will be strained."

He took an unsteady breath. "I'm beginning to see why Addison couldn't work with Mack, and it may not be his fault after all."

She nodded. "He's a good guy, Sean. You should cut him some slack all around."

"You and him. You go way back, right? So was there ever anything between you two?"

"Never. He was already dating Addison by the time we met. And I honestly believe he thinks of me like a kid sister. At least that's the vibe I always got."

"Yeah, I can see that." Sean sighed. "Now anyway."

"What?" She stared at him. "Wait, you thought

that Mack and I, that we had a thing together?"

He leaned back. "He keeps touching you, and he calls you Slim in an endearing way."

She'd also noticed Mack had been a little more affectionate than usual. "I wonder if he's lonely without Addison, so he's extra happy to see an old friend. But it's nothing more. I wish they'd get back together. You know neither one of them has filed for divorce."

Sean's eyes narrowed. "I didn't know that."

"So maybe they're holding out hope for a reconciliation." She gazed at Sean. "And you now know I don't have any feelings for Mack. I've reserved all those feelings for you . . . for all the good it does either of us."

CHAPTER 24

Sean looked out the FBI conference room window where the team and Dustee had gathered to start the day. Rain pelted the glass, and the forecast predicted a solid week of rain. Sean didn't know how anyone lived with constant precipitation for months on end. He needed more sunshine. Much more.

Mack ended his call and set his phone on the table. "Got the list of phones from the reverse warrant. Ten devices in the area. I'll get started tracking them down."

"Great." Sean took a quick sip of his fresh coffee. "And the software update?"

"Good news there." Mack smiled. "It was served to Phantom, and he's deployed it. Once he texts or makes a call, we'll have his location."

Sean nodded his thanks. He really did appreciate Mack's skills and work ethic and his dedication to the team. Maybe Taylor was right, and Sean had been focusing only on Mack's negative points.

"Good work," Sean said with enthusiasm, as it wasn't easy to accomplish these items much less do so under such a tight deadline.

The tough guy's face colored. A real shocker and proof that Sean could do a better job as a leader. He had to change. Be more positive with Mack in the future and a better leader overall if he wanted to keep running investigations.

Still, Sean ignored Mack's response to keep from embarrassing him and glanced at his watch. "Two hours until Phantom's routine text to Hall."

Taylor rubbed her eyes. "What if he doesn't text?"

Sean desperately hoped that wouldn't happen. "With control of his phone, we can remotely turn on his GPS and get his location."

Dustee cocked her head. "Why not do that now?"

"It would alert him that we've taken control of his phone," Sean said. "He could bolt before we get to his location and arrest him. But it's a fallback plan for sure."

Sean gestured to the door and smiled at Taylor. "We should get over to Hall's safe house to be ready for Phantom's text."

Taylor returned his smile, and his heart lifted. It would be amazing if he could eliminate the stress in her life so she could not only smile like this more but laugh too. Forever.

Wait, what? Did he not only want a relationship with her but a till-death-do-us-part kind of relationship? Stunned, he stared at her. Last night's kiss came to mind. Man, what a kiss. Perfection. At least from Sean's perspective. Taylor sure seemed to enjoy it too.

She got up and quirked an eyebrow. "You

coming, or are you going to let a little odor get in your way?"

The words registered in his brain, but with her adorable gaze fixed on him, he was unable to move or respond.

"You all right, boss?" Kiley's concerned tone broke through. "You seem a million miles away."

Right. Work. He was here to work, not admire the way Taylor's soft green sweater brought out the red highlights in her hair. He blinked a few times to clear his head and gathered his things. "I'm good. Just a lot going on."

"You know." Cam looked up from his computer. "We never took time to celebrate that the vulnerable witnesses have been moved and no one was murdered."

"You're right," Sean said. "We may not have Phantom yet, but we need to take a moment to savor the win." He held up his coffee cup in a mock toast. "To Cam, for his hard work in finding the vulnerable witnesses."

The others tapped their paper cups against his, and a hopeful spirit left Sean feeling optimistic. Maybe they really could bring Phantom in without any loss of life.

Sean slipped into his jacket. His phone rang and he dug it out. "I need to take this. It's Eisenhower."

"If he's calling, that can't be good," Kiley muttered, putting voice to Sean's thoughts.

"Sir," Sean answered.

"You alone?" Eisenhower's deep voice rumbled through the phone.

Sean's gut clenched. "No, the team's here with me."

"Then go ahead and put me on speaker."

"Hold on a second." Sean thought Eisenhower was sounding overly dramatic, but Sean put his boss on hold and opened the door. "Dustee, I need you to step into the hall with Snow for a minute."

She glared at him but got up and left without arguing for once.

"Keep an eye on her for a few minutes," Sean told Snow and closed the door.

Taylor had taken a seat, and Sean dropped into the nearest chair. He tapped his speaker button and set his phone on the table. "Go ahead, sir."

"Just left a briefing on the WITSEC database," Eisenhower said. "As I mentioned before, the Marshals' IT staff has been reviewing the hack too."

"And?" Sean's gut clenched. Gone was the good mood of a few moments ago.

"The administrator found large packets of data leaving the network long before the hack."

"Packets of data?" Taylor asked.

"Means someone was stealing information." Kiley frowned. "How did he miss that when it was happening?"

Sean wanted to slam a fist into the table, but he took a deep breath instead. "Administrators often focus more on watching incoming traffic. Looking for a hack. When in reality hackers long ago infiltrated businesses and organizations and are quietly stealing data."

"The FBI's been trying to educate administrators for years." Cam frowned. He once worked as a network administrator for a large retailer, and this was a sore spot with him. "Outgoing data is one of the biggest problems facing corporations today, but many administrators refuse to believe they've been infiltrated."

"This administrator will now," Eisenhower said. "In his next job."

"The guy was sacked. Good." Cam gave a firm nod. "Hopefully the new administrator will learn from this."

"But that's not why you're calling, is it?" Sean asked.

"No." The single word resonated through the room. "Records indicate that the hacker quietly downloaded the entire database long before you discovered the hack."

"No!" Taylor shot to her feet. "That's thousands of records. Every witness is in jeopardy now."

"Exactly," Eisenhower said, his tone dire.

"The obvious hack was a smokescreen to make us think Phantom took only select records." Sean curled his fingers into tight fists. "We should've known Phantom would do something like this."

"Why didn't Roger mention this?" Taylor asked. "He had to have accessed the computer twice."

Sean thought back through their interview. "We were never specific on dates. He probably thought we knew about both times."

Kiley clutched her hands together. "If only we'd dug deeper."

Taylor fell back against her seat. The shocked expressions of his teammates mimicked Taylor's bewildered look.

"Sorry to be the bearer of such bad news," Eisenhower said. "At this point, we have only one way to keep the witnesses alive. It's up to all of you to find Phantom and recover the stolen data."

Sean shoved two antacids into his mouth. With the dire circumstances they were now facing, he didn't care if the team saw him toss in a whole roll of them. Not that they were even noticing him. They'd all been staring at the table since Eisenhower ended the call with a promise of sending the administrator's report to them.

Sean felt empty inside. Hollow. Like a shell. And a failure. He swallowed and tried to come up with his next step.

Taylor rested a hand on his arm. "What are we going to do?" she whispered, and her voice broke. "My people. I need to . . . we need to . . ."

Sean took her hand and held it under the table. He might not be able to figure out proper action steps right now, but he had to be strong for her. For the devastated team. As lead on this investigation, he was responsible for their attitude and mood.

He squeezed Taylor's hand and stood. "I know this is a blow. A big one. One you don't think we can recover from, but we can."

"How?" Kiley frowned at him. "I don't know how many records are for living and active witnesses, but even if it's only fifty percent of the database, we have like nine thousand people counting on us. Nine thousand!"

"And that's exactly why we have to let go of our shock and get to work." Sean made sure he sounded confident. "As Eisenhower said, we're the only ones who can stop Phantom."

Mack sat up straight, determined. "What do you want us to do?"

"Taylor and I will still go to the safe house to take Phantom's call. Kiley and Cam, get started on the files Eisenhower is sending. Mack, review every detail from the physical investigations and come up with a lead or two that we missed."

They all nodded.

"And for goodness' sake, stop looking so devastated or Dustee will know something terrible is going on and not stop asking you about it." He smiled, hoping to lighten the mood, but received only blank stares in return.

He didn't like leaving the team like this, but he had no choice. Phantom would be calling soon. He opened the door and motioned for Dustee to enter.

She searched everyone's faces. "You all look like someone died."

Sean eyed his team. "I'll report in after Phantom makes contact."

In the hallway, he glanced at Snow. "We'll be back soon."

Taylor drew in a deep breath and let it out. Her face was tight with worry. Without giving it any thought, he took her hand as they started down the hall. Her mouth fell open, Snow's likely dropping open too, but Sean clung to her all the same.

She eased her hand free. "What's up with the hand-holding?"

"It just felt right."

"Yeah . . . well . . ." She shrugged.

They stepped into the parking garage, and she lifted her jacket collar against the damp and chilly air.

He opened her car door, and though he shouldn't keep the personal conversation going, he couldn't stop himself. "I guess it wasn't right for you. The hand-holding, I mean."

"Oh, no . . . I liked it just fine, but we're

working." Her forehead creased. "And with the recent news, we need to focus even more."

He wanted to smooth out the wrinkles with his thumb but restrained himself. "Yeah, I shouldn't have done it at all. Let alone at work and with all these witnesses depending on us. I'm sorry."

She looked into his eyes. "It's all right, but let's not do it again, okay? Even if we don't have people like Snow watching, it'll only make it harder to stay friends when this is over."

He nodded, but with her warm topaz eyes fastened on him, the vulnerability still lodged deep inside, he wanted to draw her into his arms and let her lean on him even more than holding her hand.

But he fought hard against his feelings and stepped back to wait for her to slide her long legs into the SUV. Of course she would have chosen today to wear a skirt. He watched as each shapely leg lifted into the vehicle and settled in place. She crossed her legs at the ankles, her heels resting on the carpet.

"Is there something you need, Sean?" she asked.

He found that eyebrow quirked again. She knew he was admiring her. After all, he didn't even try to hide it. He shook his head to answer her question. Maybe to clear his brain too, as he was in part letting her get to him so he didn't have to think about the added pressure. But he had to.

Focus. Focus. Focus. You have thousands of people counting on your ability to do so.

He took several cleansing breaths and slipped behind the wheel, his mind all business now. He got the SUV headed down the highway and turned into the safe house driveway without any further personal discussion.

As he parked, Taylor swiveled. "What do you think the odds are that Phantom will text and we'll pinpoint his location?"

"I'd say they're good." Sean removed the keys. "He has no reason to think Hall's been compromised."

"When we respond to his text, will he be able to tell where the text came from?"

Sean shook his head. "The only way he could do that is if he installed spyware on Hall's phone, and we confirmed his phone is clean." Sean thought for a moment. "I suppose he could have someone inside the phone company who could check the account, but the odds of that happening are slim to none."

"Still, we're talking about Phantom here. Shouldn't we assume he has a person who can track the phone?"

"You're right. We should change locations. Go somewhere with a lot of people." He smiled at her. "We'll take Hall on a field trip."

"Oh yay. Close quarters with him." She rolled her eyes and got out.

He exited the SUV, marched up to the porch, and knocked on the door. Agent Kemp, a burly guy with jet-black hair and a fierce scowl, answered the door and stepped back. Sean chose him because he was a member of the local FBI SWAT team, and his black tactical pants and shirt made him look every bit the part.

"Everything okay?" Sean asked.

He gave a firm nod. "Nothing out of the ordinary."

Sean expected him to complain about Hall's odor, but when they went into the family room and Hall rushed up to them, the guy didn't reek.

Sean spun to look at Kemp. A cocky smile crossed his mouth. Sean didn't know how Kemp did it, but he'd obviously convinced Hall to clean up his act. A refreshing surprise.

Hall locked his focus on Taylor and started in her direction. She fired him a warning look, and he stopped dead in his tracks.

"We're going for a drive," she said. "Somewhere public. Just in case Phantom can track your responding text."

Hall scratched his chin. "Nah, man. He can't do that, can he?"

"Not without your telecom's help," she said. "But we're taking no chances with your safety."

"Hey, thanks." He looked at Taylor as if he thought she was doing this for him because they had a connection.

Sean didn't correct him. Better to have him think he was indebted to them. He turned to Kemp. "I'd like you to join us."

"Roger that." Kemp didn't waste time, but led the way to the door.

Sean stood back gesturing for Hall to go first. The guy cast a longing look at Taylor, sighed, and lumbered toward the door. Sean had Hall take the back seat by Kemp for added protection, and he drove for miles to put distance between the safe house and the call. When he spotted a Starbucks, he pulled into the busy lot and parked. He removed Hall's phone from the Faraday bag where he'd stored it for protection. He quickly confirmed the battery was charged and then looked at Hall in the mirror. "Now we wait."

He crossed beefy arms over his large stomach. "I don't like sitting out in the open like this."

"Phantom has never killed anyone in broad daylight," Sean said. "Or even tried as far as we know."

"There's a first time for everything," Hall grumbled.

"Even so." Taylor swiveled to look at the guy. "It's highly unlikely that he knows our location."

The phone chimed in Sean's hand, startling him. "He's early."

Hall's worried gaze flashed up to the rearview mirror. "Do you think that means something? Like he knows something's up?"

"Not likely."

Hall frowned. "But in the past, he called at the same time like clockwork."

"Don't read too much into this." Sean opened the text. "He's asking you to dig tomorrow and will pick you up at the same location at ten a.m. What would you say in reply?"

"I'll be there."

Sean typed in the message and hit send. It took only seconds before Phantom confirmed he'd meet at the predetermined location. Sean wanted to smile at their success, but how could he when they weren't out of the woods in the least? Thousands of lives depended on this text revealing Phantom's location, and until Sean got back to the office, he wouldn't know if they'd succeeded.

Taylor stepped into the FBI conference room that was becoming her home away from home. Sean hurried after her. Cam and Kiley were missing, but a new sense of urgency hung in the air.

Mack shot them a pressing look. " 'Bout time you two got back here. I've got Phantom's location."

Taylor hurried to Mack's side of the table, Sean barreling behind her. She half expected him to push her out of the way to get to Mack first. "Where did he call from?"

Mack pointed at a single-story home in an older

neighborhood on the east side of Portland. "Place is registered to a Patrick Jorgenson."

"The same initials as Paul Jackson." Sean's breath was warm on her neck as he leaned over.

"That was my first thought too." Mack clicked on a link to property records, and detailed information on the address filled the screen. "He inherited the house from his parents. I can dig deeper into the prior owners if needed, but I thought it more important to get Jorgenson's driver's license photo." Mack clicked on a different tab, revealing a man's picture.

"He's a perfect match for the sketch artist rendering." Sean squinted at the picture. "He's, what, thirty-seven? Do we know anything more about him?"

"No criminal record." Mack shifted in his chair. "Not even a parking ticket."

Sean stood to his full height. "Looks like Jorgenson is our guy. We need to find him."

"He's driving a 2008 Dodge Ram, silver. Already got Kiley and Cam on their way to do recon on the property. If the truck isn't there, I'll issue an alert. And I've obtained aerial maps and have drafted a preliminary assault plan."

"All in an hour?" Taylor asked.

"What can I say?" Mack blew on fingernails and brushed them against his shirt. "I'm just that good."

Taylor laughed, and it felt good to break the

tense atmosphere. Likely Mack's purpose in cracking the joke.

"Excellent work," Sean said, sounding like he meant it.

That caught Mack's attention, and he flashed Sean a wide-eyed look.

Sean's lips puckered. "What? Can't a guy compliment you without you making a big deal of it?"

"A guy can, but you?" Mack shook his head. "Doesn't happen often."

"I . . . I . . ." Sean cleared his throat. "Print me a copy of the report."

"Already done." Mack picked up a packet from the table and handed it to Sean, then gave one to Taylor.

"Thanks, Mack." Taylor squeezed his shoulder, but her thoughts remained on Sean. This was the second time Sean complimented Mack today. Had Sean listened to her suggestion and opened his mind to see the real Mack?

If so, thank you for that.

Sean started reading. His forehead furrowed, and he dropped onto a chair.

"Since everyone else is busy, I can search the internet for information on this Jorgenson guy," Dustee offered. "I mean, looking at the code isn't really relevant anymore."

Sean shook his head. "I can't have you doing that. Not without someone looking over your shoulder, and as you said, we're all busy. More than ever now."

"Thanks for nothing." She directed a glare at Sean and crossed her arms, then leaned back in her chair, looking more like a petulant teenager than a grown woman.

"Besides," Sean continued, "your work on the code *is* still relevant. Anything you uncover will be used in court when Phantom goes to trial."

"Like that's any fun." She slumped down.

Taylor had just about had it with Dustee's attitude, but she wouldn't snap at her. Taylor took a calming breath and worked hard to find a civil tone. "Sean's not being unreasonable, Dustee. You shouldn't even be on a computer, and he arranged for this chance. So don't take it out on him."

"But I proved I can be trusted," she whined. "Been doing this for days, and I haven't tried a thing."

"I appreciate that," Sean said. "But I can't afford any mistakes."

"And you still think I might contact Phantom?" She grimaced. "Unbelievable."

Sean didn't respond, but Taylor could read his thoughts just by the pinched look on his face. He didn't trust Dustee because he didn't trust anyone.

No one. Not even Taylor.

CHAPTER 25

Hours passed while they finalized the assault plan with all the players involved. Sean and Taylor now stood near the SUV just down the street from Jorgenson's house, along with Agent Kemp, who held a heavy battering ram. They awaited the signal that Mack and Kiley were in position, and Sean was amped. Not only from adrenaline, but also from hopefully outsmarting Phantom. The team never had the opportunity to make an arrest in the Montgomery Three investigation, and somehow he felt vindicated by at least bringing in the man who had the potential to expose thousands of witnesses to people who wanted them dead.

"In position," Mack said over Sean's earpiece. "All quiet."

One down, one to go.

"You're jonesing to get in there," Taylor said.

"Aren't you?"

"Yeah."

"In position. No movement inside." Kiley's voice rang clear. "Still no vehicle in the garage. Curtains are closed. Do not have eyes on suspect."

"Roger that. Stay alert. We're headed to the door." Sean looked at Taylor. "Let's do this."

She nodded, and he took off, knowing she'd be right behind him. He kept his head on a swivel, his assault rifle up. They took hurried but careful steps down the street and up the sidewalk to the door. He only hoped the neighbors didn't come outside. In a perfect scenario, Sean would have evacuated the nearby homes, but he didn't want to take any chances with tipping off Phantom. He'd informed PPB of the op, as residents often spotted guns and called 911. Then local police came screaming to the scene, ruining the op, and Sean wouldn't let that happen here.

He pounded on the door with the side of his fist. "Police! Open up."

Taylor cocked her head and listened. Sean thought he heard movement inside. He pounded on the door again. "Police. This is your last chance, Jorgenson, before we break down the door."

Sean listened. Nothing. Silence. Maybe they'd heard a cat or dog. Or maybe Phantom was taking a defensive stance. If so, they needed to be ready. Sean lifted his assault rifle and signaled for Taylor to do the same. She'd told him she rarely used one in her years as a deputy, but she stayed current on her skills at the firing range. Still, her injured arm could affect her shooting accuracy.

Sean counted to ten. No response. He wouldn't stand around any longer. He leaned down to his mic. "We're going in on my signal. Stay alert."

"Roger that," Mack replied, as did Kiley.

Sean stepped to the side and signaled for Kemp to use his battering ram.

He slammed it against the door, splintering the wood. The door burst open, hit the wall with a sharp bang, and flew back. Sean pressed it out of the way and signaled his plan to enter first. Kemp gave a swift nod and stepped back. Taylor met his gaze and gave him a *be careful* look.

Heart pounding hard, Sean burst into the foyer. A small living area with a tall fireplace and overstuffed furniture sat to the right. Dining room to the left.

"Clear," he called out and headed left, the three of them packed into a tight trio of firepower. He swept the dining room. "Clear."

They moved into a small kitchen with an eat-in area and door to the backyard, with steps to the basement and the tunnel. He wanted to race down to it, but first they had to check the main floors to remove any threat from above. In the hallway, they cleared two bedrooms and a bathroom. The final bedroom was set up as a basic office with expensive computer equipment filling the desks lining the room's perimeter. The sound of whirring hard drives brought Sean to a stop.

Protocol required that he wait for computer techs to image the hard drives before he or his team touched them. The computer snapshots in their current condition would be used as evidence when Phantom sat before a jury. But with the hacker's past history of wiping drives clean, Sean couldn't risk losing the data and had to act now.

"Cover the door," he said to Taylor. Her rifle was raised in a defensive position. "Phantom likes to erase drives. I can't let that happen here."

Sean rushed over to the desk and jerked power cords from the backs of the machines. The drives powered down and stilled. "Okay, good. Any disk-wiping programs he kicked off have been stopped. Attic next."

They moved to the hallway hatch, and Kemp made quick work of clearing the attic space.

Sean turned to Kemp. "Agent Mills and I have the basement. You're up here watching our backs."

Since SWAT often led the way, Kemp looked skeptical, but he nodded his understanding.

Sean marched to the walled stairwell and took a breath before descending. He reached the solid concrete floor at the bottom and swung left. Found an empty, unfinished space. No Phantom. Swung right. Saw a washer and dryer in the corner. Laundry basket overflowing with clothing. A clothesline strung across the room, but still no Phantom or tunnel.

Had Hall lied?

Sean stepped to a door on the far wall and pulled it open. An ancient oil furnace took up most of the space, but in the corner he found a gaping hole in the floor. A sheet of plywood serving as a hatch lay open, and a padlock dangled from a hasp.

"Bingo," Sean whispered.

Taylor crept up to the plywood. "You think he's down there?"

"Police!" Sean directed his voice into the tunnel. "Show yourself now."

He waited. Counted.

Ten. Nine. Eight.

"Not a sound," Taylor said.

Seven. Six. Five.

"He might not be down there," she added.

Four. Three. Two. One.

Sean looked at Taylor. "I'm going down. You wait here."

"No. I'm not letting you do this alone." She eyed him.

He shook his head. "It could be an ambush, and I won't take you or anyone else with me. I'll toss a flashbang and go."

"But it—"

"Will be fine. The flashbang will blind Phantom for at least five seconds, and the afterimage will impair any aim he might have. Likely disorient him for longer. Plus the blast will disturb the fluid in his ears, deafening him and leaving him off-balance. Gives me plenty of time to get down there and point a weapon at him before he recovers."

"The explosion could make the tunnel unsteady

or even cause it to collapse." Panic sharpened her tone.

Sean appreciated her concern, but this wasn't negotiable. "That will happen before I go into the tunnel."

"It could still be unsafe to enter." She bit her lip. "SWAT should do it."

"Trust me, I know what I'm doing. I have more training and experience than any of them."

Her eyes widened. "You want me to trust you when you can't trust anyone else?"

"I trust . . . never mind. This isn't the time for that conversation." He intensified his expression. "Promise me you'll stay here until I give the all-clear."

Her stern expression wavered. "Oh, so you trust me to follow through on my promise?"

"Taylor, not now, okay? Just promise."

She solidly met his gaze. "I *do* promise. And you can trust me."

He nodded and took a step toward the tunnel. And then it hit him. She could be right. The tunnel could be unsafe and collapse on him. If that happened . . .

He turned back, pulled her against his chest, and gave her a hard, swift kiss, then released her. "I'll be okay. Don't worry."

She stood there breathing hard. "Promise?"

"I promise." He lowered the face shield on his riot helmet and tossed a flashbang into the hole.

The flash grenade exploded, the harsh sound rising up from the tunnel opening. He started down the rickety ladder. He was on the hard-packed dirt floor in seconds; the dirt walls were barely high enough for him to stand. The air cleared slightly and revealed a wide-open area with a narrow tunnel ahead. No sign of Phantom, and no place to hide.

Sean took a quick look around the space, which held a microwave, refrigerator, porta-potty, and a table with two chairs just like Hall described. Dirt clods were scattered on the cot, but no sign of Phantom.

Sean crept down the tunnel, expecting to find Phantom cowering at the end. It went on for a long stretch, curved a bit to the right, then continued on. Sean believed he'd walked the length of the property and had to be moving under the alley behind Phantom's house. The tunnel kept going.

He continued walking, step after step. The tunnel curved again. Then the end appeared with a ladder leading up to the surface.

Sean stood staring at it. Hall said it served as an escape tunnel, and Sean had hoped it would've been Phantom's end, but he'd finished it. Odd. Why arrange for Hall to dig today? Did he fear Hall had seen something that could lead to this place and planned to kill him? Sean wouldn't put it past Phantom. Didn't matter now.

Sean quickly climbed the ladder. The exit opened on the opposite side of the alley, three houses down from Phantom's place. No way would Mack have seen Phantom exit the tunnel here. Not with the tall privacy fence circling the property. If Phantom had parked his truck in this location, he could be long gone by now. If on foot, the team still had a chance to catch him.

At this point, Sean didn't care if Phantom figured out they'd hacked his phone. Sean got out his cell and opened the spyware app to access GPS. The app whirred, and a red dot displayed the location of Phantom's phone.

Sean enlarged the map. "No way."

The ping registered from inside this house. Phantom wasn't there, so he had to have left behind the phone he used to communicate with Hall.

Sean bent down to his mic. "Suspect completed tunnel and escaped in the rear alley. Could be on foot or in a vehicle." Sean provided the information on Jorgenson's truck. "Could have exited the alley in either direction."

Sean released his mic and took a moment to process. Phantom was in the wind, and there was no way to track him. Sean had failed. When the stakes were so incredibly high. Even more lives were on the line than with the Montgomery Three investigation, and he failed again.

He had totally failed.

CHAPTER 26

Sean finished the initial walk-through of the house to devise a plan for processing the scene. He'd noted the presence of potential evidence and would assign the forensic staff to begin working in those spots. The only surprise was the evidence of a female living in the home. Looked like Phantom had a girlfriend. But Sean hadn't located any pet hair, and the hair found in Dupont's car was unrelated, unless Phantom had picked it up elsewhere.

Priorities set, Sean stepped onto the porch and took in the crime scene. Officers had parked PPB patrol vehicles behind wooden barricades, blocking the road, their headlights spiraling into the foggy air that smelled of fresh rain. Nearby sat a sergeant's SUV with the husky sarge leaning against the hood, phone to his ear. The ERT van, a larger version of Anna's state vehicle, was parked at an angle just ahead of him. An FBI photographer stood on the lawn, snapping shots of the house's exterior and property, the flash a blinding light in the sky.

In a word, it was a circus, and Sean was the ringleader, trying not to fall from a high wire and botch the investigation. Cam was still researching Jorgenson, and Sean had sent Mack and Kiley back to the office to review Eisenhower's new information. Taylor remained on-scene to help keep the forensic staff on target.

He crossed over the damp grass and eased through swirling fog illuminated by Klieg lights brought in when the sun dropped below the horizon. He stopped next to the photographer. "You're free to shoot the inside."

He nodded. "Good timing. Just finished out here."

Sean continued on to the vans where he approached Anna. He'd been so impressed with her skills that he'd quickly brought her in to handle the top-priority areas. "You have the office. I want every bit of computer equipment dusted for prints and processed for DNA."

"Seriously," a male FBI tech grumbled. "We should do that."

"When you're in charge of an investigation, you can make that decision." Sean eyed the guy, and he backed down. Sean returned his focus to Anna. "You should know, I found both male and female clothing in the master closet."

She snapped on gloves. "Two occupants then."

He nodded and turned to assign the other techs to the remaining key evidence areas. He left them and approached the beefy sergeant with dark hair and wearing a pressed and crisp navy-blue PPB uniform.

Sean stopped in front of him. "How's the neighborhood canvass going?"

"Nearly finished." The sergeant clamped a hand on his holstered weapon, his expression carrying the heavy weight of catching this investigation. "One neighbor across the street reports seeing both a male and female coming and going from the house for months. Always late at night. The witness has insomnia and is up at odd hours. She tried knocking on their door several times during the day to welcome them to the neighborhood, but no response. She figured they worked nights and were sleeping, so she gave up and left them alone."

"Can she describe them?"

The sarge flipped open his small notepad. "Male is six feet and muscular. Woman a few inches shorter, of average size and build. Both have dark hair. The woman's is cut short."

Sean made a mental note of the details but would jot them down later to make sure they became part of the case file. "And did you show her the suspect's sketch?"

He nodded. "She couldn't confirm anything. Like I said, she only saw them from a distance."

"What about security cameras?"

"None in the neighborhood pointing at this house. I'll request traffic cams in the area and review them."

"I'd like a copy too."

"Sure thing." The sarge's phone rang, and he reached for it on his vest holder.

Sean had hoped the neighbors would help more, but he wouldn't let this get him down. With a girlfriend in the mix, he was hoping she wasn't as crafty as Phantom and would mess up. Or she could even have a record, and her DNA or prints would reveal her name.

He turned back to the scene and spotted Taylor stepping behind the ERT van. She'd been trying to get his attention since he'd come back from the alley, but he'd had too much to organize to talk with her. With everyone assigned now, he could take a few minutes away from the madness to clear his head and see what she wanted.

He found her seated on the vehicle bumper in the dark, her phone in her hand. She looked up and gave him a soft smile. He took a seat next to her. "Looking for some quiet?"

She held up her phone. "Called to check on Dustee."

He hadn't even thought about that. "Everything okay at the office?"

"Fine, but with Phantom still on the move, I can't be too careful." She ran her gaze over him. "How are you doing?"

"Trying not to let my anger over missing him take over," he said honestly.

"Yeah, I'm struggling with that too." She touched his hand for a fraction of a second, like a butterfly briefly landing and lifting off again. "I'm here for you if you want to talk."

"Thanks." He expected her to bring up the kiss in the basement, though that was the last topic he wanted to discuss.

Her eyes narrowed. "You don't look convinced of that."

"No, I'm grateful, it's just . . ." He shrugged.

"You thought I would want to talk about the kiss."

He couldn't believe how well she'd come to know him, and it was clear she had him pegged. "Yeah, I thought you would."

"A crime scene's not the time nor place."

Okay, she was acting exactly as he'd hoped, leaving it alone. So why did he feel disappointed? "Just so you know, I didn't plan it. Just acted. A spur-of-the-moment kind of thing."

"Yeah, I get that. Probably fueled by adrenaline." She seemed to shrug it off. "I keep wondering if Phantom really was here when we arrived."

"Honestly, I'd rather think he wasn't than he used his tunnel to evade us. But there's ice in the glass on the desk, so someone was recently here. Could be his girlfriend." Sean explained the clothes and other feminine stuff he'd found in the house. "Both of them could've bailed through the tunnel, I guess."

She frowned. "I didn't like you going into that tunnel."

"Far tamer than a lot of places I've been."

"I don't like that thought either." She released a shaky breath. "The thought of you getting hurt is almost too much to bear."

He had to play it down. "You've known what I do since we became friends."

"Yeah, I didn't like it then, but now . . ." She shrugged and looked away.

"Right." He took her hand. It was cold but soft. He held it tightly, a lifeline, letting her know he understood. "I thought the same thing about you when you insisted on coming along again. I can't lose you."

She put away her phone and took his hand. "What are we going to do about us?"

He knew she meant the feelings they were developing for each other, and he had no answer. Not a single one. "I'd like to think we could find a way to move on without hurting each other when this is over."

"What would you say if I told you I don't want to move on?" She transferred her focus to their hands. "That I like what's developing between us."

Say what? He wished she'd look at him so he could read her expression, but she kept staring at their hands. "Are you ready to let go of the no-dating edict?"

"Closer than I've ever been." Her words came out on a whispered breath.

"But still not one hundred percent sure?"

"No, not quite." She looked at him. Sadness deepened her golden eyes into a darker brown, and he couldn't hold back any longer. He didn't care where they were. A crime scene or the moon. He stood and pulled her into his arms. She came willingly into them, and he held her there, her head pressed against his chest. He stroked her hair and cradled her body with his other arm, her warmth providing comfort for everything wrong in his life.

Footfalls sounded close by, coming their way, and Taylor pushed back. He reluctantly let her go, felt alone, and wanted to reach out for her, but that would be a mistake. A big one.

"I should get inside," he said to cover the awkward silence as an ERT tech strode past.

"Yeah, me too, to help supervise." She started for the house.

They climbed the steps to the porch and both grabbed booties and gloves from boxes. He leaned against the wall to cover his tactical boots, then stopped to admire her graceful balance as she slipped on a bootie. He didn't know what he would tell her if she brought up the kiss again. Adrenaline wasn't his motivation. Not at all. He'd reacted to the possibility that he could die, and he'd wanted her soft kiss to be his last memory of her.

"Ready?" Her delicate eyebrow arched.

Despite wanting to trace a finger over it, he

nodded and followed her inside and down the hallway.

"See you later." She swung into the master bedroom.

He continued on to the office. A computer tech sat in the desk chair, his hand shoved into nutty brown shoulder-length hair. Sean didn't like the frustrated look on his narrow face and really didn't want to approach to hear bad news. But bad news or not, Sean had to hear whatever the tech had to say.

He joined the frowning man. "I take it our suspect was successful in wiping info."

The guy tapped one of the external drives, his lips in a distasteful twist. "I checked the first image. Nearly blank. Hopefully we'll have better luck with the other drives."

The news Sean expected. The drives could be the best source of information in the house, and Sean wouldn't let it get him down when they were just beginning to deal with the forensics. "It takes an hour or so to wipe a drive, and I got to the plug within five minutes of our initial approach. That should leave us something to go on."

"Yeah, maybe," the tech said, but his narrowed expression said something else.

Sean ignored it and stared at the guy. "I want a copy of those images before you leave here."

"But I—"

"Before you leave." Sean eyed him. "It's not optional."

Before he could argue again, Sean spun and strode over to Anna, clearing his mind of the computer tech's negativity on the way. She was wearing the typical white Tyvek suit, but due to her slight stature she'd bunched it up at the waist. She hunkered over a computer mouse, a long swab in hand, her face screwed up in concentration. Next to the mouse lay Phantom's phone in an evidence bag.

He put a smile in his voice. "I hope you're having better luck than the computer tech."

"I am." She put the swab into a plastic cylinder and stood. "Already lifted good latents, and we'll definitely collect DNA from the phone and the mouse—both places are notorious for that. Also, CPU and monitor switches have been processed."

She pointed at a water glass. "This glass is fresh so it's a no-brainer for DNA and prints too."

Sean was optimistic about that glass and hoped not to be let down. "What about Enzo's body? Were you able to get over to the morgue yesterday to do the swabs?"

She nodded and reached for a fresh swab container. "His neck and wrists were bruised. I swabbed those and his face. Collected several viable samples, but it was late in the day, so nothing's been processed yet."

"How soon can you get to it?"

"I plan to go back to the lab when I finish here. I'll need you to set the priority for me—which do you want first?" She waved the swab. "The samples found here or the ones from Enzo?"

"I want both."

"Of course you do." She rolled her eyes. "But the machines limit how fast I can work."

He didn't like the roadblocks that kept getting in his way, and yet it was how these investigations worked. One step forward and a few steps back. "Phantom likely wore gloves to kill Enzo, but not here in his home. So process the evidence recovered here first."

She gave another quick nod. "By the way, the ME confirmed the injuries in the prior murder match Enzo's injuries. We're looking at the same killer."

"No surprise there." Still, it was good news, as it confirmed Phantom had murdered both men.

Taylor entered the room. "I need to talk to you about something."

Sean didn't much care for her sour expression or grim tone, and the acid that had been roiling in his stomach since they'd arrived on-scene bubbled up his throat. He didn't want to upset her more and wouldn't let her see his concern. He swallowed the pain and made sure his tone was light. "What's up?"

"The FBI tech in the master is complaining about bedbugs." Taylor shuddered. "She really doesn't want to work in there, and honestly, I can see why."

Bedbugs. The tech's concern was just about bedbugs?

"Seriously, *that* grossed her out?" Anna bagged the swab container. "I for one am excited we found bedbugs."

Taylor narrowed her eyes. "Why on earth does that make you happy?"

"Simple." A smile flashed across Anna's face. "They're a perfect source for recovering human DNA. Just a single bug can identify multiple human hosts."

Taylor's mouth dropped open. "Seriously? DNA from itty-bitty bedbugs?"

Anna nodded vigorously. "Once they feed on a person, they retain their blood. I'm sure we'll get good DNA samples from all areas of this house. But if we really want to know who's actually living here, then bedbugs are the perfect answer."

CHAPTER 27

The next morning, blue skies dotted with white puffy clouds greeted Sean, the air crisp with a hint of recent rain and pine scent from the towering trees. Even though they'd struck out last night in their review of Phantom's hard drives, Sean reveled in the warm rays as he'd jogged alongside the team to run off stress. They'd had a sleepless night reviewing hard drive images from Phantom's office and found zero new leads. The run gave everyone a much-needed break to refocus and renew their minds.

They rounded the bend, heading back to the safe house, and veered as a group up the drive. At the top, everyone stopped to stretch and work out any kinks from the five-mile run. A perfect time to review the day's agenda, instead of sitting in a stuffy conference room to do so.

Sean gulped in a breath of the pine-scented air. "Anna called, saying forensics results from the house are in. I'll start the day with a visit to the lab."

Taylor propped a leg on the retaining wall. "I'm going with you."

He loved how she didn't give him a chance to argue about joining him. He'd always been drawn to her strength in their online conversations, and this quick decision told him she could make one when needed. Made him more hopeful that they were compatible after all.

She reached forward, and the smooth arch of her back and fluidity of her form held his attention. He loved her personality online, and now he could add a gorgeous smile and amazing legs that her neon-green leggings emphasized to his reasons for finding her attractive.

"Earth to Sean." Kiley waved her hand in front of his face.

Right. Work. "I received the evidence list from the house this morning. They recovered several boxes of .30-06 ammo from the garage."

Taylor's head popped up, her gaze tight. "So it *was* Phantom who shot at me."

"Looks like it," Sean said. "I'll email the evidence list to everyone. Let me know if you see anything we should pursue."

"It's not likely you missed anything," Kiley said.

Sean lifted a knee to his chest. "Still, I want you to review it. And I'd like Dustee to continue to review hard drives with you all while we're at the lab. Means I'll need a volunteer to keep an eye on her."

"I'll do it," Kiley offered.

"Seriously?" Sean cocked an eyebrow.

"What?" She firmed her shoulders.

He held up his hands. "Nothing. Just surprised."

"Yeah, well, maybe I'm adulting better than I used to."

Mack grabbed his foot behind his back to stretch. "The minute we get into the office, I'll distribute Jorgenson's DL picture to the press to replace the original sketch."

Sean nodded his approval. "Any other updates?"

"Maybe." Cam was bouncing like a kangaroo on steroids. "I think I'm on to something with one of the drives."

Sean shot him a look. "Why didn't you say anything last night?"

"I wanted to be sure."

"And are you sure now?" Sean asked.

"Ninety percent or so."

"What did you find?"

"MUMPS file fragments."

Taylor scrunched her eyes. "I assume you aren't talking about the disease?"

"It stands for the Massachusetts General Hospital Utility Multi-Programming System," Cam said.

"Oh, right, that's so much clearer." She rolled her eyes.

"The programming language was designed in the sixties for the health-care industry to solve the problem of massive data flowing into multiuser systems," Sean explained. "Today it's still widely used by government agencies and banks."

Taylor tipped her head, her focus intensifying.

"So the kind of system a hacker like Phantom would be proficient in, enabling him to commit the ultimate hack."

Sean marveled at how quickly she caught on. He faced Cam. "What do you know now that makes it more likely than last night?"

"I found a fragment of a record and evidence of a cloud storage account."

"You think we struck out on finding the database because he's storing it online?" Sean asked.

Cam nodded.

"Makes sense," Kiley said. "Phantom needs to be mobile and can't leave the files behind if he has to bolt."

Sean looked at Cam. "Your top priority is to find and hack that account."

"Of course." He grinned because hacking was one of his favorite activities, and he was very good at it.

"So let's get to it." Sean jogged up the steps, the others following him.

Before getting changed, they stopped for water, and Sean poured a cup of coffee. But with just one sip, acid burned a path up his throat. He grabbed tablets from his computer bag and scarfed them, the relief instant, but for how long?

A hand rested on his shoulder, and he swiveled to see Taylor looking at him with concern. "Maybe cut back on the coffee."

He nodded, but knew that wasn't the solution.

Faith. Trust. That was what he needed. Faith in God. Something Sean thought he possessed in abundance, yet he could see now that his hope and faith had taken a nose dive after Gina betrayed him.

One thing he'd forgotten, an important thing: God didn't betray. Didn't turn His back. He was always the same loving God. Always wanting the best for His children. Sean had to trust that He would lead them to Phantom. And if for some reason He didn't see fit to do so, it was because in His almighty power, He knew it was right for Phantom to evade capture.

Sean didn't like that thought, didn't like it one bit, but it was time he lived his own words. He squeezed her hand. "Honestly, prayer is what I need. What we all need."

"Let me," she said, then got everyone's attention.

Sean closed his eyes, and she led them all in a heartfelt prayer. When she finished, he opened his eyes to find Dustee watching them. No scorn or derision in her expression, just curiosity.

Could God be using this situation to make himself known to her?

Sean thought it entirely possible, and it showed him even more that God's plans were not necessarily Sean's plan. Now he felt even worse. He'd been a terrible witness for his faith.

That had to stop. Now. God just reinforced a valuable life skill—trusting Him when all seemed lost—and Sean needed to start putting it into practice. He only hoped that didn't mean God would provide the opportunity to practice it more by letting Phantom escape capture.

Taylor followed Sean and Anna into the forensic lab that smelled like caustic chemicals. Much like Taylor's high school chemistry lab, except Taylor had no idea the type of chemicals Anna and her coworkers used or how the many machines filling the room operated.

"What do you have for us?" Sean's usual urgent tone was more relaxed, and his face less tight.

Taylor had felt a change in him since her prayer. He was more upbeat and hadn't reached for his antacids again. A good sign and one she could learn from. She wanted to trust God, too, not just one day at a time, but each and every moment. That had always been her goal, but since Jeremy had died, she hadn't even managed the one day at a time. On the drive over, she'd recommitted herself again and would start by trying not to doubt Him today. Then the next day and the next, hopefully stringing them together and strengthening her faith.

"Actually, I have two things I think you'll find interesting." Anna took a stack of papers from the lab table and handed them to Sean.

Taylor looked past him and saw it was a DNA report for a male.

He quickly perused the page and flipped to the next report, this one for a woman. He looked up at Anna. "So you were able to collect DNA for both a male and female?"

She nodded. "But the bedbugs contained only the male's DNA."

"That's odd that you didn't find female DNA there too, isn't it?" Sean asked.

"Maybe not. I don't think they had this infestation for long."

Taylor still couldn't believe they could find anything from the tiny bedbugs. "How can you tell?"

Anna frowned, likely from Taylor questioning her so often. "We found very few eggs in the bedding, and females lay up to five eggs a day. If the bugs had been there for some time, we would've located a larger quantity. So it's possible that once the infestation was discovered, the female didn't sleep in that bed."

Taylor could imagine it far too vividly, and she shuddered. "I sure wouldn't."

Anna nodded. "It's also possible that the bugs I collected simply hadn't fed on her, though I took a very random sample, so I think that's less likely."

Taylor was so grossed out that her breakfast churned in her stomach. "Please, can we move on?"

Anna chuckled. "Sure. Let's talk about the people. I've put both their ages at thirty-seven."

"Jorgenson is thirty-seven," Taylor said. "Guess it makes sense his girlfriend is the same age."

Sean's attention remained fixed on Anna. "Where did you locate her DNA?"

"In the office on the computers, mouse, glass, living room tables, kitchen, et cetera."

Sean furrowed his forehead. "So Phantom shared his equipment with her. Or she's his partner. After he killed his first partner, we've never seen any evidence of his having another one, but then we don't know all that much about him."

"What about searching the hard drives to look for anything that points to her?" Taylor asked Sean.

"Yeah, sure." Sean pulled out his phone. "Give me a second to text everyone to keep an eye out for that."

He tapped his screen, and Taylor watched him attack his phone like he did everything else. Full force and quickly. After the time she'd spent with him, she could truly confirm that he was her direct opposite. Could she handle being with someone who raced through life? Wait, could she handle being with anyone?

Oblivious to her internal musings, he stowed his phone and focused again on Anna. "What else do you have for us?"

She tapped the pages Sean still held. "We didn't get hits in CODIS on either profile."

He frowned. "I'm not surprised on Phantom, but I was hoping the woman would've matched."

"I also processed the samples recovered from Enzo's body," Anna said. "Unfortunately, no hit in CODIS, and they didn't match these samples. Either Jorgenson isn't the killer or he wore gloves."

"Oh, he's the killer," Sean said with conviction. "And he's most certainly smart enough to wear gloves."

Taylor admired how sure he was about his opinion. Admired so many things about him. And she wished just one bit of forensics would break in their favor. Not only for finding Phantom but to help relieve the pressure Sean was facing. If Anna wasn't in the room, Taylor would have taken his hand and reassured him.

"One odd thing you need to know." Anna's eyes narrowed, and she took a long breath. "We found only one toothbrush in the bathroom, and it matched the male's DNA profile."

Taylor *did* find that odd. "Maybe the woman wasn't living there after all."

Sean frowned. "But why the clothes and female hygiene products?"

Anna shrugged. "My science doesn't explain that."

"Did you test for DNA on any of those items?" Sean asked.

She shook her head. "I didn't think it was relevant to the investigation. I can go back to the house if you want, but honestly, I don't see a reason to do so."

"Nah," Sean said. "You're right. What's the point? We know a man and woman were both in the house, and we have their DNA." He glanced at the pages in his hand. "This isn't much to go on. Please tell me you have more items to process."

She nodded. "Fingerprints from the house are still being reviewed, and there's a good bit of trace evidence to process still."

"Trace evidence," Sean repeated. "Like what exactly?"

"Like the phone, for example. People leave behind trace chemicals, molecules, and microbes on every object they touch."

"Okay, explain that to me, please," Taylor said, as she rarely worked with forensics in witness protection, and they were ever-changing.

Anna took another one of those long breaths, as if she were searching for patience. "Say, for example, you put lotion on your hands and then touch your phone. You leave behind traces of the lotion. Or you take a medication and leave traces of it. Or food. Just about anything that remains on our hands transfers to our phones."

"How will finding that help?" Sean asked, the skepticism in his voice mimicking Taylor's uncertainty.

Anna firmed her stance. "The skin chemistry left behind tells us what kind of lifestyle he leads. Could tell us where he likes to eat and where he might have eaten last. Give us products he uses that can be purchased only in certain locations. If we narrow down where he's been, you can look for video or eye witnesses in those locations."

"Sounds like more cutting-edge forensics," Sean said. "Does it actually work?"

Anna's head bobbed enthusiastically. "I've used it before to bring in killers, and I'm confident it can do the same thing here."

The morning turned into afternoon while the team continued to review the many hard drives, though with little success in locating a lead. The conference room trash can was filled with empty Chinese takeout containers from lunch, the spicy scent lingering in the air. The pressure was getting to Sean again, but he was working hard to keep trusting God as he prayed to be led in the right direction. Taylor's constant encouragement had also helped, and in a big way.

In the last few days, he'd let his heart rule his head too many times because of her. Typically he'd say that was a bad thing, yet now he wasn't so sure. She'd brought something out of him that his mother's lies and Gina's treachery had stolen from his life. Now he could say he trusted someone again. Taylor. And maybe he was developing a willingness to give other people the benefit of the doubt too.

He watched her across the table, her finger swiping through pictures on her phone, her full attention on the screen. He could sit and look at her for hours, get lost in everything about her. Her beauty. Her personality. Her empathy for others. He'd never felt this way before. Ever. And he didn't want it to end with the investigation. He was sure of that now. No going back to being friends. No long-distance relationship, but the two of them together, exploring their feelings for each other.

She glanced up and smiled, a soft, intimate smile for him only.

He started to get up to go talk to her when his phone rang, and he settled back down to check the screen. "It's Anna." He answered the call and tapped the speaker button. "Taylor's here with the team, and I've put you on speaker."

"Okay," she said, sounding a bit hesitant. "I've finished processing the samples from the phone recovered at Jorgenson's house."

"And what did you find?" Sean kept his gaze on Taylor as they waited for what he hoped was a strong lead.

"We detected an anti-inflammatory and food molecules that included citrus and caffeine. All routine things, but interestingly we also found DEET and wood ash."

"DEET," Sean repeated. "As in the stuff used in mosquito repellent?"

"Exactly. Which would suggest that Phantom has spent time outdoors. And since there isn't a fireplace at his house or fire pit outside, the wood ash might suggest a campground somewhere."

Taylor's eyes narrowed. "I don't remember seeing anything on the evidence list that indicated he was a camper."

"We weren't looking for camping items," Sean said as he processed the news. "Still, I don't remember it from my walk-throughs."

Taylor sat forward. "That doesn't mean we shouldn't look again."

"I agree," Kiley said.

"Me too," Mack weighed in.

Cam nodded.

"Thanks, Anna." Sean disconnected, and he felt the mood in the room lift.

Cam sat closest to Sean, so he met his teammate's gaze. "Keep an eye on Dustee so Taylor and I can search Phantom's house for that lead we all desperately want to find."

Taylor walked beside Sean up to Phantom's house. Dark clouds hung in the sky, and fog clung to the building and overgrown shrubs like little whispers of smoke. She imagined Phantom lurking behind the bushes, gun in hand, peeking through the haze, ready to take another shot at them. She shivered.

Sean glanced at her. "You okay?"

She wrapped her arms around her waist. "Feels kind of creepy knowing the guy who shot me lives here."

"I can see how you might feel that way." He removed the screws in the plywood used to secure the house after they'd broken down the door.

Sean set the plywood aside, and she ignored her unease to step inside. A musty smell hit her hard as she flipped on the nearest light switch, and the place flooded with mottled orange light from a pair of old mid-century lamps sitting on tables of the same era. When she'd first walked into the house to locate Phantom, it seemed as if they'd been transported back in time. The house and furnishings were like a time capsule reminiscent of the 1960s.

She took another look around, not surprised to see black fingerprint powder covering many of the surfaces. "As bare as this place is, it's hard to believe we'll find something here. Nothing personal in this room at all."

He nodded. "I'm thinking Phantom saw no point in it. Stay mobile, you know?"

"I doubt he even cares about that sort of thing. I'm going to start by searching the bookshelves." She crossed the room to built-in shelves that looked original to the home.

"I'll take a look in the garage." Sean left the room.

She ran her hands over the top shelves, her fingers coming away coated with dust. She bent down to the bottom shelves hidden behind doors. She opened them and shone the light from her phone inside the deep cavity. Empty. Both sets. She ran a hand over every edge, looking for a false wall. Nothing.

The garage door closed, and Sean returned. "No camping equipment."

She stood. "On to the bedrooms then."

"I've already given the office a thorough search, so I'll take the master."

"What you're saying is that I didn't inspect his room as thoroughly." She eyed him.

Sean opened his mouth to say something, but his face colored. "Sorry. I guess I am."

"If I told you to trust that I'd done a thorough job, could you ignore the room?"

He warred with his answer for a long moment. "No, but it's not personal. And I have a feeling you plan to search the office too."

"That I do." She grinned.

Smiling, he took a step in her direction, then shook his head as if changing his mind and marched out of the room.

What had he been about to do before taking the U-turn? He'd seemed pleased and then, poof, his mood changed. She'd gotten pretty good at reading him, but that look was too mysterious to interpret. She wouldn't figure it out standing here, and honestly, it didn't really matter. Finding Phantom, that was what mattered right now.

She made the short trek to the office over creaky wood floors. The desks had been cleared of computer equipment. Dust and black fingerprint powder covered the scarred wood. Down on her hands and knees, she peered under the desk for any hidden files, then moved to the drawers, finding them as empty as the bookshelves. She felt for a false bottom. Found none. She went to the closet and shone her light inside the empty space, inspecting every inch of it.

"Find anything?" Sean asked.

Startled, she jumped.

"Just a lot of dust." Backing out, she brushed her hands together to clean off the dust and powder. "Let's do the third bedroom together."

He pointed at the door. "After you."

Not a stick of furniture sat in the smaller room. The matted lime-green shag matched the carpet in the office, all over fifty years old, and she could only imagine what lived in it. She went straight to the closet and swept her light over the space. Finding nothing, she turned to leave when the beam caught something in the corner.

She squatted to study the carpet. "Am I imagining this or is the carpet loose?"

Sean joined her, and she tugged on the shag. The carpet came up, revealing a large manila envelope.

"What's that?" Sean's voice rose.

"You tell me." She handed it to him and pulled the carpet back further. "More envelopes."

Sean glanced inside the one he held. "Pictures. Grab the other ones, and we can go to the family room where the light's better."

She gathered up the envelopes and joined him on the living room sofa that smelled old and stale, as if it had sat in this same place for eons. She opened the top envelope.

"More pictures." She reached inside and pulled them out, her eyes landing on a Christmas photo with a young boy in candy-cane-striped pajamas. He sat in front of a brightly lit tree, a big frown on his face.

She flipped through the other snapshots to confirm they were all of family members. "It's odd to hide these under a carpet."

"Criminals often don't make sense."

She looked at Sean. "Do you think Phantom hid these or his parents?"

"I don't know." He paused, head tilted. "I don't see Phantom being sentimental. And I also don't see him risking leaving behind anything that could ID him. But why would parents hide pictures?"

She shrugged and thumbed through the remaining Christmas photos, giving Sean a chance to see them. "This child looks like he's about three."

"They were definitely taken in this house. Same furniture and décor."

She looked up for a moment. "You know, I don't get the sixties furniture here. When I first saw the house, I thought Phantom might have really old parents, but these pictures prove they aren't that old."

"They could've inherited the house from a parent and never changed anything. Or even bought it and liked the décor. Retro is kind of in."

"It wasn't back in the eighties when these pictures were taken." She studied the photo. This one also included a young girl with dark hair in neat braids. "His parents are wearing conservative clothing and look pretty straitlaced. Not someone I'd peg as Phantom's parents."

"I wonder who the little girl is." He turned over the picture. "Nothing written on the back."

Taylor continued to look through the stack. "It still seems totally odd to hide these."

"Maybe the other envelopes will explain it." He dumped out the next one, and photos mixed with postcards from Disneyland dropped onto his lap. The same boy, looking unhappy, stood with Mickey Mouse. "The pictures are dated 1987."

"Assuming Jorgenson and Phantom are the same person, his birth date says he would've been five here." She glanced at the back. "Nothing."

"He looks about that age." Sean squinted at the

photo, then set a few more beside it. "Do you see what's strange about all of these?"

"He's not smiling."

Sean quickly browsed through the others. "He never smiles. Not even on his birthday. How can a five-year-old not smile on his birthday? Or Christmas or at Disneyland?"

"Some kids hate having their picture taken."

"Yeah, but don't you think his parents would've caught at least one candid with him smiling?"

She did. She really did. "Let's look in the next envelope."

Sean drew out school pictures in order of year. "Again. No smiles. Not even when he was younger."

"Something seems very off about this family. Like what happened to the parents? Are they still living? We'll need to research that."

They continued through all the envelopes. The last one made Taylor sit forward. "Camping at Valley of the Rogue State Park. And he's—"

"Smiling." Sean leaned closer. "These snapshots cover several trips, and he's having a good time in every picture."

DEET and wood ash. "Do you think this is his happy place, and he's hiding out there?"

"I think it's worth exploring for sure."

Eyes wide, Taylor clutched his arm. "We may not have found camping gear because he's using it."

Sean nodded. "I'll send Jorgenson's driver's license photo to the park rangers. Ask if they've seen him. If so, I'll arrange for a helicopter and head out there."

"I'll be going with you."

"I—" Sean's phone rang. "It's Cam."

Taylor's heart dropped. Cam knew they would be back soon, so if he felt a need to call, something big must have happened. Could a witness have died?

Please, no.

Sean answered quickly and tapped his speaker button.

"You better get back here pronto." Concern deepened Cam's tone.

"Why?" Sean asked.

"Patrick Jorgenson can't be Phantom," Cam replied.

Taylor clasped her hands together. "Why not?"

"Because Jorgenson died eight months ago."

CHAPTER 28

Taylor couldn't believe Jorgenson was dead, and based on the expressions on the RED team's faces as they gathered in the safe house family room, they were also shocked. It really was unbelievable. The person they thought held the witnesses' lives in his hands wasn't the man they thought he was. They were no closer to finding him, and the witnesses remained in grave danger. Taylor feared for every person under her care.

"But the sketch matched Jorgenson's driver's license picture." Sean stared at the official death certificate from the county records office.

"So Phantom stole Jorgenson's ID." Kiley drummed her fingers on the end table. "He could easily hack the DMV to change the picture to steal Jorgenson's ID. Also change him from deceased to living if needed."

"He didn't change this." Sean waved the death certificate.

Kiley frowned. "I'll admit that's baffling."

Taylor thought so too. "Maybe all he needed was the driver's license and didn't care that Jorgenson was still officially dead."

Kiley's fingers stopped moving midair. "I'll contact the DMV and get them to check their change logs for Jorgenson's record to prove it's been changed."

Sean looked up. "How did you discover he died?"

"Actually I didn't." Kiley gnawed on her lip.

Mack rested his scuffed boots on the coffee table. "It was Dustee."

"Dustee?" Sean shot a look at Cam, who leaned against the wall. "I left you in charge of her, and you let her use the internet? What happened? She sweet-talk you?"

Scowling, Cam pushed off the wall and planted his feet wide, the most confrontational posture Taylor had seen him use. "Actually, I didn't."

Sean swung his gaze to Mack. "You?"

Mack took his time crossing his ankles. "No."

Sean turned to Kiley. "It couldn't have been you. You'd never let a woman who exhibited zero control in her life do something like this."

Kiley flinched.

"What?" Sean demanded. "You let Dustee use the internet? For real?"

She nodded, but uncertainty remained lodged on her face. "I got to thinking how I would feel if someone told me I could never use a computer again. Didn't much like the feeling. She'll be going back into exile soon enough. I figured what harm would it do if I let her search the net while I supervised."

Sean's disbelief lingered on his face, and Taylor

thought he planned to unload on Kiley in front of all of them. Better to move forward before that happened.

"How did you get the actual death certificate so fast?" Taylor asked.

"Ah." Kiley's eyes brightened. "That was all Mack's doing."

Taylor looked at her friend.

"Texas charm, what can I say?" He grinned. "The woman at the county records office was putty in my hands."

Taylor had seen him in action before, drawing out his Southern accent, throwing in a "Yes, ma'am" when needed, and batting those impossibly long eyelashes at younger women.

"Your charm isn't going to change the fact that our best lead so far is dead," Sean muttered.

"Exactly." Mack's smile fell, and he dropped his boots to the floor. "That's why I'm not waiting for the DMV records. I'm going to my computer to find every bit of information I can about Jorgenson."

"Good idea for all of us, but not yet." Sean grabbed the envelopes they'd brought back with them. "First, I need to show you the photos we found at the house."

He passed the pictures around and reminded them of the DEET, his words concise and emotionless. If Taylor had been explaining, she would've let her sadness over seeing a small child who found nothing to laugh about impact her. One more difference between Sean and her.

"There's a little girl in some of the pictures too." Kiley looked up from the photo in her hand. "But I didn't find any record of a sibling when I searched his family history."

"She's not in the majority of them, so a cousin maybe," Taylor suggested. "Or even a friend."

"Or a sibling who died," Kiley said. "I'll expand my family search and do a deep dive on Jorgenson's parents and siblings, but a childhood friend might be a challenge to locate."

"Hey, if anyone can find the information we need, it's you." Cam patted her shoulder.

"True that," she said.

Taylor knew Kiley wasn't bragging, just saying what she believed to be fact. From the information Sean shared about Kiley, Taylor knew her lack of socialization while growing up often left Kiley feeling awkward around others, and she could come across as socially out of step.

"What we really need is to know whose DNA was found in that bed," Sean said. "Could it actually have been Jorgenson's?"

Taylor hadn't even considered how the bedbugs related to Jorgenson's death. "Can bedbugs live for eight months? Maybe still have his blood in them?"

"Let me call Anna." Sean dialed her and quickly launched into an explanation on speakerphone.

"Bedbugs typically only live four to six months," she said. "But they can live longer and can go months without feeding. However, for our purposes it's irrelevant. They preserve full human blood DNA profiles for only three days."

"So it's impossible for our DNA profile to be from Jorgenson?" Sean asked.

"That's right."

Sean shoved a hand into his hair. "I would still like to have Jorgenson's DNA for comparison."

"You doubt me?" Anna asked.

"No, of course not," Sean said. "But I want concrete proof."

Taylor agreed wholeheartedly. "How would we even begin to find Jorgenson's DNA?"

"If you know where he's buried, you could have the ME exhume his body." Anna sounded less than enthusiastic about that idea.

Taylor searched for a more realistic idea. "What about one of those ancestry sites? They use DNA."

"They do," Anna said. "But after detectives used them to catch a serial killer, the sites have tightened security. Getting access can take some time."

Sean swung an intense look from team member to team member. "Let's prove we're the team to beat the odds and not only find and access Jorgenson's DNA, but do it before the day's out."

As the sun rose high in the sky and filtered through the conference room blinds, Sean took a look at his fatigued group. Finding information on Jorgenson had become a priority, along with calling the DMV and sending Jorgensen's picture to the campground. Other than restroom breaks, no one left the room. Not even to eat. Agent Snow had come through again, providing food and hauling off the trash.

"He did it!" Kiley laid her phone on the table. "Jorgenson's DL photo was updated nine months ago."

Sean gaped at her. "*Before* he died?"

Kiley nodded. "And once he died, no one brought in a death certificate so his license remained in effect. I've asked them to trace the change transmission, but they'll likely find an extensive trail of proxy servers, and in the end, Phantom will be long gone from the location where the transmission originated anyway."

Kiley's computer dinged, grabbing her attention. "That will be the original photo for Jorgenson. Let me put it up on the TV."

She clicked her mouse, and Sean stepped to the large flat-screen TV. A photo opened of a dark-haired man with similar features to Phantom's sketch, except the hair was cut short, his nose smaller, and his chin narrower.

Sean moved even closer to study the picture. "He has a mole by his ear."

"Wait." Taylor grabbed the photos recovered at the house. She flipped through them and handed one to Sean. "Look. The boy has the same mole."

Kiley's eyes narrowed. "So the kid is the real Jorgenson. Not Phantom."

"Means the state park lead won't pan out," Mack said.

Sean slammed a fist into the wall. The sting bit into his hand, radiated up his arm, and soothed the anger in his gut.

Taylor took a long look at Sean's hand and sat back, her face tight.

Great. He'd not only disappointed himself by letting his anger get to him, but he'd disappointed her too. She knew he'd let go of trusting God again. Her disappointment hurt more. Much more.

"You should still follow up with the state park," Cam said. "Just in case."

Sean nodded. "I'll do that while you all get back to work."

He stepped into the hallway so he didn't disturb the group with his call. Or maybe to avoid Taylor's continued frown.

He dialed, and the woman he spoke to earlier answered. "I wanted to follow up on the picture I faxed to you."

"Oh, right," she said. "Sorry. I got busy and didn't have a chance to look at it. Hold on. I'll grab it from the fax machine."

The call went silent, and he heard footsteps in the background.

"Hey, yeah," she said. "Yeah. This guy checked in yesterday."

Sean could hardly believe it. Could she be right or had she made a mistake? Most state parks recorded vehicle information at check-in, so he described Jorgenson's truck and gave her the plate number.

"Let me bring up his record." He heard her fumbling around. "Okay. Got it. Yep, that's his vehicle."

"You're sure the plate matches?" he asked, trying not to get too excited.

"Positive."

Sean's enthusiasm soared. "I need his campsite number."

"Sorry, can't give you that without a warrant, but I'll settle for your official ID."

Sean wouldn't send that via a fax. It would have to wait until he got there. "Do you have a yurt or cabin with a good view of this guy's campsite?"

"Let me check." He heard her fingers clicking on a keyboard. "We have a yurt available with a good view. A18. You can reserve it online."

"I'll be there as soon as I can arrange for a

helicopter." He started to disconnect when a vision of her rushing out to check on Phantom flashed in his brain. "This man is dangerous. Very dangerous. Do not approach him. Not for any reason."

CHAPTER 29

"I'm going to the campground with you." Taylor fisted her hands on her hips in the hall, away from the team's interested gazes.

Sean gave her a patronizing look. "You're injured."

She wouldn't back down. No way. "I can function just fine. I've proved that the last few days, and you're just using it as an excuse to leave me behind."

"But I—"

"Look." She took a step closer. "I'm the only one who's seen Phantom. I can ID him."

"We have his picture."

"A picture's not like seeing someone in real life," she rushed on. "Plus he shot me. Could've killed me. There's no way I'll miss being there when he's taken down."

"I . . ."

She stood her ground. "I'm an official team member and have every right to go along. So either I ride in the helicopter with you or I find my own way there. Your choice."

Sean glared at her, a glare she knew was born of worry for her safety, but she wouldn't give in. She didn't know what it would take to convince him, but she would win this argument. "You have nothing to worry about with me. I'm fit for duty. The doctor at my follow-up visit said so."

"Because you probably gave him no choice, just like you did with the ER doc."

"I can demonstrate my fitness in any test you devise." She braced her feet wide. "We could go hand to hand right now. Come on. I can take it."

"I'm not fighting you. Or testing you." Sean blew out a frustrated breath. "I'll agree to let you come with me on the recon mission, but I'll hold judgment on the takedown based on what we find."

"That's a start." Yet there was no way she'd give up on being included in the takedown.

"I'm planning to go in undercover," he said. "Posing as a camper. We can go as husband and wife, and that will be even better." He smiled at her.

With the feelings for him that she was already struggling to deal with, she didn't want to pretend to be his wife. On the bright side, she wouldn't have to act to play the role convincingly. It was time to face facts. She'd love to be his significant other at the park and in life.

If only . . .

"I've reserved a yurt with a perfect view of Phantom's campsite," he continued. "We can set up surveillance there."

"You know about yurts?" The circular domed structures with hard floors and canvas sides were common in Oregon campgrounds, but she wasn't sure about other parts of the country. "I didn't think a city boy like you would have even heard of them."

"Hey." A humorous gleam lit his eyes. "I resent that city-boy comment. My work has taken me to some pretty rustic places. I also like the outdoors, which includes camping."

She liked that he was able to lighten up at times. "We've never talked about that."

"So I can still surprise you then." He grinned, playful and nearly irresistible.

Oh, yeah, he could surprise her all right. Thankfully, he didn't know how much.

His smile disappeared. "Phantom will likely recognize us. We'll need to change our appearance. I'll get Snow working on procuring wigs and appropriate clothing. Even so, he's seen you, maybe me, so we'll have to keep our heads down at all times when not in the yurt, and stay inside as much as possible."

"Sounds perfect."

"Just give me your sizes."

It felt odd sharing her clothing and shoe sizes. It seemed almost as intimate as kissing him for some reason, but she gave him the details all the same. "In the meantime, I'll arrange for Dustee and Dianne's protection."

He arched an eyebrow. "I can't believe you're willing to leave them."

"I'll make sure Inman assigns our best deputy," she said, though she was indeed concerned about leaving them behind. "And the rest of the RED team will be with them too."

"Yeah, they'll be fine. I just never thought I'd see you put anything before your witnesses. That's all."

He had a point. A good one. Going camping like this on a whim without weighing all the pros and cons—just trusting that Sean knew what he was doing—was new for her. Maybe this was a sign that she was relaxing on that front. At least a bit. And maybe, just maybe, she'd found a man she could trust.

She took his hand, the one he'd put through the wall, and lifted it to her mouth to press a soft kiss on his knuckles. "I look forward to being your wife."

His mouth fell open. She loved that she could shock him and laughed, feeling glad to change the mood. "I thought after smashing your hand into a wall, that you might need to lighten up."

He nodded. "I'm trying to trust God here. Really, I am, but it's hard to do when Phantom keeps evading us."

He lowered his hand, but she continued to hold it. "We'll find him."

"How can you be so sure?"

"Because I have tremendous confidence in you and your team."

He frowned. "Not sure how you can after the way we failed in the Montgomery Three investigation."

She took a minute to find the right words to respond. "This is a different investigation, and you can't solve every crime."

"Seriously? You really think that?" He searched her face. "I don't agree. If we work hard enough. Smart enough. Long enough. We can do anything."

"You'll burn out thinking that way, and then you won't be much good to anyone."

He blew out a long breath. "Speaking of the Montgomery Three, will you reconsider letting me interview Harold Wilson?"

"What? Where did that come from?" She watched him as she thought about her witness. "Oh, I get it. You think I'm vulnerable now, and you're taking advantage of that." She went to pull her hand away.

He held tight. "I'm not. At least not intentionally. I just need a win right now, and I thought the interview could give me that."

"I get it. I do. I left a request on Inman's voicemail, but I think the break-in has taken all of his attention." She thought to leave things there, but at the tightening of his jaw, she added, "Let me call him. See what he's decided."

"Thank you." He squeezed her hand and released it.

She dialed Inman, and he answered right away. "Just checking in, Chief, to see if you made a decision on Agent Nichols talking to Harold Wilson."

"I've been meaning to call you about that, but the break-in . . ." A long hiss of air filled the line. "Wilson's your protectee. What's your opinion?"

"My opinion?" Taylor looked Sean in the eye. "If Harold agrees, I think Agent Nichols should be allowed to talk to him."

Thank you, Sean mouthed.

"Okay, fine with me," Inman said. "But you know I won't be happy if anything happens and we have to relocate him. Our budget just won't stretch to that."

"Yes, sir. I understand," she said sincerely. "Also, while I've got you, I need a deputy for graveyard duty with Dustee." Taylor brought him up to speed on the investigation.

"I'll send Thatcher out."

"Perfect." She trusted Thatcher.

But you trusted Roger too.

She ignored her internal warning. The odds of having another dirty deputy in the office were astronomically unlikely and not worth thinking about. She ended the call and looked at Sean. "Inman approved your talk with Harold and will send out Deputy Thatcher for Dustee's detail."

Sean grabbed her up in his arms and kissed her hard on the mouth. She clung to his broad shoulders and kissed him back, reveling in his touch and never wanting him to release her. She let the kiss go on and on, the touch of his lips filling her with longing and joy. They continued, not a fraction of an inch between them until her common sense returned.

Breathless, she pushed back and gulped in much-needed oxygen.

"You've got to stop kissing me." She attempted a stern tone, but the smile that she couldn't control belied her words.

"You say that, but . . ." He winked.

His joy wrapped around her heart. Her arms seemed to rise on their own accord to go around his neck.

What was she thinking? Kissing Sean at all, but doing so in an FBI hallway?

She stepped back, shoved her betraying hands in her pockets, and forced a professional demeanor. Still, she wanted nothing more than to be in his arms again. He would hold her tight. Maybe if he was feeling as lighthearted as she was, he'd spin her around. Happiness between friends.

No, that was wrong. More than friends. So much more.

Oh, man, she was in trouble here. Deep trouble. She had to get back on the right track before going off to act like his wife. "I know I say one thing when it's clear I don't mind your kisses at all. But we need to keep in mind how easily it could become so much more at the yurt, and how hard it will be to part if we keep this up."

His expression quickly sobered, and he gave a clipped nod. "I'm sure you'll want to talk to Thatcher. Go ahead and call him now while I update Snow on the extra supplies needed."

He opened the conference room door for her and departed. By the time she reviewed the situation with Thatcher, set up specific protocols for Dustee, and informed him of her restrictions and her tendency not to follow them, Snow bustled her into the small conference room with camping gear, clothing, and a wig for her to wear.

She studied the nearly black wig. It was quite natural-looking but would seem odd with her reddish eyebrows and fair complexion. Women dyed their hair all the time, so it should be fine. Especially from a distance, which she knew Sean would make sure she kept.

"Is there a problem?" Snow asked.

"No." She picked up the wig and clothing. "I'll just get changed."

He exited the room, and she made quick work of pairing the warm turtleneck and flannel shirt with a pair of jeans and hiking boots. She swept her hair up and put on the wig. A quick look in her compact mirror, and she knew Phantom wouldn't recognize her from a distance. Snow had also gotten a heavy jacket with a hood that she could further use to disguise her appearance, and she would keep her head down like Sean suggested. No way would she be the reason their cover got blown.

She opened the door to find Sean wearing clothes very similar to hers. He looked ruggedly handsome, and a blond wig changed his appearance so much that she had to force herself to focus on Snow, who pointed at the main exit. "Your chopper is waiting."

Snow drove them to the airport just down the road and took them to a special clearance landing area. He expedited their trip through security and parked close to the chopper with blades already turning.

Sean held the door, and together they rushed toward the helicopter as it blew clouds of dust into the air, swirling like a tornado around them. She worried her wig would go flying, so she planted a hand to hold it in place.

"You look kind of amazing in that wig," he said, the intimate tone in his voice sending her heart racing as fast as the rotors.

Sean vaulted up into the aircraft and held out a hand, but her heart was still fluttering from his warm tone, and she couldn't imagine touching him on top of that. She ignored his hand and climbed inside. A knowing look crossed his face, but she wouldn't touch that either. Not with a single word.

The plump pilot with a full beard and bushy eyebrows swiveled in his seat and smiled at them. "Flying time is less than two hours. Headsets are next to the seats, allowing us to communicate in-flight. Any questions along the way, just ask."

He turned back, and Sean picked up his headset. "You ever fly in a chopper before?"

She nodded.

"Like it?"

"Yes." She buckled her seat belt, grabbed her headset, and settled it over the wig.

"We're cleared for takeoff," the pilot said. "Enjoy the flight."

She wished the pilot wasn't in on their communications. This flight was a chance for her and Sean to talk further about the investigation. But with the pilot in the loop, they couldn't have a meaningful discussion. Instead, they sat there, the awareness of each other hanging in the air, making the next two hours seem like an eternity.

The moment the side door opened in Medford, she grabbed her backpack and hopped down. Sean gave her a funny look, then shook hands with the pilot and motioned her toward a gray Jeep Wrangler. It had a black soft top and cargo area filled with camping gear.

She eyed it with surprise. "I won't even ask how you made this happen so fast."

Sean chuckled as he loaded his backpack and two large tote bags holding surveillance equipment into the back of the Jeep. He slid behind the wheel, looking so at home in the rugged vehicle that her heart did another tumble. She nearly groaned at her betraying emotions as she stowed her backpack and climbed into the passenger seat.

"Campground's only a few miles away. Mind if I take the top off for the short drive?" A boyish grin followed his request.

"That would be great," she replied, knowing she might have to hold on to her wig. But at least it would curtail any personal conversations.

Now all she had to do was figure out how to take the top off the yurt, because she was certain she would never survive a night in the small space with this man who had totally and completely captured her heart.

"Be right back." Sean smiled at Taylor and jumped from the Jeep, excited from the ride with the wind blowing in his face. Thankfully his wig was tightly secured and hadn't even budged.

He stepped into the campground's small registration building near the road and took a moment to gather his thoughts. He might have enjoyed the ride over here, but he needed to focus on the undercover assignment facing them. He'd reserved their site and paid online, but he still had to get Phantom's campsite number. The ranger he'd talked to stood behind the counter. Average height and build, she had a pleasant smile and mousy brown hair under a broad-brimmed hat.

He stepped up to her and displayed his official ID. "Agent Sean Nichols."

"Ah," she said. "So you're the guy who called. Been wondering when you'd get here."

He stowed his creds. "Which site am I looking at?"

"A01." She handed him a campground map.

Sean had memorized every inch of the campground and the exact location of their site. Now he could place A01 in the right spot without even looking at the map. Yet he took it anyway to keep the ranger from asking questions.

"Just so you know," she said, "I drove past that campsite a few times today on my rounds, and the guy's truck isn't there."

"You didn't approach his tent, did you?" Sean asked, hoping the woman didn't scare Phantom off.

"After your warning? Are you kidding?"

He slid his business card across the counter. "Thanks for your help. My cell's listed there. If he contacts you, don't try to apprehend him, but call me."

Her firm nod gave Sean confidence that she would follow his directions. Jonesing to get his eyes on Phantom's site, Sean hurried outside. He joined Taylor in the Jeep, tossed the map on the dash, and pointed the vehicle toward the A loop.

"Everything go okay?" she asked.

He nodded. "We're in A18, and Phantom's in A01."

She picked up the map and clutched it tightly. "This is all happening so fast. Maybe we should've given it more thought before rushing out here."

"Seriously, I would've liked to have been here hours ago."

She frowned and studied the map. He understood her reason for being cautious, but he had to admit he hoped she could let it go for her own sake.

He wound around the campground, the Rogue River running through the middle, separating the property. This time of year, the park closed the camping loop bordering the river, and he could see why. The winter rains had swelled the river, and the nearby rapids were faster than normal and unsafe. Thankfully, it didn't affect their yurt site, which included a picnic table, campfire ring, and tall pines soaring to the sky.

Sean parked and looked at Taylor. "Our yurt faces away from Phantom's campground so we should be good to unload without worrying about him seeing us. Still, keep your eyes peeled for him."

She nodded, and they hopped out of the vehicle, their feet crunching over fallen pinecones as they carried sleeping bags, a cooler, and bags of food into the yurt. He took a moment to breathe in the fresh air. Taylor joined him, and he could almost believe they were on an actual camping trip.

An older couple strolled by hand in hand, telegraphing how at home they were with each other. Sean imagined himself at that age. With his current take on relationships, he'd be alone. A lonely old man. No wife. No children.

He didn't want that. Not anymore. He put an arm around Taylor and pulled her close.

"Look, honey," he said, loud enough for his voice to carry. "That'll be us in a few years."

The couple looked their way, smiled and waved, reacting exactly as Sean had hoped.

He turned Taylor to face him and kissed her tantalizingly slowly. Her lips were soft and warm, igniting a firestorm in his body. She had to know he was playacting, but she threw herself into the kiss, matching him and even deepening the intensity. Her hand came up behind his neck, her soft touch adding fuel to the fire, and his muscles tensed under her touch. His heart filled with joy, but he had to end the kiss to keep his wits about him. He lifted his head, and she honestly looked grieved over the end of their contact.

"I'm not sure what I think about the wig," he whispered as he tucked a strand of dark hair behind her ear. "You're beautiful no matter the color of your hair, but it's what's inside that counts."

"You know this isn't something we should be

doing or talking about. No matter the reason. We're here on business only." She frowned.

He wanted to trace a finger over her mouth to erase it. "I couldn't help myself. I try to keep things professional between us, and then you smile at me, and I lose all common sense."

She rolled her eyes. "You probably use that line with all your women."

What was she talking about?

"You know there aren't any other women. No one but you." He almost added *and there never will be another,* but he didn't want to scare her when she was already skittish.

Her frown deepened, and she pushed against his chest. "Let me grab my backpack, and we can get our surveillance set up."

She hurried away as if being chased by a big bad wolf. Was that what she thought of him, or was she running from her feelings? They would be alone in the small space tonight, and he didn't want to do anything that might offend her.

He went to grab the tote bags, and after they were in the rustic yurt with the door closed, he made sure the curtains on the door and the two windows were pulled closed. The space held a heavy wooden bunk bed and a futon, all boasting mattresses covered in hunter-green vinyl. The walls were made of wood lattice frames and white canvas backing. The space also had a small dining table with two chairs, and a heater.

"I'll set up the surveillance equipment, and we can take turns watching." He carried the tote to the larger window facing Phantom's site and unpacked the camera and tripod. He didn't need a zoom lens to get a good overview of the site but simply peeked out between the curtains. "No vehicle, but a small tent, a few lawn chairs, and the picnic table, which has a checkered tablecloth clipped to it."

"Wait, let me see." Taylor rushed across the room and nudged him out of the way to take a long look before facing him.

"This guy is really something else, right?" Sean said. "A stealthy hacker who's evaded the best of law enforcement for years, and he puts out a tablecloth."

"Did you bring Phantom's old pictures?" she asked.

"No. Why?"

"The tablecloth that appears in a lot of the camping pictures has a similar melted spot as this one. The lawn chairs are the same too." She put her hands on her hips, and he loved seeing how much effort she put into thinking about the developments in the case.

Sean's phone rang.

"It's Kiley." He dropped into the chair by the camera and answered.

"You are so not going to believe this." Excitement had her words nearly tumbling over each other.

"Hold on. Let me put my phone on speaker so Taylor can hear." He turned it on and set his cell on the table. "Okay, Kiley, go ahead," Sean told her.

"We've been searching for Jorgenson's DNA. Found his profile on an ancestry website."

"Good work!"

"Yeah . . . well . . . kind of. This is crazy, but his DNA is an exact match to the male profile from the bedbugs."

"What?" Sean met Taylor's baffled gaze. "Jorgenson's dead. How's that even possible?"

CHAPTER 30

Sean quickly got the team on a video conference call on his iPad while Taylor sat next to him at the table. For once he wasn't distracted by her closeness. His mind was wrapped up with trying to figure out how a dead man's DNA could be found in living bedbugs.

"I would say Phantom could have planted the DNA in the house," Mack said, "but the bedbugs prove that's not possible."

"Unless Phantom had a vial of blood for them to feed on to throw us off track." Cam laughed.

Sean knew Cam was joking, but then . . . "I wouldn't put it past him."

"Maybe Anna was wrong when she said she extracted his DNA from the bedbugs," Taylor suggested.

"We need her to join us," Sean said.

"I'll get her connected." Cam turned away to begin the process.

"Any other thoughts while he makes the connection?" Sean asked.

"Like what?" Kiley frowned. "This is just too weird. Impossible even."

Sean was starting to lose confidence in Anna, only he wouldn't let the team know that. "I'm sure Anna will have a logical explanation."

"Right, sure." Mack rolled his eyes. "This is the woman who just said it was impossible for the bedbugs to have the DNA from a man who's been dead this long."

"Got her," Cam said.

Anna came on the screen. She looked tired and a bit irritated at being summoned. "I hope this is important."

"It is," Sean said, a sense of urgency in his voice. "We found Jorgenson's DNA profile on an ancestry site. It matched the profile from the bedbugs."

"Interesting." She tipped her head in a thoughtful expression when he expected her to gape at him.

"That's all you have to say." Taylor stared at Anna. "What about 'I made a mistake, his DNA can't be in living bugs'?"

Anna frowned. "I didn't make a mistake."

"I'm sorry," Taylor said quickly, as if realizing she'd been harsh. "But what other explanation can there be for DNA in a living bedbug from a man who's been dead for eight months?"

"Off the top of my head, I'd say Jorgenson donated bone marrow to someone, and they now have his DNA."

Sean sat in quiet shock for a moment, and so did his teammates. "You'll have to explain that to us."

"Sure." Anna took a long breath. "When a bone

marrow transplant is performed, the recipient's bone marrow is destroyed. Either partially or completely. It's then replaced with the donor's marrow. The recipient could either have their own DNA completely change to that of the donor or keep some of their own DNA and some of the donor's."

Sean tried to wrap his head around this. "So in the second instance, the person could have two DNA profiles?"

"Yes," Anna said. "And this would make sense since it's Jorgenson's house."

"Jorgenson had to have been close to Phantom if he donated the marrow," Kiley said. "And it looks like he took over living in the house when Jorgenson died."

Stunned, Sean sat back. "This not only has implications for our investigation, but far-reaching ones for law enforcement."

"Like what?" Anna asked.

Sean couldn't believe she had to ask. "How can you ever be sure the DNA profiles you run actually match the right person?"

"This is a very rare condition," Anna said. "In fact, I've never personally come across it."

"That you know of," Mack said. "Makes me wonder how many people are behind bars for something like this."

Anna crossed her arms. "I doubt it's a significant number, as anyone who's undergone a transplant would know their DNA could've changed."

"Just to clarify, is there any other way the DNA from the bedbug could match Jorgenson's profile?" Sean asked.

"The reverse of what we're talking about is possible. Phantom could have donated marrow to Jorgenson. But otherwise, there's no other scientific explanation."

Sean took a moment to process. "This is good news then."

Taylor narrowed her eyes. "How can it be?"

"From what Anna is saying, odds are now very good that Jorgenson donated bone marrow," Sean replied, his enthusiasm growing. "All we have to do is locate his medical records for the procedure, and we'll find the name of the marrow or donor recipient, a man known to us as Phantom."

While the team at the office searched for the transplant information, Taylor had spent hours praying and watching through a camera lens, but now Sean was at the window. The sun had made a glorious showing in vibrant reds and blues before surrendering to the moon, with no sign of Phantom arriving back at his campsite. And she was no closer to knowing what to do about her personal feelings for Sean than she'd been before she started her long conversation with God.

She did know one thing, though. With as much

as she now cared for him, she would have to tell him about Jeremy. The telling would be painful, yet Sean deserved to understand her reason for not entering into a relationship with him.

"Are you hungry?" She squinted to try to make out his expression in the dark. They were keeping the lights out so Phantom couldn't see the camera in the curtain opening. That was, if he ever returned.

"I could eat something, sure," he replied.

She dragged the other chair to his location before taking sandwiches and bottled water from the cooler and finding plates and chips in a grocery bag. She placed the food close to him so he didn't have to leave the camera.

"Thanks." He reached for the sandwich. "I really expected Phantom to be back by now."

"Yeah. Strange, right? Why come all the way out here and not stay?" Taylor had tried not to let her imagination go wild with all the things Phantom could be doing, but she hadn't managed it. "I checked in at the safe house, and everything is fine there."

He took a drink from the water bottle. "You really do worry a lot, don't you?"

Here it was. The opening she needed to tell him about Jeremy. Her mouth was dry. So very dry. She grabbed a water bottle and chugged. She sat across the table from him. "My worry. It's . . . Jeremy. What happened to him. It was my fault."

He swung his head around to stare at her. "Seriously? I asked you if you had something to do with his death, and you said no."

"I lied. I couldn't tell you," she rushed to add before he could respond. "I'm sorry, Sean. It's just . . . I wasn't ready to talk about it."

He shook his head. "You lied to me. You really lied to me."

"Yes." She was thankful for the yurt's low light, as she couldn't make out his expression. She'd rather see nothing than witness his deep disappointment in her.

He put down his sandwich and swung his focus back to the camera.

Was that it? Wouldn't he give her a chance to explain why she'd lied?

"Okay. Tell me about it," he finally said, his tone sharp and unyielding.

She didn't want to talk to his rigid back, but she had to explain. "I was sixteen and was going to the mall with my friends to shop for prom dresses. Jeremy owed me twenty bucks. So I went to his room to get it. I found narcotic pain pills in his drawer. I figured he was just getting high on them, you know, and I could tell my parents when they got home. Never did I think he was planning to take the whole bottle."

"But something happened and you couldn't tell them," he said without looking at her, that inflexible tone still clinging to his words.

411

"Right. This was my first formal dance. I forgot all about the pills and stayed out way too late. Blew off my curfew."

Memories she'd kept at bay for years now pummeled her brain. Vivid, bright, technicolor memories. Of Jeremy. Lifeless. In a casket. The box being lowered into the ground. She tried to inhale, but it felt like the world sat on her chest, and she could barely breathe. She wanted to crawl in a hole and not go on, but she needed to explain.

"It shouldn't have mattered," she said. "Jeremy had football practice and wouldn't be home before our parents. But he'd planned things out. Came home early and swallowed all the pills. My mom found him when she got home from work. It . . . it was too late."

Taylor shuddered at the memory as tears flowed down her cheeks. She hoped Sean would at least look at her, but he didn't move.

"Later," she continued, her voice barely a whisper, "at the hospital when the doctors said he'd died, I told my parents about finding the pills. They blamed me for his death. They were right. It was my fault. If I hadn't gone shopping for the stupid dress, he would still be alive."

She hoped Sean would turn and tell her it was okay, that she wasn't to blame. But he sat there in silence.

"Sean?" she asked.

He shook his head, just one solid shake telling her he didn't want to talk. Yeah, he was very angry at her. She got it. There was no point in dragging this out, only to end up with the same result. She'd done the one thing he detested most. Lied to him.

His phone rang, and he grabbed it like a lifeline. "It's Kiley on a video call." He quickly answered.

Despite the turmoil between them, Taylor moved closer so she could see the screen.

"Boy, am I glad you're still up and answered." Her face was bright with excitement. "I located the girl in the picture with Jorgenson."

Taylor gaped at the phone. "How?"

She sat forward. "I had an age progression done on the picture and ran it through facial recognition."

"You didn't mention doing that." Sean sounded suspicious, probably the result of learning Taylor had lied to him.

"I didn't want to get your hopes up if it didn't pan out."

"So who is she?" Taylor asked.

"Patrick Jorgenson's cousin and, wait for it—" she grinned—"the person he donated bone marrow to."

Taylor jumped to her feet and stared at Kiley. "She's Phantom? Phantom's a woman? But who's the guy I saw? The guy we thought was Phantom?"

413

Kiley shrugged. "Not sure on that, but I can tell you her name. Natalie Primm. She got leukemia six years ago, and Jorgensen donated marrow. We got his medical records, and he died from lung cancer. Mack interviewed nurses via phone, and they remember Primm being there with him."

"Wow, just wow." Sean sat shaking his head. "We were so wrong. Why was her picture in the database?"

"Two reasons. She was arrested about five years ago for identity theft via hacking."

"Makes sense. And the other reason?"

"Her family once applied for witness protection but were denied."

"What?" Taylor looked at Sean, whose mouth had fallen open.

"Her parents were low-level criminals in Philadelphia who witnessed a mob murder. They testified as a way to reduce charges they had pending, but then they thought better of it. Tried to get into the program, only there was no obvious threat. So they moved to Portland to hide out. Unfortunately, they were murdered a few years later. The police never proved it was related to the trial, but the records say Primm blamed the Marshals for not protecting them."

"Another motive for hacking the database," Sean said.

Taylor could hardly believe it. She knew one thing, though. "She sounds very unstable."

"Exactly. Far more than I would expect for a woman who's able to write logical and high-level code to complete nearly impossible hacks." Kiley took a long breath. "I'm still piecing some things together, and I'll call if there's anything else you need to know. But thought you'd want to know that you might be on a wild-goose chase."

"Great work, Kiley." Sean smiled. "Text me her picture so we know who we're looking for."

"Will do the moment I disconnect." The screen went blank.

"This is unbelievable," Taylor said.

"Yeah." Sean shook his head. "Maybe we should have been more open to it being a woman all along."

"That's just hindsight talking. She's been representing herself as a man, and all visual sightings have been male. There's no way anyone would have questioned Phantom's gender. Not even a super team like yours. There was just no basis for such speculation."

His phone dinged, and he shared the image of Natalie Primm. She had short black hair, one side shaved, the other long and hanging over her eyes. A nose ring and multiple lip piercings and a deep and intimidating scowl rounded out a scary picture.

"One tough-looking woman," Sean said.

And one Taylor could believe might commit murder and not think twice about it.

"I'd say we could wrap this up, but her associate could come back and lead us to her." Sean turned to pick up the camera. "I'll keep an eye out for both of them. Go ahead and catch some shut-eye."

"Can we talk about Jeremy first?" She really wanted to talk about lying to Sean, but she couldn't say the words.

"I need to think about it first." His voice was devoid of all emotion.

Though she preferred his anger to this, she thought she deserved whatever she got from him. She crawled into the bed and pulled her knees up to her chest. She forgot all about Primm, and tears welled in her eyes. Sean was just like her parents. He knew she deserved blame for Jeremy's death, and on top of that, she lied to him. He still warred with the pain of betrayal, and she couldn't have done anything that would hurt him more.

And this thing between them? This beautiful, wonderful thing that had her feeling hope and joy for the first time in years was over. Over before it even got started.

Sean kept his attention trained out the window and heard Taylor moving in her sleeping bag behind him. He wanted to discuss the fact that he'd been all wrong about Phantom, but he couldn't talk to her right now. His brain couldn't let go of the fact that she'd lied to him. Lied!

He'd come to trust her, and she lied. Everyone lied to him. Everyone!

He'd been foolish to think she would be different, and now he had a big gaping hole in his heart where his feelings for her lived. And even with that, the pain she carried over her brother tore out another giant hole, and he'd wanted to comfort her.

Was he just a glutton for punishment? Sure seemed like it.

I finally open up and this happens? Why? Why?

With his trust broken and heart crushed, he wanted nothing to do with her, or with trusting God. And now here he was with hours until daylight to think about it. If only Primm or the guy posing as Jorgenson would show up. Give Sean something to do other than sit in the dark and think.

Where was Phantom anyway? Would she show up here, or was this all about the impersonator and nothing about Primm?

Sean closed down his mind and stared ahead. Focused on the tent. On his career. On what he wanted in life. Things he wanted before spending this week with Taylor. He could go back to concentrating on that. But it held no appeal. None.

Shut it down. Toughen up. Be the man you used to be. The one who didn't let anyone in.

He clenched his hands and emptied his brain. The night passed, the hours, like weeks in his mind. Finally, the sun was starting to rise, and there was still no sign of anyone at the campsite.

Sean pulled back from the camera and rubbed his eyes. Taylor hadn't moved lately. Hopefully she'd finally fallen asleep, and he wouldn't have to look her in the eye for some time and see the cold light of betrayal. A look he could never have imagined seeing there.

His phone rang. He quickly answered before even looking to see who it was. "Sean Nichols."

"Dustee's missing," Kiley blurted out.

"What?" He blinked to process the news. "What do you mean *missing?*"

"She took off. Split out her bedroom window. Not sure what time. Dianne just reported it."

"Let me put this on speaker so Taylor can join in the conversation." He tapped the button and held out the phone to Taylor. "Dustee's missing."

She shot up. "Do you think that's where Primm is? That she took Dustee?"

"There's no sign of forced entry," Kiley said. "And I know the lock was engaged. I checked all of them before bed. So it doesn't look like she left under duress."

Sean asked Taylor, "Any idea where she would go? What she would do?"

Taylor shook her head. "She doesn't do much outside of work other than shop. I can't imagine she got up in the middle of the night to go to the mall."

"What if we were wrong?" Kiley said. "What if she *is* working with Phantom, and she went to meet him?"

Taylor clasped her hands together, her gaze wild and unfocused. "I just don't see that happening. She has issues, but she wouldn't do that."

"Did she take her phone?" Sean asked.

"Yes," Kiley said.

"Get a warrant to ping it," Sean instructed. "And get locals out there to do a grid search. Call Anna to process the area. We'll keep an eye out for Dustee here. If Primm or the other guy shows up with her, we'll let you know."

"Roger that," Kiley replied. "And I'm sorry, Taylor. I know you trusted us to take care of her."

Sean snorted. "Trust. What's that?"

"Something else wrong, boss?" Kiley asked.

"No." Sean ended the call and turned his attention back to the camera.

"Do you really think Dustee betrayed us?" Taylor asked.

"Honestly, no. I bought into her story and her sincerity." He met Taylor's gaze and held it. "But then people lie, and some are very good at it."

Taylor came over and sat in the chair next to him. "I know you mean me."

"Everyone is capable of lying." He gave her a pointed look, and she cringed. He should feel bad about that, but his heart ached. Like a knife blade had pierced it. He got that he wouldn't feel such pain if he didn't love Taylor. But could he forgive her?

He looked back into the camera. A rusty blue pickup with a small boat fastened upside down on the bed pulled into the campsite and parked.

"We have action," Sean said.

Taylor jumped up and came over to peek out the window.

"Female driving the vehicle. Female passenger." Sean focused the lens on the driver. "It's Primm."

Sean switched to the other woman and took a sharp breath.

"What is it?" Taylor asked. "Let me see."

He backed away from the camera to let her look and decide what to do next.

"It's Dustee." Taylor jerked back. "Her mouth is duct-taped." Taylor drew her sidearm and started for the door. "I'm going after her."

Sean grabbed her good arm. "Hold on. Primm has a gun."

"Gun!" She jerked free. "We have to save Dustee. I can't let someone die again. It's my fault. I should've been with her, but I let my selfish desire to be here take over."

"Stop!" Sean raised his voice to break through her panic.

She looked at him.

"Let me see what Primm's doing before we go rushing off." Talk about role reversal for

420

them. He focused the camera wide again. Primm marched into the tent. "We might have a moment before she comes back out."

Taylor was at the door and around the building before Sean could even stand. He caught up to her in time to see Primm charge back out of the tent carrying a tote bag that she flung into the truck bed. Her phone rang.

"What?" she answered, sounding irritated by the interruption. She kept her free hand on her weapon and glared at the truck. "Yes. I'm fine. We're here. I've got her." She frowned. "Look. I've told you like a million times. Revenge is mine. Only mine. You may be the face of Phantom because everyone expects a man, but someone betrays me and I get to take care of it. Me. Me alone. If you don't start accepting that, I'm going to cut you loose."

CHAPTER 31

"Primm's leaving." Taylor glanced at Sean, panic clutching at her stomach. "We have to do something."

"We'll follow them." Sean didn't waste time, but ran into the yurt. He came out a few seconds later with an ammo bag and charged for the Jeep.

Taylor jumped into the passenger's seat. "Hurry."

Sean held up a hand. "Wait. We have to give her a bit of a lead so she doesn't see us."

Taylor didn't want to hang back, but Sean was right. Their being seen wasn't in Dustee's best interests. Sean gave it a minute before pulling out behind the truck that barreled down the narrow road, kicking up dust. He kept his distance but remained close enough for them to see Primm turn onto North River Road.

Not the river road.

"I don't like this." Taylor checked the clip in her gun. "Is Primm planning to take Dustee downriver? Or maybe take her out in the middle and dump her overboard while she's tied up?"

"Could be, but we'll intervene before that happens." Sean sounded confident.

Taylor would feel a lot better if they had backup from Sean's teammates. "Why didn't we bring the whole team?"

"We were on a scouting mission. Everyone showing up would draw attention. No way could we have planned for something like this to happen." He frowned. "Or maybe I should have."

Taylor got a sinking feeling in her stomach. This was just like Jeremy. She'd thought she had time and then she didn't. Would this end tragically as well?

"I pray you're right," she whispered and hated hearing the panic in her own voice. "She's my responsibility, and I can't fail another person."

"First, you didn't fail your brother." He sounded understanding instead of angry. Not at all like her parents had reacted. "Jeremy chose to end his life. Even if you'd told your parents about the pills, there's no way of knowing he wouldn't have tried and succeeded later. So you can't blame yourself for that. And this? This is nothing like your brother. Dustee chose to leave. She would've done the same thing even if you'd been there. And now you're here where you can help her. You can't take personal responsibility for everyone under your care. You can do your best and then that's it."

"And is that how you feel about the Montgomery Three? You did your best and that's it?"

"No, but I—"

"No buts. It's the same thing. We have the same problem, you and I. We can't trust ourselves, because we can't trust others or God. We spout the words. Go through the motions. But actually trusting? Nah, we don't succeed."

He glanced at her, sadness in his eyes. He didn't speak, but returned his focus to the road ahead.

No matter what he said or might say, Dustee's safety was Taylor's responsibility. She would like to believe his claim that she wasn't responsible for Jeremy, but what did it matter? By lying to Sean, she'd also blown any chance of a future with him. That didn't matter now, though. Not when Dustee deserved Taylor's very best. And that meant letting all of this go and focusing on the one task in front of her.

She stared through the dust down the road where Primm's truck made a sharp right turn.

"She's pulling into that white-water rafting business." Taylor pointed ahead at a small building with a *Closed for the Season* sign out front. Just to the side of the building, a ramp or driveway ran down to the river, and a chain was stretched taut across it. But Primm plowed through the chain, made a quick three-point turn, and backed toward the water.

"She's going to unload the boat." *And Dustee too* came to Taylor's mind, but she couldn't say it out loud.

Sean slowed the Jeep. Primm jumped out and went to the other side of her battered truck.

Her face was glazed with anger as she dragged Dustee out of the vehicle. Her hands were bound with the same tape, her eyes wide with terror.

Taylor thought she might throw up, but she ignored the feeling and lowered her window to listen to what Primm was saying to Dustee. The wind caught Primm's words, and they drifted out of reach.

Dustee vehemently shook her head. Primm backhanded her, causing her head to whip backward. Primm spoke again. Dustee nodded, and Primm shoved her into the back of the truck. Dustee lifted her hands to the boat. Primm rushed to the other side. Together they removed the small rowboat.

"Primm's going to take Dustee out on the river." Panicked, Taylor scanned the area, looking for a solution. She spotted a caution sign ahead, and her stomach dropped. "No. Oh no. This is a class-four rapids area. This is bad. Really bad. How could I let Dustee get into this position?" She grabbed Sean's arm. "We have to do something."

"Not yet. We'll wait a few more minutes until we can approach without being seen."

"No. Now!" Taylor bolted out of the Jeep, crossed the road, and slipped into the edge of the woods before Sean even got his door open. He watched her, shock in his gaze. Primm must have heard Taylor, as she stared in their direction, which meant Sean had to stay put.

Taylor kept moving, passing Primm, who was now setting the boat into the water. Seeing that Primm was too busy to notice her, Taylor sprinted across the road and into the scrub alongside the boat ramp.

"Ready for that ride now?" Primm laughed, high and shrill. "Class-four rapids with your hands tied should be fun."

"Mmmm," Dustee said behind the tape. She squirmed, her eyes frantic.

Primm nodded, looking determined. "Guess you're wishing you hadn't responded to my email, but how could you refuse when I took the fall for both of us back in the day? Back when we were friends."

Taylor stared at them, incredulous. Dustee knew Primm? Crazy. So that was why she'd left the safe house. To see an old friend.

"Poor little Dustee. You had no idea I'm Phantom," Primm said. "But I knew who you were. Was just biding my time until I could end your life. Then the stupid Marshals take you into the program when decent people can't even get into it."

Dustee started to cry, big tears rolling over her high cheeks and dripping to the dew-covered ground. Taylor silently made her way closer and glanced back to check on Sean. He remained with the Jeep.

Primm's expression suddenly cleared, and she

clapped her hands, the sound echoing into the sky and sending birds flapping. "But now . . . now I exact my revenge. On you. On the Marshals. Into the boat, my little pet."

Please, God. Please show me how to save Dustee. Dustee shook her head.

"Would you rather I blow your brains out?" Primm lifted her gun. Placed it on Dustee's forehead. Leaned her face toward Dustee, just inches away now, and pressed her backward. "Or gut you like Enzo? You did hear about him, right? It's a little messier, but it's my preferred method."

Dustee shook her head hard.

"I'm already cutting you slack because you're a woman, and it's hard to get ahead in the hacking world—any world—as a woman. Men just don't take us seriously, do they? Don't think we're capable of enforcement when someone screws up." Primm lifted her shoulders. "I might have brought Linc in to be the face of Phantom, but *I* do the killing." She jabbed her thumb into her own chest. "Me. I do it. Got it?"

Dustee nodded, her eyes wide like a wounded animal seeking comfort.

Primm stood back, a cool gaze now fixed on Dustee. "Then be a sweetheart and get in the boat."

Dustee trudged slowly forward. Primm followed and helped her climb in.

"Revenge is the sweetest." Primm gave the boat a shove, and the current caught the bow. "Buh-bye, my pet."

Primm spun and charged up the ramp, her back to Taylor. She didn't think twice. She had her opening. Her chance to save Dustee. She bolted out of the scrub and shot down the incline to plunge into the water. She hit hard. Icy, sharp. Shocking, it stole her breath.

"No, Taylor! No!" Sean yelled. "It's too cold."

As the water took her, she had to agree with his assessment. The frigid water paralyzed her muscles, and she couldn't move. Not a fraction of an inch.

CHAPTER 32

Sean stood horrified for a moment. Frozen in place. Watching. Fearing.

Taylor clung to the edge of the boat and hauled herself in. She was out of the water but facing class-four rapids with an injured arm and soaking wet clothes. He had to go after her, but he had to get through Primm first. And Sean had blown his cover when he called out.

Stupid mistake, but it just happened. He'd think about how and why later.

Primm lifted her gun. Aimed it at Taylor.

Sean had to intervene. "Stop!"

She spun and aimed at Sean. Then turned back to Taylor, who was slipping fast down the river. Sean charged ahead, running full force. Launched himself into the air and slammed into Primm. They hit the ground hard. He grabbed her wrist, but she was strong and motivated by revenge. The gun fired. The bullet went wide.

Sean lifted Primm's arm and pounded it into the ground. The gun fell free. He flipped Primm onto her stomach and secured her wrists with the cuffs.

Taylor.

He glanced at the water. The boat slipped away, spinning and disappearing around a bend. No time to lose. He jerked Primm to her feet.

"Hey, man, take it easy," she whined.

Anger flooded Sean, and he wanted to jerk harder but controlled his impulse. He got Primm into the Jeep's back seat and zip-tied her wrists to the door. Then for good measure, he zip-tied her ankles together. She wasn't going anywhere.

But Sean was.

He was going after Taylor.

"I'm here, Dustee. I'll untie you, and together we can get through this." Taylor shivered as she crawled toward Dustee in the back of the boat.

On a rush of water, the dinghy rose into the air, the current strongly propelling them toward frothy white water rushing around boulders and fallen trees. The boat fell hard, slamming her into the bottom, and water crashed over the top. Her injured arm banged against a wooden seat. Her vision darkened, and the world spun.

She coughed out the water and blinked to fight the darkness. To gain control. To believe that God wanted her to save Dustee. To trust.

Drenched and freezing, Taylor scrambled to her knees and over the seat to Dustee. "It's okay, Dustee. I'm here. I'll get you out of this."

Taylor glanced ahead. A huge boulder stood in their path.

Decision time. Dustee's mouth or hands?

Hands. She'd need them if they capsized.

Taylor grabbed the edge of the tape with ice

cold and stiff fingers that wouldn't cooperate. The boat crashed into the rock before Taylor could remove the tape, dumping Dustee on top of Taylor. She landed hard, and Taylor's breath left her body.

She frantically sucked in air and rolled Dustee to the side.

The current caught the boat. It turned. Spun. Whirling with the rushing water.

Taylor looked over the rim. Saw the rapids approaching. Water surging. Rising. Destroying.

She had to free Dustee now. It was her only chance to survive.

Sean hung up from calling the local sheriff for backup and raced the Jeep down the river road, glancing out to check the boat's progress downstream. He came parallel with them but had to get ahead of them. He floored the gas and searched for the right spot to stop and effect a rescue.

"You're never going to get to them," Primm said from the back seat, her tone satisfied. "They're both goners, and good riddance."

"Another word out of you and I'll gag you."

"Nah, you won't waste the time." She laughed, but there was no humor in it. "I might be going away, but before you lock me up, I get to see my revenge carried out."

Sean wouldn't let that happen. But he couldn't save them on his own. He knew that now.

Help me rescue them. I can't lose Taylor. I can't. I need her in my life.

Yeah, and how was he going to accomplish that?

By giving up the lack of trust and the need to live only for punishing lying and cheating criminals.

But she lied to you. The words niggled at his brain.

So what? She lied to protect herself from more pain. She didn't mean to deceive him. To hurt him. Had his mother been the same? Did she need to keep his father out of their lives for a reason that was valid to her? And what about Gina? She said she wanted to tell him about falling out of love with him, but she couldn't bear to hurt him. Was that the truth?

Did it matter anymore? Any of it? When he'd found a woman as wonderful as Taylor? Her ability to take things slow, to savor the moment and not rush past life in search of the next thing like he often did. She would balance out his haste and had so many good qualities that would make for an amazing relationship. He had to let go of his distrust and move on in life. Embrace his feelings for Taylor. And tell her.

Once he saved her.

He saw a wide clearance alongside the road with direct access down the bank to the river located just before the worst of the rapids. He swung the vehicle off the road and glanced back at Primm. She was well secured, but if Sean left the Jeep, he was still risking her getting free.

Too bad. Taylor and Dustee came first. He'd risk losing Primm.

"Don't be a fool," Primm said. "You're gonna get killed, and for what?"

For the woman I love.

He shed his jacket, jumped out, and locked the car, then double-checked the locks. One last look at Primm, and Sean rushed down the incline to the river. His feet and legs caught on scrub and brambles, but he barreled ahead toward the angry swirls of water.

He searched the rocky shoreline. Caught sight of a fallen tree jutting out into the water. If he could get them close to the tree, they could cling to it. But they'd have to ditch the boat and get into the icy water to do so. Maybe not such a good idea.

He looked upstream. Their boat bounced through the rapids, surging his direction at high speed.

What could he do?

Father God, please! I can't fail them.

The boat suddenly spun, the bow headed for a boulder.

Sean couldn't just stand by. He grabbed a branch and waded into the current.

The icy water bit into his legs. He could hardly

breathe. He couldn't imagine how Taylor had managed to cling to the boat. If she could do that, he could keep going. He took step after step. Feeling for the murky bottom of the river, planting his feet firmly so he wasn't swept downstream.

Waist-deep now, he focused on the spinning boat, picking up speed and whirling faster. They hit the boulder. Bounced. The current took them. Flipped the craft, expelling the two women.

"No!" Sean shouted. Discarding the branch, he didn't think twice but plunged deeper into the water. He swam toward the women. Both of them came up for air, gasping, wide-eyed, panicked.

"Dustee!" Taylor swiveled.

"Mmmm," she got out before she went back under.

Taylor dove for her witness.

"No!" Sean's shoulders burned with the effort of swimming against the current. He got close to them. Was about to dive himself.

Taylor popped up. Alone.

"I've got Dustee. Grab onto the tree."

She looked at him frantically for a moment, then nodded.

Sean dove underneath the murky water. Could barely see. Focused hard and spotted Dustee's white jacket. He grabbed the fabric. His chest screaming, he kicked to the surface. He gulped air. Taylor latched on and helped get Dustee above the surface of the water.

She sputtered and coughed hard. *Good.* She was breathing.

"Hurry!" Taylor called out. "The current's pulling us downstream."

Sean tucked Dustee in a protective hold and backstroked toward the tree. Taylor remained upstream, moving at a good pace. If she grew too fatigued, his body would keep the current from carrying her past him.

He reached the tree, sagged against it, and lifted Dustee up. Taylor swung her arm over the wood and coughed, her teeth chattering.

He heard sirens in the distance. The best sound he'd ever heard.

"Hold on, honey," he said to Taylor. He slid his hands along the tree trunk to reach her.

"I . . . I'm . . . s-so c-c-old."

He looped an arm around a branch and drew her to him with his free hand. "We'll be fine. It's almost over. Once we're warm, I plan to tell you how much I love you."

Her eyes flashed open as he hoped. This wasn't the way he wanted to tell her how he felt, but he had to shock her into staying awake before she gave in and let the current take her.

CHAPTER 33

The ambulance pulled up to the nearest ER. Heated blankets covered Taylor when all she wanted was to be cradled in Sean's arms as he looked at her from the bench seat. He'd obviously forgiven her. Why, she didn't know, but she was overjoyed.

He clutched her hand and kept encouraging her, his voice soft but insistent. He was an amazing man. Tough and soft at the same time. Handsome. Oh so handsome, even with his waterlogged look. And his incredible eyes. She couldn't pull her attention from them now that Primm was heading to jail and Dustee had already arrived at the ER in another ambulance.

How could Taylor have known him for six months and not fallen helplessly in love with him until now?

Fear. Guilt. Feeling unworthy.

After her near-death experience, she was done with all of that. Life was short. Certainly too short to waste it on regrets and fear, if a man like Sean was offering love instead. And their difference in personalities would complement each other. His passion and zest for life simply deepened his ability to love fiercely.

The ambulance came to a stop, and the back doors opened. Sean grabbed her hand again, and she was rushed toward the doors. She wasn't critical. Dustee was in worse shape, but the medics said all they needed was warming and should hopefully be able to go home today.

They wheeled Taylor into a small room. "Dustee Carr. She was brought in before me. Is she still doing okay?"

The nurse nodded. "But let's focus on you right now."

Thank you. Thank you.

The nurses and medics transferred her to a narrow bed. Her hand slipped from Sean's, and she looked at him, keeping her eyes firmly on his. Something she wanted to do for the rest of her life. But what could they do about logistics? She loved her job and didn't want to leave her witnesses. Still, she could care for witnesses in any city with a U.S. Marshals' office, as long as there was an opening. She could even switch to judicial security or investigations if she had to. She didn't want to be in criminal apprehension, though she'd do almost anything to be with Sean.

He didn't have that same flexibility in his job. The RED team worked out of one location: Washington, D.C. Of course, she was getting ahead of herself here, when they hadn't even had a chance to talk beyond his confession of love.

"We need to get you out of those wet clothes," the redheaded nurse said before looking up at Sean. "And you should too. Soon as Taylor's set,

437

I can grab something dry for you to change into."

"Sure, fine." His gaze never left Taylor. "After I'm sure Taylor and Dustee will be all right."

"Change, Sean," Taylor encouraged. "You have to leave anyway while I do."

"Then I'll go check on Dustee for you." He smiled and squeezed her hand.

Arguing wouldn't change his mind. He was a grown man and could decide what to do on his own. After he left, the nurse helped Taylor remove her soggy clothes and get into a gown.

"The doctor will be here soon, and we'll get your temperature back up." The nurse smiled and quickly exited.

A few minutes later, Sean slipped back into the room and brushed her hair from her forehead, a glint in his eyes. "Alone at last."

"Sounds like you're glad of that."

"I am. So I can do this." He bent lower, and his lips landed on hers. They were cold and warm at the same time, and shock traveled through her at the foreign sensations of love flooding through her body. She'd never loved a man before, and she didn't want the kiss to end. She brought her hands up and around his solid neck to pull him even closer, deepening the kiss.

A man cleared his voice behind them, and yet she wouldn't let go. She loved his touch. His taste. The joy.

Sean eased free but kept his focus on her. She

spotted the doctor grinning at them. His nametag read Randall Gibson.

"Maybe we won't need those warming blankets after all," the doctor joked.

Heat flooded Taylor's face. Sean didn't seem embarrassed at all but stood strong by her bed, holding her hand again as if he thought she might disappear if he let go.

Gibson looked at Sean. "I'll need you to step back so I can examine Taylor."

"Oh, right. Yeah." Sean moved to the other side of the bed and took her hand.

Gibson put his stethoscope around his neck. "You two newlyweds or something?"

"Not yet," Sean replied.

She was shocked he was even thinking that way, but overjoyed too. Her heart rate likely gave away her emotions to the doctor. But he completed his exam and said she would be fine. That once her temp rose, he would release her. He gave them both a warm look and departed.

"Before that nurse comes back," Sean said, "I want to tell you again that I love you. Just in case you didn't hear it over the rush of the water."

"Oh, I heard you all right. It probably saved my life." She drew him closer. "And I love you too, Sean Nichols. More than I ever thought possible."

A wide smile radiated from his face. "What do you think we can do about that? I mean, you don't want a relationship."

"Neither do you."

"I've changed my mind."

"Me too." She took his hand and held it tight. "Nearly dying really puts things in perspective."

"And nearly seeing you die did the same thing for me."

She wanted to pinch herself to see if this was all real, but she had some hard work to do yet to be with Sean. "I plan to contact my parents and tell them that I'm done feeling guilty. Tell them I want to be part of their lives, and if they don't want it?" She shrugged.

"That's my girl." He gripped her hand tighter. "So what about the long-distance thing?"

"If there's a job open in the D.C. office, I could move there."

"I can't ask you to do that."

"Oh, Doctor, aren't you a cute one." Dustee's voice came from the next room. "I know I look like a wreck at the moment, but I clean up really well. Honest. We should grab some dinner after this is all over."

"Somehow," Taylor laughed, "it's seeming like less of a hardship right now."

"I don't have a ring, but I know what I want, Taylor. Will you marry me?"

"Yes," she said without having to think about it.

He grinned. "That's probably the fastest decision you've ever made."

"That's because I've never known anything as

certainly as I know this." She traced her finger over his lower lip, and he gave a soft groan.

"We're meant to be together, Sean," she said, lifting her head for a kiss. "Forever."

The next morning, Sean and Taylor met Harold Wilson in the Marshals' waiting area. Taylor had been gracious enough to arrange the interview before Sean hopped the redeye back to D.C. He couldn't believe he was leaving Taylor behind only a day after declaring their love. But the team already had another assignment, and as much as love had rocked his private world, as part of the RED team, lives depended on him, and his life was often not his own.

"Harold." Sean shook hands with the man who he hoped held the key to finding the Montgomery teens.

Harold's palm was moist, and his deep-set eyes were tight with worry. Sean noticed that Harold had gained a bit of weight in the last few months, though he was still on the lean side. He was wearing jeans pulled up high with a wide belt and had a Bible tucked under his arm.

"I really appreciate that you're willing to talk to Agent Nichols." Taylor smiled at him, and Sean could hardly believe he would have a lifetime of those smiles.

"No sweat." His high forehead, leading up to a bald head, narrowed even more.

She handed him a small bag of groceries that she insisted they stop at the store to buy. "I got your favorite dried fruit assortment and some chocolates."

"You spoil us." Wilson gave her a fond smile. "We don't deserve it."

Sean was surprised at how humble the man sounded, a man who used to be such a braggart. Was he putting on an act for Sean or had he genuinely changed? Maybe the Bible hinted that he'd found faith and had taken on a new life. Sean wanted to believe people changed, but his experience said they really didn't. He still wondered, had his mother lived, if she would have eventually told him that she'd purposely kept him from his father.

"Of course you deserve it." Taylor squeezed Wilson's arm.

Sean was even more impressed than before. She really was very good at her job, and it was such a hard one to do. Take Wilson, for example. He'd been in and out of prison for burglary and had a warrant out for his arrest when Sean spotted him in the crowd of onlookers outside Becky Vaughn's house. He only agreed to talk if his priors were dismissed, and if he was protected from the possibility of the killer coming after him.

"Let's go in." Taylor swiped her card on the reader by the door.

If Sean hadn't seen the damage from the break-in, he wouldn't know anything had happened from looking at the busy office. Taylor nodded a greeting at her coworkers and entered a small room with four comfy chairs.

Wilson took a seat and looked up at Sean. "So how can I help you?"

While Sean was antsy and wanted to stand, he sat in order to seem less intimidating. "Take me back to the day you saw the van. Close your eyes and pretend you're reliving it."

Wilson squirmed in his chair. "I don't like to do that."

"We know this is hard for you, Harold." Taylor smiled and sat across from him. "But can you try? For the missing girls."

He nodded but didn't immediately close his eyes. He crossed his feet at the ankles and leaned back, then placed his Bible on his lap and clasped his hands over his stomach as if trying to protect himself.

"Take your time, Harold." Taylor's voice was so soothing, Sean imagined Wilson couldn't resist her advice. "When you're ready, go ahead and tell us what you see."

He exhaled loudly. "It was a Friday night. I did what I always did back then after a week of thankless work at the machine shop. Stopped at the grocery store for a six-pack and a frozen pizza." He gulped in air as if he were drowning.

"I got home around five-thirty. It was almost dark, and when I got out of my car, I saw the girls through their dining room window."

Sean would never forget the small bungalow from where the girls went missing. Chipping white paint. A sagging front porch with a rusty iron swing. One broken window covered with plastic film to keep the winter cold out. A dismal exterior, and an equally dismal interior filled with dirty dishes, laundry everywhere, trash overflowing, and tons of makeup and hair products for the flashy mother, Vivian.

"It wasn't unusual for a bunch of girls to be at Viv's place," Wilson continued. "She didn't supervise them well on the weekends. Often went out and left them alone. Then she'd come stumbling home drunk in the wee hours of the morning. Sometimes with a guy, most times not. She even came knocking on my door a time or two. I hate to admit it, but I let her in, and we . . . well, you know. The girls did what they wanted. Had boys over. Parties that always included alcohol."

He lifted his head, a frown drawing down his face like a bulldog's jowls. "I should've reported Viv. Then those girls would be all right today."

"It doesn't pay to focus too much on the past and what could've been," Taylor said. But the unease in her voice told Sean her past still had a hold on her and would until she talked to her parents. Even then, she would still have to fight her feelings, just as he was doing with his mother and Gina.

"You're right," Wilson said. "The Bible says to forget the former things and don't dwell in the past." He clutched his Bible to his chest and closed his eyes again. "The night was cold. Crisp. I hurried into my house and let Oscar out in the backyard. He did his business lickety-split, came back in, and I watched the news while the pizza cooked. And I downed my first two beers."

He sighed, a long drawn-out affair filled with regret. "I'm not proud of that now, and I don't drink anymore, but that night I grabbed a third can of beer and started on the pizza. It was my favorite, cheese and pepperoni. I'd usually give Oscar a few pepperonis, but he ignored me and went to the window facing Viv's house and growled. He was always making a racket over the squirrels, but he never turned away from pepperoni. Still, I figured it was just the girls being wild, and I was tired from work and didn't want to get up. Then when my beer can was empty, I stood and glanced outside. That's when I saw the van pull away from the sidewalk."

He drew in another long breath and sat there quietly. Sean wanted to nudge him into speaking, but he was clearly reliving the past and prodding him wouldn't help any.

"White," he finally said. "The van was white.

But splattered with dirt by the wheels like it'd been on a country road. A Ford. Full-sized cargo van. The streetlight above illuminated it. I saw Becky in the passenger side. She looked worried. I figured Viv finally took her to task and had busted up the party."

He'd never described Becky this vividly before. He was in the zone, or he was projecting something onto the memory. Embellishing it. That was always possible and happened after witnesses read newspaper articles or watched TV reporters detailing the incident they'd witnessed. They suddenly recalled seeing things they'd never actually seen. Sean was hoping the additional information came because Wilson was relaxed, allowing him to remember other facts.

"And there was something on the side of the van too. A logo that was painted over."

Sean shot upright. This was the first time he'd heard anything about a logo. "Tell me about the logo," Sean encouraged, curtailing his enthusiasm to keep from pushing Wilson.

"I saw it, but couldn't make it out very well. It looked like it was from a business, and they sold the van so it was painted over." He squinted, then pressed his fingers over his eyes. "Oh. Oh. It has letters in a big circle. Green letters. Red circle. The bottom one has something written in it." His eyes flashed open, and he sagged in his chair. "Yeah, capital letters. *T* or an *I*. And below it, a

W or maybe a *V*. Not positive on the letters, but this should help, right?"

Sean nodded. They were heading in the right direction, yet he needed more to figure out which company might have owned the van. "Hypnosis can often bring back additional details. Would you be open to doing that?"

"Hypnosis," he muttered. "Man, I don't know."

Sean wasn't surprised by Wilson's reluctance, and he wouldn't try to force the idea. If Wilson felt at all coerced into it, the hypnosis wouldn't likely work anyway.

Sean smiled. "Think about it for the rest of the day. I'll have Taylor call to see what you decide to do."

Wilson scrubbed his hands over his pants. "Okay. Yeah. Sure."

"Remember." Sean locked gazes with the guy. "Hypnosis might be the very thing that helps you remember enough to finally bring these girls home where they belong."

Taylor wanted the day alone with Sean. She didn't want to share him with Harold, and yet she did want to help bring those missing girls home. So she didn't stand when Sean did, but instead looked at Harold.

He frowned. "You want a decision now, don't you?"

She shook her head. "I want to see if there's

anything I can do to help you make the decision."

He eyed her skeptically. "Go ahead."

She was vaguely aware of Sean sitting back down, but she wouldn't look away from Harold and remind him that Sean was still in the room. "You know what I always say when making a decision?"

Harold chuckled. "Yeah. Ask yourself what's the worst thing that could happen."

"So . . ." She let the word trail off. "What's the worst thing here?"

His good humor vanished. "I would be under the control of someone I don't know and can't trust."

There was that word again. *Trust.* She couldn't very well tell him about her recent transition regarding it, but she could press him. "You trust me. Would you like me to attend the session with you?"

"You'd have my back, that's for sure." He let his eyes wander the room as if looking for an answer.

She sat forward to gain his full attention again. "I'm not trying to pressure you. I'm honestly just trying to help."

"I know," he said. "That's the way you always are. Never telling me what to do, but helping me find my way. I wish we could talk about faith and how it plays into this."

She'd like nothing more. "But you know I

can't. My job forbids that." She smiled so he didn't see how much that bothered her. "But I can ask you to think about your beliefs, and if this process goes against your beliefs . . ."

He tapped his chin. "No. Nothing that I can think of."

She couldn't either, but she had to let him discover that for himself. "Would you like to go home and think some more?"

"No. No. I've decided." He planted his hands on his bony knees. "I'll do it if you're there with me."

A sense of relief flooded her. "I'll be there every step of the way."

"I'll get it set up," Sean said.

Harold switched his focus to Sean. "Like how soon?"

"I'll have to find a psychiatrist experienced with hypnosis who has an appropriate clearance level, but the minute I do, you'll be the first to know."

Sean escorted Taylor through the front door of the safe house. Sean and the team had paperwork to complete and a few loose ends to tie up before heading home, and he wanted to spend as much time with Taylor as possible so he'd dragged her along. He had to admit she'd come along willingly and no dragging was needed, though that didn't stop him from doing a lot of hand-holding.

They entered the family room to find Kiley next to Mack on the sofa, her face buried in her laptop.

Mack was filling out forms on a clipboard. Cam sat in a chair, his phone in hand.

Kiley looked up, a worried frown on her face, and she jumped to her feet. "About time." She set down her computer and rushed over to Taylor. "You're really okay after your crazy trip down those rapids?"

"Fine."

"And I hear you may be moving to D.C."

Taylor shot Sean a look.

He shrugged. "She wormed it out of me. What can I say?"

"Well, I for one will be glad to have you there," Kiley said. "I've been the only woman on the team since Addy left."

"Wait. You misunderstand. I won't be on the team."

"Not officially, no, but if you're going to marry Sean, you're as good as part of the team."

Taylor's mouth fell open.

"Don't be so shocked, Slim." Mack crossed over to her and knuckled her shoulder. "We all kinda like you."

"Speak for yourself." Cam didn't look up, but he was grinning.

Mack handed the clipboard to Sean. "For you to review and sign so we can get out of Dodge today."

Sean nodded and directed Taylor to sit. "I know this will be boring for you."

"No worries. I just didn't want to say goodbye yet."

Sean squeezed her hand.

"This isn't going to get all mushy, is it?" Mack dropped back onto the sofa. "Because I don't know about the rest of the team, but I'm not paid enough to put up with that. Killers. Bombers. Terrorists, yeah. But kissy-face. No way."

Taylor laughed and playfully punched his arm.

"See?" Kiley said. "Part of the team already."

Sean loved seeing how they were opening their arms to Taylor and welcoming her into their little family.

"There." Cam sat back. "Cloud files wiped and the WITSEC database is secure again."

"Perfect," Taylor said. "And Inman told me this morning that since you all were able to access Primm's dark website and capture the remaining data she sold, our deputies have been able to move the remaining compromised witnesses."

"Also, in case you haven't heard," Kiley said, "we brought in Primm's buddy Linc Vines. He explained the REL tattoo Primm made him get. Means *Remember Every Liar*. She wanted him to be reminded of what she'd do to anyone who betrayed her. He's finally had enough of her control and agreed to cooperate against her."

"Great," Sean said. "That, along with Dustee's and our testimony, plus the forensic evidence, will put her away for a very long time. Maybe for life."

"Case closed." Mack planted his hands on his knees. "Feels good to successfully close one. Especially one with such high-stakes consequences."

Sean agreed, but then the Montgomery Three investigation was still outstanding. "You should know," he said, "I just spoke to Harold Wilson, and he'll undergo hypnosis at my request to see if he can recover additional memories."

Mack's eyes narrowed. "I can't believe you even suggested that."

"Why not?" Taylor asked.

"Because it's not often admissible in court, and it can contaminate *real* memories with ones that are conjured up during hypnosis."

Sean had known that before suggesting it to Wilson, but it didn't matter. "Hypnosis can also be very effective in gaining new information. Sure, it doesn't happen all the time, but at this point, what do we have to lose?"

Kiley bobbed her head. "I agree with Sean. The case is closed, so anything we do to help Wilson remember more is worth the risk."

"Yeah, I'm on board with it too," Cam said.

Sean smiled his thanks for their support. "You'll be happy to hear he did remember something else. Even without the hypnosis."

"What?" the three of them asked at the same time.

"A business logo on the side of the van that the

girls disappeared in." Sean described both the vehicle and the logo.

Cam sat forward. "I'll get started writing a search program with the three letters and logo colors. Hopefully it'll produce a few leads to follow up on."

"And I can search business vehicle registrations," Kiley offered. "Something we never did because we didn't know the van was previously owned or could still be owned by a business."

"Once that's done, I'm glad to take a weekend and head down to Montgomery to dig into the businesses," Mack offered.

"We can all go," Kiley said.

Cam nodded, and Sean was thankful that all of them were willing to continue investigating the girls' disappearance. He would do it without them if he had to, but they would get much further much faster with everyone's skills employed.

He met Taylor's gaze. "After Harold's hypnosis, I'll hop a flight back here to interview him again. We'll have to keep after this, and it might take some time, but I know we're going to find those girls."

Taylor squeezed his hand. "I'll help in any way I can, and we'll find them. I know we will."

"It's only a few hundred dollars," Dustee snapped as she came down the hallway with Dianne. "I won't wear those old clothes in my new job, and you can't expect me to."

"Problem, ladies?" Taylor asked.

Dustee sniffed and lifted her head. "If I'm going to work as a computer analyst at the FBI, I need to dress the part."

"Your clothes are fine," Sean said. "Especially since this is on a trial basis."

He didn't add that he had no idea how long Dustee would manage to follow the strict computer-use rules and buying new clothes was really a premature step.

"I won't mess up. Believe me. This is exactly what I need." She looked at Sean. "Thank you for arranging it."

"Don't thank me. Taylor's the one who got your MOU changed."

She flew across the room and swept Taylor into a fierce hug. "I'm going to miss you. You've been, like, the very best."

"Ditto," Dianne said. "I hope you enjoy living in D.C."

"I haven't officially resigned from my job here yet." Taylor looked sad, and Sean wondered again if it was wrong for her to move to D.C. Not that he asked. She'd volunteered. And readily.

"Oh, come on. Like you're staying here." Dustee rolled her eyes. "What woman in her right mind would say no to that?" She jerked a thumb in Sean's direction.

"Yeah." Sean grinned. "Who?"

"Not me." Taylor returned Sean's grin, and his heart tripped. "Definitely not me."

EPILOGUE

Taylor wanted to believe she could face this day without crying. She couldn't. The fifteenth anniversary of Jeremy's death was almost as hard as the first. But today, as she got out of her car at the cemetery, Sean walked beside her, his arm around her back, holding her close.

"I wish I could make this easier for you." He drew her even closer.

She smiled up at him. She couldn't get enough of seeing him after being apart for three weeks. "You have. By being here, and by helping me let go of the guilt."

A steady mist was falling, just like it had on the day of the funeral, though she hadn't noticed it much then.

"And I promise, no matter what's going on in my life, I will be here with you every year," he said.

She looked up at the man she loved, and her heart overflowed with gratitude. He was currently involved in a high-priority investigation, plus the team was still working on the Montgomery Three leads, and yet he'd found a way to be here for her. He had to fly back to D.C. that afternoon after only arriving an hour ago, but they had four hours together, and for now, that was enough.

She'd be moving to D.C. at the end of the month. A WITSEC deputy's job awaited her, and they were planning a summer wedding, so they'd be together again soon.

He brushed a strand of hair from her face. "I missed you."

"Missed you too." She turned to face him and wrap her arms around his trim waist.

"If I wasn't getting so much grief from the team, I'd probably call more often."

"Is it Mack?"

"Surprisingly, no. We've got this new understanding. Kiley's been the worst. Nonstop jokes and harassment," he said fondly. "But then I've known her the longest so that makes sense."

"You sure you two never had a thing?" Taylor searched his face.

"Kiley?" He shook his head. "Never even thought about it."

"Maybe she did."

"Nah, she's been one of the guys from day one."

"I was one of the guys too." She grinned.

His gaze warmed. "Only until I laid eyes on you. That changed in a heartbeat."

"Yeah, for me too."

He chuckled. "What? You mean I'm not one of the guys anymore?"

"No, you're *the* guy. The only guy. Forever."

He looked like he wanted to kiss her but was

holding back because of their location. She cupped the side of his face, then sighed and rested her head against his broad chest. She listened to his heartbeat, the solid thump reassuring. When she was ready to move again, she pulled back and took his hand, and they started down the walkway toward Jeremy's headstone.

"Taylor, is that you?" Her mother's voice cut through her like the bullet that had pierced her arm.

Taylor turned to see the woman she'd missed so very much. She'd aged in the fourteen years Taylor hadn't seen her up close, but her face was as familiar as Taylor's own face in the mirror. Beside her stood Taylor's father. His hair grayer, a few more wrinkles, but that horrible sadness lingering in his eyes—their eyes—when Jeremy died was gone.

Taylor's heart sang with the thought that they might've been able to move on. They'd stayed together when so many couples split under the pressure of such a tragedy, and they deserved happiness now.

"Mom, Dad," she said, her voice catching on being able to speak those words after so long a time.

"I always wondered if we'd run into each other here one day." Her mother's voice trembled.

"I made sure it wouldn't happen." Taylor gnawed on her cheek to keep from crying. "I came early in the morning or late at night so you didn't have to see me."

"What? Why would you do that?" Agony laced her dad's voice.

Sean squeezed her hand, giving her the courage to go on. To say what she'd planned to say to them when she contacted them before she moved. This meeting just moved it up. Who knows, maybe she came today in hopes of running into them when she had Sean by her side.

"Toodles." Her dad used his nickname for her, bringing tears to her eyes. "Why?"

"You made it clear that you blamed me for Jeremy's death," she got out through a throat that was closing fast. "And I figured you didn't want to have anything to do with me."

"That's just not true." Her mom planted her hands on her hips, jutting one out as she did when she felt a need to defend herself. "Did we handle losing him the best way possible? No. Did we get upset when you first told us you'd found the pills? Yes. Not because of what you did, but because it was just one more chance that could've stopped Jeremy. But we tried so many times while you were still living at home to tell you that it wasn't your fault."

"I don't remember that."

"You were in such a bad place that you never heard it," her dad whispered.

"I . . ." She started to argue, then let her voice fall off.

Were they right? Had they told her that and she couldn't see it? Maybe, but did it matter? No. Fifteen years had passed, and now they could end the rift between them.

Her dad took a step closer. "We want nothing more than to have you in our lives."

"I planned to come see you this week to say the same thing."

"Really?" Her mother's expression perked up, and ten years disappeared from her face.

"Really. And so . . ." She drew Sean forward. "It's only right that you meet the man I'm going to marry this summer."

"Sean Nichols." He held out his hand to her father, who took it like a man offered a precious gift.

"I'm Vern Mills." Her dad pumped Sean's hand, hard. "Glad to meet you, son. Glad to meet you. This is my wife, Grace."

He released Sean's hand, and Sean extended it to her mother, who was a bit more reserved, but a wide smile remained on her face.

Her mom held up a bouquet of flowers. "Would you mind if we joined the two of you at Jeremy's grave?"

The request closed off Taylor's throat. Not a word would come out. She nodded and turned to take the last steps to where Jeremy rested. She quickly placed her own flowers by the headstone, and as she let the tears flow, she stood back.

Sean slipped his arm around her waist and pulled her so tightly to his side, not a hair could fit between them. Together they watched her parents settle their flowers. They stood alone for a moment, before her mom kissed her fingers and laid them on the stone. "I love you, my sweet, sweet son and miss you as much today as I did fifteen years ago."

Her dad clutched her hand and led her back to stand next to Taylor. Tears rolled down her mother's face, and Taylor felt her own running down her cheeks.

Her mother silently took Taylor's hand, and they stood there crying together. Reunited in grief and in hope.

She was home with her parents. With her future husband. She'd given up her guilt to fully trust and was finally at home with God again too. All was well.

ACKNOWLEDGMENTS

Thanks to:

My family, for your support and the many sacrifices you make that enable me to continue to write the books of my heart. God has blessed me mightily with each one of you, and you are the reason I'm able to write. A special thanks to Mark. God has blessed me with such a supportive husband, and I couldn't keep writing without your encouragement.

My fabulous agent, Steve Laube. Your advice is always spot-on, and I appreciate it more than you can know. It's wonderful to have such a godly man in my corner.

My editors, Dave Long and Luke Hinrichs. I'm so blessed by your insights and suggestions for crafting a stronger novel and am honored to work with you and the other staff at Bethany House.

The amazing romantic suspense author Elizabeth Goddard, for always being my sounding board and a friend through thick and thin. I am blessed by our friendship, Beth, and I couldn't do this writing thing without you!

The very generous Ron Norris, who gives of his time and knowledge of police and military procedures, weaponry details, and information technology. As a retired police officer with the

La Verne Police Department and a Certified Information Systems Security Professional, the experience and knowledge you share are priceless. You go above and beyond, and I can't thank you enough! Any errors in or liberties taken with the technical details Ron so patiently explained to me are all my doing.

The Portland FBI agents, for sharing your knowledge, expertise, and heart for your jobs at the Citizens Academy. I still smile when I think about our day at the firing range. I hope the FBI agents in the HOMELAND HEROES series are reflective of your incredible dedication to the job.

Pastor Samuel Wilson, for bringing an inspiring message each and every Sunday to enrich and deepen my faith. And to Kasey Sanchez, for music that lifts my soul and rejuvenates my heart each week. You both are so instrumental in helping me to share God's love.

And most important, thanks to God for giving me the opportunity to share stories filled with the hope He gives to all of us, and for the ability to write them. You have blessed my writing in ways I could never have imagined, and I look forward to seeing what you will do next.

SUSAN SLEEMAN is the bestselling author of more than thirty romantic suspense novels with sales exceeding one million copies. She's won several awards, including the ACFW Carol Award for Suspense for *Fatal Mistake*, and the *Romantic Times* Reviewers' Choice Award for *Thread of Suspicion*. In addition to writing, Susan hosts the popular Suspense Zone website, www.thesuspensezone.com. She's lived in nine states but now calls Portland, Oregon, her home. For a complete list of the author's books, visit www.susansleeman.com.

Books are
produced in the
United States
using U.S.-based
materials

Books are printed
using a revolutionary
new process called
THINKtech™ that
lowers energy usage
by 70% and increases
overall quality

Books are
durable and
flexible
because of
Smyth-sewing

Paper is
sourced using
environmentally
responsible
foresting methods
and the
paper is acid-free

Center Point Large Print
600 Brooks Road / PO Box 1
Thorndike, ME 04986-0001 USA

(207) 568-3717

US & Canada:
1 800 929-9108
www.centerpointlargeprint.com